Five & Dime Christmas

Four Historical Novellas

Susanne Dietze
Patty Smith Hall
Cynthia Hickey
Christina Lorenzen

A Merry Little Christmas ©2022 by Susanne Dietze
A Home for Christmas ©2022 by Patty Smith Hall
The Light of Christmas ©2022 by Christina Lorenzen
Lunch with Maggie ©2022 by Cynthia Hickey

Print ISBN 978-1-63609-365-9

Adobe Digital Edition (.epub) 978-1-63609-366-6

All scripture quotations are taken from the King James Version of the Bible.

Cover images: Lee Avison / Trevillion Images

Published by Barbour Publishing, Inc., 1810 Barbour Drive, Uhrichsville, Ohio 44683, www.barbourbooks.com

Our mission is to inspire the world with the life-changing message of the Bible.

Printed in the United States of America

A Merry Little Christmas

Susanne Dietze

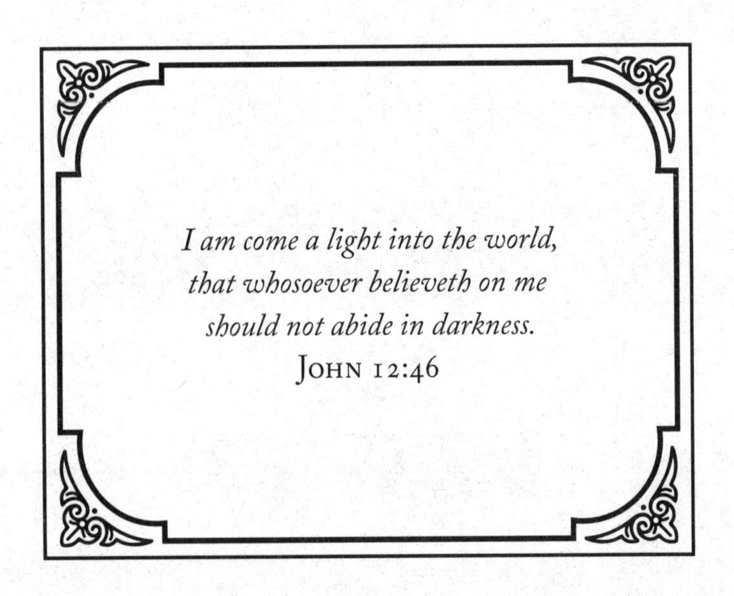

I am come a light into the world,
that whosoever believeth on me
should not abide in darkness.

John 12:46

Chapter One

125 Penn Avenue
Scranton, Pennsylvania
Late November 1881

One false move, and Hattie Scott would surely ruin Christmas.

"I daresay I've never seen such care taken with anything I've ever purchased, Miss Scott." The handsome Englishman leaning against the mahogany shop counter was a teasing sort, and he was probably smiling that dashing grin of his that made her stomach flutter.

Hattie didn't dare look up at her favorite customer to prove herself right though. The German glass Christmas ornament he'd just bought from her at the Five and Dime was so fragile that if she fumbled at all, it could easily fall and shatter into a thousand pieces.

Slowly, gently, she placed the paper-wrapped decoration in a small box. "I don't wish anything to happen to your ornament, Mr. Branson. 'Tis precious."

"And how is that?" His British accent sounded both foreign and familiar to her ear. "Because it is the only of its kind in the shop?"

The bauble, shaped like a cluster of grapes topped with a brass cap, was indeed unique among the ornaments for sale at the Woolworth Brothers' Five and Dime where she worked and so vibrant a cobalt blue that she had never seen its equal.

But that wasn't what she'd meant. "Because it is your American Christmas."

He'd told her of his intention to set the lone ornament in a small dish with a candle and a sprig of pine to add a dash of holiday spirit to his cozy rented room. That single decoration would suffice because he'd be returning to England with the new year.

Hattie and her family's simple holiday decor would be on par with Mr. Branson's, but not because of an upcoming transatlantic journey. Baubles were a luxury they could not afford, not with her late father's debts weighing so heavily on their shoulders. Nor could Hattie work full time. Mother's legs were too weak to carry her more than a few steps, so she couldn't be left alone more than the few hours each morning Hattie worked at the Five and Dime.

Therefore, most of the family's financial burden was on Hattie's brother, Zebedee, whose long shifts at the Slocum Iron and Coal Company often left him exhausted. If he'd been grumpy the past few weeks though, it had less to do with fatigue than frustration, since he'd once again deferred his wedding to his ever-patient fiancée, Cora. When Hattie heard the news that Zeb had postponed the wedding yet again, she'd scolded her brother, accusing him of dragging his feet. Then he'd shown her the newest tears in his Sunday clothes, not the sort of thing that could be mended even by her fine stitching.

"I won't marry Cora dressed in rags."

She understood then. With every penny they earned marked to pay off bills, Zebedee couldn't afford a new suit. . .and, in his mind, couldn't afford a wife either. Although that was nonsense. Cora didn't want riches. She wanted Zeb.

Her brother's plight was enough to make a shopgirl gloomy, but Hattie had come up with a plan to speed her brother to the altar. Thinking of it now, she smiled, but in truth, it was also impossible to feel downcast around her favorite customer, Timothy Branson. He came into the shop each morning, an oddity that her family and coworkers teased her about, but she didn't mind. He never failed to make her laugh, and seeing him was a bright spot in her days.

While most of the male customers who shopped at the store where she was employed made a brisk business of paying for their purchases, the Englishman with the dark wavy hair and cheerful manner had been friendly from the start. Conversational on topics both light and heavy. She'd learned both of their fathers had passed on, both were the youngest among their siblings, and both were close to their mothers.

But Tim also bantered with her, and today he was clearly in a playful mood. His lips curved upward as his eyes narrowed to study her.

"You're saying this blue bauble here is the extent of my American Christmas?"

She met his mischievous gaze squarely. "Isn't it?"

"Surely it is not the only trapping of the season I shall have. Don't Americans attend church or sing carols? Exchange gifts or eat roast goose?" His teasing smile widened, and he shook his head as if pitying her. "What dreary holidays you must have."

"Pish-tosh, Mr. Branson. We engage in the lot. Church and hearty suppers and carols and gifts. Miles of ribbons and swags of greenery. But what I meant is, this bauble is a *symbol* of your American Christmas. The one memento of it you will take back to England with you. Next year you will hang this on your Christmas tree and be reminded of your time here. Of the friends you made."

His eyes twinkled. "I could never forget my time here, nor you, Miss Scott, no matter what keepsake I possess. But I will treasure this bauble all the same."

His words might have made her heady had his tone not been so lighthearted. Nevertheless, she must be careful, or she might actually believe he held her in high regard.

Such a fanciful thought. In her twenty-four years, she'd never had a beau. And Timothy Branson's time in Scranton was temporary while he undertook some sort of business. She'd never asked his occupation, but his well-tailored clothes and polished shoes suggested he spent his days in an office.

His hands, however, told a different story. They were dotted with scars, as if he'd worked too close to a sparking fire.

She mustn't stare though, nor did she wish to dampen the cheerful mood between them. "What else does one require for an English Christmas?"

"Plum pudding, of course." He didn't hesitate for a second. "Everyone loves plum pudding."

"Mm." Her answer was noncommittal.

His dark brows knit together. "Don't tell me Americans do not like plum pudding."

"I cannot speak for the nation, but I have never tried it."

"A travesty."

"Because it is delicious?"

"Because it is a tradition. An experience, one might say. It's prepared weeks early, and every member of the household is involved by taking a turn stirring the pudding and making a wish. Then, before it is presented on Christmas Day for, yes, a delicious dessert course, one or more tokens are hidden inside."

"Tokens?"

"Most often a coin but also silver tokens. Wishbones, anchors, and a shoe, for example. They each symbolize something in the year ahead for the person who receives it in his or her slice. In these instances, a boon in one's finances, a dream fulfilled, the safety of home, or a journey."

"Did you receive a shoe in your pudding last year, then, since you undertook a journey to America?"

He laughed. "No. It's all in good fun."

"Unless one doesn't notice a token on one's fork and bites into it. That is not what I would call good fun." She gave an exaggerated shudder to make him smile. "Perhaps Mrs. Oswald will make a pudding for you. Your landlady is known about town as a good cook."

"Or perhaps I shall make one myself. I might even be persuaded to share it with you."

She did something she'd never done before with a fellow. She giggled.

Oh dear, was this flirting? She glanced at the others in the shop for signs of disapproval. Her employer, the young and handsome Mr. Charles "Sum" Woolworth, exchanged pleasantries with a customer, while her coworker who normally tended the lunch counter, Maggie, adjusted the holiday decorations in the display window. Two other women who worked at the shop were busy at their tasks too. Essie set out glass jars of tooth powder, while Lizzie unpacked a crate of dishes. Not a one of them seemed to be paying Hattie a lick of attention.

Nevertheless, she should probably remember she was at her place of employment and behave accordingly. "Mr. Sum"—as they called their employer—was kind, but she didn't wish to test his patience. Many folks in town would eagerly snap up Hattie's job at the popular Five and Dime if she were foolish enough to lose it.

She altered her smile to one she hoped was more polite and businesslike and handed Mr. Branson his parcel. "I hope the rest of your day is a happy one, Mr. Branson."

Rather than leave, he leaned across the counter. "Now that we've been acquainted for a few weeks, I don't suppose you might call me by my given name. You remember it, don't you?"

Of course she did. He'd used it when he first introduced himself, and she remembered everything about that day. The weak autumn light streaming in the shop windows. The way his smile took her aback, and she felt as if she'd never be the same.

It was unusual to address one another by their Christian names after so short an association, but he was leaving the country soon, which made her feel like there was no harm flouting convention.

"Timothy." It sounded strange but pleasing on her lips.

"Tim, please."

"Very well. And I am Hattie."

"Until tomorrow, Hattie." He tipped his hat and exited the store, letting in a draft of cool air and the unmistakable whistle of a train leaving the nearby station.

No other customers required her assistance, so she pulled a feather duster from beneath the counter and joined Maggie at one of the front windows. While Hattie's duties included tending the front of the store's general and seasonal merchandise, Maggie had been given the task of decorating the front windows. "The holiday display looks lovely."

"Not as lovely as you do when your suitor's been in the store. You're all rosy-cheeked and bright-eyed." Maggie's gray-blue eyes twinkled with mirth.

Hattie swept the duster over a stack of boxed games, displayed strategically with other holiday gift ideas. "He is nothing more than a customer, and if I am flushed, it is because I am nervous. I start a secretarial position this afternoon."

"That's today?" Maggie's eyes went wide. "I shall pray for you."

Hattie touched her friend's arm in a gesture of gratitude. "I have never done anything like this before, of course, but Cora agreed to sit with Mother while I work, and the agency found the perfect assignment. It only lasts a few weeks for a few hours each afternoon. Just what I needed to be ready for Christmas."

"Where are you working?"

Hattie rattled off the address, an office building not far from the Five and Dime. "I know nothing of my contracted employer, only that I'm to appear at office number four at the given address at one o'clock."

"Your brow is bunched." Maggie frowned. "What worries you? That you won't like it?"

"I'm not overly concerned about that, because it's for such a short length of time, but I confess to a certain sense of guilt." Her hand pressed her belly, directly over the spot where her insides ached. "I haven't been entirely honest with my family or Cora."

"How can you be if your earnings are to pay for Christmas gifts? You don't wish to ruin the surprise."

The door opened, admitting two older women, both wearing eager expressions as they took in the holiday displays. Hattie exchanged brief smiles of understanding with Maggie before she stepped toward the ladies. "Welcome. May I be of assistance?"

"The window display drew us right in," the older of the two ladies said. "We couldn't resist."

As the morning progressed, Hattie helped several customers

with the same sentiments. The calendar might read November, but there was truly a sense of Christmas in the shop today. It was more than the decorations Maggie set up in the window. More than the crisp air swirling around Hattie's ankles each time a customer opened the door or the knowledge that she had a secret plan to give her brother the merriest Christmas of his life.

It was knowing that her family's holiday, though not dripping in shiny baubles or fragrant pine boughs, would be rich in joy and love as they celebrated the birth of their Savior. She didn't want a single gift for herself. If she could bless her loved ones, it would be more than enough for her.

Nevertheless, throughout the rest of the morning, one pang of longing struck repeatedly at her heart. She couldn't help recalling how Maggie teasingly referred to Tim Branson as Hattie's suitor... and how lovely the idea had sounded. Like a dream.

How silly. She didn't even want a suitor, what with her family's needs so extreme. Not to mention Tim wasn't staying long in America.

Nevertheless, if she were to have a suitor, she'd wish for one just like him, with his cheerful manner, warm smile, and dark, wavy hair. And yes, his accent, which charmed her at once—

But it was not to be.

Even if, as she was so often told, Christmas was a time of miracles.

"I received some of your correspondence by mistake, Branson." Armand Dudek, the fair-haired, round-faced accountant who worked in the adjacent office, popped his head into the small chamber Tim occupied during working hours. "Looks personal."

"The only personal mail I receive is from my family at home."

Tim rose from the desk to take the missive from Armand, surprised by the elaborate penmanship looping over the envelope. There was no return address. "This seems odd. Is such high-quality paper like this standard in America?"

"Not for sending letters to an accountant like me." Armand chuckled.

"It's all ledgers and tally sheets for you?" Tim leaned against his desk.

Armand's scoffing sound came from deep in his throat. "My life is not all about arithmetic, you know. Numbers alone only tell part of the story, and I'm often relied upon to interpret what I see. Like a historian, looking to the past and pondering patterns for the future."

"There's art in your science. I suppose in mine too."

In no apparent hurry to return to his work, Armand leaned his back against the cream-and-brown-striped wallpaper beside the door. "My Luisa says I'm a nosy fellow, but what do you think that fancy letter is? A wedding invitation, perhaps?"

"I don't know anyone getting married." Not in America. Or back in England, for that matter. His three older sisters were happily settled with families of their own. Making quick use of the sharp letter opener on his desk, he opened the envelope. "An invitation to dine on Friday at the home of one of my business associates."

"A dinner party? Unmarried ladies will be present, I am certain." Armand waggled his eyebrows.

Tim had to laugh. "You're as bad as my mother, pushing me into the marriage mart."

Armand's jaw dropped. "What sort of place is England? There is a marketplace to find a spouse?"

Tim laughed. "'Tis an expression, my friend. As if the

unmarried among us are on display like wares at the Five and Dime."

The store was one of his favorite places in Scranton. His first full day at work, he'd taken a morning constitutional to collect his thoughts. The three-story building bore a banner that read 5¢ & 10¢ WOOLWORTH BROS' STORE, and, in need of boot blacking, he stepped inside, never expecting a shopping experience like it provided. While some of the merchandise was kept behind the counter or in glass cabinets, other goods were displayed on tables and shelves so customers were permitted—no, encouraged—to handle them, and each item cost only a nickel or dime.

"An interesting comparison." Armand's lips twitched. "But perhaps your mother just wishes to see you happy."

"She wishes to see me *married*. Happiness is secondary." It wasn't completely true, but it felt like it when she nagged him.

"You don't wish to marry, then?" Armand's pale brows drew low. "A pity. I highly recommend the institution."

"I'm not opposed to marriage at all, but I will consider it only on my own terms. The past few weeks I've come to realize that may not be as easy as it sounds—"

A shadow manifested in the hall beyond the empty doorway, indicating the imminent arrival of an individual who didn't need to hear Tim's thoughts on matrimony. Good thing he stopped talking when he did, because a woman in a brown skirt and deep green coat with matching bonnet swept into the doorway, eyes wide, as if looking for a signpost.

"Is this number four?"

"Hattie?" She looked a little different, with her hair hidden beneath the bonnet, but he'd know her anywhere. Her hazel eyes, the curve of her cheek. . .the way her presence made his heart pound.

Those hazel eyes widened in delight. "Tim? Er, Mr. Branson," she corrected when she saw Armand standing inside. "What a surprise to see you here."

"Hattie, meet Armand Dudek, accountant. Armand, this is Miss Scott."

Armand bowed at the waist. "A pleasure to meet a friend of Tim's."

"Likewise, sir, but in truth, I have not come to visit anyone. I am here to work. My secretarial services have been engaged by an employment agency, and I am to report to office number four at this address at one o'clock. Is this your office, Mr. Dudek?"

"It is mine whilst I am in Pennsylvania." Tim gestured at the space. "I had no idea you had other employment outside the store."

"Today is my first day."

"Then I wish you well, Miss Scott." Armand's smiling gaze took in the clutter of books, files, and stacks of papers teetering atop Tim's desk. "You might require the use of a shovel to tidy his desk."

"I have seen worse messes," she said as Armand left, leaving the door slightly ajar for the sake of propriety. Then her cheeks flushed. "Not that you are untidy, Tim. Sir. I meant no offense."

"We established that you must call me Tim. And I am not offended in the least. I am aware how disastrous the piles of paper appear, but I assure you, the clutter is organized. I know where everything is. You need only concern yourself with the table by the window." Tim had set it up this morning for the person the employment agency sent his way. The small desk was clean, topped with a fresh blotter, writing set, and small lamp.

He couldn't pretend he was unhappy to see her, but he was somewhat confused. "Your secretarial help is an unexpected but welcome surprise, but I must know, what of your mother?" Several days ago, Hattie mentioned she lived with her brother and infirm mother and that she worked mornings at the store only so she could care for her family the rest of the day. "Is everything all right?"

To his relief, she smiled. "Oh yes. I mean, Mother is the same, but Cora, my brother's fiancée, has graciously agreed to sit with Mother while I undertake this temporary assignment. You see, I told them I wanted to earn additional money for Christmas gifts. But what none of them know is Zebedee's present will be a new suit to get married in. I shall sew at night, and none of them will be the wiser."

Two jobs, plus sewing in secret? "I am impressed. That sounds to be a massive undertaking."

She waved off his praise. "I am highly motivated. His good suit is too worn to be mended, and he won't marry Cora in shabby clothes. He won't buy anything for himself, not when he suspects Mother or I have a need. Well, it is time he puts himself—and Cora—first. They have delayed their wedding a few years already because of. . .because of our situation at home."

Their mother's health? Or financial difficulties? From their conversations, Tim only had bits and pieces of information, but he had suspicions. An ill mother, deceased father, and now Hattie took a second job. Clearly, each penny they earned was precious.

And she was spending those precious pennies on others, not herself. She was truly the loveliest woman of his acquaintance—in appearance and in heart. "You aren't giving him a suit for Christmas, Hattie. You're giving him your blessing."

Her smile was soft. "I suppose I am."

He didn't want anything for Christmas but to help Hattie achieve her purpose. To that end, he indicated the small desk.

"Shall we begin, then, so Zebedee may have his fine suit?"

Her smile lightened the room. Lightened his heart.

And like a moth to the flame, he was drawn in.

Even though, like the moth, he was in danger of being scorched if he moved too close.

He mustn't forget. In just over a month, he'd be returning to England.

It was his duty, and there was no getting around it.

Chapter Two

As she settled at the writing table in Tim's office, Hattie's heart was full of gratitude. She'd trusted God to provide temporary work for her, but she never could have imagined how He would answer her prayer, placing her with a friend.

Friend? Where had that word come from? Hadn't she just told Maggie he was a customer and no more?

Never mind that now. She had work to do, so she looked to Tim. "How may I be of assistance?"

"The work will probably not be exciting to you. However"—his tone grew more serious—"it is important to me, and my report is due on the twenty-third of December. When I enlisted the help of the employment agency, I had two requests. First and foremost, I wanted a person of character who will not discuss our work here with outsiders until the job is finished. I assure you, it is a matter of professional courtesy, because we are working on a business proposal that is intended to be private until a decision has been made. Are you able to keep matters confidential until it is finished?"

"Of course." She sat straighter.

"Excellent. That leads to the second request I had of the agency. I need someone with neat penmanship. On occasion I would appreciate you handling my correspondence—there is not much—but the main task before you is rewriting a neat, legible draft of the report I am to present to those who hired me. I'm still writing it, but the portion I've completed is illegible."

"I'm certain it cannot be that bad."

"You may retract your words once you get an eyeful of it. My penmanship is as muddled as my desk." His smile was so charming, it warmed her cold toes. With a self-deprecating "I-told-you-so" chortle, he handed her a half-inch-high stack of papers. "Before you get to the meat of it, see if you can make heads or tails of this chart."

She peered down. Squinted. The letters looked like scratches. "Is this word. . .magnesite?"

He grinned as if he'd been bestowed a gift. "You've cracked it, Hattie. Yes, magnesite. Also known as magnesium carbonate. I'm a metallurgist, so you'll no doubt be bored to tears with the report unless you're as fascinated with alloys and metals and engineering as I am. Which, of course, you probably are not. I've not met too many who share my passion. Even my loving mother thinks I'm eccentric."

"That is not the word I would use. We are each fashioned by God for a special purpose, so naturally, we are passionate about different things." She'd never heard of a metallurgist before, but it made sense that there was a discipline devoted to metals. "God's world is wide and wonderful. How boring it would be if everyone cared passionately about the same aspect of His creation."

"A kind thing for you to say, Hattie, and a beautiful perspective. Gifts are gifts, whether they have to do with healing or teaching or, in my case, a keen interest in the properties of metals. That said, my gifting doesn't make for the most sparkling dinner conversation."

His tone was carefree, but she couldn't let it pass. "One mustn't look down on anyone's gifting, including one's own. The Bible is clear on that point."

"Ah yes. Paul's first letter to the church in Corinth." His eyes flashed. "Alas, I have no gifting in penmanship, as you have noted, so in the new year I intend to learn to use one of those typing machines so no one ever need be subject to my scribbles again. Have you seen the advertisements for the Remington apparatus?"

"The 'type writer,' I think it is called. I've yet to see one in person, but a customer told me about them in the shop." Costly items, but they supposedly sped up the writing process threefold.

"Lacking one, I am glad you are here to rewrite the report for me. First, though, would you please jot a note of acceptance to this work-related dinner party? A response to such a formal affair would be far better received in your handwriting than mine."

"Of course." She took the invitation from him. The heavy stationery told her it came from a person of great wealth.

Little surprise, then, to recognize the name at the bottom as the wife of one of the richest men in Pennsylvania, Percy Flynn. Flynn and his partner, Lloyd Nielson, owned one of America's largest iron producers. Her brother's employer. "You work for Slocum Iron and Coal?"

"Not *for* them." He sat behind his desk and moved a stack of papers. "I am in America to advise them. They've set me up in the boardinghouse and rented this office through the end of the year while I serve as a consultant."

Who was he, to be so important to the likes of Mr. Flynn and Mr. Nielson? Curiosity burned from her core to her fingers, but she was here to work, not pry. She picked up a pen and jotted down a cordial response on Tim's behalf, accepting Mr. and Mrs. Flynn's invitation to dine Friday evening. In her finest, most careful penmanship, of course.

That simple task completed, she turned to the far more daunting pages of Tim's report.

The work was slow at first but picked up speed as she learned to decipher his lettering. The first several pages were introductory, listing his qualifications, including his studies at the Government School of Mines and Science at Imperial College in London, before describing his impressions of Slocum Iron and Coal Company, and offering an alternative course for the future—

"This cannot be right."

She didn't realize she'd spoken aloud until Tim looked up from his desk. "Sorry, I tend to get engrossed in my work. On such instances, you have my permission to shout to get my attention. Have you encountered a block of particularly poor penmanship? Allow me to translate for you."

"That is not the problem." Her voice quavered. "You're a protégé of Henry Bessemer."

"I am." He beamed, clearly delighted to speak of his mentor. "I have been in Sir Henry's employ in Sheffield six years now. You know of him?"

"A little. I read an article about his recent knighthood by Queen Victoria for his method of steel production." Henry Bessemer—rather, *Sir* Henry Bessemer—was celebrated for his innovation. But hearing his name now sent her stomach roiling. "This report is on changing Slocum Iron and Coal to steel production, isn't it?"

"Aye."

She couldn't return his smile. "The process isn't without dangers, as I recall. Sparks, white flame. Splashes of hot metal. . ."

Her voice trailed off as he held up his hands, revealing his scars to her. "In my years as a metallurgist, I have received a few injuries, but none from my encounters with Sir Henry's process. His initial experiment was dangerous, yes, but the converters were quickly redesigned for safety. Sir Henry's process is the way of the future—a fast, inexpensive way to mass produce high-quality steel from pig iron, and it requires less skill and time to produce than other methods."

Less skill and less time? "That means it will require fewer workers, doesn't it? People will lose their jobs. People like my brother, Zebedee."

He was quiet for a moment. "It is possible, yes, and I am sorry for that, but mills in Pittsburgh have converted to Bessemer's methods, and Mr. Nielson, for one, does not wish for Slocum to be left behind."

"What about Mr. Flynn?" Hope fluttered in Hattie's chest. "Are you suggesting he is resistant to the conversion? As they are equal partners in Slocum, Mr. Nielson cannot go forward without Mr. Flynn's approval."

"Mr. Flynn is hesitant to make the initial investment, yes, but I agree with Mr. Nielson that without the change, Slocum will lose contracts and languish, and then jobs will be lost anyway. At least with the conversion to Bessemer's process, there is potential for growth."

She saw his point, but there was so much more to consider.

"Firing workers will not go unnoticed. You have no way to know, but five years ago there was a strike over low wages. It turned violent. People died, and in the end, not one of the strikers' requests was met. If it happens again? Our memories are not so short here that we have forgotten that terrible time, nor has everyone forgiven."

His face hardened. "A tragedy, but that doesn't mean it will be repeated. This is a time of great change in the world, and—"

"I cannot do this." Hattie rose and grabbed her coat and hat. "After my shift at the Five and Dime tomorrow, I shall inform the employment agency that they must send someone else to assist you with your work."

"Hattie. . ."

His voice trailed behind her, but he didn't follow her out the door. Thankfully. There was nothing more to be said. No argument he could make to change her mind.

Earlier today she'd experienced joy and hope. A second job to provide cash for the holidays so she could bless her family. A gift for Mother. A suit for Zebedee.

Now the promise of a happy Christmas sputtered and died like a neglected candle.

And beyond the holidays? Hattie had no idea what was to come. Would Zebedee have a job in the new year? What of their friends who also relied on Slocum Iron and Coal for employment? Cora's father and brothers. . .all their neighbors. . .

Hattie swiped a tear from her cheek as she hurried home. Her family mustn't know she'd been crying. She'd agreed to keep Tim's work secret, but oh, how she wished she could confide in her family now. Not to burden them, but so they could pray.

Although she wasn't sure what to pray for. Tim's plan to be thwarted by Mr. Flynn? The elder partner at Slocum was not enthusiastic about making the conversion at the steel mill. There was still hope, wasn't there?

A slim ray, perhaps.

Meanwhile, she would have to beg the employment agency to offer her something, anything, tomorrow so she could still earn money for Christmas. . .and so she wouldn't have to explain to her family that she'd lost her secretarial job on the first day.

Oh Lord, I thought You answered my prayer in the most delightful of ways, providing me with work and a friend and a way to bless my family. But now? I can't see why this is happening. Please help me to have faith.

Even though, when faced with impending difficulties for her family, it was far easier said than done.

The next morning, Tim pushed open the door of the Woolworth Five and Dime and strode inside, just as he had done each working weekday since he began work in Scranton.

He hadn't expected to make a daily habit of shopping there, but that first morning he stepped inside, the young woman with the reddish-blond hair behind the counter—Hattie—had drawn his eye at once. Not because of her looks, although she was lovely. Not because she had been so kind when she assisted him with his purchase either. It was the way she knelt to comfort a crying lad who had lost a toy soldier in the store and promised to help him find it, as if there was nothing else in the world she would like to do.

He'd seen a glimpse of her beautiful heart in that moment, and he admired it.

So of course he'd returned to the shop every day. It wasn't hard to find an excuse. He was a foreigner in a strange country, and the store carried a wide assortment of items. When a button came loose, where but the Five and Dime to buy needle and thread to mend it? When his landlady, Mrs. Oswald, mentioned her broken pepper box, what else but replace it as a gift to thank his hostess for his first and only American Thanksgiving meal?

He had purchased an odd assortment of things at the store, to be sure. A baseball, to see what the fuss was about here in the States. Shoelaces. A blue four-in-hand tie he didn't need and more candy than he could possibly eat. All as excuses to get to know Hattie Scott better.

But today's purchase was perhaps his oddest yet: a metal whistle, like those used by the police.

There was no trace of smile on Hattie's lips. No brightness in her hazel eyes. Just the dull recognition that she had to do her job.

"Five cents, please."

Her lackluster tone drew the eye of her employer, Mr. "Sum" Woolworth himself, a fine-looking man and a young one too. Younger than Tim's eight-and-twenty, certainly. His thick mustache and slicked dark hair were fashionable, as was the cut of his clothes. While generally amiable, he frowned as he looked up from straightening a stack of tin cups. "Anything amiss?"

"No, sir." Hattie's smile didn't fool Tim, but it was enough to make her employer nod and return to his task.

"Hattie." Tim's voice was low as he handed her a nickel. "Was your evening as wretched as mine?"

"If you are asking whether I told my family that you are about to destroy the livelihoods of a large percentage of people in town, no. I promised you I'd hold my tongue. Although I did break confidence in one thing. I had to tell them who you are. They pestered me about who I'd gone to work for, and I had to say something. I did not think your identity needed to be secret."

"Not at all, but what I meant was, I hate how we parted yesterday. I have come to say I'm sorry."

"As am I for losing my temper, but I make no apologies for my beliefs." She deposited his nickel into the till and nudged the whistle back toward him. "As I said yesterday, when I finish my shift here, I shall visit the employment agency and claim all responsibility for bowing out. They should send you a new secretary at once."

"I do not want anyone else. I want you."

"You and I hold opposing views. There is no compromise."

"I think there is." He shoved the police whistle back across the counter toward her. "This is for you."

"You are giving me a whistle." It wasn't a question. More a statement on the absurdity of his gift.

"It is to get my attention. I didn't listen as well as I should have yesterday, but I wish to do better. To execute my task in a way that honors God and all concerned parties."

She tucked her hands into her apron pockets. "I don't understand."

"I know you would far rather I abandon my task, but it will not make the problem go away. Change is coming to Slocum sooner or later. Wouldn't it be better for us to find a way for that change to be accomplished without resulting in heartbreak? That is why I need you."

Her lips parted in surprise. "How so?"

He stared deep into her hazel eyes, imploring her to hear his sincerity. "I am a metallurgist. Cause and effect are only relevant in my brain if it has to do with science, and I don't always see beyond formulas. You reminded me of the effect this conversion to steel will have on those who rely on Slocum for work. I need help to find a way to make the company more productive and efficient while maintaining jobs. The help of someone who knows people and can counsel me on their needs in all of this."

"You truly believe all the jobs can be saved?"

"I cannot promise it, but I know steel and you know people, and I believe that together we can come up with a way to present the partners with that option, yes."

Although he hadn't the slightest idea yet how to do that.

He'd been hired to assess Slocum's facilities and make recommendations, including educating Mr. Flynn on the benefits of Bessemer's process. Tim's task was far more complicated now, but God had pricked his conscience throughout the night. Tim had hardly slept for thinking of Hattie's words.

All he could do now was pray for God's wisdom and ask once more for Hattie's help. "Will you continue to work with me, Hattie?"

"If—if change is coming to Slocum, as you say, I should prefer it be executed the way you described. With care."

Her agreement was a balm to the ache in his chest. "You'll come back to the office this afternoon, then?"

"I shall, but I cannot guarantee that I will have any ideas to convince the lofty company partners. I hold no sway with anyone. My voice is unimportant."

"Not to me it isn't. I wish to hear it often, for I work best when I can discuss challenges with a friend. Someone who will use this whistle to bring me back to the present when I am lost." He tapped the counter beside the whistle.

At last there was a twitch in the corner of her lips. "You cannot possibly wish me to blast a whistle when you are preoccupied." She passed the whistle back to him.

"I do, Hattie, so please take it."

"I can't pocket it here without looking like a thief, can I? Leave it on my desk at the office, and I shall put it to use this afternoon if I deem it necessary."

He couldn't hide his smile. "Thank you. Truly."

"I should be thanking you. If you can accomplish these changes without sacrificing jobs or safety, Christmas will be all the merrier."

A difficult prospect, but his heart felt light as he tucked the whistle into his coat pocket. He was not alone in this task. He had Hattie, and he had God, who would show them what to do, wouldn't He?

He tipped his hat. "Until one o'clock, then."

"One o'clock."

Lord in heaven, he prayed as he walked back to the office, *I'm beginning to feel as if You brought me to Pennsylvania to do more than give my opinions on Slocum. There is so much more at stake. I ask You to show me and Hattie how to best get this job done. I have every hope in my heart, but in my head I know we are but two people who are not business-minded. We are not accountants or investors or skilled orators, gifted in moving men's wills from one thing to another. We are not equipped for this task.*

But as he entered the office building, he was reminded that God had used individuals who thought themselves ill-equipped in the past. Moses and Isaiah among them—not that Tim counted himself as the peer of such heroes of the faith. But surely he could follow their example of relying on God as they went about His business.

To do that, he must stay close to God and seek His direction.

Help me stay faithful to You and Your call, Lord. I don't wish to fail You by missing what You put right in front of me.

Not again.

Chapter Three

A few hours later, Hattie glanced at the mantel clock in the snug parlor of the little rowhouse she shared with her mother and brother. And gulped.

Twenty minutes to one. She had best hurry so she wasn't late to Tim's office. It might be her second day of work, but it was a fresh start in her eyes. Their first day working together on ideas to convince the Slocum partners to retain the entire workforce.

Her hand pressed against her nervous stomach, where her lunch threatened to revolt. *Lord, I pray I'm doing the right thing, going back to work with Tim. Will You please help us find ways to keep everyone working at Slocum?*

What was it Tim had said in the store? That he knew steel, and she knew people. She could only pray that would be enough.

Forcing a smile, she turned to where her mother lounged on her favorite chaise. "Time for me to go. Cora should arrive any moment, but do you require anything first? Tea? Another quilt?" She'd already tucked one around her mother's thin, feeble legs.

"Not a thing." Mother's cheeks were as pale as the bleached cap she wore over her fading red hair, but her eyes were bright. "You fuss over me so, Hattie."

"I don't wish you to catch a chill. This morning at the store, I heard talk of an influenza concern in town."

"Illness comes in with the cold weather, doesn't it?" Mother's hazel eyes gazed out the window at the gray sky. "Do not fret about me. I may not be able to walk more than a few feet, but I don't have so much as a sniffle."

True, but Mother was prone to illnesses. They would do well to exercise caution.

It was probably just as well Hattie was barred from disclosing Tim's purpose in Scranton, because it would have ruined her family's merry mood last night. She should have known they'd crow with laughter upon learning her afternoon job was for the same Englishman who visited the Five and Dime each day, Tim Branson.

They'd guessed that Tim was somehow engaged with Slocum Iron and Coal, seeing as it was the largest employer in the valley, but they hadn't probed further when she told them their work was confidential for the time being.

She endured their teasing last night, holding her tongue about quitting too, because she'd hoped to find a replacement job. Besides, the last thing she wanted to do was worry her family. They had enough troubles as it was, so she'd determined to find another job, any job, with them none the wiser.

Thankfully, this morning she'd settled things with Tim, so she no longer need concern herself with that, but she really must hasten out the door so she could get to the office building by one. "Stew is simmering on the stove for supper. If Cora wouldn't mind giving it a stir or two—ah, I think I hear her at the door now."

"Hello." Cora's warm greeting carried from the front door.

"We're in the parlor," Hattie called.

The room was just off the hall, and within a moment Zebedee's fiancée entered, carrying a straw sewing basket over her arm.

The pretty, round-figured brunette bustled over to kiss Mother's cheek, then Hattie's.

Hattie took Cora's brown cloak and hung it on a peg while Cora approached the stove with extended hands. "Wear an extra scarf, Hattie, for the wind is brisk today. Cold enough for snow, but alas, nothing but gray skies." She glanced at the well-worn copy of *A Pilgrim's Progress* on the table beside Mother. "Shall we read again today, Mrs. Scott?"

"Only if it will not keep you from mending. I don't wish to interfere with your work."

"Not at all. Oh, Hattie, before you go?" Cora's question tugged Hattie's gaze up from tugging on her mended mittens. "I met Zebedee on his way to the mill this morning, and he said you're working with your Englishman in the afternoons."

"He is not my Englishman." Hattie donned her coat, hiding so they couldn't see her cheeks flush. "And my working with him is pure coincidence. I was sent by the employment agency."

"I still say he is your Englishman," Cora said. "What is his name again?"

"Mr. Branson." Mother answered for Hattie, and her tone sounded calculating. "I agree, Cora. Once I learned he came into the Five and Dime each day, I knew he was either an inefficient shopper or wasn't really there to shop at all."

Regretting that she'd ever told them about her daily visitor at the store, Hattie tied the bow of her bonnet beneath her chin. "Tim thinks better when he walks. The Five and Dime is just the right distance from his office for a short, round-trip constitutional."

"*Tim*, is it?" Mother's thin eyebrows rose to meet the lace edge of her cap. "He is no longer *Mister Branson* to you?"

Oh dear. Why had Hattie just admitted to her newfound familiarity with Tim? "He is a friendly sort and—it isn't what it seems."

Neither Cora nor her mother believed her, she could tell. But she didn't have the time to argue that her relationship with Tim Branson was not romantic. Nor would it ever be. "Farewell. I love you both despite your teasing."

"And we love you despite your too-adamant protestations that he is not *your* Englishman," Mother called after her.

Hattie hurried out into the cold afternoon, embarrassed and unsettled. Mother and Cora didn't have all the facts. And they seemed to have forgotten that Tim would be leaving the country in a month. Even if there was something between them beyond light flirtation, it wouldn't go anywhere. How could it?

But if it could, would she wish for it to?

Yesterday she'd been convinced Tim was her opponent in a high-stakes battle. Now everything had changed. They were teammates of sorts.

She was grateful for the opportunity to preserve jobs, but she nevertheless had concerns. Not just about their ability to save the mill but about her heart. She must smother her attraction toward him now, before she developed deeper feelings toward him. The security of the mill and job positions were far more important than her minor, harmless attraction toward the handsome Englishman.

After all, he was in her life for a brief season, with the aim of helping her family and friends.

As she neared Tim's office building, a stiff gust of wind nipped her cheeks and nose with the icy promise of winter. She hadn't realized until this moment how cold her feet were, but it was little surprise, seeing as how her stockings had grown thin. She would ask for new ones for Christmas. Perhaps mittens too, since new holes appeared as fast as she could repair old ones.

But the only present she really wanted for Christmas was

saving her brother's job.

At two minutes to one o'clock, she rapped against the open door of office number four. Tim looked up from his work, and a lock of dark hair fell over his brow in a curl just big enough for her to wrap around her finger.

Goodness, she must work harder to put a stop to such dangerous thoughts.

"No need to knock." He beckoned her inside. "This is your office too."

Not quite, but she appreciated the sentiment.

The little stove in the corner of the room put off a blissful amount of heat. Her toes would thaw in no time. "How shall we proceed?"

He indicated for her to take her seat. "I thought today we might simply talk. Discuss ideas, no matter how far-fetched they may seem. Tomorrow we can narrow down options so that I may come up with the most viable ones to present in the report for the investors."

"A report? Why can't you give them the information in person, rather than in a report?"

"I wish I could speak to them, really discuss the Bessemer process as well as the concerns you broached, but the partners do not wish to be involved with minutiae. Including me." He leaned against his desk, a picture of ease and confidence in his gray tailored suit and azure silk tie that brightened his pale blue eyes. "That's why I am grateful for the invitation to dine at Mr. Flynn's house Friday. I'm not certain the evening will be conducive to discussing business, but I hope to at least plant a seed."

She understood what he was saying. This might be a slower process than she wished it to be. "I am not always a patient person, but I'm trying to be more so."

God's timing was not her own. How well she knew it, yet how often she struggled against it. Her attitude was less often *Thy will be done* than *Now, please, Lord? My way?*

Mercy. Now that she thought of it, she hadn't sought God's will in this at all. She believed she was right, wanting to save jobs, but she hadn't surrendered the matter to God.

"Tell me your concerns once again from the beginning, if you please." Tim's voice cut through her realization, and she had to pocket it away to pray about later. "I will listen closer this time. I am prone to interrupt on occasion, as you know."

His teasing smile elicited a grin from her. He was always so lighthearted—except for yesterday when they disagreed, of course. And today when he'd come to the store. Which reminded her. . .

She looked on the desk for a particular object. "You promised you'd leave a whistle for me."

He burst into laughter and retrieved it from his pocket. "I forgot. Forgive me. Here you are, to use at your discretion, although I shall endeavor to ensure you have no need of it. Imagine poor Armand next door, hearing it and hastening to our door."

With a playful pat of the whistle, she rolled her eyes. "Perhaps I shall simply wave it at you if I feel you are not listening well."

But he did listen. Without interruption. Since she had already told him her thoughts yesterday, she wasn't sure she had much to add, but once she began, she found herself elaborating.

As he had warned her he might, Tim moved about as she talked. At various times, he paced, jotted notes, nodded, and rubbed the back of his neck. As restless as he seemed, she would not have been surprised if he'd been thinking of other things while she spoke, but when she finished, he had thoughtful questions for her. Points of clarification.

And a few arguments, which he expressed with civility and

consideration. His thoughtful dialogue was as crisp as the wind that rattled at the window and just as unceasing. Question followed question, idea followed idea, until a howl of wind drew them both up short.

He peered out the second-story window. "Looks as if Old Man Winter has arrived."

From her vantage at the writing desk, she could see leafless tree limbs swaying as the afternoon light retreated. "Like clockwork, on the brink of December."

"With a roar too." He turned back to smile at her. "I don't like the look of it, so I should be gratified to see you arrive safely to your hearth."

She almost begged his pardon. Was he offering to escort her home? Walking her to the house she shared with her family?

What if they saw her with *her Englishman* and got the wrong impression? Or teased her relentlessly? Her refusal formed on her lips.

But this was an excellent opportunity for him to view the homes inhabited by Slocum workers and their families. It might give him more perspective on those whose lives were affected most by the upcoming changes to Slocum Iron and Coal.

Perhaps that would communicate her position far more strongly than anything she could say. And if her being walked home by Tim was misinterpreted by her family?

It was worth it to give them all a Christmas.

Tim regretted leaving his thick woolen muffler back at the boarding house. As he walked beside Hattie, the wind's cold teeth bit into his neck and nipped his earlobes. It was cold enough for snow to fall, but the clouds held back, leaving the scene bleak and bare-boned, all gray skies and yellow-brown vegetation.

He glanced at Hattie out of the corner of his eye. Not everything in his view was bleak, was it? She was truly the comeliest female he had ever met.

She also appeared to be cold. She crossed her arms over her chest as if trying to warm her hands.

The impulse to take her hands in his ran strong through him, so he stuffed his own deep into his coat pockets. He must pound all fanciful thought of romance from his head.

When he first met Hattie, he'd seen how special she was. How kind. He'd recognized how much joy his daily visits to the store brought her, and he'd decided a lighthearted flirtation couldn't hurt anything.

But he'd been fooling himself. He had never been flirtatious in his life. He was not one of those fellows who bantered with females and left without a second thought. Romance was, in his mind, serious business. That was why he'd never formed an attachment back in England. He'd never met anyone he cared for with any intensity.

Until he met Hattie. He'd recognized the danger of flirting with her far too late, because now his feelings were engaged. Feelings that had no place returning to England with him.

But more significantly, now he knew God hadn't brought her into his life because they had any sort of future together. Their friendship wasn't about feelings or romance or even so his holiday would be a smidge less lonely in a strange country.

God had introduced Tim and Hattie for one reason only: so they could work out a way to improve the mill and save jobs at the same time.

But that didn't mean he couldn't enjoy being with her while their task lasted, did it?

He gave her arm the tiniest nudge. "When you are home, you must promise to warm yourself with a hot cup of tea—"

A strong gust of wind hit them full force in the face, and Hattie let out a laugh. "We are being blown about like kites."

"I'm English. These puffs of breeze do not bother me."

Laughing, she eyed him askance. "Puffs, indeed. What an understatement."

He adjusted his coat collar to better cover his neck. "There is no use complaining about the weather. 'Tis almost December. And one cannot have Christmas without first enduring some cold."

She peered up at him, all traces of merriment gone from her eyes. "You have every reason to complain, Tim."

"About the wind? Bah."

"About the way I've complicated your life. Extra work beyond the reason you came to Scranton in the first place. In addition, you're spending the holiday season away from family and friends in a foreign country with naught to brighten your holiday but a blue bauble and pine sprig on a dish."

"I like my bauble." He'd been proud to have come up with the idea for the decoration. "And the work is not bad at all. I'm rather looking forward to our time together." He smiled down at her. Then regretted it because his heart took off like a stallion at full gallop. He must make more of an effort to stop thinking about her in a romantic light.

He shifted his thoughts to deeper things. "How can I not see blessings all around me at Christmas? It is a season of joy, of recalling the great gift of Jesus and why He came. All the traditions and trappings, the plum puddings and pine garlands might not have anything to do with His birth, but they can be reminders for us to turn our gazes toward His coming. And at this time of year, the reminders are everywhere. See?" He pointed.

Her gaze followed his finger to the shop window behind her. In it the proprietor had posted a printed sign bedecked with holly leaves announcing a Holiday festival.

"The festival is new this year, to raise funds for an orphan home. The children are always in need, of course, but a fire recently damaged their school building."

"How horrible." In every way. "Those children deserve a happy Christmas."

"The festival serves a double purpose for them, I suppose. Fun on the day of the event, and then the profits will support repairs to the school."

"The cause is worthy, and it would be a good idea to get to know more people who work for the Slocum company. Besides, I love a good village fete—which is what I imagine your festivals are like. Food, entertainments, and games among the townsfolk."

She led him around a corner. They were close to Slocum Iron and Coal now, on a road of rowhouses fashioned of yellowish brick. "They sound similar, but this one will have a holiday flair to it, of course."

"Of course. Will there be a pantomime of St. George and the Dragon, I wonder?" At her blank look, he laughed. "I suppose it is too English of a story. Pity, because it's smashing good entertainment."

"There will be carolers," she offered hopefully. "Surely that is similar."

"Indeed, where one can sing along or enjoy whilst consuming the delicacies sold off carts from the street. Roasted chestnuts are a seasonal favorite, but I'd not pass up an eel penny pie or pease porridge, and... Why are you grimacing? You do not eat penny pies?"

"Porridge? Eel?" She shuddered comically.

Her laugh was the most pleasant sound in all the world, and he wished to hear it again and again. "Do you have plans to attend the festival?"

Her smile froze. "I hadn't thought of it yet, but... We are here. This is my house." She indicated a plain wooden door. "Thank you for walking me home."

Much as he'd like to keep talking, he wouldn't dare keep her out in the cold. "Of course. Go inside and warm yourself, Hattie."

As she reached for the knob, the door flung open, revealing a wiry young man with a sly smile and hair a few shades darker than Hattie's. Zebedee, no doubt. After giving Tim a thorough once-over, he opened the door wide. "Hattie, won't you invite your friend inside on such a cold day?"

She blinked, clearly hesitating, before offering him a tight smile. "Please, come in."

It would be impolite to refuse, and Tim burned with curiosity about anything related to Hattie. He followed her inside, immediately finding himself on a blue patterned rug in a narrow hallway. He extended his hand to Zebedee. "Good evening, sir. I'm Tim Branson."

"We know who you are. I'm Zebedee. Come meet the family." He gestured that Tim should precede him into a snug room furnished with simple but comfortable pieces. "Step here into the parlor. Mother? Cora? Hattie's friend is here."

Hattie's face went scarlet, and Tim knew it was not from the rush of blessed heat they felt emanating from the stove.

Hattie's mother, a thin woman of middle years, lounged on a chaise near the stove. Swathed in blankets, her faded red hair topped with a warm cap, she gave the impression of illness, but her hazel eyes shone with keen interest. There was plenty of spark in her yet.

Cora was rounder in build than the Scott family, and her smile was just as friendly as theirs. He liked her at once. The mood was jovial, but Hattie stood stiff as a frozen flag, not even removing her mittens or bonnet.

Zebedee eyed her. "Come now, Sis, and tell us what was so amusing a moment ago."

He'd been watching them, eh? Clearly, her family was as curious about him as he was about them.

Hattie blinked, breaking her impression of a marble statue. "Nothing really. Just discussing the differences between American and English cuisine and what might be found at the Holiday Festival."

She made it sound like an essay topic, and her family clearly wasn't persuaded by her matter-of-fact dismissal.

When all eyes landed on Tim, he shrugged. "Like most of my fellow countrymen, I have bought my share of meals from vendors on the street, and I wondered if similar fare would be sold at the Holiday Festival. Alas, Hattie did not think eel pies and pease porridge sounded appetizing."

"Eel?" Zeb's incredulous tone matched Hattie's. "Never tried the likes of that."

Tim shrugged. "The meat is sweet, rich."

"How does one eat porridge on the street? A borrowed bowl?" Cora's brows knit in confusion until Tim nodded.

"I have not eaten pease porridge since childhood." Mrs. Scott tapped her chin. "But Hattie is right. The festival will probably sell candies and treats. Perhaps roasted chestnuts, another seasonal delicacy I've not tasted for some time."

Hattie removed her mittens. "Do you crave roasted chestnuts, Mother? We shall have some for Christmas, then. Imagine the fun we'll have, roasting them over the fire."

"Why wait until Christmas?" Tim couldn't help himself. "If your family has no other plans to attend the festival, I'd be honored to accompany you, where it would be my pleasure to procure roasted chestnuts for you, Mrs. Scott."

"Imagine how fun that would be, wouldn't it, Hattie?" Mrs. Scott reached for her hand. "But much as I should like to go, Mr. Branson, I do not walk far without growing quite weary. You all go without me, however."

"Nonsense." Hattie knelt at the side of her mother's chaise. "Zeb and Cora should go, of course, but I'll stay here with you."

Understanding dawned. Mrs. Scott was not left alone for long, and Hattie wanted to ensure everyone in her family was cared for.

Mrs. Scott was having none of it, though, shaking her head even as her daughter spoke. "I insist. You can tell me everything when you come home."

"I'd rather you came along with us, Mrs. Scott, if you can tolerate a wheelchair for a short time." Tim didn't want a one of them to miss the event, and if this idea didn't work, then he'd sit here so Hattie could go to the festival.

Hattie's smile was sad. "You are most kind, but we do not have a wheelchair."

"But I know someone who does. A doctor at my boarding-house has a cupboard full of contraptions, crutches and things, all gathering dust at present. I am certain he will lend one to me."

"It might be too cold for Mother though—"

"Nonsense, Hattie, not if I dress warmly." Mrs. Scott's voice was full of spunk. "I should like that very much, Mr. Branson."

"Then it is settled." Tim rubbed his hands together. "I shall collect you all here on the night of the festival, where we will gorge ourselves with roasted chestnuts and enjoy the carolers and indulge in whatever holiday festivities present themselves."

Cora clapped. Zebedee rocked on his heels. And Mrs. Scott had more color in her cheeks than when he arrived.

Hattie walked him to the door. "Thank you, Tim."

"For the chair? It is nothing."

"It is everything if it allows Mother out into the world again after two long years." Hattie stood on tiptoe as if she was going to kiss his cheek.

But instead, she whispered in his ear, "You deserve an eel pie for this."

Minx. Laughing, he bade her farewell, and the memory of her warm smile and teasing eyes kept him toasty the whole windy, cold walk back to his boardinghouse.

Chapter Four

Friday evening as the sun dipped below the horizon, Tim rushed into his office building, taking the stairs to his rented room two at a time in his haste—and smacking straight into a figure rounding the hallway.

"Ho, there." Armand jumped backward, clutching a case to his chest.

"My apologies." Tim gave his friend a quick once-over in the golden glow of the hall gas lamps. "Did I wound you?"

"Startled, is all. Aren't you supposed to be at your dinner party? Poor form to be late on such an important evening."

Didn't Tim know it. "I left the invitation here. I don't know the address, and I'm expected in ten minutes."

Armand grimaced. "Shall I light a lamp for you so you may find it easier?"

Though his office would be dim at this time of day, Tim shook his head as he unlocked the office door. "I know precisely where it is." The corner of the desk, where Hattie had stacked important correspondence. Snatching it, he hurried out and locked the office door.

"I shall pray for you." Armand patted Tim's shoulder. Yesterday over lunch Tim admitted to his new friend that he'd encountered a challenge in his work and tonight's dinner could prove beneficial. "Tell me on Monday how it turns out."

"I shall. Thanks, friend. I mean that, truly."

He practically flew down the steps, out of the office, and into the carriage he'd hired to convey him to the Flynns' home. Though he had a full night ahead, his worries lessened, knowing both Armand and Hattie prayed for him tonight.

He wished Hattie was with him. The past few days of working together had been invigorating, and he knew they both had hopes for his success tonight, talking to Mr. Flynn. Once he arrived, however, he saw an even greater opportunity, for the dinner party was large, and Mr. Nielson was in attendance as well. He might be able to speak to both company partners.

After a rich meal, the party moved from the dining room into a large, sumptuous parlor. The women drifted away to sit near the fire crackling in the hearth, leaving the men to their own devices. Was this his opportunity to broach the topic of his concerns for the workforce at the mill? Tim followed the other gentlemen to the coffee urn across the room, praying for words.

Mr. Nielson, a tall, imposing man in his middle years with lead-dark eyebrows, folded his long frame into an overstuffed chair. "When do you leave for New York, Percy?"

Mr. Flynn was a good foot shorter than his business partner and perhaps ten years older, with a shock of white hair and thick muttonchops down his cheeks, but his eyes sparkled with youthful vigor. "The seventeenth, for a solid three-week visit with my grandchildren over the Christmas holidays."

Tim schooled his features so his disappointment wouldn't show. "I didn't realize you would not be here when my report is submitted." The partners had requested it to be turned in on the twenty-third of December. If Mr. Flynn was leaving the seventeenth, Tim couldn't go over it with them. Nor would he know if Slocum would adapt to the Bessemer process in a way that allowed men like Zebedee to maintain their jobs.

"I shall look at your report upon my return. But that is not a topic to discuss at present." Mr. Flynn reached for a cup of fragrant black coffee. "Speaking of Christmas, tell me what the holiday is like in Sheffield. That is where you are from, is it not?"

Before Tim could answer, Mr. Nielson leaned forward. "First, how is the report coming?"

"I meant to ask Branson about himself," Mr. Flynn chided. "To learn more about our guest, not talk business."

"That is kind, but I do not mind." Much as Tim enjoyed sharing about his home, he had prayed for an opening to discuss steelmaking so he could voice his and Hattie's concerns. Mr. Nielson had given him that opportunity. "The report is progressing well. In fact, I should like to discuss—"

"No business talk, gentlemen." Mr. Flynn shifted in his chair, grunting from the exertion. "Heady topics after a fine meal will only sour our stomachs."

Mr. Nielson grimaced. "I should think the prospect of growing richer would only make you happier, Percy. Andrew Carnegie's been making steel through Bessemer's process since '75. He's richer than Croesus, and we could be too."

"I have heard rumors of Mr. Carnegie that are not to my liking," Mr. Flynn continued. "Animals receive more time to sleep and eat than his laborers."

Tim could have applauded the perfect opening to broaching his concerns. "On that topic, sir, I wish to address ways Slocum Iron and Coal can move forward making steel while preserving the workforce—"

"No more business, please." Mr. Flynn's tone turned hard.

"My wife will have my head if she overhears us. Now, tell us about your family in Sheffield, Mr. Branson."

More words formed in Tim's throat. *May we please discuss this in person on Monday, sir?* Or *just one more moment of your time, Mr. Flynn, whilst I express similar concerns of my own*. But he was a guest here, and he'd been cut off. Pushing the matter wouldn't get him anywhere and might, in fact, prevent him from doing so in the future.

"Lose the battle to win the war," his late father used to say.

So Tim swallowed the words down in a painful lump.

As disappointed as he felt about his inability to bring Hattie's concerns before the partners, he knew Hattie would be even more so.

Your timing, not mine, Lord.

Nevertheless, it was difficult to enjoy himself the rest of the evening. Despite Mr. Flynn's hospitality, something was missing. True, the fire blazing in the hearth was warm on a chill night, and the elegant guests displayed fine manners, but he would have far preferred the corner stove in Hattie's parlor tonight, in company with her family, with her smile in his view instead of his memory.

Waiting until Monday for news of Tim's dinner at the Flynns' house was agony for Hattie, a constant reminder to grow in patience and trust in God.

You will provide, Lord. I know it.

But when Tim entered the Five and Dime Monday, she could tell by the set of his shoulders something was wrong.

She rushed to meet him, feather duster in hand. "What happened? Did Mr. Flynn say no to our ideas?"

"No, we didn't get that far. The talk was shifted from business at every turn. I'm sorry, Hattie." He looked crestfallen.

Disappointed as she felt, all was not lost. They must be patient, and in the meantime, she wished to cheer him. "You warned me it would be a social evening. We will not give up."

Tim puffed out a breath. "No, but we have a new challenge ahead of us."

Hattie's throat tightened. A new challenge? It sounded ominous. No wonder he looked grave.

"Hattie will be delighted to help you. I believe there are more silver Christmas ornaments in a box behind the counter."

At the mention of her name, Hattie spun around. Mr. Sum gestured a stout woman toward her—a woman Hattie hadn't even noticed entering the store because she'd been so fixated on Tim. Shame pooled in her belly.

She flashed a brief look of apology at Tim before beckoning the woman toward the counter where the extra ornaments were stored. "Of course, madam, right this way."

It didn't take long to help the customer select a dozen ornaments. Once Hattie had finished wrapping them and bid the woman farewell, Tim returned to the counter.

To her surprise, he snatched up a ring from the small jewelry display near the till. The Five and Dime didn't sell precious jewels or gold bands, of course, so it was not the sort of ring a man proposed marriage with. But it was pretty with its green gemstone.

And clearly for a woman. Hattie's stomach did a flip.

He handed her a coin. "Sorry we can't speak freely, but I suppose it is best we wait for privacy anyway. Until one o'clock, then?"

"Yes, of course."

Hattie kept her smile bright as she came out from behind the counter to tidy the toy display, but inside, her emotions were as scattered as autumn leaves in a stiff wind. A new challenge, Tim had said. What did that mean?

And who was the ring intended for?

He hadn't mentioned a lady friend, and the way he flirted with Hattie, there had better not be another female in his life. He didn't seem like a bounder.

But the ring had to be for someone. Her? A shiver climbed up her spine and down her arms.

If it were indeed for her, she mustn't overthink the gesture. It was not *that* sort of ring, and it would surely not be intended as anything more than a gift of thanks for the work she was doing with him. Work that could have lasting impact in Scranton—

This line of thought must cease now. Hattie mustn't forget she was working, and Mr. Sum had already had to get her attention once today. She didn't want it to happen a second time. She was grateful for her job and wished to keep it.

And as important as she felt her work for Tim was, this job at the store was the position she could least afford to lose, because it would be here long after Tim boarded ship and sailed back to England. She must be mindful to do her job well when she was here. And she mustn't forget this. . .relationship with Tim, this friendship, was temporary.

Lord, my focus is straying. I think of Tim more often than I should, and when I am with him, I lose track of time. Help me stay fixed on the path You have for me. The work with Tim, yes, but also making Christmas brighter for my family and being of help to them. I cannot do that if I act like a moon-eyed miss over a visiting Englishman.

Thus resolved to concentrate on the matters set before her, Hattie worked extra hard at the Five and Dime until the end of her shift, when she went home for a hasty lunch of scrambled eggs and toast with Mother. Once the dishes were cleaned, she donned her coat once more and bustled to Tim's office, arriving promptly by one o'clock, ready to work, determined to focus on their work, not the ring he'd bought.

After greeting Tim, she took her seat. "You said we have a new challenge."

Tim's hair was mussed, like he'd taken out his frustrations on it. "Mr. Flynn is celebrating the holidays at his daughter's home out of town. He intends to leave the day of the Holiday Festival. But if we can submit the report the day before, on the sixteenth, then he will have a chance to look at it before he goes. It is six days earlier than we planned and will require a good deal of hard work."

Her spirits deflated, but she would not be defeated. This was about Zebedee and their friends, after all. "We are up to the task. What can I do?"

"I'd be grateful if you opened and sorted my correspondence. There was a lot for me in the post today, and I've been so busy on the report, I haven't had time to look at it." He gestured at the ten or so letters on his desk. "Forgive me, though, for not asking how you have fared these past few days. Tell me, how you are coming along with your Christmas gifts? Zebedee's suit, for example."

She took the mahogany-handled letter opener from the writing set on his desk. "Quite well. The fabric is purchased and cut and a few pieces stitched together. Mother's gift is books. Not as grand a gesture as Zeb's gift, perhaps, but I trust she will enjoy new reading material."

"Books are the way to my heart too."

He spoke as if she was curious how to win him. My, she had to look away or she'd surely blush. "I thought eel pie was the way to your heart."

He laughed. "Plum pudding is far preferred."

The tension in the room dissipated, and she thought it

wouldn't hurt to continue their conversation while she opened his mail. "Have you spoken to Mrs. Oswald about making a pudding for your Christmas?"

"More than that. When I mentioned it to her the other evening, she expressed a desire for one for herself, so Saturday I took a few hours off from working on the report and we made a fine afternoon of it. I purchased the ingredients and we stirred them up in her pots, a fair exchange. We steamed four puddings, and now they are resting in her pantry, awaiting Christmas."

"What fun." With a soft *scritch*, she sliced the knife through an envelope and withdrew what looked to be a financial statement. She smoothed the paper and laid it to the side. "A taste of home for your holiday."

"Hmm."

She looked up. He stood at his desk, scribbling quickly. An idea must have come while she was speaking. She wouldn't interrupt his train of thought, so she turned back to the letters. A greeting from the pastor of a local church, a bill, and a business letter from a coal company down south. A few of the letters bore postage depicting the profile of Queen Victoria, and she set those business letters atop the financial statement. The last letter was also from England, and she couldn't help noting the large, feminine script on the pages she pulled from the envelope.

The pages slipped from her hand, and she had to bend to pick them up from the floor. She smiled to see the signature read *Your fondest Mama*.

She placed the pages in correct order and smoothed them, happy for Tim to get a letter from his family, especially at Christmastime. Letters from far-flung relatives were treasures in her home, and surely Tim would be—

Married. Her eye locked in on the word. Then the sentence surrounding it.

Soon you will come home, be married, and give me more grand-children, my darling Tim. . . .

Hattie's senses went numb. Sight darkened, sound hushed, and the letter fell from her limp fingers again. She couldn't move, but oh, she could feel. The ache in her belly stretched like a black maw, swallowing her body into an abyss of pain.

She forced herself to breathe and stop this nonsense.

Hadn't she just had a discussion with both God and herself that she needed to focus on what was important? Not on her infatuation with Tim or the woman he intended to give the ring to. It wasn't as if they were courting. He was to escort her family to the Christmas festival, yes, but not her alone. They were attending as friends. Or whatever it was that they were.

Yet here she was. Unequivocally jealous. Despite the fact that he was not staying in America more than a few weeks and his personal life was none of her business.

Before she could stop herself, she stared at him and her lips parted.

"You're to be married?"

Chapter Five

Why, oh why, had she blurted it out? Loud enough to draw Tim's attention from whatever he was madly scribbling on the pages.

Tim's dark eyebrows drew low as he set down his pen. "I beg your pardon?"

Hattie grew so hot, she certainly flushed as red as one of the baubles hanging in the Five and Dime's window display. "Forgive me, 'tis none of my affair."

"I'm getting married?"

She tried to act as if it didn't bother her. "It's in the letter. I didn't mean to read it, but I dropped the page and there it was, right in my line of sight. I was surprised to learn you are betrothed, that is all, but I wish you happy."

Not really, not at this embarrassing moment, but it was the polite thing to say. "Now, if we are to submit the report before the festival, we must return to that task. What can I do for you now that these are organized?" Her trembling hands landed atop the correspondence.

"Oh no, Hattie. How can I concentrate on work when I've just learned I'm to be married?" He came near to peer over her shoulder. His proximity was palpable, and the embarrassing nature of this discussion made her skin prickle. "It's from my mother, I see."

"Yes." She pointed at the letter. "I— Well, there it is."

He read aloud in a skimming sort of way. "Come home, soon to be married, have a dozen children. Yes, that's my mother, all right, plaguing me to wed. She's not stating fact, Hattie. Only her wishes to see her remaining unmarried child settled, as happy as she and my father were before he passed."

Was he telling the truth? It was no more her business than it had been a minute ago, but Hattie couldn't help herself. "If you are not betrothed, then why did you buy a ring today from the Five and Dime?"

"Oh, that." His lips twitched. "'Tis for Mrs. Oswald."

Mrs. Oswald was old enough to be his mother. "For Christmas?" Jewelry seemed a rather personal gift for one's landlady.

"Not precisely. You see, she and I got to chatting about the tokens hidden inside the plum pudding."

Confusion muddled Hattie's brain, but then she remembered. "You told me about this. The charms you press into the pudding and pray no one chokes on."

"No one chokes if one is looking for a token. And everyone looks, I assure you, because of the silly traditions associated with it." Tim's grin was amused. "I mentioned some of the tokens to you previously, a wishbone or shoe, but there is also a bell or ring to indicate marriage for a woman. Mrs. Oswald and I spoke of the tokens, and she joked that she'd never receive a ring of any kind again, not even in a pudding. I thought to make her smile with a small gift, an amusing memento, nothing more. But I can easily see why you might think it was for someone else. Particularly after seeing that message from my mother."

"Well, I cannot see you wearing so feminine a piece of jewelry yourself." Still flushing hot, she returned her attention to the writing table, even if she couldn't focus on the letters themselves yet.

He laughed. "I daresay not. But I assure you, Hattie, I am not betrothed, nor do I have a sweetheart—that is what you Americans call it, isn't it?"

Her heart fluttered. "I suppose."

"Do you have a sweetheart, Hattie?"

It was hard to speak, her mouth had gone so dry. "No."

"The day we met, I noted that you wore no ring. Not on either hand—not even one from the shop."

He'd noticed her bare hands that first day? She hid her hands on her lap, lest he see her trembling fingers. "My father bought me a ring once, years ago, but it was always catching on things. I don't wear it often because of that."

That, and the memories were too painful.

"What happened just now, Hattie?" He shifted, gazing at her. "Something has upset you."

She couldn't lie. "Two years ago, my mother fell ill, and the strength went out of her legs. Then a carriage accident robbed us of our father but left us saddled with debts we didn't know existed, including a large loan. It was a difficult time made harder by the fact that we had no idea what had been going on in his life."

His face hardened. "What a shock that must have been. I had one of my own with my father, when I learned how ill he truly was. He tried to protect his children from worry, as I suppose your father tried to protect you."

"It sounds as if our fathers wanted our best." She looked down. "Even if my father chased dreams where he no longer had to work. The irony is, now Zeb and I must work so we may someday have the ability to dream again."

His warm fingers gently tipped up her chin. "You mustn't ever stop dreaming, Hattie."

Dream? She couldn't even think with him gazing into her eyes like this. She was almost overcome by her growing feelings for him.

Feelings she must snuff out before the flame grew any brighter. He may have made note of her unmarried state, they may have flirted, and his smile made her knees weak, but they were only together to complete a job.

And they had only eleven days in which to do it if it was to be submitted by the festival.

She forced herself to look away from him. "Perhaps we should get to work."

His fingers fell away. "Yes, of course. While I've been mucking through my assessments of the existing facilities, I've had an idea for the conclusion to our report."

She picked up her pen. "Tell me about this idea."

"People." He returned to his desk, leaving a wide berth between them. "I'd like to describe some of the people in town whose livelihoods trace back to Slocum Iron and Coal. Show how their lives will benefit or falter based upon the partners' decisions."

"I think that's a wonderful idea."

She organized his messy files until he produced new pages for her to copy, and she worked diligently until the hour arrived for him to escort her home—something that had become their daily routine.

And she would continue to work diligently until their project was finished. It was all she could do. Because in eleven days, her work with Tim would be over.

And life would somehow, some way, return to the way it was before he entered her life.

Friday afternoon, with seven days until they planned to submit the report, Tim shut the cover of the thin writing book he'd purchased from Woolworth's store that morning—an object he hadn't really needed, but the sort of thing a fellow could always put to good use. The truth was, his purchases from the Five and Dime were naught but thin excuses to see Hattie, and he was running out of things to buy. As a single man lacking a kitchen, he had no need of a gravy strainer or apple corer, plates or napkins.

He would buy every last plate off the shelf, however, if it meant seeing Hattie each day. He relished wishing her good morning, enjoying a few moments of pleasant conversation, nodding at Sum Woolworth and the other menfolk at the store, and pretending not to notice how her friends Maggie, Lizzie, and Essie made a point of ensuring Hattie was the only one who could assist him with his purchases.

Then there was their time in the office. He enjoyed working with her, being challenged by her, sharing time with her. The time spent together was—

"Almost finished." She gazed over at him from her little table.

Delightful, was what he'd been thinking.

But her words—which were meant about her work on the report—were appropriate regarding their time too. In just over two weeks, he'd board a ship back to England. Back to his family, who needed him.

A slender lock of her ginger-blond hair escaped its pins, and he had the urge to wrap it around his finger. Instead, he forced his gaze to land on the stack of pages she'd just completed. "Your efficiency is a blessing."

"Needs must, if the report is to be ready in one week."

Over the past few days, they'd worked diligently on the report, from the requested information on steel production with its information on raw-steel ingots, sheet mills, and the generation of pipe, to the details about the people of Slocum for the report's conclusion. Together they also created a plan to keep on every employee at Slocum, at the same wages, while also managing to improve working conditions. By limiting the number of hours a single person could work per week, employees wouldn't be so exhausted, and the path would be open to create additional shifts. The Slocum partners might balk at the expense at first, but they would quickly make up any deficit once productivity increased, which wouldn't take long at all.

Tim was confident that the report would be in the hands of Mr. Flynn and Mr. Nielson in one week, the day before the festival, leaving almost a full week before Christmas. Plenty of time for Tim to go over any areas of confusion with them and answer their questions—and spend time with Hattie.

Speaking of which, it was time to walk her home. In a few minutes, they'd donned their coats and hats. All too soon, they arrived at her doorstep. As she opened the door, a familiar female laugh caught his ear.

"Mrs. Oswald?" He looked to Hattie for enlightenment. What was his landlady doing here?

"How curious," she said before inviting him inside.

He followed her into the narrow hallway through to the parlor, where Cora and Mrs. Scott sat in armchairs across from his landlady. Wisps of thin gray hair poked from beneath a bright blue hat that matched Mrs. Oswald's twinkling eyes.

"I had no idea you were so well acquainted with the Scott family, Mr. Branson." Mrs. Oswald eyed him carefully as he took a seat beside Hattie on the sofa. "Imagine my surprise when my oldest friend, Julia, here told me Hattie works each afternoon for a Mr. Branson. 'Surely, he is not my Mr. Branson,' I said."

Mrs. Scott nodded. "But I informed her he is one and the same. Be assured, we have not been gossiping about you, Tim. Only exalting your character. I told Nancy you are borrowing a wheelchair for me so I can attend the Holiday Festival."

"It is nothing." Tim brushed it off. "Do you have plans to attend the festival, Mrs. Oswald?"

"I have not given the matter much thought, to be truthful."

"Come with us, Nan," Mrs. Scott insisted. "It will be like the old days. Remember the summer entertainments by the river, back when we were in school together?"

The reminiscences continued between the older ladies, and Hattie leaned toward Tim, carrying the faint swirl of lavender and summer with her. "I knew they were girlhood friends, but they have not spent much time together in recent years. Mrs. Oswald is so busy, and Mother is. . .confined here."

Tim's heart softened. "A diverting evening will do us all good. You have worked hard, Hattie, and I don't just mean your two jobs."

Could she read in his eyes what he meant? Since she had shared the story of her father's debts with him, he better understood how hard she worked for her family. Not just to provide for their physical needs but to bless them as well. If anyone deserved an evening of fun and diversion, it was she.

Besides, they would have much to celebrate once the report was submitted and its heavy weight was off their shoulders.

After firming plans to attend the festival together, Mrs. Oswald hefted herself to her feet. "Would you be so good as to escort me home, Mr. Branson? Your fellow tenants will be none too pleased if their supper is late."

He was on his feet before she finished her question. "It would be my pleasure."

"I must be gone as well." Cora joined them at the coatrack. "I'd hoped to see Zebedee, but I knew he might work late today. He mentioned covering for an ill friend."

"Hattie said influenza is in the air," Mrs. Scott said with a shudder.

Mrs. Oswald grimaced. "I do not have time to fall prey to it. My house is full of tenants, and I've also received word my late husband's nephew and his family are coming for Christmas. There is much to do, not the least of which is finding seats for everyone at the supper table."

"Perhaps Tim should come here for Christmas so you will have one less mouth to consider." Hattie's mother looked happy at the prospect. "Do say you'll spend the holiday with us."

Christmas with Hattie? Tim wished to with all of his being, but. . .

"I would hate to impose."

"You're not imposing. No eels, perhaps, but we shall have a merry little Christmas." Hattie's smile was all the assurance he needed.

"Very well, but I should like to bring a plum pudding."

"I've read about them and always wished to try one." Mrs. Scott clapped. "What a treat. Cora, you must come sample it with us after you finish supping with your family."

Their prolonged farewells were a jumble of happy voices commenting on pudding and Christmas, and Tim found himself loath to leave, as if he carried a magnet in his chest that pulled him to the parlor. Where Hattie was.

"A lovely family, the Scotts." Mrs. Oswald jiggled his arm once they were out on the street.

"Most hospitable," he said. It was an understatement, but what could he say? That he was finding it harder and harder to say goodbye to Hattie? To hold back his feelings for her and prevent their lives from intertwining tighter and tighter by the day?

Enough of that, lad. You may enjoy this time with her, but you mustn't tread beyond the boundary of friendship.

But even as he thought it, he knew he was doomed. The boundary of friendship and romance had been torn down in his heart, and it was far too late to do anything about it.

Chapter Six

"Oh, look at these." Hattie opened the lid off a box of new stock the following Friday. It was impossible not to sigh with longing. "I haven't wanted a single thing for Christmas until now."

Beyond making Christmas bright for her family, of course. In the week since Mother invited Tim to Christmas, she'd kept busy in the few spare hours she didn't work either at the Five and Dime or in Tim's office. She'd purchased novels from the bookshop for Mother and hidden them beneath her bed. The suit for Zebedee was half finished and folded neatly in her hope chest. She'd even purchased a little something for Cora, who would soon be her sister. Hattie selected three new handkerchiefs from the shop and would embroider Cora's first initial in each hankie's corner, leaving space beside the "C" to add an "S" once Cora married Zebedee.

Those gifts, and saving as many jobs at Slocum as possible, were all she wanted for Christmas. Nothing for herself. Until now.

She couldn't help it. Each little handbag in the box she unpacked was the same style, a textile pouch large enough to hold a handkerchief, coin, and perhaps a pencil, cinched by a metal clasp. No two were alike when it came to the fabrics or trims though. Lacy, beaded, beribboned, or plain, they were all works of art.

Her friend Lizzie looked up from her inventory of cake turners. "Are those handbags?"

"They are indeed."

Since the store was quiet, Essie and Maggie made their way over for a closer look. "I don't blame you for wanting one, Hattie," Essie said as she admired a creamy lace bag.

Maggie nudged Hattie's arm. "Should we give your brother a strong hint this would be a good Christmas gift for you?"

Hattie's stomach twisted with embarrassment. Zebedee had already purchased something for her—something practical, she was certain—and she'd hate for him to hear she had her eye on something so frivolous. "Oh no. I'm inspired to try sewing my own, actually." She turned back to setting the purses out for display, and if her grasp held too long on a bag sewn of red and pink rose-strewn fabric, well, it was the prettiest of the lot.

The one she sewed for herself wouldn't be this fine, with the shiny chain or rose-bedecked clasp, but it would be hers and ready for spring.

"New stock?" a familiar voice said from behind her. She'd become so engrossed in the purses, she hadn't noted it was time for Tim's morning visit to the Five and Dime.

She didn't miss the sly smiles on her friends' faces as they returned to work, leaving her and Tim alone. "Just in time for Christmas shoppers."

"It truly feels as if Christmas is upon us with the festival tomorrow. Mrs. Oswald and I will collect your family at the appointed hour with the wheelchair." He looked around the store as if scanning for a specific item. Then he peered at one of the toy shelves behind her and reached for a small doll in a blue gingham smock. "What do you think of her?"

Far be it from Hattie to question anyone's choice of purchases, but she didn't understand why Tim would buy a doll. The one he selected was no porcelain-headed lady, but a batting-stuffed rag doll with a simple smile stitched to her cotton face. Just the sort of thing Hattie would have cherished as a child. "She is sweet."

"I hope whoever she goes to finds her sweet as well."

"You do not have someone in mind?" Hattie abandoned the purses to move behind the counter, where she took his coin for the purchase.

"I saw there is to be a donation box at the festival. For educational supplies as well as toys for Christmas for the orphans who lost their school. My sisters always wanted dolls, so I hope one of the lasses at the orphanage will like it."

"I should say so. I always liked dolls too." Hattie finished wrapping the doll in brown paper.

Tim tucked it into his coat pocket. As he withdrew his hand, a small, flat box came out with it, landing on the floor with a soft *thwack*. He retrieved it and shoved it into his other coat pocket as if hoping she wouldn't see it.

"I have a gift for you, Hattie." His eyes twinkled.

The strange box? "Not another whistle, I hope."

He laughed. "A little better than that. You now have more time to work on Zebedee's Christmas suit, for this morning, I submitted the report to Mr. Nielson's assistant at the Slocum offices."

It took a moment to fully understand what he was saying. "I thought we were to finish it today." In time for Mr. Flynn to read it before he left for his daughter's.

"That was our intent, yes, but last evening I went through it, and it was ready. You've done such a good job translating my horrible handwriting that it looks perfect. Neat and tidy. All I did was extend a chart, and I thought, why not be rid of it? More time for Nielson and Flynn to look at it. The assistant said he would show it to them right away."

"It's really done, then." Done and over. He looked so happy she couldn't help but return his smile, but her heart did not engage with her lips. No more work together? No last day to go over the project, to bid farewell to their time together in his office. No more teasing or smiles or even a prayer together to ask God's blessing on the report.

Tim rapped his fingers on the mahogany counter. "Isn't it wonderful? And you need not worry about losing a week's worth of wages." His voice was low, for her ears only. "I paid the agency for your full time, as contracted, plus an addition. Your help has been invaluable to me."

"Thank you." But pay wasn't at the forefront of her mind. They'd only worked together a few weeks, but she really would miss seeing him every day, wouldn't she?

Of course, they still had tomorrow's festival. Still had Christmas supper. Still had time together without the constraints and burdens of this project. But the completion of their work was a milestone she hadn't thought she'd face for a few more hours. It meant that soon he'd be gone.

"Until tomorrow, then, Hattie?" He tipped his hat.

"Tomorrow." Her gaze followed him out of the Five and Dime.

When she turned around, Maggie was watching her with wide eyes. "Did I overhear that you're going to the festival together? And you said you two weren't courting."

"It's not like that. He's going with my family." Hattie busied herself with the purse display once again.

"What will you wear?"

Hattie and her friends at the shop didn't normally talk about such fripperies as fashion, but why not? There weren't any customers to assist now. "My bronze mohair suit." A few years out of fashion, perhaps, but it was her best cold-weather ensemble, and the flattering cut of the coat-and-dress combination complemented her figure as well as her coloring.

"The one with the knife pleats down the skirt?" Maggie's brows rose. "If you aren't wearing your finest ensemble for him, then for whom?"

Oh brother. "I promise, he is not my suitor."

"For the moment, maybe."

"For*ever*."

"I never took you for a liar, Hattie Scott." Maggie's grin told Hattie she was teasing.

"Nor did I take you for a meddler," she teased back, but her heart ached.

She'd tried to prevent this from happening, this anguish in her chest. Tried to hold back her growing feelings for him. Now, despite her best intentions, she would mourn when he returned to England after Christmas.

But that didn't mean she couldn't enjoy the time they had left. The festival. Christmas. Made even better by his kindness to her family, his help ensuring her mother could participate. She would make memories and tuck them away in a quiet corner of her heart, and someday she would look back on them with fondness.

But for today, she would embrace Christmas and all the trappings of the season.

"One more," Tim coaxed Hattie Saturday evening, enjoying the happy look in her eyes. "Just one. It is Christmas."

"Christmastime or not, I cannot eat another doughnut." Her hand pressed the flat front of her coat as their little party strolled down the thoroughfare. "We have eaten our way through the festival."

Not quite, for they hadn't even been through half of it thus far. Tim had paid their admissions, dropped the doll into the donations box, and then paused with Hattie's family and Mrs. Oswald while they got their bearings on the wide street that had been closed off for the Holiday Festival. Benches had been set up around a large bonfire, and beyond it, booths and tables lined both sides of the street—food on the north side, wares on the south. Down the middle, games and entertainments, like a puppet theater, had been set up. The street came to a dead end at the orphanage, where Hattie said carolers would perform.

Many options were available all at once. It was almost overwhelming—almost. Even though they'd all had their fill at supper, it took only a moment for their group to decide to start the evening with food.

Roasted chestnuts for Mrs. Scott. Sticky, sweet popcorn balls for Mrs. Oswald. Zebedee and Cora insisted Tim try a stick-pierced apple dipped in thick caramel, and the combination of tart apple and rich caramel tantalized his tongue. He'd found a new American favorite, until Hattie pointed to the woman selling fried cakes beneath a homespun banner that read *OLY KOEKS*.

"That's what the Dutch call them, but we call them doughnuts," she said.

Hot, spiced with nutmeg, and dusted with sugar, the circular treats were delicious. And addictive. He had to have another.

But he didn't want to be the only one. Not if Hattie would join him. "Shall we stop for another on our way back? Perhaps your appetite will have returned by then."

"I might be persuaded to eat another then, yes," she teased.

Mrs. Scott looked over her shoulder at him as he pushed her in the wheelchair. "Thank you, Tim. For the chestnuts, for the use of the wheelchair, for everything. I cannot tell you what it means to me to be out and about. It truly feels like Christmas."

"To me too." This might not precisely be like his holidays back home, and yet at the same time, it was achingly similar. The happy noise of the crowd blended with the trill of Christmas carols on the cold night air. Every face shone with happiness, from the bundled-up children to the oldest among them, eyes aglow at the puppet show and trinkets for sale. Tim took a deep breath, catching pine and woodsmoke and cinnamon wafting from the spiced-cider stall.

Hattie walked alongside him as he pushed her mother in the wheelchair. Mrs. Oswald strolled beside Mrs. Scott, and Zebedee and Cora wandered alongside, hand in hand. Everyone's mood was merry, and Hattie's eyes glowed like the gas lamps illuminating the street from above. "So which is better, a doughnut or eel pie?"

He laughed. "You win. The doughnut is champion."

"You like American food, then?"

"Not just the food. I like America and its people very well indeed."

He shouldn't have said it. Shouldn't have gazed into her eyes while he uttered words that could be interpreted several ways, but the truth was, he meant them in any and every way she might interpret them. He'd grown quite fond of Hattie. Fonder than was wise, considering his short stay in America, which had him wondering what to do about it. His life was in England. His work, his home, his family.

And yet. . .and yet. . .

When he arrived at her house with Mrs. Oswald and the wheelchair an hour ago to gather them for the festival, he caught sight of Hattie in a fine bronze dress that complemented her hazel eyes, and his breath caught in his chest. It wasn't her attire, for she was equally as fetching in a simple ensemble and shop apron at the Five and Dime, but something was different tonight.

Perhaps the excitement in her eyes. Perhaps the way she allowed him to help her into her coat and didn't protest when his hands lingered a fraction too long on her shoulders.

Perhaps it was just him admitting to himself she was not just lovely but beautiful. Achingly so.

He didn't wish to leave her side. There was something unfinished here. He felt it in his bones. Asked the Lord what it meant. Because he had a duty at home.

"What are you thinking about with such a serious expression?"

"I do not mean to look serious. Just thinking of my mother. I wish she were here." Then he wouldn't feel so guilty about leaving her alone.

"Rather than you being there?" Hattie brushed a spattering of sugar from his sleeve, a gesture so much like ownership that his heart skipped a beat. Maybe two.

"Yes." He came out and said it. The honest truth. The others in their party were engaged in conversation, not listening, so he had a reasonable amount of privacy with Hattie at this moment. "I have always felt I failed God, failed my family, by not noticing the signs when my father first took ill. I could have been of better help, could have been a better son, had I not been so absorbed in my own interests. I told you that I get engrossed in work and I miss things."

"I think your father was as good at hiding his troubles as mine was."

"I still feel as if I failed my parents. Failed God. I don't wish to do that again, and that is why I needed your help, Hattie. You help me see things I've missed. But that is also why I've never questioned my plan to return to England. My mother is alone, and I feel responsible. Duty-bound to her. All she wants is for me to be settled in England. But these past few weeks? I've wondered."

Hattie's eyes went wide. "Wondered? If you can stay?"

Mrs. Scott twisted in her chair. "Tim, this is the grandest night I've had in ages. Thank you."

Tim inwardly groaned at the ill-timed interruption, but perhaps he was being saved from making an utter fool of himself. What had he been about to do? Declare his affection for Hattie here and now, in the middle of the festival? "You're most welcome, ma'am."

"Perhaps you can borrow the chair for Christmas Eve," Mrs. Oswald said.

"An excellent suggestion." Tim smiled. "I shall ensure you can attend church, Mrs. Scott."

Hattie's hand went to her heart. "That would be so kind, Tim. Thank you. But you must come to Christmas Eve service with us, of course."

"I attend the same parish," Mrs. Oswald said. "The service on Christmas Eve is always a special one, singing hymns in the late afternoon by candlelight."

He met Hattie's happy gaze. "I would be honored to worship with you. Thank you."

They reached the carolers then, and after the performance, they turned around to visit the trinket stalls. Their group was admiring tin stars to hang on the Christmas tree when a familiar voice called his name.

"Armand." He greeted his friend, then nodded to the

well-rounded woman on his arm. "Is this your wife?"

"Luisa. And you have quite a group with you."

Tim made introductions, and he was glad Hattie and Luisa seemed to take to one another at once. After a few minutes, however, Zebedee gestured to the wheelchair, as if to take it from Tim. "There's a juggling act ahead. Why don't we meet you two there?" His eyes darted between Tim and Hattie.

"We'll not be but a moment." Hattie waved as her brother escorted the three women down the way and then returned her attention to Luisa. "How are you enjoying the evening?"

Armand nudged Tim's shoulder and drew him aside for a quiet word. "Winter might be upon us, but a rose is blooming before our eyes."

Tim speared him with a look. "A poet as well as an accountant?"

"I told you already, my friend. I am not trained in arithmetic only. I was taught to look for patterns, to interpret what I see, and here I see you two and have but one conclusion. You and the miss are, shall we say, a matched pair."

"What's a matched pair?" Luisa spun. "Do not say you bought me mittens for Christmas. I have three sets already."

Tim caught Hattie hiding her worn, holey mittens in her coat pockets.

Armand pressed a kiss against Luisa's fingers. "No, *kochanie*. No mittens for you this year."

"Not much else is matched except for horses." Luisa rolled her eyes at Hattie. "My Armand cannot wait to buy our own carriage."

"How grand," Hattie said.

Tim felt relief that the women hadn't heard the full context of his conversation with Armand. He and Hattie, a matched pair? Much as he liked the sound of it, he didn't see how it could be. Still, he resolved to enjoy their time together tonight, and once they parted from Armand and Luisa, Hattie took his arm, walking close beside him.

As if they truly were a matched pair, they slowly meandered in the direction her family took, pausing along the way to look at a wide variety of goods for sale in the stalls: handmade items like knit woolen caps, jars of preserves, lace angels and antimacassars, as well as books, candlesticks, toys, and tiny looking glasses.

"It reminds me of the Five and Dime." Tim pulled her a fraction of an inch closer as he bent his head to speak to her. "There is a little bit of everything here."

To his delight, she didn't pull away but instead looked up at him. "This is wonderful, isn't it? People coming together to help the orphanage in such a fun, festive way. Every face is bright with goodwill, and every person has given something to help the orphanage, from purchasing admission tickets to donating school supplies and toys."

"Or buying those doughnut confections."

She laughed. "Speaking of which, we discussed stopping for another on our way back."

"So we did. Are you ready?"

"It is said that it is unladylike to express hunger, but I cannot lie. I wish for another."

"Whoever invented that ridiculous saying is a cretin. Or never tasted one of these doughnuts. Come on."

Laughing, they sauntered across the street toward the vendor's stall. Halfway there, Hattie turned at the call of her name. Cora bustled through the crowd. "There you are."

Hattie released Tim's arm. "Oh, I took too long, didn't I? Mother hasn't been out in two years, and here I am dawdling. She must be cold."

"She is nothing of the sort." Cora rolled her eyes. "It is your brother who twisted his ankle. He is fine, but your mother insisted he sit for a spell, so we are on the benches on the far side of the bonfire. When you are ready, you know where to find us."

"If Zeb hurt his ankle, perhaps we should go now." Hattie bit her lip, then looked up at Tim.

"Why don't you go check on them while I purchase a few doughnuts, and we'll eat them walking home."

"I like this idea," Cora said. "Thank you, Tim."

Thus resolved, Tim parted from the ladies, whistling a carol as he strode toward the stall. Then he realized someone was staring at him, a figure in a gray topcoat the same leaden hue as the man's thick eyebrows.

"Mr. Nielson?"

Lord, is this an answer to prayer? Tim approached the company partner, grateful for the opportunity to talk to him about his and Hattie's report. To think Mr. Nielson might tell him here and now that he and Mr. Flynn accepted Tim and Hattie's suggestions. There would be no waiting for answers, and tonight they could celebrate the security of the millworkers' jobs. Tim rubbed his hands together in anticipation.

"Branson. Here alone?"

"I've come with friends, seated just beyond the bonfire. One of them, Zebedee Scott, works for you." Tim wished Zeb were at his side right now, that he might introduce him.

"My wife and her sister are over yonder, buying out the lacemaker's stock by the look of things. As if the missus doesn't already spend a fortune on trims and fripperies." Mr. Nielson tipped his head at a table where Tim and Hattie had admired lace angel ornaments. "These festivals are a lot of bother, if you ask me. Vendors with hands out at every turn. Litter underfoot.

And all the shrieking children give one a headache. Alas, one must attend these things or risk appearing uncaring. I envy Flynn being out of town as an excuse not to come."

Tim's excitement flickered with every passing word, until the last sentence, when he felt as if the floor was tilting beneath him. "He's gone? But I submitted the report today so you both might have opportunity to read it and make a decision before Christmas."

"I don't need to read it. My mind is as fixed as it was before your visit that Slocum must change." Mr. Nielson waved his hand in dismissal. "But Flynn had a look at your report before he left."

Hope sprung anew. "Did he say what he thought, if I may ask, sir?"

"He flipped to the financial pages, saw the figure you presented, and turned purple. Naturally, he balked and said no to everything."

Shock reverberated through Tim's being. All that fuss bringing him to America, all that work he and Hattie had put into the report, and nothing was to come of it? "I admit to some surprise, sir."

"Bah, I'll talk him out of it in the new year. We may be equal partners in the company, but I'll get my way. There's too much to lose, financially, by going stagnant. By spring thaw, we'll begin altering structures to prepare for the conversion, trimming labor—"

"Firing workers?" *No, Lord, please.* "That is not my recommendation at all. If you would look at my report, you will see how to keep on the entire workforce—"

"The whole point is to make money, Branson. The company grows richer when the payroll is cut." Mr. Nielson gestured at two women in fur-trimmed coats waving at him from the lace table. "My wife requires my presence, or at least my wallet. Merry Christmas to you, Branson." He clasped his hands behind his back and began moving in the direction of his wife.

"It is not a merry Christmas for those who will soon lose work."

Mr. Nielson turned around. "I beg your pardon?"

"Please, read my report. You and Mr. Flynn, both. Not just the financial pages. The methods described will provide the most efficient, effective, productive mill, where Slocum will profit and the workers can all keep their jobs."

Mr. Nielson's eyes narrowed. "You forget yourself, Branson. I brought you here to assess the property and show us how to best convert our facilities, not share your opinion on how we do business. If you persist in forcing it upon me, I shall inform Sir Henry Bessemer myself of your outrageous conduct."

Tim didn't care about that. All he could do was pray for calm before he punched something. "I beg of you to reconsider. It is Christmas. Will you not hear me out?"

"I've heard enough." Mr. Nielson stomped away.

Much as Tim wished to follow, he knew in the core of his being it would do no good. Nielson was a rigid man, and while Flynn's main concern seemed to be about money, he had mentioned his dislike of the methods of other steelmakers who overworked laborers to save costs. Tim might have been able to persuade him to read the full report, but he was already gone.

God in heaven, what is happening?

Tim wanted to pummel a wall. Wanted to yell. But he had to collect himself before he talked to Hattie. Had to formulate words.

It was too late. She hurried toward him, wide-eyed and smiling. "Zebedee told me that was Mr. Nielson you were with. He's seen him and Mr. Flynn a time or two. What did he say? Has he read the report?"

Tim's deep breath shook in his chest. "No."

"He will on Monday, I am sure."

"I am not. Hattie." How to tell her this? "Flynn said no to the Bessemer process, but Nielson is going ahead with it anyway. As planned."

"As planned? What does that mean?"

He hated himself for what he was about to tell her. Staring into her hazel eyes, however, the only thing he could do was tell her the truth. "In the new year, he'll be firing workers."

Chapter Seven

A groan welled up within Hattie. She covered her mouth with her hands to hold it back.

How many people would lose their jobs? Would Zebedee? Even if he managed to maintain a position at Slocum, how many of their friends and neighbors could say the same?

Tim's eyes were sad. "I know it may sound hollow, but I believe God will provide." He reached to lay a comforting hand on her shoulder.

She shrank from his touch. Sometimes it was too difficult to understand why God allowed such things to happen. To trust Him through such valleys. Far easier to wrest control back for herself. "I still do not understand. Could you not convince Mr. Nielson to read the report?"

"My attempt was not well received. He made up his mind and reminded me that I was hired to assess their property and make recommendations, but my opinion was not welcome."

"And that's that? It's over?"

"Much as this scenario infuriates me, yes. We knew our effort might not work."

"I believed it would. I thought you did too." How could he give up so easily?

"I never lied to you, Hattie. Much as I hoped and prayed for better results, failure was always a possibility."

She had failed, all right. And not just with the report. She'd allowed herself to hope, and hope was such a fragile thing. It melted faster than the first flakes of snow, vanishing so quickly it was as if they'd never existed.

"You're right, Tim. Looking back, I suppose I should have known the partners wouldn't be interested in anything but profit."

"It was never guaranteed that they'd listen, but we tried. I have no regrets." His light eyes narrowed. "But I can see that you do."

"Not about our attempt. It was the right thing to do."

"Your regrets are about me, then. I thought our friendship was based on far more than our project for Slocum. Was that all it was to you?"

"No." She couldn't pretend she hadn't enjoyed his company, that seeing him was always the best part of her day. "But you must return to England. You have duties to your mother, do you not? Besides, our failure with Slocum's partners would cast a pall over our time together. Our friendship, as you call it, may have begun at the Five and Dime, but it is forever linked to the all but certain loss of my brother's job. Our future's uncertainty is rooted in. . .this."

A muscle worked in his cheek as if he held back words. "The future is always uncertain, Hattie. One never knows what tomorrow holds, and we must do the best we can in the here and now."

"You know what I mean."

"Yes, that even if I were staying, you would not wish to be friends with me."

"There is no point in discussing it. You are not staying, and there is no way to change the unchangeable."

Any response he might have had was squelched by Zebedee and Cora's approach. Hattie's throat pinched at the sight of them, smiling and happy. "Their hearts will break when we tell them."

"We cannot." Tim's voice was sad but firm. "Our work was confidential. If Zebedee can be encouraged to find new work without you sharing what is to unfold, I think it wise, but beyond that, we must hold our tongues. At least until a formal decision is announced."

She was no actress. How could she pretend everything was all right? How could she get through Christmas, presenting her brother with a suit to be married in, knowing once he took on the responsibility of a wife that he might lose his livelihood?

Upon studying her and Tim's faces, Zebedee's grin slipped. "No longer hungry, eh?"

Hattie shook her head. "If you wish for another treat, by all means."

"Just as well if we don't, I suppose. Mother could stay on for hours, but Mrs. Oswald is complaining her toes are cold."

"We mustn't have that." Tim did not offer Hattie his arm again but led them back toward the older ladies, marching a half step ahead.

Hattie didn't miss the cringes Zeb and Cora exchanged.

No one voiced a word of suspicion about the change in her and Tim's behavior, but it was clear they'd gathered the two of them had argued. Once Hattie was in bed that night, she overheard her mother's voice through the thin bedroom walls. Something to Zebedee about a lover's quarrel between Hattie and Tim.

Hattie wadded her pillow into a ball and buried her face in it.

Lovers? Ha.

Quarrel? What was there to quarrel about? Not a thing. They'd failed at their task. Tim was leaving. Their friendship, as he'd called it, was doomed to fade.

Friendship. What would she have called it? Infatuation? Flirtation? More?

Whatever it once was, now it was finished.

The next day was Sunday, and Hattie and Zebedee's custom was to take turns attending church each week so one was always home with Mother. Although it was Hattie's week to join Cora's family at worship, she shooed her brother out the door. He didn't argue once he saw her eyes, red and puffy from crying overnight. She spent a quiet day reading scripture to Mother. Her family didn't press her for details about what transpired the night before, for which she was grateful. If they had, she might have broken her promise to keep her work confidential.

Shouldn't I break it though, Lord? Isn't this the sort of thing where the end justifies the means?

Or was that saying rotten and deceitful, displaying a lack of trust in God's provision?

I don't know what to do, Lord. So she did nothing outwardly, but inside she didn't stop praying. Not hoping, perhaps, but wanting to hope. Wanting to trust.

Wanting to talk to Tim and—what? Apologize?

The truth was, she held the upcoming change at Slocum against him. And it wasn't fair of her. Slocum Iron and Coal Works would be changing whether Tim had come or not. For good or ill, change was the only constant in the world, aside from God's love. He was the only steadfast thing she could cling to when everything around her eroded, shifted, ebbed, or sparked.

And even in dark times, His light shone through the darkness. She knew this from her own experience with her father dying. When he was lost to them, she and Mother and Zebedee thought they'd never smile again, but God had never left them, and in time, they had found a sense of healing.

They'd emerged from their grief different people. Stronger in some ways, although at a steep price.

She and her family and friends would survive an uncertain future too.

And Hattie would survive the pain of Tim returning to England, but not by denying it or burying it. She had to accept that her feelings for Tim were strong and could have turned to love faster than a wink. And at the festival, he'd said some things that gave her the impression there might be a way for them to be together.

It was impossible now, of course. She'd said such awful things about not wanting to be friends because of the changes at Slocum. She regretted them now. She'd have stayed friends. . .or more. . .with Tim if he didn't have to return to his mother, a duty she fully understood.

Lord, I can't change the mill. Or his leaving. But I can at least change the way we say farewell.

Eager to see him, she rushed to work at the Five and Dime Monday morning, smiling every time the door opened to admit a customer. But despite his weeks-long pattern of coming each morning, he failed to come.

There was nothing for it, then, but to hurry to his office building.

"He's gone," Armand said after poking his head out of his office when he heard her knocking on door number four. "Your business concluded, he said."

"Yes, but I thought. . . Never mind." She couldn't admit to Armand that her business today was of a personal nature.

"If it is urgent, he may be at the boardinghouse."

Hattie knew where Mrs. Oswald lived, and though it was not

far from her own home, Mother was home alone, awaiting lunch. "I shall call there tomorrow." It might not be precisely proper for her to visit a single man, but Hattie didn't care at the moment.

Cheered by her plan, Hattie waved farewell to Armand. "Merry Christmas to you and Luisa."

"*Wesołych Świąt*," he said, which she could only assume meant roughly the same thing.

The next day, Tuesday, she donned her best work dress, a red-and-white-striped ensemble that made her feel seasonal. Her spirits were high, despite the strange emptiness of the Five and Dime. It was as if all the shoppers had come in yesterday to make Christmas purchases after Hattie's shift ended. Even the pretty rose-strewn purse was sold. She could only hope it had gone to someone who would appreciate it.

As she unpacked the last of the Christmas ornaments, a familiar figure strode past the window. She knew that coat and hat, that long stride. Tim.

Her heart leaped high up her chest, and she hurried toward Mr. Woolworth. "Sir? May I take a moment for some fresh air?" She'd never asked for a break before. It felt forbidden, but she was desperate.

His brow bunching, her employer nodded. "By all means. You look a little flushed.

"Thank you, sir." Without taking the time to don her coat, she rushed out the front door onto Penn Avenue, following after Tim. He turned right onto Lackawanna Avenue, and for a brief time she lost sight of him while she bustled to catch up. The cold snuck beneath her cuffs and down her neck, but she folded her arms against the chill and hurried on.

The crowd thickened the closer she grew to the train station. Judging by the plume of the smoke rising from a locomotive waiting behind the station, it was almost time for the departure of the midmorning eastbound train. A number of the folks rushing toward the station carried valises or satchels.

Even Tim, she realized. He carried a leather case in each hand. The bags were far too small to be the entirety of his luggage if he was returning to England, but perhaps he'd sent his trunks ahead.

As he disappeared into the station, Hattie's stomach twisted into a knot. He was leaving Scranton. He'd finished the job he was hired to do, and nothing tethered him here any longer.

But Hattie wasn't finished with him. Not yet. She had to talk to him first. Had to settle things between them.

The shrill train whistle pierced the cold air like a mother's call, once, twice, then a third impatient blast, indicating the train's departure was imminent. The hour must be later than Hattie thought. *Oh no, Lord, don't let me miss him!* Hiking up her skirts, she broke into a most unladylike run.

Did anyone stare? She didn't care. She ignored everyone and everything, focused only on the train station. She would run through it to the platform and—she didn't know for certain what she'd do. Call his name? Clamber aboard the train without a ticket?

Right as she reached the station though, new sounds joined with the whistle, hissing and rolling and puffing, creating the chorus of a departing locomotive.

It was too late. He was gone. And, much as she hated it, she had to let him go even though she grieved everything. Their failure. Their parting.

Her broken heart.

It broke a little more when a boy around ten years of age delivered a wheelchair to their house later that afternoon with a red ribbon tied to one of the handles. It wasn't the same as the one Tim borrowed from his doctor friend at the boardinghouse. It was new, with a note attached, addressed to Mother.

"This is yours for today and every day, Mrs. Scott. Your humble servant, T.B."

"How thoughtful of Tim." Mother's eyes misted. "I only wish he had delivered it in person."

"So do I, Mother."

"Then enough of this moping. Help me get into this contraption, and let us go to Mrs. Oswald's so you two can settle your differences."

"I can't, Mother."

"Of course you can. You love that man."

Did she? "Mother, there's no use."

"You are my own darling daughter, but you're behaving like a muleheaded miss. Now fetch my wool cap for me, please."

"No, Mother, I truly cannot. He's not in Scranton anymore. I saw him enter the train station today, and the train left seconds later. He's. . .gone."

"Without so much as a fare-thee-well?"

"I think we said our goodbyes at the festival."

"I see." The fire in Mother's eyes doused, replaced by sympathy. Reaching for Hattie's hand, she gave her a sad smile. "I am here to listen if you wish to talk through what happened."

Hattie shook her head. "Thank you, but I'm not ready." Nor was she free to say everything yet, still bound by her vow to hold their work in confidence. "Soon though, I promise."

"Then let us speak of something else, something cheerful. Like Christmas. What do you wish for this year, dear one? New mittens? Or perhaps stockings? I noted a few pairs of yours are looking worn."

"No, I want for nothing."

"Surely there's something at the Five and Dime that tempts you."

This was a far more comfortable conversation to have than one about her complicated feelings, so she described the rose purse in detail. "It was sold, alas, but now I know if I find fabric I like, I can sew one."

"Is there nothing else you want?"

"Only things that cannot be bought at a store. A happy family and community." What had she told Tim? To give her family presents and then to save jobs at Slocum.

She might be able to accomplish the first, but her second wish was not to be.

If she could add one more thing to her Christmas list though, she would.

A fully mended heart.

Tim turned up the collar of his coat against the biting cold of the New York City afternoon. The walk from his hotel to this block of Thirty-Fourth Street was longer than he'd expected, but he would gladly walk the length of the city and back if it meant there was any hope of making things right.

He could only hope he wouldn't be turned away.

At the correct address, he stared up at the house, chocolate-dark in color and elegant in design. Tim took the stone steps to the wide porch and fixed his collar so he'd look more presentable. He lifted the brass knocker on the wide front door and let it fall with a loud slap.

Within seconds, a liveried servant opened the door, staring at him with an impassive, haughty expression. Tim was accustomed to seeing servants like this back in England if not in Scranton. He withdrew a silver case from his breast pocket and pulled a calling card from it. "Timothy Branson for Mr. Flynn."

"Have you an appointment?" The servant's words were clipped.

"I do not, but the matter is important."

The servant stepped aside, allowing Tim into a marble-floored, circular entry decorated in white and gold. Signs of the season were evident everywhere, from the kissing ball hanging from a chandelier to the pine garland festooning the staircase. The house was warm, fragrant with greenery and spice, and, from upstairs, the sounds of laughing children made Tim smile.

"Wait here." The servant withdrew through a side door rather than the yawning arch that led to a gold-papered hall, leaving Tim the choice of sitting on a hard-looking white settee or walking the perimeter of the room to admire the landscape paintings. Instead, he removed two boxes from his case, one eight inches square and the other a much smaller cube.

He expected the servant to return and usher him into a library or parlor, but instead, Mr. Flynn himself bustled through the archway, white eyebrows high in a surprised expression. "Mr. Branson? Last person I expected to see in New York."

"Thank you for seeing me, sir. I regret interrupting your time with family so close to Christmas." Tim handed him the square box. "Chocolates for you and your family to enjoy, sir."

"I see they are from my favorite confectioner in town." Mr. Flynn chuckled as he took the box. "Do tell, who spilled my secret?"

"No one, sir. I happened past the shop on my way here."

"Not that secret. I meant, who told you where to find me?"

"Again, no one, although I did ask your assistant at Slocum.

He is highly protective of your privacy, I assure you. He was also kind enough to oblige my request for the return of my report. I carried it with me and boarded a train for New York, armed only with the names of your daughter and son-in-law. Thankfully, they are well known in town, and their address was not difficult to learn."

"I am not certain if I should be impressed or alarmed by your sleuthing ability." Mr. Flynn's smile told Tim that he wasn't upset, but notably, he still did not invite him further inside. That meant he did not intend to prolong this meeting, and Tim would be wise to hurry it along.

"I shall hasten to the point, sir. I ask you to read the report I prepared for you."

"Nielson told you I skipped to the end, eh? Well, sorry as I am for your trouble, the price you estimated is too high for my comfort. You are sent from the bosom of Bessemer himself, so I know what you will say next to me. That the method is the way of the future. That Slocum will fall behind in industry without it."

"Those things are true, in my estimation, and Mr. Nielson agrees, so much so that he saw no need to read the report. But I wish you both would look at it before you make your final decision on the matter, because there is a good deal at stake." As Mr. Flynn watched, Tim set the small box on a round mahogany table in the room's center so he could pull the report from his case. "The woman I hired to transcribe my writings opened my eyes—she is the sister of one of the men who works in your mill. Zebedee Scott. You can learn more about him in the conclusion of my report, where I introduce him and several others in your employ who could lose their jobs if you go ahead with the conversion as Mr. Nielson plans—yes, he is confident he can persuade you to agree."

Mr. Flynn took the report but didn't open it. "This is about a woman? Saving her brother's job?"

"It is far too late to impress her. I was foolish, blithely ignoring things that have caused her great anxiety. I never should have assumed we could move forward as if this was not the most important thing to her family—"

He stopped himself. Mr. Flynn didn't need to hear this romantic claptrap. "I am a man who must listen to the conscience God has given me. A man whose mind is set on something far more than profit or steel, but I do not ignore it entirely, sir. The report details how to preserve all the jobs and still make a hefty profit."

Mr. Flynn sighed. "I am not a man of faith myself, but that does not mean I am heartless. Still, the numbers do not lie, Mr. Branson."

"A friend of mine—an accountant—said something that has rattled around my brain the past few days. Numbers only tell part of the story. The methods outlined in this report will cost more at first, yes, but you will make it up soon. Production could quadruple within a few years, which, of course, is reflected in the projected profits, as described here." He pointed to the page open in front of Mr. Flynn. "Such vibrant growth would help the people who rely on Slocum Iron and Coal Works at the same time. They are good people. Hardworking, honest. So in their honor, I have brought this to you." He indicated the small box on the table.

Mr. Flynn set down the report and chocolates, trading them for the cubed box. With a half smile, he pulled a silver bauble from within, round and gleaming. "A Christmas ornament. A thoughtful token of the season, to be sure."

"It is from the Five and Dime on Penn Street, run by Charles Woolworth. The woman I told you about works there. I hoped this small token would remind you of your neighbors in Scranton."

"Then it shall have pride of place on the Christmas tree in the parlor." Mr. Flynn carefully tucked the bauble back in the box. "Would you care to help me hang it, Branson?"

"Sir?" What was he saying?

Mr. Flynn tipped his head toward the archway. "You look like you could use a hot cup of coffee to warm your bones once we hang the ornament. Then perhaps we could further discuss this report of yours."

"Thank you, sir."

Tim knew better than to expect the best outcome, but he hoped for it.

Then he could return to England, his conscience clear. Even if his heart was empty.

Chapter Eight

Christmas Eve, to Hattie, had always been the most beautiful church service of the year, and this year was no exception. It had been a precious reminder of the significance of the holiday, and she'd added her voice to the others gathered to thank God for what the scriptures called His indescribable gift—His Son, Jesus.

The Light of the World, shining into darkness.

She was not immune from a darkness of the heart, and it weighed heavily on her as she, Zebedee, and Mother left church as twilight fell. While Zebedee pushed Mother in the new wheelchair, joining her in a Christmas hymn, Hattie gazed up at the lead-dark sky. She couldn't see the heavenly bodies beyond the thick cloud cover, but she trusted they were there, bright and shining.

Sometimes she felt that way about God. Her vision might be obscured by her anxieties and circumstances, yet she knew He was always there. Faithful. Tender.

Hattie bit her lip. *I haven't trusted You, Lord, but I want to now. Please forgive me for focusing on the clouds of my troubles rather than on You. I pray You would guide me as I navigate forward, no matter what comes, following the path You've set me on, walking by Your light.*

A sense of hopefulness warmed her chest. She didn't know

how God would work out her family's future, but He was the One who held it in His hands. There was no safer place to be.

Smiling, she joined in the last verse of "Silent Night" with her family.

At its end, Mother sighed with satisfaction. "It was wonderful to be in church again. Hearing the sermon, singing together, and seeing friends."

They had chatted with quite a few of Mother's old friends after the service concluded, but not Mrs. Oswald, who rushed out with a group that must have been her nephew and his family. She was probably in a hurry to return to her boardinghouse and serve supper to her tenants. Nice as it would have been to meet her family, it was just as well they went their own ways tonight without speaking. Undoubtedly, Tim would have come up in conversation, and Hattie wasn't sure she wanted to talk about him. Not yet.

Far better to continue the current topic. "Now you can attend church every Sunday, Mother."

"And I shall." Mother twisted in the wheelchair to look up at Hattie and Zebedee. "I knew I missed church, but I didn't realize just how much until I crossed the threshold tonight. I wish I'd come back sooner. You two tried to get me there, I know."

"I offered to borrow a wagon to get us there, and I'm more than strong enough to carry you inside to a pew," Tim reminded her.

"I know, dear boy, but I didn't want to cause a fuss. Nor did I wish to see anyone after your father died. I was ill, and I did not want it to be known how bad a shape he left us in. For so long, my illness robbed me of the will to do much of anything. But lately I feel. . .invigorated. Perhaps God's healing is bubbling up in me. Things are changing, children."

Now that Hattie had chosen to fix her eyes on God's goodness, she joined Mother in concentrating on future blessings. "You are right. Winter will pass to spring, Zeb and Cora will marry. Happy changes indeed."

"The wheelchair is a wonderful change." Mother's eyes shone in the glow of the streetlamps. "I'll always be grateful to Tim for such an extravagant gift."

Hattie ignored the pang in her belly at the mention of his name, choosing to focus instead on Mother's newfound mobility. "And now that you have means to be out and about in town, where else would you like to go?"

"The Five and Dime, of course. Mrs. Oswald showed me the ring Tim gave her. It was an amusing gesture, but it's quite pretty for a ring of that price."

Everything came back to Tim, didn't it? Maybe someday her heart wouldn't ache when she heard his name.

"If I'd known you wished for a ring, I'd have purchased one for your Christmas, Mother."

"I think half the fun will be going and selecting it for myself." Mother sounded giddy at the prospect.

They turned onto their street. A lone figure stood on the walk outside their house, his tall frame leaning against the lamppost. The stance, the height, the hat and coat, all so achingly familiar, Hattie lost the ability to breathe.

His head turned. Even in the dim, she could see the gleam of his smile.

He lifted an arm in greeting. "Happy Christmas."

As Hattie struggled to get enough air, Mother reached for him with both hands. "Oh, and what a wonderful Christmas it is too, Timothy. I cannot thank you enough for the chair."

"The pleasure was all mine, ma'am." He shook Zebedee's hand.

If his smile was tight for Hattie, well, she was certain she looked strained as well. How could she not? Her heart was pounding so hard and fast in her throat, she wouldn't be surprised if she'd come to resemble a bullfrog.

"Come in, do." Zebedee unlocked the door. "Sorry you missed church."

Tim gathered parcels from beneath the lamppost. "Forgive me, but I just arrived back in town. I traveled out of the state."

"Where?" Hattie blurted, and her face grew as hot as the corner stove. These past days, grieving him being gone, she'd imagined what she'd do and say if she was ever given the chance to speak to him again. At first, she'd been rendered incapable of speech, but now that she had the opportunity, *that* was what she'd asked?

"New York City."

Questions tumbled one over another as Mother ushered him into the parlor, but none of them were really important. Not when Tim was here, as she'd prayed and hoped. She would not let him leave without speaking to him privately. Making things right. . .

If only he'd meet her gaze so she could get an inkling of what he was thinking. Instead, he admired the beribboned pine bough on the mantel, draped with strung popcorn, pine cones, and dried orange slices. "Such festive decorations."

"Christmas comes but once a year," Mother said in a singsong voice. "Do take your coat off and make yourself comfortable, Tim. Hattie, put the kettle on for tea."

Much as she wanted to talk to Tim, she was grateful for the chance to collect her thoughts and pray. Happy chatter reached Hattie's ear as she stripped off her coat and filled the kettle with fresh water. Then she pressed her hand against her fluttering stomach, smoothing the fabric of her bronze suit.

As she returned to the parlor, Mother's face was aglow with excitement. "Look, Hattie. Tim brought us a plum pudding." She gestured to the dessert on a plate centered on the table. Dome-shaped, it was brown and speckled with purple currants. White icing drizzled down from the top, which had been crowned with a sprig of holly.

She smiled at Tim. "One of the four you made with Mrs. Oswald?"

"It is indeed. I promised you one for Christmas. I hope you don't mind that it's one day early."

"I count this evening as Christmas, dear boy." Mother beamed. "I cannot wait to taste it."

"Shall we have supper first?" Hattie had plates of cold ham and pickled vegetables waiting in the icebox.

Mother waved away the suggestion as if it were the height of silliness. "If ever there was a day to have dessert first, 'tis Christmas Eve. Would you please bring some plates and spoons in with the tea?"

Mother was not behaving her usual self at all, but Hattie was not about to spoil her happiness. Especially since happy moments might be few and far between soon. "Of course."

Tim hopped to his feet. "I'll help."

"No, please. Sit and warm yourself." She'd prefer their conversation to have more privacy than what the thin wall between the parlor and the kitchen afforded, especially since so much of what she had to say was rooted in things her family wasn't supposed to yet know about.

She prepared the tea and set the pot on a tray with cups, small plates, spoons, and napkins. Her stomach shook like a dish of jelly as she carried out the tray.

Lord, please help me find the time to speak to Tim tonight. Make it clear when that moment is to be, that I might seize on it, and that I won't spoil my family's happy Christmas.

When she returned to the parlor, however, her family's happiness already appeared to have been spoiled. Zebedee and Mother's faces bore twin expressions of shock, and Zeb's hands curled into fists on his lap.

Her feet rooted to the rug. "What has happened?"

Tim rose and took the tray from her, setting it beside the plum pudding on the table. "I am explaining to your family that I was paid to assess Slocum's existing property and instruct them how to best transition to steel production using Bessemer's process, and you were hired to assist me. And that the changes would entail firing a large percentage of those who currently work at Slocum. Possibly including Zebedee."

As she met her family's sad gazes, she wrung her hands at her waist. "I am sorry I could not tell you. The business was confidential, and I had given Tim my word that I wouldn't speak of it. Please know how hard we tried to persuade the partners to keep everyone employed. Tim had the most wonderful ideas for adding shifts but making them shorter so everyone could keep working but not be so tired. And at the same wages too. Shorter hours and Tim's safety features would have improved conditions and morale at Slocum."

"Hattie's ideas were amazing," Tim said with an admiring smile. "She was the torch who lit the way, and together we produced a solid report for the partners to address the changes."

"Alas, Mr. Flynn didn't read it beyond the financial page's bottom line." Hattie couldn't meet her family's gazes as she took a seat beside her mother.

Tim sat by Zebedee. "Actually, Mr. Flynn did read it, from introduction to conclusion."

Hattie's chin lifted so fast she'd probably have a crick in her neck tomorrow. "I thought he said no and then left for the holidays. Was Mr. Nielson mistaken?"

"No, Mr. Flynn did leave Scranton after a mere glance at our report. So I chased him to New York City."

"That's what you were doing there?" Her pitch rose two octaves.

Tim's smile grew. "All I knew was his daughter lived somewhere in that large city, and though the task seemed impossible, I had to try. I took the report back from the Slocum office, boarded a train, and prayed."

"What happened?" Mother's hand was on her heart. "The suspense is unbearable."

"I do not mean to prolong the story, forgive me." Tim's smile was apologetic. "Thankfully, Mr. Flynn received me in every sense of the word, and together we went through the report. He is not a man of faith, but he was never comfortable with the prospect of laying off so many workers. Alas, he was even less comfortable with spending money. However, he listened when I explained that, yes, there will be a higher cost at first, but if Slocum employs the methods Hattie and I propose, they will soon begin turning an even larger profit. My friend Armand, an accountant, verified all the numbers for me before I left."

"Spending money is required to make money." Zebedee relaxed a fraction. "So you spoke to Mr. Flynn in a language he can understand—money—and he is thinking about the matter, I take it?"

"Not thinking about it. He agreed to it. He sent Nielson a telegram that very day, and before I left New York, they had come to an agreement. Every job is spared as Slocum Iron and Coal Company moves forward in making quality steel. And it is all due to Hattie."

Zebedee stood and let out a whoop. Mother clapped, her face pink with excitement. Hattie gaped at them, then at Tim.

He smiled at her. Tentatively, as if he wasn't sure how she felt about his announcement. How could he not know? How could he not read everything in her eyes?

She couldn't help rushing toward him for a brief embrace. A thank-you, short and sweet.

But then she was enveloped in his warm, strong arms, her head pressed against his pounding heart.

Oh, but it felt like coming home to a snug parlor after a long, cold walk on a winter's day. He smelled of cedar and spice, an intoxicating mixture she could happily breathe in for the rest of her life.

Shocked at the direction of her thoughts, she shifted back, out of his warm embrace into the cold of reality. Happy as she was that the company partners accepted their proposed ideas, nothing else had changed. Tim was still leaving for England in a matter of days. Tears stung her eyes, and all she could do was hope her family misinterpreted them as tears of happiness and relief.

"Thank you." Zebedee shook Tim's hand and then reached for Hattie. "Both of you."

"Yes, you dear ones, thank you." Mother took both of Tim's hands in hers. "You've made this a merry little Christmas."

"What is Christmas without presents?" Tim picked up the parcels he'd brought. "These are for you."

Hattie's heart warmed and panged at the same time. They had no gifts for Tim. She could do something overnight so he'd have something to open tomorrow though. Embroider his initials on a handkerchief. Yes, she had all she needed for that.

"We shall open them tomorrow with our other gifts." She

gestured at the small pile beside the hearth: the completed suit for Zebedee, the books for Mother, and gifts from her family that she suspected were new mittens and wool stockings. "Will you come to supper?"

"I would like it above all things, thank you. But I would also like it very much if you opened your presents now."

"If you insist." Mother opened hers, oohing over the fancy box of confections from New York City. Zebedee's gift was a pen set, also from a New York retailer. But Tim's gift for Hattie was from much closer to home.

"The purse." She fingered the smooth, rose-patterned fabric. "How did you know I'd set my eye on it?"

"Your friends at the Five and Dime told me on Monday afternoon. Do you truly like it?"

She clutched it to her chest. "I do. Thank you."

Mother leaned back in her chair. "Since you are coming tomorrow, Tim, shall we save the pudding until then? As a grand finale to our Christmas feast?"

Did Tim go pale? "I think we should carve into it now if you don't mind. It is here and ready, after all."

"I do not require persuasion." Mother reached for the large serving spoon on the tray. "Do I slice or scoop, Tim? I don't know how this is done. Hattie, pour tea while I portion this out."

Tim lunged—there was no other word for it—to the tray and gently put his hand on Mother's. "If you don't mind, I thought Hattie could do the honors? Since she is the true heroine of the hour?"

"I am not the one who went all the way to New York." Besides, Hattie didn't know the first thing about plum puddings and how they should be served. Sliced or scooped—what was it Mother was going to do with the pudding? And it was really Mother's place to do the serving if she wished. Why was Tim acting so strangely?

Mother didn't seem to mind though. "Yes, Hattie, please serve it up for us." She handed Hattie the spoon.

"Very well." Hattie picked up a small plate to begin serving.

Tim rotated the plate so the holly berries faced her. His shrug was so casual, she wondered why he'd bothered at all.

She slid the spoon into the pudding so the serving would receive a good share of the icing from top to bottom. "Here we are, then. Our first plum pudding." It smelled richly of raisins and spice. "Mother and Zeb, I must warn you that there are sometimes tokens hidden inside, according to Tim, so be fair warned that you don't choke. A shoe for a journey, a coin for fortune, an anchor for safety at home, I believe, and a ring for—"

The sound of metal on metal was unmistakable. A token! How enjoyable that would be for the recipient. "Who should receive this slice?"

"That is your slice, Hattie." Tim's lips twitched.

Shaking her head at him, she plopped the pudding onto the plate without looking at it. "The server always takes the last piece. Mother?" She extended it toward her.

"Hattie, I am certain that portion is not for me." Mother's eyes were on the plate.

Hattie looked down. Silver sparkled from the pudding, no surprise since she'd heard the faint sound of the spoon against a token. But there was not *a* token. There were many, pressing through the sides and bottom, impossible to miss. One slid from its precarious position on the side of her serving and plopped onto the plate with a metallic clink.

Not wishbones. Not coins or shoes or anchors or whatever else Tim had mentioned when describing the lore of the tokens to her. "Rings."

Her gaze met Tim's hopeful one. His uncertain, sweet, loving one.

"Do you remember what a ring means?" His voice was quiet. Soft.

Her throat was so full of emotion, all she could do was nod.

"I wish someone would enlighten me," Zebedee muttered.

"Shall we step outside for a moment?" Tim extended his hand.

Nodding, she took it, and without stopping for coats or mittens or any sensible protection against the cold, they hurried out the front door as night was falling. The intensity of Tim's gaze made her feel as if he could see to the very depths of her being.

"A ring, Tim?"

"Dozens of rings. I didn't want them to go unnoticed."

There was no missing them. "Oh, Tim. I have so longed to speak to you."

"And I you. I owe you a lifetime of apologies, Hattie, for glossing over the uncertainty of the future you were facing. I should have been more sensitive to your family's needs. When you said the failure of our project would cast a pall over our friendship, it tore me to the quick. That is not the reason I went to New York—I went in the hopes of getting Flynn to see sense—but I only hope now that Slocum doesn't cast a shadow over us, you might reconsider. Could you bear to be my friend, more than my friend, now?"

"Bear it? Being without you is what I find unbearable, Tim. When I spoke those words about Slocum and our friendship, I did not speak true. I lashed out in pain and fear. I am sorry and have wanted nothing more than to make things right between us, but I saw you get on the train and I thought..."

"You thought I left, never to return."

"Believing I no longer wished for us to be friends."

"I came to America for a brief season, but the moment I saw you, I knew my life was forever changed. You make me a better man, and I don't want to spend another day without you, never. I wish to face the future together, as a team, the way we do best. I love you, Hattie. More than I ever thought it possible to love another. Have I any hope that you feel the same?"

"I love you so very much, but—"

"But what? We can figure it out together."

"It does not change that your home is England. I know you're concerned about your mother, who wishes you close and settled. I cannot leave my mother either. How do we manage that?"

He smiled as he pulled her into his arms, not so close that she couldn't see his eyes but near enough that it seemed only natural to place her hands on his chest. "Funny thing. While in New York, I contacted my mother via transatlantic cable. Told her I regretted my failure to notice how sick my father was and that it pained me to fail in my duty to care for her now, being in America. But then I asked if she would be willing to come here for a while and why. Because of you."

Hattie's pulse ratcheted. "What did she say?"

"She responded immediately, scolding me for my guilt over not recognizing Father's illness when he worked so hard to conceal it. Then she upbraided me for worrying about her. All she ever wanted was to see me happy and settled, wherever it is. Even if it's not in England." His eyes blazed. "My home is you, Hattie."

"You're willing to stay here?"

"Actually, I must, because Mr. Flynn has offered me a job overseeing the transition at Slocum."

"Truly? And you accepted it?"

"Yes, just as he accepted my invitation to attend church with me in the new year." His gaze fixed on her lips. "I don't wish to sever ties with England altogether though. I thought we might go for our honeymoon so you can meet my family, and we can bring my mother back with us, if she likes. Although it's just dawned on me, I have yet to ask for your hand."

He dropped to one knee on the walkway, pulled a gold ring with a blazing red ruby from his pocket, and offered it to her. "It is not from the Five and Dime."

She laughed as tears blurred her vision. "No, it is not."

"Will you marry me, Hattie? Let me show you how much I adore you today and all the days to come?"

"Yes, Tim, yes! Now get up off that freezing ground and kiss me properly."

After sliding the ring onto her finger, he obliged her request, and with great enthusiasm too. The pressure of his lips was gentle at first, then firm, and he rendered her senseless.

"A merry little Christmas, indeed." Mother's voice came through the front window.

Jolting back to the present, Hattie spared a peek and saw the curtain fall. Her family had been spying, but she didn't mind. Before she could comment, she made another realization. Flakes of snow dusted Tim's shoulders and dark hair. "It's snowing?"

"I suppose it is." He cupped her face in his scarred hands. "And I suppose it's beautiful too, but it doesn't compare to the beauty within my arms. Alas, we should probably go back inside. I am sure they will have questions about my intentions."

She snuggled against his side as they made their way to the door. "I certainly have questions."

"About me?"

"About the rings in the pudding—were they in that box that fell from your pocket that day at the store?"

He laughed. "I didn't lie when I said I'd previously purchased them. They just weren't purchased from you."

"I didn't realize you shopped anywhere else in town," she teased.

"Only for surprises, my love."

His love.

Something she never would have put on her list of Christmas wishes, but now that she had received this most precious gift? How could she not cherish it forever?

"I wouldn't blame you for having serious doubts about me though." Tim grew serious, stopping in front of the door. "I tend to get too engrossed in my work, as you know, but I'd never wish you to think I don't care. You, my dearest darling, are the most important thing in the world to me, so will you help me break that habit?"

Silly man. He was the most important thing in the world to her too. "How do you propose I accomplish that? Blow the whistle you gave me?"

His lips quirked. "I'd rather hoped you'd try kisses first."

"Are you certain?" she teased. "The whistle is so handy. In fact, it's just inside the house. I can fetch it right now—"

His kiss banished all thought of whistles from her mind.

Epilogue

December 24, 1882

Candlelight caught on the cobalt-blue ornament that resembled a cluster of grapes, causing it to gleam on the parlor Christmas tree as if lit from within by a sapphire flame. "Perfect," Hattie proclaimed.

"My American Christmas bauble." Tim moved behind her and wrapped his arms around her. "A precious reminder of our mornings in the Five and Dime, way back when."

"Last year is not that far back, my love."

"But so much has happened in the past year." Tim kissed the top of her head. "We married and moved into this lovely house with our mothers, and now we need a bigger house. A *much* bigger house once the little one arrives."

Their baby would arrive midspring, soon after Zebedee and Cora's baby. Mother was thrilled by the prospect of two grandchildren coming so soon.

Slocum Iron and Coal had changed too. Tim's work as adviser to Mr. Flynn, as well as bringing on his friend Armand in the finance department, had initiated many positive changes in the company. The first blow, or pouring of molten steel from the Bessemer furnace, occurred to great success—and every employee shared in the celebration.

They rejoiced that Mr. Flynn had joined them at church soon after they married, and now he and his wife were regular members. They continued to pray for Mr. Nielson's faith as well.

But tonight they celebrated Christmas. After the candlelight service, a small group of friends and family gathered to trim the tree and feast at Tim and Hattie's house. The scents of pine and apple cider blended in the air along with the festive chatter of their mothers, Zeb and Cora, and even Mrs. Oswald, giving the house a rich, festive atmosphere.

Tim released Hattie to hang a silver ball on the tree, a twin to the one he'd purchased for Mr. Flynn last year. "Every year let us buy a new ornament from the Five and Dime for our tree."

"To remind us of where we started?" Hattie stepped back to admire the ornaments.

"And how far God has brought us."

I asked You for help last year, Lord, and You gave me so much more. You gave me a rich and wonderful life with this man at my side.

She would never take it for granted. Hattie reached for her husband's hand. "Merry Christmas, my love."

"Merry Christmas, and many more to come."

Tim sealed his promise with a kiss.

Author's Note

Thank you for joining me in a celebration of Christmas past! I hope you enjoyed spending time with Tim and Hattie as much as I did.

We writers seldom work on Christmas stories during the holidays themselves, but I was grateful for the keen reminders of Christmas this story brought to me "off-season", namely, that Jesus—God with us—was sent not only to save us and shine His light on our weary world but to walk alongside us on our journeys. What a privilege we have, to be invited into such an intimate relationship with the living God!

Now for a few tidbits on the story itself. Readers may notice that creative license is used from time to time. For example, the Slocum Iron & Coal Company is fictional but loosely based on the real Lackawanna Iron and Coal Company. I invented it so I could time the adoption of the Bessemer process to the appearance of the Woolworth's on Penn Avenue, and I named it after an early settlement in the area, Slocum Hollow. The riot Hattie refers to is a real event that took place in 1877.

There wasn't a lunch counter at Woolworth's for a few decades yet, nor were there specific departments, but "Sum" Woolworth was an active presence on the sales floor of what was already referred to as a "Five and Dime" (according to Merriam-Webster), and everything sold for either a nickel or a dime. Every item Tim buys in the shop was sold at Woolworth's during this era, except for the ring, although "jewelry" is documented as having been sold.

Many thanks to the Lord for His faithfulness to me; to editors Rebecca Germany and Ellen Tarver; to agent Tamela Hancock Murray; to my coauthors Cindy, Patty, and Christina; to my family; to those who prayed for me; and to you, dear readers. Thank you for picking up this book! You've blessed my socks off!

Merry Christmas!

Susanne Dietze began writing love stories in high school, casting her friends in the starring roles. Today, she's an award-winning, RWA RITA®-nominated author who's seen her work on the ECPA, Amazon, and Publisher's Weekly Bestseller Lists for Inspirational Fiction. Married to a pastor and the mom of two, Susanne lives in California and enjoys fancy-schmancy tea parties, genealogy, the beach, and curling up on the couch with a costume drama. To learn more, visit her website, www.susannedietze.com.

A Home for Christmas

Patty Smith Hall

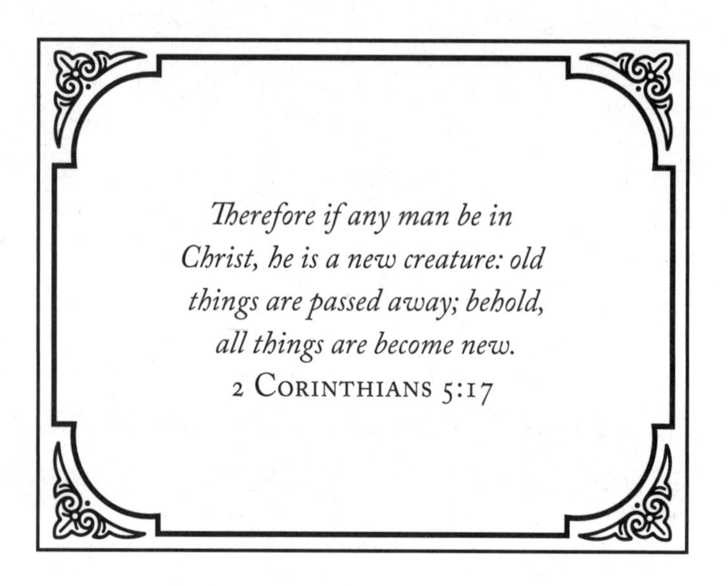

Therefore if any man be in Christ, he is a new creature: old things are passed away; behold, all things are become new.
2 Corinthians 5:17

DEDICATION

To my husband, Danny. The man who loves Christmas more than anyone I know. I love you most.

Chapter One

"Essie, that man is here again."

Estella Banfield looked up from the box of buttons and sewing notions she'd been working on to find her friend Maggie hurrying toward her. "Who?"

"You know, the one you've been talking about." She must have noticed Essie's confusion. "The one who buys six of everything."

"Oh." Essie's stomach did a little flutter, not that she knew why. She and Pastor Warner had only exchanged pleasantries the few times she'd rung up his order. Still, she found herself looking forward to his weekly visits and possibly uncovering the reason behind his unusual purchases.

"So?" Maggie asked, her expression expectant. "Are you going to go and talk to him?"

Her ears burned at the thought. "I don't know. Doesn't that seem a bit forward?"

"Not if it comes with the offer to help, and you are in charge of the personal care counter, after all." She leaned closer so only Essie could hear her. "He's studying those toothbrushes as if they were the Declaration of Independence."

Her lips twitched at her friend's ridiculous comparison. Still, Essie had a job to do, and happy customers meant returning customers. After putting the box behind the counter, she slipped through the gate and joined Maggie on the sales floor. "Toothbrushes section, correct?"

A playful smile lighting her face, Maggie nodded. "He was there the last time I checked."

"All right." Essie took a few measured steps down the aisle, giving her leg time to adjust. Since the accident, the brace she'd worn helped steady her, but she had to walk slowly or risk tripping over her lame foot. She glanced back to find Maggie watching her. "Don't you need to go back to work?"

"I just wanted to make sure you spoke to him this time," she replied with an impish gleam in her eyes.

"I will."

"Promise?"

Essie gave a little huff. "I promise. Now go, before Mr. Sum discovers that you're not at the lunch counter."

"He's the one who sent me over here." Maggie couldn't contain the laughter in her voice.

Essie froze. Charles Sumner Woolworth was a kind boss, but he held high standards for his employees. "He's not angry with me, is he? I mean, I don't want to lose this job."

"Calm down," her friend replied as she hurried toward her. Taking her hands, Maggie met her gaze. "He didn't say it in a mean way. Only that he thought you two would make a handsome couple if only one of you would get up the nerve to speak to the other." She leaned in closer. "Who would have thought Mr. Sum was such a romantic?"

Not Essie, but then she hadn't been working there very long. Besides, she didn't even know the man Mr. Sum wanted to pair her with. All she knew about him was that he was a minister and that he had the peculiar habit of buying six of everything.

"You will tell me everything that happens, won't you?"

Essie couldn't see any harm in Maggie's request, not that there would be that much to tell. "I didn't know you were fascinated by oral hygiene," she teased.

Maggie squeezed her hands, then let her go. As she walked back up the aisle, she called out over her shoulder. "The man is too interested in you to talk about some silly toothbrushes."

Essie laughed. Such a description of herself would amuse her family and friends. Since the carriage accident that left her right leg lame, "poor girl" and "unmarriageable" had been the only words whispered at suppers and in ballrooms to describe her. If only she could be more like the women she'd befriended here at the store. They had a confidence that came from providing for themselves, something she'd never had to do and, if her mother had a say in it, never would.

Her foot slipped, and she grabbed hold of the nearby counter to keep from falling. Mother's latest campaign to get her married off had been a disaster. Most of the men in their social circle knew of her physical defect and had taken a wide berth. But her mother wouldn't be deterred. Papa's contacts in Washington and New York were invited to dinner, where they suffered through awkward conversation, during which Mother expounded upon Essie's attributes. "She sings like a bird and plays the piano as if she were born to it," and "She's been educated in the art of running a large household and can hold a conversation with the best of them." To be fair, some showed interest—until she got up from her chair and walked, and they discovered what everyone else already knew.

Poor girl.

Essie righted herself and kept moving forward. Wasn't there more to life than playing a song correctly or organizing a menu for Cook? What about helping the poor or teaching others how to read and write? She wanted a purposeful life, but what did that look like? How could she find meaning in her life if she didn't know where to look?

She turned down the personal care aisle and stopped, her heart skipping a beat. There, studying the toothbrushes as if his life depended on it, was Pastor Max Warner. He picked up one, glanced at it for a moment, then returned it to the shelf where he picked up another one. She'd caught him doing this kind of thing several times before, his dark head bent over the soap packaging as he read it or weighing a hairbrush in his strong, very capable hands. A spendthrift, the other girls had called him, because he bought six of each product he sought.

And if she didn't help him, he might never buy a toothbrush. Essie moved toward him. "Pastor Warner, how are you today?"

"Miss Banfield, I didn't see you there." His lips parted into a wide smile as if he was truly glad to see her. Her heart did another little hiccup. "How has your day been thus far? Good, I hope."

"Lovely, thank you. May I help you with something?"

"Toothbrushes!" His outburst surprised not only her but him, by the look on his face. He took a deep breath then began again. "I'm looking for toothbrushes. Six of them."

She kind of liked this befuddled look on him. It made him more human instead of a man of God. Essie nodded to the shelf. "This is all we have in the way of toothbrushes. Maybe if you could tell me who they are for, I could show you different sizes."

He showed her the one he was holding. "I was trying to figure out why some were larger than others. Why is that?"

The way he watched her, as if she were the most important thing in the room, caught her off guard. She swallowed, and when she spoke, the words came out breathy. "The smaller ones are for children while the larger ones are for adults."

"A child would need a smaller brush." His blue eyes gazed into hers. "That makes all the sense in the world. Thank you, Miss Banfield. I'll take six child-sized toothbrushes then."

The tiny bubble of happiness popped. Good heavens, she was making cow eyes at a married man! She turned and counted out six of their finest toothbrushes, then grabbed a large container of tooth powder and handed it to him. "This should be everything you need. Is there anything else I can help you with?"

"Well. . ." He paused as he pulled a piece of paper from his pocket. "To be truthful, I have quite a few things I need to pick up and not a lot of time." His gaze snagged hers again, and for the briefest of moments, she forgot to breathe. "I could really use your help if you have a moment."

He's married, remember. Essie gave herself a mental shake and straightened. "Of course. What's next on your list?" She glanced over it. "You didn't like the soap you bought last time?"

The pastor blushed at the question. "Well, yes, but the boys complained it smelled too much like a girl for them. Maybe we could look for something with a little more lye and a little less perfume."

"You have boys?" She wasn't asking for her own sake. She was just doing her job. Mr. Sum himself often said, "Build a relationship with the customer, and they'll keep coming back." She glanced down at the toothbrushes in his basket. "How many girls do you have?"

"None, thank the Lord." He chuckled as they walked up the aisle. "I wouldn't know what to do with them. No, it's better I stick with boys."

That was a strange comment. Almost as if he thought he had

a say in the matter. "Wouldn't your wife like a little girl to dress up and pet over?"

Pastor Warner stopped in the middle of the aisle, a look of amused bewilderment on his face. "I'm not married."

Why did the news make Essie so happy? "You're not? I just presumed when you talked about the boys that you were married."

"That's understandable." He hesitated for a moment as if collecting his thoughts. She wagered he was a wonderful pastor, not like stuffy old Pastor Henderson who preached where her family attended. "The boys are children I found living on the streets. They had no family, no way to keep warm or be fed, so I opened my home to them. I know what it's like to not know where your next meal is coming from, and I don't want any children to have to suffer like that."

"That's so kind of you," Essie replied. "How old are they?"

"John is the oldest; he's almost twelve. Then there's Jacob, Noah, Neal, and Billy. Tommy is my youngest at six."

Six years old and out on the street. What had the poor boy lived through to be fending for himself at that age? She had no clue. She who had so much, with her Paris-designed gowns and elaborate dinners, while others prayed for a scrap of bread or to be warm. Without realizing what she was doing, Essie reached out and touched the pastor's arm. "What can I do to help?"

Was this woman serious about helping him?

Max had heard this question before, usually from a well-to-do member of his congregation wanting to donate money for absolution of wrongdoing or some marriage-minded mama volunteering her daughter in hopes that sparks would fly. But Essie Banfield didn't fall into either category. So why did she want to help him and the boys?

Maybe it would be best to dissuade her. "You don't have to do that."

"I know I don't have to, but. . ." She nibbled on her lower lip as if she was nervous. "I want to have a purpose."

He blinked. Of all the answers he expected, this was not one of them. He turned to face her. "I'm not certain I understand."

Essie glanced around to ensure their privacy, then met his gaze again. "I've attended church with my parents since I was old enough to walk. I've heard the Bible taught, and I pray occasionally at holidays and such. I thought it was enough."

It was a story Max had heard time and time again, and it broke his heart. It was what drove him to preach the Gospel from his pulpit so that everyone would know the saving grace of God. He focused more intently on Essie. "But it wasn't. Enough, I mean."

She shook her head. "A few months ago, we had a visiting pastor, and he spoke about having a relationship with God. I wanted that with everything in my heart. So I prayed, and when I opened my eyes, I knew everything was different. I was different because of Him."

" 'Therefore if any man be in Christ, he is a new creature.' " Max gave her what he hoped was an encouraging smile. "Second Corinthians."

"I haven't gotten that far in my reading yet." Her cheeks went a delicate shade of palest pink. "Anyway, I found that all the things I volunteered for before weren't enough. I want to do something that will help others, something that will give my life purpose. But I'm not exactly sure how to do that."

A sense of excitement rolled through Max. This kind of response to the Word was what he longed for in his own congregation. A call to action, to live out the scriptures he'd taught.

Essie understood that, and he could help her. "Have you prayed about it?"

"Yes, though I'm not very good at it." She shifted away from him, her gaze darting around, breaking the thread that bound them together. "I shouldn't have bothered you with all of this. You yourself said you were short on time." Essie gave him a perfunctory smile. "You were looking for soap."

As she gracefully walked ahead of him, Max found that he couldn't move, not until he knew the answer to one question. "Why did you offer to help me and the boys?"

Essie turned to face him, her expression peaceful. Almost serene. "I don't know. I just felt this nudge inside me, pushing me to help out if I could."

"That was the Holy Spirit," he replied. Like a bull in a china shop, he was. But he was still learning how to be a pastor. Now came the big question. Could he swallow his pride and allow Essie Banfield to help him and the boys? He wasn't sure. How would his congregation feel about their pastor taking help from a woman who didn't attend their church? How would the boys feel about it? Max scrubbed his chin with his hand. "Can I think about your offer?"

"Of course," she answered, then turned and proceeded down the aisle.

Max watched her for a moment. She walked, her movements graceful, each step measured. Thick curls were drawn up at the back of her neck, shimmering with each step. He might enjoy the look of a beautiful woman like any other man, but Essie was different. There was an innocence to her, a calm spirit that seemed to call out to him. But there were other people who needed his attention. Six of them, to be precise. Romantic entanglements would have to wait.

Still, he felt he owed her some kind of an explanation. "Miss Banfield, I shouldn't have bombarded you with questions. I just haven't had very good luck with people helping in the past. They offer, but then they don't follow through. The boys end up disappointed, and to be honest, I do too."

"I wouldn't do that."

He wanted to believe her, but he had to think about the boys. The last time this had happened, a prominent businessman in town had offered new clothes for school only to withdraw his offer two days before classes started. The disappointment the boys felt had been hard to swallow. "I'll let you know in the next day or two, if that's all right with you."

She nodded, but there was a joyful anticipation in her expression that made it hard to breathe. "Now, let me show you the soaps we carry."

Chapter Two

"You're late again." Merritt took the hat from Essie and tossed it on an overstuffed chair. "Your mother came up a little while ago and asked if you were all right because she hadn't seen you all day."

Essie jerked around, her cloak flaring in a wide circle. If Mother found out she had taken a job. . . "You didn't tell her anything, did you?"

"Of course not, but I didn't lie. I told her you'd given me the afternoon off and gone downtown to the shops."

A soft chuckle escaped her lips. "That was clever of you."

"I don't understand." The maid started on the cloak's buttons, stealing glances at Essie as she worked. "Why don't you simply tell them the truth? Most parents would be thrilled to know their daughter could support herself if need be."

"Maybe my father would, but Mother would have a fit." Essie pulled out one hairpin and then another as Merritt freed her from her cloak and led her over to her dressing table. "She would think I ruined my reputation on purpose."

Merritt met her gaze in the full-length mirror as she bent down to untie Essie's boots. "Is that what you're trying to do?"

"Of course not." She pulled the last pin and let her plaited hair fall to her waist. It was difficult to explain what had led her to apply at the Five and Dime when she had dropped in one day, searching for a ribbon to match her new dress. It had felt. . .right. She didn't have much to occupy her during the day, so why not work? She didn't need the money—she'd already decided whatever she earned would go to help the poor—but she needed the company of women like herself. Women trying to figure out their purpose in this life. That was something money couldn't buy.

"You saw the pastor again, didn't you?"

Essie's breath caught in her throat. How could Merritt know about her conversation with Max Warner? Did she wear a sign around her neck like the men who paced up and down the sidewalks, advertising various businesses downtown? Yet she knew she could never keep a secret from Merritt. She might be Essie's maid, but she was also her dearest confidante. "He came in looking for toothbrushes."

Merritt pushed Essie's hair out of the way and began working on the buttons of her gown. "Did you find out why he buys six of everything?"

"He's taken in six boys who were living on the street." Essie pushed her sleeves down, her bodice pooling around her waist. "Isn't that kind of him?"

"Yes, but six boys! That's a lot of mouths to feed on a pastor's salary." Merritt unfastened the last button, then helped Essie out of her gown. "I hope his congregation is helping him out."

"I got the impression they weren't, at least not in any permanent way." Essie hesitated. Should she tell her maid her plans to help Pastor Warner? Would Merritt think she was being prideful? "I would like to help them out for Christmas."

Merritt smiled up at her as she gathered the dress and stood. "I think that's a lovely idea. What are you hoping to do?"

Essie shrugged. "I'm not sure. Never having any siblings, I don't know what boys that age would want or need."

"Boys any age just want something that can get them into a bit of trouble. At least, that's what my brothers want." Merritt chuckled. "James, my youngest brother, took the sled I gave him last Christmas and slid off the roof of our parents' house. Broke his arm in two places but said he'd do it again if he had the chance."

"I didn't know you had brothers."

"Sisters too." Merritt hung the dress on a hanger and placed it in the wardrobe. "I'm the oldest of five, two sisters and two brothers younger than me."

"That must have been fun growing up." Essie meant it. She'd often longed for a brother or sister to play with. To experience the kind of love Merritt obviously felt for her siblings. But it wasn't meant to be. She changed the subject. "I'm not sure how Max. . .I mean Pastor Warner would feel about it."

Merritt gave her a knowing look. "It's Max now, is it?"

"He is a regular customer, so it's only polite that we use our Christian names." But even as she said it, heat filled her cheeks.

"If you say so." The corners of Merritt's mouth lifted slightly as she brushed out Essie's hair, curling the thick waves in her hands. "Why do you think the pastor wouldn't appreciate your help?"

"I don't know. He just doesn't seem the type to accept charity."

Merritt pinned Essie's hair high on the crown of her head. "What you're planning on doing is not for him but for the boys, yes? So why would it bother him if you helped them out?"

"That's a good point." One she'd have to remember if the matter came up. "I guess it's that Pastor Warner strikes me as the type of man who made his own way in life and might feel obligated if I help with Christmas."

Merritt pried another pin open with her teeth. "Then ask him why he'd want to steal a blessing from you."

Essie glanced up at her maid in the mirror. With her faith so new, it had been wonderful to learn Merritt was also a believer. "I don't understand."

"In the Bible, we're told to do good works. It's a way of showing those around us that we're followers of Christ." She stuck the hairpin into the growing mass of curls. "If you feel led to help those boys out, but the pastor refuses your help, he's robbing you of the blessing God intended for you."

"He wouldn't want to do that."

"He may not want to, but most times we let pride get in the way of asking for or accepting help, and when we do, we rob others of the chance to serve."

"I see." Though she understood what Merritt was saying, she wasn't sure it would help her with Max. As her father was known to say, a man had his pride, and he wasn't much of one without it. Yet Max seemed different from most men. He'd do anything for those boys, even at his own expense. Would he accept her help? She'd already asked once. If he turned her down, she'd find another way.

Merritt finished with Essie's hair, then stood back to admire her work. "You look quite lovely if I do say so myself."

Essie glanced in the mirror. Her maid was always trying out the latest fashions on her, much to her dismay, yet this one, with her curls piled high on her head with tiny wisps of bangs, looked rather pretty. It showed off her high cheekbones and softened the edges of her heart-shaped face. "You'll have to do this one again when we have company."

Merritt met her gaze. "You're having company tonight for dinner."

"No we're not." Essie opened her vanity drawer and pulled out the small calendar where she kept up with the social obligations her mother accepted on her behalf. After glancing through it, she shook her head. "There's nothing listed."

"I believe it was a last-minute addition." Merritt went to the closet and pulled out an evening dress of turquoise trimmed in blue satin. The skirts were gathered in the front by neyron-red rosebuds. "Your mother asked that you wear this dress."

Jerking around in her chair, Essie glared at her. "Where did that come from?"

Merritt's eyes met hers in a sympathetic gaze. "Your mother ordered it from Paris months ago. It's supposed to be the latest fashion."

"Well, I won't wear it. The skirts are drawn tight against the legs." Essie pulled a pin out of her hair, then another. Though the dress was lovely, Mother should have asked her opinion before sending all the way to France for something she couldn't wear. "I'll fall flat on my face if I wear that."

"No, you won't. I let out the gatherings in the skirt to give you room to move, and it won't show your brace." Merritt touched her shoulder. "I would never allow you to be embarrassed like that."

"I know." It was true. Once all of Essie's so-called friends realized her limitations, there had been fewer calls and invitations, but this woman had stood by her. Held her when she cried over her losses. Pushed her into rejoining a life she'd thought was over. Merritt had proved to be a true friend. Essie rubbed her forehead. "Why does Mother do this?"

"What do you think? She's rustled up another husband prospect for you and doesn't want you flying the coop before you meet him." Merritt shook the dress out and placed it on the bed.

"Why she won't wait and let you find the man you love, I don't understand."

"You know the answer to that. No one wants me."

"You don't believe that, do you?" Merritt rolled her eyes. "From where I sit, I would think any man would be honored to marry a woman like you. Not only are you easy to look at over the breakfast table, you're kind and compassionate and don't mind a little work."

"You can add crippled to that list, and that's something no man wants in a wife."

"You just haven't met the right one yet."

If only Essie could believe that. Not that she wanted to get married, but it would be nice to think that a man could like her for who she was rather than for what her mother called her "accomplishments." Thus far, she'd only been disappointed. "So who is this gentleman my mother is certain can't live without me?"

"I don't know. Some business acquaintance of your father's from New York." Merritt took the dress off its hanger. "The butler said he's a businessman who is setting up his office here in town."

A friend of Papa's and probably just as old if not older. She grimaced at the thought. True, Papa had done business with some very attractive older men, but Essie always felt like a child in their presence. No, she needed someone closer to her age, someone like Pastor Warner.

The thought sent a tingle up her spine. She found Max an attractive man with an easy smile that made her heart skip a beat and her skin flush. What was it that made her want to know more about him? Maybe it was his kindness or the way his eyes sparkled when he spoke of the boys. She only knew that when she was with him, she wanted more from her life, a purpose, and something else she couldn't quite put her finger on.

Essie shook her head. It was preposterous, thinking of him in this manner. He didn't travel in the same social circles she did. Not that it mattered to her, but her parents would never approve. To them, her marriage was a business connection, not a love match. Cold and clinical, without the tenderness and love a marriage should have.

"It's going to take some time to get you into this dress, so we need to get started." Clouds of fabric rested across Merritt's arm as she stepped closer to Essie. "Are you ready?"

Giving herself a mental shake, Essie nodded. Merritt gathered the dress in a circle then helped her step into it, bringing the soft material over her hips, then her upper body. As she pushed her arm through one sleeve then the other, she glanced down. The skirts moved easily, and there wasn't the slightest outline of her dreaded brace. "You did a fine job, Merritt. How will I ever repay you?"

Merritt didn't hesitate. "Find the man you love and marry him."

Essie busied herself with the lace at her neckline, then turned to face the mirror. Whatever she thought of her mother, there was no arguing about her fashion sense. The dress's color made Essie's skin glow a rosy pink and enhanced the pale blue of her eyes. Merritt had worked a small miracle with the skirts, giving her room to maneuver with her brace. For once, she almost felt beautiful again.

If only Max Warner could see her like this.

Essie's eyebrows furrowed. Where had that thought come from? Max was simply a customer, nothing more. Besides, he was a pastor. The woman he chose to marry needed to be almost perfect, someone who could serve alongside him. The mother of his children, not some half-crippled woman. Only she got the feeling that Max wouldn't care about the outside appearance but rather the woman's heart.

Why was she thinking about this nonsense anyway? Probably because he'd been the last customer of the day, and she'd decided to help his boys for Christmas. Yes, that had to be it. How had he responded when he opened his delivered packages and found the woolen cap she'd snuck in? Hopefully, he saw it for what it was—a gesture that expressed her interest in helping them for Christmas. The items Max had ordered had been simple—combs for the boys, a baseball, and a set of jacks. The simplicity of the items told Essie there wasn't much money to spare. If Max would allow her to help, she'd give them the best Christmas of all.

Only she had an urgent problem of her own to face right now.

Several moments later, Essie stood outside the parlor, the itch to run growing stronger with each passing second. She drew in a fortifying breath. Maybe this time, things would be different. Maybe this was nothing more than being kind to her father's business associate and not her mother's matchmaking. With a twist of the knob, she opened the door and stepped inside.

The two sets of eyes turned to her, sweeping over her, looking for the tiniest flaw, and Essie's heart sank. Why couldn't her parents love her unconditionally as God did? Then they wouldn't care about her brace or the fact that she was lame, only that she was their child and they loved her.

Mother moved forward to greet her. "Darling, we were beginning to worry. Where have you been?"

"I was at a shop in town." She wouldn't lie, but she could let them jump to their own conclusions. Essie walked over to her father and brushed a kiss against his cheek. "Good evening, Papa."

"Sweetheart." He kissed her forehead, circling one arm around her waist. "Did you have fun shopping?"

She simply smiled, then turned her attention to her mother. "I hear we're to have another guest at dinner tonight."

Instead of looking at her, Mother fiddled with her gloves. "Yes, he's a business associate of your father's from New York. He's moving to Scranton, and we thought it would be a lovely opportunity to get acquainted."

But Essie wasn't buying it. "You mean to sink our claws into him before the other marriage-minded mamas discover there's a new man in town?"

"Estella Anne Banfield," her mother scolded. "There is nothing wrong with asking a family friend to come to dinner, and if he happens to be single and available, that's just a happy coincidence."

"Is that what you call all these men you've been inviting over all these months? A happy coincidence?" Really, if the situation wasn't so sad, she'd laugh.

"Now, Essie. . ." her father began, drawing her closer. "Your mother is only acting in your best interests. Emory is a fine young man with a bright future ahead of him. Just the kind of man who could make you happy."

Essie backed away from her father. "I don't even know the man, and you already have me married to him."

"Estella." Her name came out clipped and harsh when her mother spoke again. "You know as well as I do that marriageable men are hard to come by and even more difficult to find in our" —Mother glanced down at Essie's skirts with a grimace— "circumstances. Because of that, we must take what is offered."

A sharp pain plunged through Essie's heart. Is this what she was left with? Men other ladies wouldn't have? The thought of it made her go cold. "Why bother then? Why not accept the fact I will be an old maid rather than marry me off to a man who sees me as damaged goods?"

Her mother rushed toward her, but whatever words she intended to say died on her lips as the butler stepped into the room. "Mr. Emory Davidson."

With one last glare, Mother turned, the false smile plastered on her face sickening Essie. Mother hadn't always been like this, determined, almost driven, to get Essie married off and out of the family home. But she didn't have time to think about the past, not with Mr. Davidson and her father coming toward her.

"Sweetheart," Father said, giving her an encouraging smile, "I'd like to introduce you to a business associate of mine, Mr. Emory Davidson. Davidson, this is my daughter, Estella."

"Miss Banfield, it's a pleasure to finally meet you." He bowed over her hand, his hair a dark golden blond in the lamplight. "Your father has told me so much about you that I feel as if I know you already."

"Don't believe everything he says," she said with a hint of humor. "I just happen to be his favorite daughter."

"What are you talking about?" Father glanced down at her, a glint of pride in his eyes. "You're my only daughter."

"Need I say more?" They all chuckled softly. Essie turned toward their guest. "What brings you to Scranton, Mr. Davidson?"

"I manage investment properties, and I'm very interested in purchasing here. With the town growing by leaps and bounds, I want to be in on the ground floor." He glanced at Father. "Your father has given me a lead on a neighborhood near the city limits that might work for this project."

"But won't that put families out of their homes?" Essie asked.

"Yes, but it's a small price to pay considering what I intend to do with the vacated lots." Davidson turned to her father. "High-rise apartments."

A neighborhood where families lived and planned and children grew. The thought of those people being put out of their homes sobered what good feelings she had. "That sounds extremely industrious of you."

He nodded. "Yes, but worth it in the end."

The conversation drifted into business, giving Essie the opportunity to study the man. Emory Davidson was handsome enough. Blond hair, green eyes that didn't appear to miss much. His suit was of the highest quality, a midnight black that he wore with confidence. Yet there was a hardness about him as if he carried a heart of stone beneath his rib cage.

Essie stole a glance at her mother. Good heavens, she looked as if she hung on his every word! Poor thing, she thought she'd made a match. Well, she'd have to do better than Emory Davidson if she wanted to marry Essie off.

Chapter Three

The neighborhood street was full of kids squeezing out the last few minutes of play before the sun set on another day. The boys played stickball while the girls watched from nearby, playing with their dolls. Though no snow had fallen, there was a sharp nip in the air as if Jack Frost would pay a prolonged visit soon.

Max watched the homey scene play out in front of him and lifted a small prayer of thanks to the Lord. This location just outside of the city limits was the perfect place for his boys to rediscover their childhoods and grow into the men God wanted them to become. Not that he would have the house much longer if he didn't come up with benefactors. His pastor's salary would only stretch so far. He had tried to educate the community about the need for a good home for abandoned children, but if his meeting with the local business owners was anything to go by, he'd have to rethink his plan. Couldn't these men see that a loved child made a better citizen and was a good investment in tomorrow? Obviously not, from their response. . .

The mudball came out of nowhere, hitting Max square in the chest. He glanced around, but seeing no one looking in his direction, continued down the sidewalk. The next mudball knocked his hat off, followed by another that glazed his jaw. He only knew one kid with that kind of pinpoint accuracy. "Tommy Miller!"

The small boy peeked out from behind a bush and grinned, his front teeth noticeably missing. "I'm sorry, Pastor Max. It's just we hain't had no snow in a coon's age, and I didn't want to get out of practice."

Max pressed his lips together to keep his smile at bay. Since arriving four months ago, Tommy had spent more time outside than inside the house. "Why not play stickball with the boys then? I can't imagine anyone could get around your fast pitch."

Tommy glanced at the boys, then away, but not before Max saw the hurt in his eyes. "I didn't want to."

He put his arm around the boy. Rejection was tough on anyone, but for these boys, it was all they had ever known. Abandonment, whether through the death of their parents or from neglect, hardened a young heart. An older one too, Max thought. "How was school today?"

Tommy shrugged. "Good, I guess."

"Have you finished your homework?"

"I've got most of it done."

"Most of it?"

The towheaded boy kicked at a rock. "Well, maybe not most of it."

Max figured as much. "What's the rule about homework?"

"It has to be finished before we can go outside," Tommy answered reluctantly. Anxiety lined his expression as he glanced up at Max. "I'm sorry, Pastor Max."

"I know you are, Tommy." He ruffled the boy's hair. "I understand how hard it is to stay in and work on math problems when you'd rather be outside. I was a boy once too."

"Really? Did you like school?"

Max didn't know how to respond. School had provided the

basics, but most of his education had come from living on the streets, foraging for food and finding a place to stay warm on cold, snowy nights. But then God had sent Pastor Boling to help him, and it changed his life. "I only went to school for a short while."

"I don't know why I have to go in the first place. I can read and cipher as good as any of the other boys."

He couldn't deny what Tommy was saying. Both Max and Miss Endicott, the boy's teacher, were surprised by Tommy's skill at mathematics. Miss Endicott had even mentioned college in his future. Max sighed. They had to get him through grade school first. He opened the front gate, then joined Tommy in the yard. "You're right. You can do all those things, but there's so much more for you to learn. You wouldn't want to miss out on that now, would you?"

"No, I guess not."

He ruffled the boy's hair again, then stopped. "Where's your hat?"

Tommy shrugged. "I don't know. I had it this morning, but when we started home this afternoon..." He grimaced. "I couldn't find it."

"I'll add it to my list." A list he already couldn't afford, but what could he do? He couldn't send Tommy out in the bitter Scranton weather without a knit hat to keep him warm. Max would just have to tighten his already tight belt. *God will provide.* The words eased him somewhat. Yes, God had certainly taken care of their needs so far and would continue to do so.

The two of them walked up the dirt path to the front step just as Neal, one of the older boys, opened the door. He glanced first at Tommy, then Max, before slamming the door in their faces. This didn't bode well. Max looked down at Tommy. "Do you know what's going on?"

Tommy shook his head. "I've been out here. I swear it on my mother's grave."

"No swearing on anything," Max answered as he drew in a deep breath. What was that smell? Smoke? Fearing the worst, he turned the doorknob and pushed, but there was something heavy blocking the door.

A window overhead opened. "Don't worry, Pastor Max. We're just cleaning things up."

Max tipped his head back to see Billy Mathis dangling out of the upstairs window. "What's blocking the front door?"

"Neal must have pushed the couch in front of the door," he answered, swinging one leg over the windowsill. "We didn't want you to get upset if you came home and smelled smoke in the parlor."

"I can smell it out here too."

Billy clucked his tongue. "We didn't think about that."

Another acrid breath filled Max's lungs. "What happened?"

The boy hesitated as if weighing his options, then spoke. "The fire in the parlor was going out, and all the wood at the back door was wet so. . ." He drifted off, grimacing as if he expected a hard rap to his head. "We broke up that extra chair in the kitchen and put it in the fire."

Oh no. Not one of the Hensons' chairs. They'd been so gracious to lend them to him. They weren't much as chairs went, but the Hensons had wanted to help in whatever way they could. How was he going to explain this to them? He'd have to reimburse them for the chair. How he would do it was another thing.

"Anyway," Billy continued, "there must have been varnish or paint on it because it smoked up the parlor real good. We opened all the windows, but it got so cold, we closed them again."

If he could smell the smoke at the door, it had to be twice as bad inside. "Open the door."

"You're not mad, are you?"

The note of fear in the boy's voice was Max's undoing. This was a safe place, and no matter how much trouble the boys cooked up, he would never let his temper get the best of him. He shook his head. "You were only trying to stay warm." He pointed to the windows. "Now close that window and let us in. We need to build up the fires in the other rooms to warm up the house for the night."

"Yes, sir." The window slammed shut, followed by a muffled call throughout the house.

In a matter of minutes, the remaining boys greeted them at the door. The sight of them on the threshold lifted Max's spirits. Even if some businessmen didn't see the worth in his plans, these boys mattered. They would do great things. As he deposited his coat, hat, and gloves on the hall table, the boys squirmed into a line in front of him. This was most definitely the best part of his day.

Finally, Max turned his attention to them. "How was school today?"

For the next few minutes, they discussed the events of their day. Max congratulated Billy on acing his spelling test, then promised Tommy he would listen to him read that evening. Being a makeshift father to these boys was the greatest gift he'd ever received outside his salvation. If he could find a way, he'd help them and others like them for the rest of his days.

"Oh, I almost forgot." Tommy ran over to the dinner table and picked up a small box. "This came for you."

It was from the Five and Dime.

Putting the box under his arm, Max shooed them into the parlor. "Boys, go get washed up. I'll get the fire going, then we'll decided what to have for supper."

"One of the ladies from church left a pot of chili on the front step," Tommy said. "Maybe we could make some corn bread to go with it."

"I think we've got a little cornmeal left." Max nodded, giving the boy a smile. "And I do like chili."

Everyone but Billy agreed. Max bent down to meet the boy's gaze. "Don't you like chili?"

"Sure, I do." He nodded toward the box under Max's arm. "I just want to know what you got from Woolworth's first."

Jacob, one of the older boys, grabbed Billy by the arm and dragged him up the stairs. "If Pastor Max wanted you to see it, he would have shown it to you. Besides, it's Christmas." Jacob winked at Max. "Santa may be sending Pastor Max a present for us."

That seemed to appease Billy. Once everyone had left the room, Max went to the small desk in the corner and untangled the piece of string securing the package. Pulling the cord away, he carefully unwrapped the heavy paper, then opened the box. Miss Banfield had followed his list to a T. Toothbrushes and powder. Combs. Everything was there. He raised another piece of paper from the bottom of the box. Hidden there were small bags filled with peppermint and hard candies cushioned by a winter cap just the right size for a young boy.

How did Miss Banfield know I'd need a cap for Tommy?

She didn't, but God did. Max bent his head. *Thank you, Lord, for knit caps and Miss Banfield.*

Chapter Four

"That's the second time you've made wrong change today, Essie," Rose whispered from behind the glass counter. "That's not like you."

"I'm sorry." Essie shoved her order book and pencil into her apron pocket. "I don't know where my mind is today."

Her friend leaned out and touched her on the arm. "You're not feeling poorly, are you? The influenza is going around."

"It's not that. It's just. . ." Essie stopped herself. Rose worked hard to make her way in the world after her parents died. Hearing Essie was an heiress whose mother was pushing her to marry an equally wealthy man would be a slap in the face, and she refused to do that to her friend. No, she'd keep last night's disaster to herself.

"Is your leg bothering you?"

Essie felt the blood drain from her face. She'd worked so hard to hide her disability from everyone else. What had given her away?

"You have a small limp when you're tired, but nothing anyone else would notice," Rose whispered to her in a comforting voice. "The only reason I did is because my mother had arthritis on top of everything else." She patted Essie's arm. "I always liked to see her limp. It meant she felt well enough to be out of bed."

Essie glanced toward the front of the store, then back at Rose. "That must have been difficult for her."

"I don't know." A soft smile tinged in sadness graced her friend's face. "Mama always said it was one of the greatest gifts God ever gave her."

A gift? Rose must have misunderstood her mother, because there was nothing good about feeling less than everyone else. "What did she mean by that?"

Rose's smile grew. "From what Mama told me, she was quite a handful as a young girl. Always getting into things she had no business in. She just about ran her mother crazy with worry. Then one day, when she was about fifteen, she woke up and could barely move. The doctors didn't know what it was or how to treat it. For the next two years, Mama wasn't far from her bed, and when she was, she had to move slowly so as not to exacerbate her condition."

"That must have been horrible for her."

Rose straightened a box of what-nots that sat on the counter. "Mama didn't think so. She said she realized that in slowing down, she was able to focus more on what was going on around her rather than just speeding through life. She learned to enjoy being in the moment. The limp kept her grounded. She was able to focus on what was most important."

Essie nodded, not certain she understood. Had she been looking at her shortcomings the wrong way? Could God be using it as a way of getting her to focus on what was most important? Why? He could have led her to this new purpose without having to make her a cripple. So why cripple her?

Anger stiffened her spine. "I didn't realize everyone else knew."

"They don't think anything of it," Rose replied, studying Essie's face before finally stepping back. "A limp doesn't make a woman. It's who you are inside that counts." She gave her an encouraging smile. "You're our friend, Essie. That's what matters."

Tears gathered in Essie's throat. Friends. She didn't have many. Most of her so-called friends had abandoned her when the full extent of her injuries was revealed. Only the best would do for them, and with her impediment, she didn't qualify. Yet these women she worked with had taken her in and called her friend. And what had she done to repay them? Withheld the truth about who she truly was.

"I'm sorry. I shouldn't have ever told you about Mama," Rose said. "Everyone sees things in different ways. That's just how Mama saw her infirmity."

The concern in her friend's expression touched Essie. Maybe she should share a bit more about herself. Who knew? Rose might even have an answer to her problem. "Last night, my parents introduced me to the man they want me to marry."

Rose blinked as if she hadn't heard Essie correctly. "Isn't it generally customary for the bride to pick out her own groom?"

"You would think that, wouldn't you?" Essie pushed a loose curl behind her ear. "But my parents feel that my disability might not garner me acceptable suitors, so my mother has taken it upon herself to hunt them down. Last night was only the latest one."

"That sounds positively medieval. Do you like the man?"

Essie shook her head. "He's not a very caring person."

"Well then, that settles it. You can't marry someone you don't even like." Rose grinned at her as she handed the organized box back to her. "So there's nothing to worry about."

If only it were that simple. In her social circles, most marriages were based on business or financial gain. Some of her "friends" had even married titled noblemen in exchange for their healthy dowries. It was all very neat and tidy, with no emotional attachments involved. But Essie craved more than being a business asset. She saw the way her father looked at her mother, as if she was the most wonderful thing in his world, and she knew Mother felt the same way. So why wouldn't her mother allow her the opportunity to find that kind of happiness for herself?

Essie sighed. How would she know she was in love? She wasn't even certain she knew what it was like. She glanced over at Rose. "Have you ever been in love?"

"Me?" she squeaked, then cleared her throat. "Of course not. I haven't had time for such things."

"And now?"

"Now, I plan to work and make my own..." Her words drifted off, and a faint blush flushed her cheeks as her gaze settled on something behind Essie's shoulder. Essie turned around to see Evan Elrod high on a ladder, storing a new Christmas shipment. Was there something going on between Rose and Evan? They would certainly make a sweet couple.

Essie studied her friend for a moment. Was this what love looked like? Staring all glassy-eyed at someone as if they hung the moon? Maybe, but what did it feel like to love someone completely and to be loved in return? Was it possible for a man to look past her physical imperfections to the person she'd become in Christ? So many questions. Maybe she needed to make an appointment with her pastor and discuss these things.

First, they needed to get back to work before Mr. Woolworth found them. Essie touched her friend's arm. "I've got to go make my rounds."

A soft gasp escaped from Rose. "Oh yes. I best get back to work too." She hurried off in the opposite direction, only looking back once as Evan descended from his perch. Yes, there was most definitely something going on between those two.

As Essie turned the corner, she saw a tall, broad-shouldered man standing in the center of her section, his worn hat clenched between his fingers. Essie smiled. She hadn't thought to see Pastor Warner today, it being Wednesday and all, but she was happy to see him. What had brought him into the store today? Were his young wards out of hair tonic? Or was he doing more Christmas shopping, perhaps for a lady friend? The thought bothered her—not that it was any of her business, of course. Her job was to provide good service at a low price.

Essie stepped forward. "May I help you?"

He turned, and Essie's heart fluttered like a baby bird on its first flight. He smiled then, the corners of his eyes crinkling into well-worn lines. "Miss Banfield. I was hoping to speak with you about the box you filled on Monday."

Oh dear, had she made a mistake? Left something out of the package? They could check his original list. For some strange reason, she couldn't bear the thought of throwing it away. "Was there something wrong?"

He shook his head. "No, everything was perfect. I just wanted to thank you for the candy and the knit cap you sent with the order." His dark eyes studied her. "They were from you, weren't they?"

Her cheeks grew uncomfortably warm. "I have a sweet tooth and thought the boys might enjoy some treats on Christmas morning."

"And the cap?"

Essie wasn't sure what had prompted her to include the hat. She'd just felt it was needed. "Don't children lose their hats a great deal?"

"I don't know." There was a smile in his voice as he leaned closer. "Did you?"

She blinked, her tongue so knotted up, it made it difficult to respond. "Did I what?"

"Lose your hat."

"Oh." She startled, her skirts swaying as she stepped back. "Of course. All the time, actually. So I thought it might be nice if you had an extra lying around."

His warm chuckle sent a wave of tingles across her shoulders. "As it was, one of the younger boys lost his on the way home from school that very afternoon, so it didn't lie around for long."

"I'm so glad." Warmth flooded her heart. Was this what it was like to help someone, this rush of emotion knowing that a small deed had provided such comfort? Whatever this feeling, she wanted more of it. The boys deserved a happy Christmas, and she was just the person to help. But would Max allow her?

"The box arrived just in the nick of time, and then to have the candy and the hat. . ." He bowed his head slightly toward her. "We are forever grateful."

"I should be thanking you." She clasped her hands behind her back. "I've never had the opportunity to help others, and I find I quite enjoy it. Besides, it wasn't that much."

"It was to Tommy."

Tommy? Amusement bubbled up inside her. "Oh, he must have been the one who lost his hat."

"Yes, and he sends his thanks." The smile in his eyes sent her heart aflutter again. "He said his ears weren't quite as cold."

Essie's smile grew wider. "I'm glad it worked out."

The pastor glanced at the mantel clock, then rubbed the back of his neck, a hint of worry flittering across his features. "I hate to ask this, but is there any way I could have a line of credit until next Friday? I wouldn't ask, but there are some things we need before I'm paid next week." He handed her a piece of paper.

Essie glanced over the list. Paper, string, pencils, some food items, and personal care products. She had more than enough to cover the order in her change purse. She smiled up at him. "I don't see a problem with this. Would you like me to help you with your order?"

"I wish I could take care of it now, but I have a very important appointment and I'm already late."

Was there reluctance in his voice? Something about the meeting must be troubling him, and as Pastor Williams said, there's only one thing to do when there's trouble. Without thinking, Essie touched his arm. "I don't know what your appointment is about, but I'll be praying for you, Max."

He glanced down at her hand, then covered it with his. A smile played along the corners of his mouth, and for a moment, she caught a glimpse of the boy he once was. "Most people don't think to pray for their pastors. I guess they feel like we have all the answers, but we don't. At least it feels like that sometimes."

Essie grasped the tips of his fingers and gave them an encouraging squeeze. "You may be a pastor, but you're a man too, and don't we all need prayer sometimes? At least that's what I think."

He studied her as if seeing her for the first time. "I'm humbled to have you pray for me, Essie."

The world shifted, and in that moment, Essie realized she'd be honored to pray for this man not just for today but from this minute forward. She bowed her head. "Heavenly Father, You know what's on Max's heart. Please help him with his appointment and let Your will be done. In Jesus' name I pray, amen."

"Amen," Max murmured beside her. Cool air rushed over her skin as he lifted his hand from hers. "Well, I better get going."

"Of course." She took a step back, then seemed to hover in midstep before teetering to the right. She pushed her leg down, hoping to catch herself, but only heard cloth tearing in response. Raising her arms up, she braced for impact.

Instead, a pair of strong arms surrounded her, pulling her into an equally muscular chest. Max's heartbeat beneath her cheek as well as his whispered words soothed her frazzled nerves. "You're all right. I've got you."

She buried her face in his chest, embarrassment burning her cheeks. That stupid leg brace! Why did she have to wear it if it did her no good? She wanted to take it off and throw it into the garbage heap, or better yet the fireplace, and watch the leather and metal contraption burn to ash.

"Essie, are you all right?"

Dear heavens! Of all the times for Charles Sumner Woolworth to pay a visit to the floor, and her in a man's arms! With what dignity she had left, Essie stepped down hard on her right leg, completing the tear to her petticoats, and pushed herself out of Max's embrace. Tugging at her apron, she turned around to face her employer. "I'm fine, Mr. Sum. I tripped, and Pastor Warner was kind enough to catch me."

"Well, I'm glad you weren't hurt." Mr. Sum held out his hand to Max. "I don't believe we've met, Pastor. I'm Charles Woolworth, but most people just call me Sum. I want to thank you for rescuing Miss Banfield. I wouldn't want to see anyone get hurt in our establishment, particularly one of our leading salesclerks."

"Max Warner." The men shook hands, then Max glanced down at her and gave her a bone-melting grin. "No need to thank me. Miss Banfield has always been quite helpful to me and my wards. I was just returning the favor."

"Warner." Mr. Sum pointed at him. "You wouldn't be the preacher who's taking in the boys from the streets, would you? I've been wanting to talk with you about your plans for them."

"He is, Mr. Sum, but I've already made him late for a meeting." She met Max's gaze. "Maybe another time?"

"Of course. Let me know the next time you're in the store. Or better still, why don't I walk you out?" Mr. Sum asked.

Max drew in a deep breath, then turned to her, the warmth in his eyes making her knees a bit wobbly. "Good day, Miss Banfield, and please, be careful. I wouldn't want you to fall."

She couldn't help but smile at him. "I'll be praying for you, Pastor."

Essie watched as the two men made their way down the aisle toward the front exit, her emotions scattered like glass marbles on the floor. Max hadn't questioned why she'd tripped, only been there to catch her and help her stand on her feet again. No one had done that since the accident. Most seemed to see her as less of a person, like she needed protection from the rest of the world. Was that the real reason her mother wanted her married, so that Essie would be cared for in the years to come?

Still, she wanted to live her own life. Fulfill the purpose God had planned just for her. She took one last glance at Max as he shook hands with Mr. Sum and walked out the front door. Something inside her quieted. Peace like she'd never thought possible flowed through her. Whatever her purpose in this life was, she was certain of one thing. Max Warner would play a major role in it.

Chapter Five

Essie breathed in the cold air and forced herself to relax. What had Sum Woolworth been thinking when he came up with the idea of opening the store an hour before his competitors? And putting everything on sale too! Who ever heard of five pencils for a penny? Was the man trying to put himself out of business?

What she needed was a nice lunch away from the store, somewhere she could rest before tackling the afternoon rush. But where? She stepped onto the sidewalk and looked around. McIntyres was good for an evening out, but she wasn't dressed for lunch there. Maybe the drugstore for a sandwich and soda water...

"Miss Banfield!"

She turned to find Pastor Warner—Max—strolling down the street toward her, his wool coat flapping around him with each step. Her heart did a funny little skip at his smile, so genuine and real, she almost believed he was happy to see her.

Essie couldn't help but smile back. "I wasn't expecting to see you today."

"Oh, I come downtown every day."

She was surprised at this information. "Why?"

His smile dimmed, and there was a hint of sadness in his dark eyes that troubled her. "I come to see if there are any children who might need food or a place to stay. A lot of them are wary of taking handouts, so I build a relationship with them. That way they can trust me and know I only want to help."

"That's the kindest thing I've ever heard." It truly was. Oh, she'd watched others throw their money at a problem, then preen around as if they had single-handedly saved the world, but she'd never seen someone actually do the work.

He brushed the compliment aside. "I thought you'd be busy working."

"I'm on my lunch hour." She had a crazy idea. "Would you like to join me?"

He studied her for a long moment, and she thought she'd made a mistake. Social etiquette forbade a young woman asking a man to lunch. But she was pretty much already an outcast in her own social circle, so what did she care what they said? The only opinion that mattered to her right now was Max's.

If he sensed her nervousness, he didn't show it. Just took her hand and threaded it through his own. "That's funny, because I was about to ask you the same thing."

Her heart did another somersault in her chest. "You were?"

"Miss Banfield." He covered her hand with his. "Essie. It's not every day I get to share a meal with a lovely lady."

Her cheeks warmed at his compliment. "That's very kind of you."

"Not kind. True."

She smiled to herself. The truth was she hadn't felt lovely since the accident that crippled her leg, only ungraceful and stilted. But Max made her feel like his words were true. She cleared her throat. "Where would you like to go?"

He thought for a moment. "The Langley Café is good, and

the prices are reasonable."

"That's sounds wonderful." She glanced around. "Is it very far from here?"

"Just behind the courthouse, about a block or so."

Essie pressed her fingers into his forearm. She couldn't walk that distance and finish her shift at the store. Already, the muscles in her leg were tightening into painful knots. "I can't go that far from the store."

Max didn't ask any questions but glanced around. Finally, he pointed to the building at the corner. "How about Dupree's Drugstore? They serve soup and sandwiches."

Essie nodded. "That would be perfect."

Fifteen minutes later, they were settled in a booth with a panoramic view of the park. Essie glanced out the window as she peeled off her gloves and placed them with her coat and reticule on the chair next to hers. "Isn't the park beautiful? I've never seen so many Christmas decorations."

"Me either. Something about it just gives me a feeling of joy."

"What part do you like the best?"

"Most people expect me to say the nativity, but I'm a sucker for a Christmas tree. When I was little, my mother would spend the entire day popping corn for us to string for the tree." Max stared off, as if reliving the moment. "We had a great time making decorations."

"Then you'll like this one. Mr. Sum donated an entire case of glass Christmas ornaments for the tree." She lowered her voice. "Next year, when the town gets electricity, he's offered to buy twinkling lights. Says it will make our little park look like the North Pole itself."

"He's a good soul." Max glanced over at her. "What's your favorite decoration?"

Essie took a sip of water. How could she tell him that her parents didn't really celebrate the holidays? Oh, presents were exchanged, and they hosted a small dinner party Christmas Eve, but there wasn't any of the little things that made Christmas so fun. So, she said the only thing she knew. "I love to make gingerbread houses."

He propped his chin in his hand. "I've only seen one, but it was amazing. A lot of attention to the details, and it was very artistic."

"Plus, gingerbread is the best Christmas cookie of all time."

"I wouldn't know," he answered with a laugh. "I've never had any."

"You're teasing me. How could someone in this day and age have never tasted gingerbread?"

He rubbed the back of his neck. "My mom was more of the oatmeal-raisin type."

"Well then, we'll just have to do something about that." She knew exactly what to do. Cook would let her borrow the kitchen one evening to make a batch of gingerbread men. Then she would slip them in the next delivery for Max and the boys to enjoy.

The waitress came and took their orders. When she returned to the kitchen, Max faced her. "I thought you generally take your meals at the lunch counter."

"I do, but I just had to get out of there today." She leaned across the table. "Mr. Sum and his ideas for boosting Christmas sales is about to drive all the clerks crazy."

His dark brows furrowed. "A Christmas sale? Never heard of such a thing."

"It's a new idea of his." She unfolded her napkin and laid it across her lap. "He thinks that by opening the store an hour early and cutting our prices, we'll make more money."

Max sat back, relaxed. For some reason, it gave her a sense of peace. "It's not a bad idea."

"No," she agreed. "It isn't, but it's very trying for the clerks." She drew in a deep breath and sighed. "I never knew there were so many penny-pinchers in Scranton until this morning."

"For some people, it's the only way they can get by."

The way Max said it, as if he understood these people completely, made her feel like a heel. How insensitive could she have been? Here was Max, putting every penny he earned into caring for abandoned children, and she acted like people saving money was too trying for her. "I'm sorry, Max. I wasn't thinking."

"It's all right."

"No, it isn't," she argued. "My life has been a lot easier than most, and I forget how hard it is for some people."

He shook his head. "Don't worry about it."

But she did. Every night since she'd started working at the Five and Dime, she'd found herself praying for her newfound friends. Maggie, Hattie, Lizzie, and Rose were amazing women, working hard to support their families and themselves. With each passing day, she'd come to respect them more and more.

And then there was Max. She'd never met a man like him before. His heart for the homeless children of Scranton made her want to do more for her community. But where could she start? All she wanted was a life lived with purpose.

She had a feeling Max might be able to give her some answers. "You have a heart for the poor."

"Yes, I guess I do." He took a sip of the soda water the waitress had served them. "But then, I know what it's like to be poor myself."

"What did your father do for a living?"

"He owned a livery right outside of Erie." A ghost of a grin softened his expression. "I remember one time this old man gave my dad a horse because he couldn't afford to care for it anymore. That horse was in terrible shape. Papa let me care for him. I fed him, brushed him out, exercised him every day. I was so sure Papa was going to give him to me." He shook his head. "But it wasn't meant to be."

After all that work, it didn't seem fair that his father would deny him the horse. "What happened?"

"The old man returned and demanded that my father give the horse back to him." Max shrugged. "So, he did."

"That's terrible." Essie leaned forward until she was almost touching his arm. "What did you do?"

"Nothing. Papa explained that the man had nothing except for that horse, and that if he sold it, the money might keep him fed and warm for a while." He grew somber. "It was the first time I realized what being poor meant."

She wouldn't soon forget his story. Essie gave him a soft smile. "Your father sounds like a wise man."

"He was." Max glanced down at the table. "My parents were killed in a fire when I was ten."

Her heart broke for him. Max didn't just understand the boys he worked with. He was one of them. She fought the urge to reach out and take his hand, but the need to comfort him won out. "I'm so sorry, Max. That must have been difficult for you."

"It was," he admitted. "But looking back now, I can see how God used the loss of my parents to make me into the man I am today." His boyish grin tugged at her heart. "Do you know what I mean?"

"Umm. . ." She really didn't. How could God use something as terrible as losing his parents to make Max the person he was today? Wouldn't Max be the same man if his parents had lived?

She shook her head. "I'm sorry, but I don't understand."

Max leaned forward, resting his forearms on the table. "I've told you about the boys I've taken in. The reason I have such a need to help them is that I understand how they feel. I know what it's like to go hungry or be cold." He met her gaze. "I also know what it's like when someone takes you in and loves you like their own."

"You were adopted?"

He nodded. "Preacher Boling and his wife took me in when I was fourteen. I'd been out on the streets for four years and was as tough as a dried-up piece of old leather." He gave her another gentle smile that turned her stomach into knots. "They poured their unconditional love onto me and showed me a different way to live. For that, I'm eternally grateful."

"And now you give a home to other boys on the streets."

"I try to, but like I told you on the way over here, some are suspicious of my offer."

The waitress arrived, bearing plates loaded down with thick meat sandwiches and German potato salad. After a quick prayer to bless the food, Max dug in, but Essie couldn't stop thinking about what he had said about his parents. Was it possible that God could use her crippled leg to grow her into a woman after His own heart? Rose had said being disabled had given her mother's life meaning. Would Essie's crippled leg give her life purpose where she'd found none before? The thought gave her a sense of peace she had long been searching for, and for once she looked forward to what God had in store for her.

Yet she had so many questions. Max had obviously found his calling in helping homeless children. But what was hers? God had to have something in mind for her, but what could it be?

"Not hungry?"

Essie glanced up to find Max watching her. "I was just thinking."

"About what?" He forked another bite of potato salad into his mouth.

Should she share what she was thinking, or would he find her silly? As a pastor, he'd probably heard worse. "When I applied for the job at the Five and Dime, I did it because I wanted my life to have some kind of meaning or purpose, and though I've learned a lot about myself, it's not what I imagined my life's purpose would be."

Max stopped eating and gave her his full attention. "A lot of people try to find their purpose in their jobs, and when they don't, they get frustrated."

"Exactly!" She pointed her fork at him. "I love my job, but there's got to be more to life than this." She peeked at him. "You probably think I'm a silly woman."

"No, I don't." He removed the fork from her hand, then took her hand in his. Her heart caught in her throat at his touch. "Everyone should take the time to figure out what it is that God wants him or her to do."

She drew in a shuddered breath. "So, you don't think I'm silly."

"No."

How such a simple word from him could soothe her, she didn't know, but it did. "All right, then, how do I find my purpose?"

Max picked up a dill pickle and munched on it as if it somehow helped him to think. "What do you like to do? What gives you joy?"

She hadn't ever thought about that. For the most part, she had lived a sheltered life, especially after the accident. Until she'd started working, her only enjoyment was in baking, and what could she do with that? "I don't really do much besides work."

"Okay then." He thought for a moment. "What is it about your work that you enjoy?"

"Well, it's not the early mornings or the sales, that's for certain." She chuckled softly as she leaned back in her chair. "It may sound silly, but I like helping people find what they're looking for, even if it's something as small as a pencil for school. For one brief moment, I helped make a difference in their lives."

Max sat back, folding his arms over his chest. "You don't ever take home a full pay envelope, do you?"

Essie blinked. Her pay envelope? Of course she took home her entire— She thought for a moment, then glared at him. "How did you know that?"

His smile gave way to a laugh. "Do your pastor a favor. Never volunteer for the benevolence committee. The church would go broke."

Laughter broke through her, a soul-cleansing laugh that brought tears to her eyes and caused the muscles in her stomach to ache. Some of the other customers stared at her, but she paid them no heed. The only person she didn't want to offend was Max, and he seemed to be enjoying the spectacle.

When she wiped the last tears from her cheeks, she dared a glance at him. "I'm sorry. I don't usually behave that way."

"Why are you apologizing?" He handed her a clean napkin. "Everyone needs a good belly laugh every now and then. It's good for the soul."

Essie had never heard anything preached on the subject at her church, so she'd have to take Max's word for it. "What does my giving have to do with finding God's purpose for my life?"

"Now that you know you're a giving person, you must figure out where and what you want to give. Some givers offer their time and talents as well as their money. You also need to know who you want to give those gifts to. Pray about it. God will lead you in the direction He wants you to go."

Essie nodded. She didn't need to pray on the matter. She knew. Like a lightning bolt, the answer struck her with a clarity she couldn't ignore. The Lord knew her heart. How could people understand God's love with an empty belly or no shelter from the cold? These were the people she wanted to help, and she knew just where to start.

With Max and the boys.

Chapter Six

Max glanced around the secretary's stuffy office, feeling like a duck out of water. Being caged in a room to work, without the benefit of the sun's warmth or a breath of cold fresh air, would never suit him, but God had known that. Walking around the city to visit the members of his congregation and playing a game of stickball with the boys before sharing a bit of food and God's Word with them was more to his liking. The elders had offered him an office at the church for writing sermons, but he found the words flowed more freely outside, where he could admire all of God's creation.

Yet sometimes he enjoyed being cooped up. The memory of his lunch with Essie was still fresh in his thoughts. She was such a lovely woman, but it was her heart that had caught him by surprise. If only more people would do as she did and spend time searching for their God-given purpose, the world might be a different place. Maybe that was what had attracted him in the first place, that and the sweet way she'd prayed over him.

"Pastor Warner?" The bespectacled young man stood in the doorway. Max stood and made his way across the room to join him. "Mr. Davidson will see you now."

"Thank you." Hat in hand, Max followed the man down a

short passageway to an even stuffier office. After thanking the man again, he took a seat in front of a massive oak desk. He'd never met Emory Davidson, only knew that the man who handled his rental agreement, Stephen Gardner, had retired and Davidson had taken his place. He drew in a deep breath. He wanted to renegotiate his lease agreement to include a purchase stipulation and wasn't sure how his request would be received.

The door opened. "I'm sorry. I was held up with another client."

Max watched as the man tossed a file onto his desk and took a seat. He was ten, maybe fifteen, years older than Max expected, with a hardness in his features that hinted at a difficult upbringing. He stood and offered his hand. "It's I who should apologize for my tardiness. It's not a habit of mine."

"Let me get right to the point. You're leasing a house on Lemon Street, are you not?" Davidson reached for another file and flipped it open.

Max dropped his hand down to his side, an odd sensation of foreboding filling him with dread. "Yes, I've been there four years."

"I see you've never missed a payment."

"Yes, and that's what I'd like to talk with you about. I'd like to have a purchase stipulation written into our next lease agreement. For now the house is perfect for us, and I'd like to own it."

Davidson leaned back in his chair. "I'm sorry, but that's impossible. You see, I bought up all of Gardner's landholdings. The only stipulation Gardner had was that I continue his agreement with you." He pulled a paper from the file and handed it across the desk to Max. "Here's the new rental agreement."

Max glanced over the paper. "You've raised the rent by fifty percent."

"That is the going rate in Scranton, Pastor Warner." He shut the file and pushed it to the side before settling back. "Gardner barely charged you enough to keep the place up, but I mean to make a profit."

Max tossed the paper onto the desk. "You do know why he did that, don't you? He knew I'd started a home for abandoned boys, and the house on Lemon Street has enough room for them to grow and become the men God wants them to be."

Pressing his arms into the desk, Davidson leaned forward. "Pastor Warner, I was one of those boys on the street. Cold during the winter months and half starved most of the time. But no one helped me. I realized early on that the only person who could help me was me. So I got small jobs, sweeping out stores or collecting garbage, and I saved my money. I'm a self-made man, Pastor, and I didn't get to where I am giving away money. Either come up with the new rental amount or I'll be forced to toss you and your boys out onto the street."

Vile, ugly words rose to Max's lips, but he held his tongue. This man was unbendable. Well, just as Davidson wanted a profit, Max knew the Lemon Street house was where he and the boys belonged. "What if I buy the house from you?"

The man chuckled, but there was no humor or joy in it. "What makes you think you can buy the house if you can't afford the rent?"

He couldn't afford it, but losing the house wasn't an option. The boys were settled into school, and he wouldn't uproot them now. "How much?"

Davidson studied him for a moment, then grabbed a pen and paper and scribbled on it. Folding it, he handed it to Max. "That's the price."

Max unfolded the paper and glanced down at the number.

"This is twice what the house is worth."

"As the owner, I decide what the worth of the house is." Davidson nodded to the slip. "That's good for three weeks, then it goes up by ten percent."

The man was being unreasonable, but he was correct. As owner of the property, he had the last word. Max scrubbed his hand across his face. The boys needed stability, and the house played a huge part in that. Maybe he could take out a loan. But what could he use as collateral?

"Pastor Warner, do we have an agreement or not?"

Without thinking, Max replied, "Yes."

"Good. So, you will have the full amount for the house to me on. . ." He flipped through a small calendar on his desk. "Christmas Eve."

That seemed appropriate. The situation felt like something out of a Dickens novel. But he had no choice. The boys depended on him. The question was, how would he come up with such a sum in three weeks' time?

He hoped Essie said another prayer for him tonight.

"Miss Banfield?"

Essie glanced up to find Mike, the delivery boy, rushing up the aisle toward her. She turned and handed her customer her purchase. "I hope the new scrub brush works out for you, Mrs. Clark. If not, please let me know."

"Why, thank you, miss, and I appreciate your help. You have a wonderful day."

"You too, Mrs. Clark." Essie moved out from behind the counter as Mike reached her. Bending over, the boy sucked in large gulps of air as if he'd run a great distance. "Mike, you know you're not supposed to be on the floor during business hours, especially on a Saturday. What if Mr. Sum sees you?"

"I know, but it's important." He stood, then pulled a stained handkerchief from his coat pocket and mopped his face. "It's about the package you wanted me to deliver. I couldn't do it."

"You mean the box for Pastor Warner?" Max had been on her mind since they'd prayed together the other day. She'd wondered how his meeting had gone and had even talked Cook into helping her bake gingerbread cookies for the boys. "Why not?"

Mike took another gulp of air. "Every time I got close to the house, they'd throw rocks at me. It got so bad, it was like a hive of bees had been set loose on me."

"Bees aren't active in the cold weather." Boys, on the other hand. . . She placed a hand on Mike's shoulder. "Don't worry about it. I'll drop it off on my way home this afternoon."

Mike stared up at her with worried eyes. "I can't let you do that! What kind of man would I be to send you into that? They'll pulverize you!"

Essie pressed her lips together to keep from smiling. Poor Mike. Eleven years old and already the man of his house, he took his job as delivery boy quite seriously. Providing for his widowed mother and younger sisters was no easy task, but didn't he deserve to go to school and be a child too? Twelve-hour days, six days a week, would make him old before his time. That was why Max worked so hard to provide for his boys, to give them a childhood and hope for the future. Maybe she would ask him about a way to help Mike.

Placing her hand on his thin shoulder, Essie gave him an encouraging squeeze. "It's all right. I need to talk with the pastor anyway, so it's no trouble at all. I'm sure the boys will think twice before throwing a rock at a woman." At least she hoped so. She nodded toward the back room. "Now go, before Mr. Sum realizes you're out here."

"Can't have that." The boy shrugged her hand away, then turned. "I need this job."

Essie couldn't help the sigh that escaped her as she watched the boy go. So many children like Mike, forced to be an adult before they were ready. Her heart ached for him and for the boys Max had taken in. For all the children begging on the street. She'd never noticed them before, but Max's mission had torn the scales from her eyes, and she saw things clearly now. The urge to help them, whether to provide a meal or a warm coat or even a place to sleep at night, grew with each passing moment. Maybe Max could help her figure out how to put her plans into motion.

The day felt like it would never end. With Christmas just over two weeks away, the store was busy with their regular customers and shoppers looking for a perfect gift. By the time five o'clock rolled around, Essie was ready. She slipped into the employee locker room and grabbed her coat, gloves, and hat. Then, with the package and a few treats she'd tucked away in her reticule, she waved goodbye to her friends and headed down the block to where her driver waited.

Essie handed Allen a slip of paper with Max's address on it. "If you don't mind, I need to make a delivery first."

Allen glanced at the address, then back at her. "That's a good half hour from here, miss, and in the opposite direction."

Which meant she wouldn't be present for dinner with her parents and Mr. Davidson. Essie smiled to herself. What a wonderful way to get out of spending another evening listening to that horrible man go on about how much money he'd made today. Max and the boys would be much better company. "We'll send a message to Merritt that I've been delayed. She's good at coming up with excuses for me."

"Yes, miss." His gray head bowed slightly as he handed her up into the carriage and shut the door.

Essie sank back into the cushions, the heated brick at her feet warming her. It had been a long day, and though her leg pained her, she'd enjoyed helping people find Christmas presents for their loved ones. Watching her customers' eyes sparkle, witnessing the happiness unfurl in their expressions, put her in the holiday spirit more than any present she'd ever received. If she felt this way about a small trinket, imagine what joy God must have felt when she accepted His gift of Jesus Christ!

Later, the carriage rolled to a stop. Allen climbed from his post, opened the door, and helped Essie down. "Are you certain about this, miss?"

She glanced down the row of neat little houses. In the waning dusk, with the glow of lamplight flickering in the front windows, they looked like the homey Christmas cards they sold at the store. Pulling her coat tightly around herself, she turned to Allen. "I shouldn't be very long, but I do need to speak to the pastor. Will you be warm enough?"

He gave her a crooked smile. "Always worried about others, aren't you, miss? I'll be fine."

Essie drew in a breath of cold air, then walked over to the front gate. Max had a sweet little place, though the yard was bare in spots, and the house looked like it could use a fresh coat of paint. But the festive wreath on the door and the jolly tree that filled the large window gave the place such a welcoming look, she almost felt at home. As she started up the worn pathway to the front door, second thoughts came to mind. What would Max say, her just showing up like this? Would he think less of her for coming alone?

She was delivering a package for the store, that was all. Yet there were so many things she wanted to talk over with him. Where do you start when you want to help children abandoned on the streets? How do you find the purpose God has for you?

How do you know you're in love?

Her heart fluttered at the last question. Talk about love with Max? She should be blushing to her roots at the thought. Instead, it felt natural, almost right, to discuss such tender feelings with him. His love for the boys was evident in every action he took. Surely he understood about the love that happened between a man and a woman.

After stepping up on the small porch, Essie knocked on the door. There was a loud clatter, like a herd of reindeer had landed on the roof, and for a second, Essie thought the house might come down on her. Then the door opened to a boy much younger than Mike, with what looked like cookie dough caked on his fingers.

"Who is it, Tommy?" a familiar male voice called out from somewhere inside the house.

The boy stared up at her, unruly hair falling in his eyes. "Who are you?"

Was that flour in his eyelashes? Essie cleared her throat. "I'm Miss Essie from the Five and Dime. I have a delivery for Pastor—"

"Pastor Max, it's a lady," Tommy hollered.

Essie took a step closer. "How can a boy so small yell so loud?"

He gave her a snaggle-toothed grin. "Practice, I guess."

"Tommy, does the lady have a name?"

Essie glanced over the boy's head as Max bounded into the hallway. Wearing an ill-fitted apron and a layer of flour on his clothes, he met her gaze, his eyes sparkling in surprise and something akin to wonder. Joy splashed over her at the sight of him.

She wouldn't have to ask him about falling in love because she already had.

She was in love with Max Warner.

Chapter Seven

She looked like an angel standing there in the doorway.

Of course, Max knew that was impossible. Angels were heavenly creatures, and a human didn't become one once they passed from this world to the next. But if God ever made any exceptions, it would be Essie.

"I thought it wasn't polite to stare."

Tommy's statement broke through Max's muddled thoughts. He straightened, though for the life of him, he couldn't stop smiling. "Miss Essie, I wasn't expecting you this evening."

She returned his smile with a shy one of her own. "Our delivery boy wasn't able to leave your package this afternoon, so I thought I'd bring it by on my way home."

"That's very kind of you." But then Essie had a kind spirit about her, always helping people even when it might be inconvenient for her. He cherished the moments she'd stopped in her busy day to pray with him. An angel, really. With her light blond hair and brilliant blue eyes and lips that were meant for—

"You're staring again." Tommy smirked.

Heat rushed up the back of Max's neck, and he cleared his throat. "Go help the other boys with the cookie dough."

Tommy glanced at the both of them, then shook his head.

"Yes, sir."

Max turned back to Essie. "I'm sorry about that. We're trying to learn manners, but it's not going so well."

"It's all right." Her laughter was musical, like the loveliest Christmas carol, as she scanned his clothes. "So, you're making cookies?"

Good heavens, how did he get so much flour on himself? He dusted off his apron, then gave up as a thin cloud of white powder rose around him. "We're trying, but we haven't had much success thus far."

Her eyes glimmered with humor. "How do you mess up cookies?"

"You should try it with six boys and all with ideas about what they want to add." He laughed because, really, it was funny now that he thought about it. Max folded his arms over his chest. "I take it you know how to cook."

"Cooking is different from baking," she informed him. She handed him the package before untying her hat and placing it on the hall table. "Cooking takes practice. Baking just requires one to read the recipe."

Essie unbuttoned her coat, and Max helped her with it, hanging it on the coatrack. "So which one do you do?"

"Bake. I don't get to do it as much as I like, so when I have a chance, I take it." She pointed toward the parlor. "Is this the way to the kitchen?"

"It's past the parlor to the right." Max took her arm, her slender bones so dainty and delicate in his grasp. A wave of protectiveness came over him. "You didn't walk here this time of the day, did you?"

She shook her head and walked through the parlor to the hallway on the other side. Maybe a friend from work had shared a cab with her. He hoped so. A carriage ride would have set Essie back an entire day's wages. Still, the idea of walking her home made his heart skip a beat.

By the time he arrived in the kitchen, Essie was at the head of the table, tugging on a white apron and circling the ties around her trim waist twice. The boys were lined up on either side like soldiers waiting for the general's command.

Neal spoke first. "Is this the lady you were goggling at the door?"

The other boys snickered while Essie flushed a lovely pink. Max took a place at the table opposite Essie and stared at the boys. "Is that any way to talk in front of a lady?" He met her gaze over the bowls of failed batter. "This is Miss Essie. She has graciously volunteered to help us with our cookies."

"She looks too pretty to know how to cook." Billy leaned over, dumping a pasty mixture out of a bowl and onto the table.

"I don't cook. I bake." She pulled a bowl with their latest attempt toward her and glanced inside. "This looks more like soup than cookie dough."

"Jacob thought it was too dry, so he added a little bit of water," Tommy replied.

"I don't like hard cookies," Jacob snorted.

A smile teased her lips, and Max thought his heart might stop. "Let's mix up another batch, and I promise they won't be dry. What kind of cookies are we making?"

"Oatmeal," Max said. "We've run out of the ingredients to make anything else."

"Then oatmeal it is." She glanced over the used bowls. "First, we need to clean out some of the bowls and get our ingredients organized."

"Let me take that for you, ma'am." Noah took the bowl from

her as well as two others from the table. He tossed the contents out the back door, then rinsed and dried the bowls. Meanwhile, the other boys gathered the flour, butter, eggs, and other ingredients necessary for the recipe and organized them around the table.

"First, we need to cream the butter and sugar together," Essie said as she took the tub from Tommy and measured it out. "And could two of you each take an egg and break it into its own bowl?"

Neal took one egg and handed the other to Max. "If you're going to eat the cookies, you have to do part of the work."

"Right." He'd rather be watching Essie. She seemed to be a natural with the boys, not taking any of their guff but treating them with respect, as if what they had to say mattered.

"Do you want me to measure the flour, Miss Essie?" Neal asked, reaching for the bag.

"That would be lovely." Essie added the first egg to the mix.

"Are you a baker?" Billy asked as he eyed the bowl. "'Cause you sure know what you're doing."

She shook her head as she added some flour, then went back to mixing. "No, I'm a salesclerk at the Five and Dime."

"Wait a minute." Tommy glanced up at her. "You're the lady who gave me my new hat."

"I thought you might need one." Essie took a dish towel and wiped a spot of flour from the boy's face.

Tommy leaned into her hand as if to prolong the contact. Essie cupped his face, then bent down and brushed a kiss against his clean cheek. Max glanced around at the other boys. All work had stopped, each child absorbed in watching Tommy and Essie, a look of longing etched in each face. She seemed to sense it too as she met each child's gaze and gave them a soft smile.

"Time for the flour. Neal?"

The boy looked almost smitten when he handed Essie the

measured bowl. "Here you go, ma'am."

As they continued to work together on the cookie dough, Max took in the homey tableau. It felt nice having her here, spending time with him and the boys. Almost as if she belonged. He liked the idea of Essie here. Was he in love with her? Maybe. He couldn't deny he found her attractive. It had taken him weeks to work up the nerve to approach her at the Five and Dime. And he wanted nothing more than to see her happy.

Max blinked, joy splashing onto his soul. He was in love with her, very much so. But he couldn't marry her. Finding funding for the house had been more difficult than he'd thought, and without it, he'd have to find another place for himself and the boys. Not exactly how he wanted to start a marriage.

"Let this set for an hour, then pinch the batter and roll it into small balls and bake them until they're golden brown." Essie placed a thin layer of cheesecloth over the dough. "Now, time to clean up."

"You don't worry about that, Miss Essie." Tommy grabbed a pair of dirty bowls and headed toward the washbasin. "Come on, fellows. Let's get to work."

Max vacated his place at the end of the table and walked toward her. "It looks like the boys have taken a shine to you."

"I like them too." Essie untied her apron, a shy smile lifting the corners of her mouth. "I didn't mean to take over like that. I just wanted to help."

He took the apron, still warm from her, and hung it from a nearby nail. "The boys loved it. They think you're wonderful." Max hesitated for a moment, then added, "I think you're pretty wonderful too."

Color stained her cheeks as she dusted off the remains of the baking lesson from her skirts. "That's kind of you to say."

Either she didn't believe him, or he hadn't communicated his feelings very well. He felt it was the former. Max folded his arms over his chest. "You can't take a compliment, can you?"

"Not if I think I don't deserve it. All I did was make a batch of cookies."

He came up beside her, and she turned to face him. "Are you joking? What you did was more than make a batch of cookies. You mothered them, and that's something they haven't had in quite some time."

Her eyes met his, and any doubts he had about his feelings for her evaporated. He loved her and would until the end of his days.

"They're sweet boys, Max. You're doing a fine job with them."

Her compliment gave him a sense of satisfaction. "I hope so. I can't afford to make any mistakes with them."

"Everyone makes mistakes." Laughter danced in her eyes. "Even pastors."

"Especially this one," he laughed. He couldn't remember having such a good time as he'd had in this last hour. Maybe she would stay while they finished up the cookies and decorated the tree. "Once we bake the cookies, I was going to make hot chocolate, and we were going to finish decorating the tree. Maybe you could stay and help us?"

"I can't." She walked through the parlor to the hallway and picked up her coat from the hat stand. "I've already stayed too long as it is."

Max reached for his coat. "Then let me walk you home."

"There's no need. I have a ride waiting for me right outside the door. Besides, I can't walk very far. I was in a carriage accident a few years ago and have some paralysis in my right leg. It's nothing much, but I have to wear a brace to steady myself."

Max stepped closer. "Is that why you tripped the other day?"

She nodded, her gaze falling to the rug. "My brace got caught in my petticoats, and I couldn't get it out." She drew a deep sigh. "I had to tear them to get free."

Taking her chin between his thumb and forefinger, he lifted her head to meet his gaze. "You're a brave woman, Essie Banfield."

Her lips trembled slightly. "I don't feel very brave."

"Well, you are." His fingers spread out and caressed the soft skin of her jaw. "Look at all you've done. Working at the Five and Dime. Taking time out of your day to teach a group of boys how to bake cookies. You're a wonder."

Her lips parted on a soft sigh. Max lowered his head, his heart drumming in his ears and blocking out every other thought but one: she belonged with him.

"Are you going to kiss her or just stare at her?"

They both jumped back. The voice of reason came from Billy, who stood in the kitchen door along with all the other boys, cackling as if they'd caught Max's hand in the cookie jar. Well, he couldn't let the child embarrass Essie like that. "Billy, that was rude. Apologize to Miss Essie."

The boy pointed to the front door. "I can't. She's gone."

Max turned, then shoving his arms into his coat, followed her out into the cold. Essie was halfway down the walk when he caught up with her. "Why did you leave?"

"I didn't want to give the boys the wrong impression." She nodded to the carriage in front of the house. "Plus, I need to get home. I don't want my driver to catch that flu that's going around."

"Will you let me walk you to your carriage then?"

Her shy smile melted his heart as she took his offered arm. "I would like that very much."

They slowed their pace as if wanting to savor every second they had together. Essie glanced up at him. "How did your meeting go?"

He didn't want to talk about his appointment with Davidson or the bargain he'd made for the house. Still, looking into her pale blue eyes, he felt as if he could bare his soul to her. "It didn't go as I'd hoped. The new landlord wants to raise my rent by fifty percent."

"That's terrible, Max. Don't you have a lease that states how much you're required to pay?"

He nodded, clasping his hand over hers. "But this is a new owner. He feels that the property has been undersold and wants to make a profit. That's part of the reason I offered to buy the place."

"You're going to buy it?" Essie glanced back at the house and smiled. "That's wonderful. It's perfect for the boys, and the neighborhood is so homey and charming."

"That's part of the reason I wanted us to live here in the first place." Should he tell her the rest of it? "The truth is, I can't afford it. The price is twice as much as the house is worth, and though I've come up with some of the asking price, I don't have enough."

"Oh, Max." Essie leaned into him, her body warm against the frigid night air. "Is there anything I can do?"

"Not really." He loved the feel of her head against his shoulder. "Just pray when the situation comes to mind."

When they reached the carriage, Essie turned, standing close, and placed her hands on his chest. "You're always in my prayers. Just as the boys will be from now on. God will provide."

Always in her prayers. Did that mean he was in her thoughts just as she always was in his? Lowering his head, his lips met hers. She tasted of Christmas and cinnamon and everything wonderful about the season. She leaned into him, and he loved the feel of her against him.

Essie broke off the kiss but didn't move away from him. "I should go."

"Yes, you probably should." He leaned his head against hers. "Not that I want you to."

He could almost see her smile. "Will you come by the store this week?"

"Nothing could keep me away."

She seemed satisfied with his answer as she stepped out of his embrace. "And please let me know if there's anything I can do to help raise funds for the house, all right?"

Max loved her caring heart, but this was one battle he had to face alone. "I will."

With a slight nod and a smile, Essie gave him a peck on the cheek, then with his help, got into the carriage. *An eye-opening night,* he thought as he waved at her one last time, then watched as the coach drove down the street and out of sight.

Chapter Eight

Max glanced around the crowded sanctuary from behind the pulpit. There was a far greater number than what he'd expected when he called this special meeting to discuss his future plans for the boys' home. Fundraising to purchase the house had fallen far short of Davidson's asking price, so he'd come to his congregation for help.

People hurried to their seats as Max rose and took his place at the podium. "I know some of you are wondering why I called this meeting this afternoon, so I'll get to the point. As you know, I've been renting a house on Lemon Street where I've been caring for six boys who were living on the streets of Scranton. You know these boys. They've been attending church with me for the last few months and have become a part of our church family. Which is why I'm coming to you today."

The crowd seemed attentive, so he continued. "The new owner of the house has the desire to sell the place, and I would like to purchase it. I have most of the funds needed to buy it, but I'm short fifty dollars." Some sharp gasps came from the audience, but he needed to finish. "I know it's a lot of money, especially at Christmas, but if you could find it in your heart to do this for the boys, it would be much appreciated." Max took a deep breath. "If you have any questions, I'll be happy to answer them."

Several hands rose. He had anticipated questions, though not so many. He motioned to Otis Rakestraw, their Sunday school director. Otis stood, scratching his head. "I don't understand. We give you a salary, which, I must say, is very generous for our small church, and now you need another fifty dollars to buy a house? Why?"

Max could understand the man's frustration. He'd felt the same way several times over the past few months when the boys had needed something and he'd been unable to purchase it. "Otis, this is very difficult for me. I wouldn't ask for myself, but the boys are my first concern in this matter. The house on Lemon Street provides a good neighborhood with lots of children for the boys to make friends."

He glanced over and acknowledged Frank Shelby.

Frank stood. "I understand you wanting a place where the boys can make friends, but the parsonage is larger and has a bigger yard. It's paid for, so you'd have extra money for the boys' necessities."

Max grimaced. Frank was always looking for ways to save a dime. "It's also in dire need of repairs. The floor in the kitchen is rotted out, and a new well would have to be dug. Not to mention that the front yard is the church's graveyard."

"But the church owns it free and clear." Frank glanced around at the others in attendance. "I don't know about you, but I'd rather collect fifty dollars to make repairs than purchase another property. The church doesn't need two houses."

A low rumble rose like a rain cloud over the congregation. If Max didn't turn this around and quick, he would lose their house. For some of the boys, it was the only security they'd ever known. But was his congregation ready to hear his solution? It wouldn't hurt anything to try. Max stepped down from the podium and joined them. "I agree with you, Frank, which is why we should consider selling the parsonage."

An eerie silence fell over the crowd, and Max glanced around. If stares were daggers, he'd be a wounded man by now. But there was also something else in their expressions. It was almost as if he'd hurt them by making such a suggestion. How could that be? They were only talking about a house.

Otis glanced back at the crowd, then turned to face Max. "Pastor Warner, I think I can speak for all of us. We're a small congregation. Most of us don't have much. A few of us own our homes, but many live with other family members or pay rent, as you do. Yet I can say we all give what little we have to the Lord."

Max nodded. His church had given far beyond what other, larger churches had.

"When our pastor refuses to live in the house we've provided and then puts forth the idea of selling it, well. . ." Otis drew in a shuddered breath as if he were in pain. "It hurts us, Pastor. It's as if you don't believe we're taking care of you."

The pain in the man's voice struck Max with the swiftness of a blade. "That was never my intention. You've been very kind toward me and even indulgent when it comes to my ministry to help the homeless. I am truly sorry and hope you'll forgive me. Now go and enjoy the rest of your afternoon." He'd have to find another way to come up with the funds, but how? It was ten days until Christmas Eve, and he'd exhausted all his usual benefactors. Essie would probably know what to do, but he couldn't tell her. It would be admitting there was no future for the two of them.

A small hand touched his arm, and Max looked up to find Rebecca Rakestraw, Otis's wife, standing in front of him. A godly woman, she was respected throughout the church and their small community. "I'm sorry, Pastor. I know it wasn't the answer you were hoping for."

He shook his head. "I'll find a way to get the rest of the money for the house. The boys are depending on me."

"Yes, we'd do anything for our children. I remember when our youngest was small, she begged for piano lessons." She gave him a gentle smile. "We couldn't afford them, of course, but Jane was so adamant about learning to play. Otis took in some side work, and I did people's laundry to earn enough money for a secondhand piano and some music lessons, and guess what?"

"What?"

"Jane decided she didn't want to learn how to play. She just liked the idea of playing an instrument because all her friends were."

"I'm not sure I understand."

The older woman chuckled softly. "Every time you spoke of the house on Lemon Street, it was just that. A house. Not one time did you refer to it as your home."

Had he done that? Did it make a difference one way or the other? "Why does it matter? It's a house where the boys can make friends and grow into the men God wants them to be."

"Ah, but there is a difference." She leaned in closer until he had to bend down to hear her. "A house is just four walls and a place to lay your head at night. A home is wherever the people you love live and share their lives with you. It has no walls because home is wherever they are. You see the difference?"

"Yes, and that's how the boys and I feel about the place. I just want them to have a sense of what is normal. You know, making friends and watching other families on our street. It will help them feel like they're not missing anything."

"And if you can't come up with the funds to purchase the house?"

Max didn't want to think about that yet. He patted her

delicate hand on his arm. "Thank you for sharing with me. I will be praying on it."

"That's all I can ask." She slipped her hand from his arm, then lifted her reticule, opened it, and withdrew a five-dollar silver coin. "Those boys will be hoping for presents on Christmas morning, and we can't disappoint them."

"That's very kind of you, Mrs. Rakestraw, but you don't have to do that."

"Of course I do." She handed him the coin. "I care about those boys too. And remember, you want a home, not a house. One can be cold on even the warmest of days while the other will always have a place for you by the fire."

As the crowd dispersed, a few more came by and slipped him money for the boys' Christmas, a kind gesture considering how little they had to give. Yet he sensed their hurt, and once again, guilt knifed through him. Had he been so focused on his ministry with the boys that he'd overlooked his own congregation?

The sun hung low on the horizon, the purples and reds of late evening overshadowing the vivid blue of the day, when Max stepped out of the church an hour later. He shrugged deeper into his coat, the sharp nip in the air needling his unprotected ears and neck. The scent of woodsmoke hung in the air, taking him back to his conversation with Mrs. Rakestraw. Could he make the parsonage into a home?

He thought back to his time with the Bolings. He'd always known he was welcomed there, even when he'd first arrived in the back of a police wagon. There had been no scolding or beatings like he'd endured on the street. Only love and compassion. Of course, Pastor Boling had kept a firm hand on him, but it was out of concern, not the need to control. Over time he'd come to trust the pastor and his wife, to believe they had his best interests at heart, and eventually he accepted the love they shared.

But the Bolings had a house—four walls, as Mrs. Rakestraw called it. How could he earn the boys' love and respect if they found themselves back out on the streets? The thought weighed heavily on his soul, and he prayed the rest of the way home.

The silence in the yard jarred him as Max opened the front gate. He glanced around. Tommy was probably hiding behind a tree, waiting for the perfect opportunity to unleash a handful of mudballs at him. As he walked to the front porch with Tommy nowhere to be found, he worried. The boy always met him at the front gate with stories about his day or just to talk. Maybe he'd finally made friends with one of the neighborhood kids. The thought lifted Max's spirits.

When Max opened the door, distant noises upstairs drew him through the empty parlor and kitchen, up the steps, and down the hall. He opened the bedroom door to find them all huddled around Tommy's bed, and a different fear fell over him.

"Boys?"

They turned as one, and it hit Max like a load of bricks. Love. He loved these boys, just like his parents and the Bolings loved him. Whatever happened, wherever they found themselves in this world, they were his family. His home.

"Pastor Max," Neal called out, fear in his young voice as he ran across the room and threw his arms around Max's waist. He buried his face in Max's side. "He's so sick."

Max leaned down and picked Neal up, then carried him to join the others. It wasn't like Neal to show emotion. Whatever had happened frightened him badly. "What's going on?"

"It's Tommy. He's sick." Billy's own cherry cheeks worried Max. "He wasn't feeling so good this morning after church, so he came up here to lie down. But then he threw up, and now he's hot enough to fry an egg on and says he hurts all over."

Max put Neal down, then knelt to check out Tommy. Billy was right. The child was burning up with fever. The sheets were knotted on the floor, victims of Tommy's constant tossing and turning. Max laid a hand on his thin shoulder. A pair of glassy eyes opened in tiny slits to meet his. "Did you eat anything today, son?"

Tommy shook his head and began to shake. "I'm so cold."

Max retrieved the quilt at the foot of the bed and tucked it around the boy's small body. "Better?"

"A little," he whispered, closing his eyes again.

"Is he going to die?"

Max looked up to find five young faces staring at him, the stark fear in their expressions causing him to choke up. They had lost so much in their lives, it had become almost expected, as if death followed them around like a loose penny.

Max put his arm around Billy and pulled him close. Even through the thick clothing, heat radiated off the boy. "I don't think it's anything to worry about. Influenza is going around, and it looks like Tommy picked it up somewhere."

Billy leaned his head on Max's shoulder. "I got nervous there for a minute. My parents died of a fever when I was small."

"Well, that's not going to happen here. I've got some willow bark tea down in the kitchen that will help with the fever and help Tommy get comfortable so he can sleep." He glanced down at the boy in his embrace. "You look like you could use some too."

Billy nodded, his body going limp against Max. "Can I lay down? Not that I'm sick or anything."

"You do that." Max helped Billy to his bed. After taking off the child's shoes, he tucked him into bed. "Is that better?"

Billy's eyes were already closed. "Oh yes. I just need to rest for a while, and then I'll get up and help."

Max glanced from one bed to the other. Two sick boys. If it was the flu, as he suspected, the rest would drop like flies over the next few days. How was he going to care for all of them if they got sick? He needed help, but who? He couldn't very well ask his congregation for a favor, not after he'd mucked things up today. With no family or friends nearby, he was hopelessly on his own.

Essie would come.

The thought caught him off guard. He didn't doubt Essie would be here if she knew of his situation, but he wouldn't ask her. If it was the flu, he wouldn't risk giving it to her and ruining her Christmas. No, he'd handle this on his own. Everything would be just fine. Still, he offered up a word of prayer.

Lord, please help me care for these sick boys. Protect me from this illness. And if things get bad, please send help!

Essie glanced in the vanity mirror, checking her hair to make certain it would meet her mother's strict standards. No guest was expected tonight, but Mother believed one should dress for company no matter what. She glanced over to where Merritt stood brushing out her attire for the evening. The pinstriped shirtwaist with the dark green skirt might not be Mother's idea of dinner clothes, but Essie found them comfortable, and that's what mattered.

"You look beat, Miss Essie. Did you have a long day?"

She glanced into her mirror to find Merritt studying her. Nothing got by the young woman, though she wished the maid was less observant, especially tonight. "I'm fine. The store was more crowded than usual, but that's to be expected."

Merritt plucked the clothes off their hangers and draped them over her arm. "Everyone's getting into the Christmas spirit by spending money they don't have on things they don't need."

"When did you get to be an old Scrooge?" Essie laughed as she shrugged into the blouse and buttoned it. "Don't you like getting presents?"

"I like them as much as the next person." After laying the skirt across the back of the chair, Merritt picked up Essie's work clothes. "But it shouldn't be all about what we get under the tree on Christmas morning. We should focus more on the gift God gave us almost nineteen hundred years ago. Christ is the only gift we should celebrate."

Essie nodded. Merritt was right. Christ was the only gift that mattered. *Lord, help me to stay focused on You and the precious gift of Jesus.*

"Did your pastor friend come by to see you today?"

"No, he didn't." Another reason why the day had felt so long. Max always came in on Mondays, but it was Wednesday, and she hadn't seen him since he'd kissed her last week. At the time, held tight in his embrace, Essie had been confident that he cared for her. A man like Max didn't kiss a woman unless he felt something for her. Yet as each hour dragged by, her confidence waned.

"That doesn't sound like him."

Why couldn't Merritt simply drop the subject? It hurt just to think about him after the other night. How could she have read him so wrong? "No, it doesn't. Maybe something came up with the boys, and he didn't have time to come by."

After bundling the clothes up and throwing them down the laundry chute, Merritt came back to the vanity and began to brush out Essie's hair. "I hope they're not sick. Cook says there's a nasty influenza going around Scranton. Said Mr. Deaver, the butcher, has had to shut down his shop, he's been so ill with it."

"Influenza." One of the girls at the store had mentioned her mother had it, but Essie hadn't realized it was so bad. What if one or more of the boys had come down with it? She couldn't expect Max to leave them alone just to pay her a visit. Or worse, what if Max had fallen ill? How would he ever be able to take care of himself and the boys? The thought almost made her weep. A bad case of flu could kill a person. She gasped, tears crowding her eyes. The thought of Max dying. . .

Grabbing her skirt and pulling it over her head, Essie hurried to do the buttons. "Could you get my wool cloak? I have to go back to the store."

"Did you leave something there?" Merritt asked as she walked to the closet. "Can't you get it tomorrow?"

Essie shook her head, grabbing her reticule from the vanity. "Is Allen here? He knows the way to Max's house."

"Have you lost your mind?" Merritt clutched the cloak close to herself. "Your mother will take to her bed for a week if she hears you went to a man's house unescorted. We're lucky she didn't find out about you being there Sunday."

"Then you'll just have to go with me." She slid on one glove, then the other. "If the boys are sick, Max will have his hands full."

Merritt gave her the cloak, then turned to grab her own. "And how are you going to help? You've never taken care of a sick person a day in your life. Do you know how to check for fever? What will I tell your mother if you come down with it yourself?"

"I don't know, and I truly don't care." Essie pulled her rabbit fur hat over her head. "If the boys or Max are sick, I'll be there to help."

"And what if they're not?" Merritt's question stilled Essie's movements. "What if the young pastor has decided to pay his attentions elsewhere?"

Pain much worse than her leg shot through her. If she'd read Max wrong, if he wasn't interested in courting and possibly marrying her, her heart would never heal. She loved him and only him, and there would be no other suitors as far as she was concerned. For the moment, all she cared about was his and the boys' well-being. "I'll handle that when it happens. Right now I want to make certain they're all right."

Merritt put her arm around Essie's waist. "Then that's just what we'll do. Let me get a few things and tell the maid that we've gone to help a sick friend, and I'll be ready."

"You don't have to go. I don't want to put you in a bad position with my parents."

"Of course I'm going. Can't have you traipsing around town all alone." She threw her cloak over her shoulders, then picked up a pair of woolen gloves. "Besides, I want to see this fellow who's got you all aflutter."

"You don't have to make it sound so dramatic," Essie answered as she walked over to the door, Merritt close on her heels. "We'll go down the back stairs and out through the kitchen. Allen will be in the stables.

"Do you think they might need food? Cook fixed a big pot of vegetable soup today that smelled heavenly."

Why hadn't Essie thought of that? "Maybe she can fix us up a basket while Allen gets the carriage ready."

Cook was more than obliging. A large jar of soup along with fresh bread and cheese found its way into the basket along with an apple pie and some of her homemade cough syrup. After she thanked Cook and helped Merritt with the basket, Essie prayed Max and the boys were safe and healthy and that her worrisome notions would come to nothing.

It hurt to move.

Max collapsed into the kitchen chair, his eyelids so heavy, he feared if he closed them he would be asleep for days. He leaned forward and rested his forehead in his hands. He had a fever—not a high one, but enough to make him miserable. Well, he'd have to be sick later. The boys were as weak as watered-down tea, and if Neal's cough didn't subside soon, he feared pneumonia would set in.

A quiet knock at the door drew his head up. It was too late for any of his parishioners to stop by with dinner or an offer to help, and no doctor had been called. He didn't have the money to pay one. So who could be at his door this late at night? He stood, catching the edge of the table, then sank back into the chair.

"Is someone at the door?"

Max forced his eyes open. Tommy stood in front of him, his hand-me-down nightshirt barely covering his knees. Another item he'd have to add to his ever-growing shopping list. "Go back upstairs and get in bed, young man, before you catch a chill."

"I'm not sick anymore, Pastor Max. See." The boy took Max's hand and placed it on his forehead. "No fever."

He couldn't tell if the child was running a temperature or not, his own body was so cold. Max closed his eyes against the headache raging behind them. "How are the other boys?"

"Asleep. Neal got sick once, then fell back to sleep."

There was another knock on the door, this one more insistent. Max tried to stand again but couldn't get his arms and legs to move. A small hand came down on his shoulder as if to comfort him. "I'll get it."

The boy hurried from the room, and Max relaxed in the

silence. A few moments passed before he heard the sound of skirts moving around him, then felt a cool hand against his forehead. "Max darling, you're burning up."

"Essie?" He groaned, forcing his eyes open again. It took him a few seconds to focus, then there she was, her face pale with concern, yet she was the most beautiful woman he'd ever seen. "What are you doing here?"

"When I didn't hear from you, I got worried that you and the boys might be sick." She removed her hat, her blond hair tumbling down in waves around her shoulders. "So Merritt and I thought we'd come by and check on you."

"Merritt?" He couldn't continue as he let out a hoarse cough. He bent forward to catch his breath, but the coughing wouldn't stop.

Glass clinked against glass nearby, then Essie held a cup to his lips. "Drink this."

He took a tentative sip, then another. The water felt wonderful against his parched throat. When he was finished, he pushed the glass away and closed his eyes again. "Thank you."

The steady rustle of her movements as she moved around the kitchen comforted him. "Let's warm up the soup and see if we can get them to eat something. It might do them some good."

Whose voice was that? Then he remembered. "Who's Merritt?"

Essie placed a cool cloth on his head. "She's a good friend of mine. When I told her I wanted to check on you, she wouldn't let me come without her."

Max relaxed back into the chair. At least this Merritt character wasn't a man. The thought of Essie with someone else caused a pain in his chest that had nothing to do with the flu. Essie was his, and as soon as he recovered, he would make his intentions known. It may take a while, but together they would find a way to build a family and a home.

"Nice to meet you, Pastor. I only wish it was under better circumstances." The young woman sat a steaming bowl on the table. "Here's some vegetable soup."

"Thank you, Merritt." Essie drew a chair close to him and sat down. "I'll make sure he eats. Could you go check on the boys?"

"Of course, as long as this strapping gentleman will go with me." She ruffled Tommy's unruly hair. "What do you say?"

Tommy nodded. "As long as I can have some of that apple pie when we get finished."

The young woman thought for a moment, then held out her hand. "Deal."

Tommy took it and gave it a quick shake. "Deal."

"Come on then." Merritt held the boy's hand as they walked out of the kitchen. "And what are you doing running around in nothing but your nightshirt? You don't want to be sick again, do you?"

Essie took a napkin from the table and tucked it into the front of his shirt, then loaded a spoon with soup. "Let's get some of this into you."

Max studied her as she struggled to keep the soup from splashing all over the table. She truly was the sweetest woman. "I can feed myself."

Big blue eyes stared into his, and for a moment, he was lost. What had he ever done for God to put such a wonderful woman in his life? Nothing, absolutely nothing. Yet here she was. He cleared his throat. "Why are you here? What if someone saw you? Visiting here at night could get you sacked."

"I doubt Mr. Woolworth would fire me for tending to the pastor when he's sick, and if he did, I could find another position."

She stood up and walked over to the stove where a teakettle whistled. After lifting it from the heat, she poured the boiling water into a cup. "We'll let that set for a few minutes, and then you need to drink it. It will help with the fever."

But Max wasn't ready to drop the subject yet. "Essie, do you know how dangerous it is for a woman to be out on the streets alone at this time of night? You could have been hurt."

She leaned back against the countertop. "Do you worry about everyone this way or just me?"

He palmed the back of his neck, pushing his fingers into the tense muscles. "Of course, I'd never want anyone to come to harm, but if you want the truth, then yes, I do worry about you."

"I see." She brought him the steaming cup and set it in front of him. "Then you understand how I felt tonight. The thought of you sick here with the boys undid me, Max. All I wanted to do was make certain you were all right."

"But the reason I fret over you is because I. . ." Max stopped. He worried about Essie because he loved her. Was it possible she felt the same about him? The question settled on his lips, but his stomach had other ideas. Covering his mouth with his hand, Max jolted out of the chair and hurried to the back door.

"Max?"

"Don't!" he called out over his shoulder as he threw the door open. The cold shocked his febrile state, the wind a welcoming balm to his fevered skin. Another wave of nausea hit him, and he ran to the corner of the house and emptied his stomach.

A blanket fell over his shoulders, and he glanced up to find Essie holding out a washrag for him. He swiped it across his face, then pressed it into the nape of his neck. "I'm sorry, Essie."

Her hand rubbed comforting circles on his back. "It's all right. You can't help that you're sick."

No, but a woman like Essie didn't need to be out in the cold caring for him. Still, he had to admit he liked Essie fussing over him. It reminded him of his mother and the way she took care of their little family before the fire had taken her and Papa away. Since then, he'd been on his own, fending for himself, then the boys. To have someone care for him felt like a great gift.

Max straightened, his head pounding. "I'm fine now."

"Let's get you back inside." Essie wrapped her arm around his waist and leaned into him, her body cool against his. "We'll get you some willow bark tea, then off to bed."

That sounded lovely. "What about the boys?"

They walked over to the back door, and she opened it. "You don't worry about the boys. Merritt and I will take care of them."

"Essie, you can't stay. People will talk."

She helped him to his chair, then retrieved the tea from the countertop. "I don't care what people say. I wouldn't be much of a friend to leave you here with the boys in your condition. So, no more arguments. Is that clear?"

She was a bossy little thing when she wanted to be. He raised his hand in a salute. "Yes, ma'am."

A soft smile played along her lips. "Good. Now drink your tea. It will bring down the fever."

Max took a small sip, then grimaced. "I hate this stuff."

"Me too, but it works, so drink up."

Max drained the cup in a couple of gulps, then set it down. "I'm feeling better already."

"Then think how much better you'll feel once you've had some sleep." She took the cup to the washbasin and rinsed it out. "Now, off you go. You can manage by yourself, can't you?"

"And if I can't?"

Essie turned around and planted her hands on her hips. Max's breath caught for a moment. She was magnificent. "Upstairs, Max Warner. Now."

"Yes, ma'am." It felt good having someone boss him around. He stood and, with a brief good night, strolled across the kitchen. At the door, he turned back to her. "Thank you, Essie."

There was a smile in her voice when she spoke. "You're welcome."

While Tommy felt better, the same could not be said for the other boys. The two oldest still had high fevers. Billy and Jacob couldn't hold down their tea, and all were as weak as water. Over the next few hours, Essie and Merritt worked changing bedding, brewing willow bark tea, and caring for their small patients. Essie checked on Max twice throughout the night. There was something so intimate about standing at the door, watching the man she loved sleep.

By the time everyone was settled, the sun was threatening to dawn. Essie sat at the kitchen table and closed her eyes, a bone-weary tiredness penetrating her being. Some people might call her a fool, caring for Max and the boys as she did, but she didn't care. All the money in the world couldn't buy the happiness she found in this place. If Max would have her, she'd be content to live here for the rest of her days.

"Drink this," Merritt said, placing a cup of steaming coffee in front of her. "You've earned it."

Essie took the cup between her cold hands and glanced over at her maid. "If anyone has earned something, it's you. How did you know how to care for the boys like that?"

Merritt sat down across from her and stretched her legs out under the table. "I do have a family, you know."

"Yes, I know." Essie chuckled softly. "Why have you never talked much about them?"

"I thought you probably didn't want to hear about them." She moved her head from one side to the other, stretching her neck.

Essie leaned forward in her chair. "What are they like?"

The young woman took a sip from her cup. "They're like most people. My oldest brother is married with a little boy, but the rest are still at home."

"You're an aunt, Merritt."

A faint smile graced Merritt's face. "Little Emmett is our pride and joy. Both of his parents work, so on Sundays I take him to church, then spend the rest of the day with him."

"No wonder you're so good with the boys." Essie stood, grabbed her cup, and headed to the washbasin. "You've had years of practice."

Merritt took a shortening bread cookie from the tin Cook had sent and popped it in her mouth. "I don't know. You caught on quickly. It's like you have the gift of service."

"I don't know about that, but I do like to help people." Essie put down her tea and busied herself by cleaning out the washbasin. "It feels like something I was meant to do. The purpose of my being here."

"It's your spirit gift, Essie." Merritt must have seen the confusion in her eyes. "When you became a believer, God gave you gifts to use for His glory. Some people have the gift of service while others have discernment or are called to preach or to teach."

"I never heard that before." Essie studied her maid over the rim of her cup. "So do you have the same gift for serving others?"

"No."

The answer startled Essie. "But you've been wonderful to me all these years, and you do it so effortlessly."

"It's my job." Merritt hesitated as if searching for the right words. "Serving others doesn't come naturally to me, but I want a better life for my younger brothers and sisters. The only way that happens is through education. Thus, I work." She smiled. "Though it's not too hard. The woman I work for is very kind and has a soft spot for pastors and little boys." She took a sip. "May I ask you something?"

Essie met her gaze. "Of course."

"Why can't you see your own worth?" Merritt pressed her lips together as if she was thinking. "You're a lovely person, Essie. You always have been, but you're too busy worried about how others see you. You've let what happened with the carriage accident take over your life."

Essie took another sip of her coffee, the taste suddenly bitter. Is that what she'd done? Had she let her accident define her? "I don't know. Even my own parents can't see past what the accident did to me."

"You mean the suitors?"

She nodded. "It's as if they don't think it's possible for a man to love me for myself."

Merritt snorted. "They should see how the pastor looks at you. That would change their minds."

Essie stared into her cup, heat bursting in her cheeks. Max deserved so much more, not a cripple like her. *Then why did he kiss you?* "You're imagining things."

Merritt laughed and pointed toward the stairs. "The way that man looks at you is scandalous. Even sick as he is, he stares at you as if you're his present on Christmas morning and he can't wait to unwrap you."

"Merritt!" She shushed her, glancing up the stairs, then back at her. "It's not like that. Max has been nothing but a gentleman."

"Maybe, but he wants something more. I'd bet my teeth on it." Essie squirmed under her perusal. "The first night Allen brought you here and you made cookies, did the pastor kiss you?"

Essie stopped breathing. That kiss had been so special, so precious, that she hadn't shared what happened with anyone, not even Merritt. "How did you know he kissed me?"

Her maid tilted her head. "You came in floating on air. I almost had to scrape you off the ceiling."

"Stop it," she chuckled. Merritt was wrong. Why would someone like Max look at her that way? He was wonderfully handsome with his broad shoulders and ready smile. But more than that, he was good and kind. Loved those most people forgot. Gave with everything he had. She had nothing to offer him. She was a woman crippled by a bad leg.

"Don't do that." Merritt glared at her from across the table.

Essie blinked in astonishment. In all her years of service, Merritt had never spoken harshly to her. "What do you mean?"

"Don't sell yourself short." Merritt rubbed her forehead as if the discussion was giving her a headache. Finally, she dropped her hand and stared across the table at her. "For someone who doesn't want others to judge her for her impairment, you do a pretty good job of doing it yourself."

"That's not true," Essie retorted. "I live with my limitations the best I can."

"Ha!"

"Ha?" Her temper rose a notch. "What do you mean by that?"

"I mean ha if you believe that."

Essie pressed her lips together. Of all the people she knew, she'd expected Merritt to understand her dilemma the most. "Give me one example."

"All right." Merritt leaned back in her chair with her arms

crossed over her waist. "Your dresses."

Had Merritt gone mad? "What about my dresses?"

"When I first came to work for you, you loved trying new styles. In fact, it was quite fun watching you wear a new dress or angle your hat differently than everyone else." Her expression grew somber. "But after the carriage accident, you refused to wear the new fashions. You're afraid someone will notice the brace and say something about it."

"That's not true," Essie argued, though it sounded weak even to her ears. "I just favor the old styles."

Merritt glared at her. "I've seen you at the dressmaker's, poring over the latest drawings from Paris. You look like a kid in a candy store. You looked smashing in that blue gown your mother ordered, and you know it."

"I don't think. . . ," Essie started.

"And your shoes. Surely, you can do better than boots." Merritt picked up steam like a locomotive heading out of town. "You may not be able to wear heels, but I don't know why you're afraid to wear slippers."

"Is that all?" Essie wasn't sure whether to laugh or cry.

"Yes. No." Her friend leaned forward and met her gaze. "Don't let your mother bully you into marrying Mr. Davidson or any other man when it's as plain as the nose on your face that you're in love with the pastor." She drew in a deep breath before sitting back. "And the lovely thing is, he's in love with you too."

"You don't know that."

Merritt barked with laughter. "Didn't you hear all that talk about saving your reputation? A man doesn't care about such things unless he cares about the woman. Then there's the way he looks at you like you're a piece of chocolate he can't wait to take a bite of."

"Really, Merritt." Had her maid always been this dramatic? "He's a pastor, for goodness' sake."

"He's a man first, and you'd best remember that."

Essie didn't need any reminders. She'd been attracted to Max since the first moment she'd seen him. But for him to feel the same way as she did, for him to love her. . . "Are you sure he cares for me?"

"Of course he does." Merritt rolled her eyes in frustration. "Isn't that what I've been telling you?"

Joy splashed over Essie. To love Max and be loved by him in return was more than she ever dreamed. All at once, she could see their lives laid out before them. A home where they'd raise the boys and shower them with love. Maybe a baby or two of their own. And Max, always Max. His arms would be her home. Was this the purpose God had made for her? To be Max's wife? A mother? The thought brought her more happiness than she'd ever dreamed possible.

A rapid knock on the door stirred Essie from her daydream. She glanced over at Merritt. "Who could that be? It's barely dawn."

"There's only one way to find out." Merritt pushed back from the table and stood. Essie rose also and followed close behind her as they walked through the parlor to the front hall. Whoever it was couldn't be bearing good news.

The knocking started again as they reached the front door. Not knowing what to expect, Essie grabbed Max's umbrella from the stand in case they needed a weapon. Merritt glanced at her, then opened the door. The umbrella clamored to the floor as recognition settled in. It couldn't be. How would he know?

"Papa? What are you doing here?"

"I could ask you the same thing, Estella." He glanced past her to the parlor. "Are you going to ask me inside, or shall we talk out here?"

Essie turned to grab her coat, but Merritt beat her to it, draping it over her mistress's shoulders. "Don't let him bully you, Essie."

Essie winked at her, then joined her father outside. The day was brisk but not too terribly cold, and for a second, she wondered if they'd have snow for Christmas. The boys would be disappointed if they didn't.

"Why didn't you invite me inside, Estella Anne? Are you ashamed to allow your father into the house where you've sullied your reputation?" Papa huffed, white clouds of smoke surrounding them as if to hide them from neighboring onlookers.

"Please calm down." She glanced around, relieved that it was still too early for most folks in this neighborhood. "There are sick boys inside trying to get some rest."

Her answer settled him for the moment. "I don't understand. How do you know these boys, and why are you and your maid here caring for them instead of their own people?"

So many questions. She'd best start at the beginning, but first she had a question of her own. "How did you know I was here?"

"Allen. He came to me early this morning when you didn't return to the carriage last night. He thought you might be in trouble. I should fire him for leaving you here in the first place."

Poor man. She had put him in a horrible position. "But you won't. Allen only did as he was told. The same thing goes for Merritt. Without her last night, I'm not sure how I would have managed."

Papa pulled his scarf closer to his neck. "You've stalled long enough. Tell me why you're here."

Essie pressed her lips together. She was about to disappoint him. "Did Allen also tell you that I've been working at Woolworth's Five and Dime for the last few months?"

Her father stared at her in shock. "Why would you do that? All you've ever had to do is ask for something, and it's yours."

"I know, Papa." Essie wasn't sure how to explain it, but she had to try. "After the accident, I felt small and insignificant, as if my inabilities suddenly made me less of a person. My friends cemented that idea with their comments and pity, and I began to wonder if God had any real purpose for my life."

"Oh, Essie. I didn't know you felt that way." He walked to her and tucked her coat more closely around her. "I've never once thought of you that way."

"Then why do you and Mother seem so set on marrying me off to the first willing man you can find?"

Papa rubbed her arms. "That was more of your mother's doing, but I understood why. She's been worried sick about you for months now and thought if you were to marry and have children, it might take your mind off what you've lost."

Essie wasn't sure that was her mother's only motive, but she'd take Papa at his word. "Anyway, I applied for a position at the Five and Dime a few months ago and was hired." She went on to tell him about meeting Max and how knowing him and the boys had changed how she saw her own life as well as given her insight about her own future. She didn't tell him she'd fallen in love. Max deserved to hear it first, but her father's expression softened as she told him about spending time with Max and the boys. "When Max didn't show up at the store like he normally does, I knew something was wrong. When we arrived last night, most of the boys were recovering, but Max had a terrible fever. We stayed to watch the boys while Max got some rest."

Her father pushed her back so he could see her face. "Does

this pastor know who you are?"

"Of course he does. I've never hid that from anyone."

"Yes, but there's a difference between Estella Banfield, socialite and heiress, and Essie Banfield, shopgirl."

She hadn't thought of it that way. She'd always just been herself, but if Max hadn't made the connection, he'd look at things quite differently. "I need to tell him."

"Yes." Concern shone from his gaze. "Be prepared that he might not take the news well, may even think you played with his affections as a prank. But you owe it to him and to those boys. They need to know everything about you."

She nodded as he pulled her into his embrace. Max had to know she loved him and the boys. That Estella Banfield and Essie were one and the same person, and nothing would change how she felt about them. But what if he didn't understand? What would she do then?

Dear Lord, I know that my purpose in life is to be a mother to those boys and a wife to Max. Please let him understand.

Max stepped away from the slightly opened window. He'd only wanted a breath of fresh air and to cool his heated body. Instead, a profound sense of loss swept through him. He'd known Essie wasn't poor. A shopgirl didn't hire a carriage and have it wait for her. She was right when she'd told her father she'd never hid the truth about her social status from him, but he'd never bothered to ask what that was.

He paced across the room. It was his fault his heart was broken. She'd always been too good for him, but now? There wasn't any hope for the two of them, not the future he'd dreamed of for them and the boys. It was all ashes now.

The pain deepened as he thought of the boys. They loved her too. How could he explain this loss to them? He waited for the words but just heard silence.

Chapter Nine

Max trudged down the sidewalk near the Lemon Street house, his legs heavy from all the miles he'd traveled today. It was Christmas Eve, but for the first time in ages, he couldn't muster up a reason to be jolly. The number of abandoned children grew with each day, each story more horrible than the last. Today he'd found a toddler, not even two years old, huddled up against a building, her soiled diaper and dirty clothes a sign she'd been there a while. He'd taken her to the hospital, where the nurses were spoiling her when he left. In a few days, she'd be taken to the orphanage, and then, if she was lucky, the orphan train would take her to where someone would adopt her.

He stopped in front of the house and studied it. How was he going to tell the boys that they had to move? It was the first place where they'd come together like a family, the perfect neighborhood for the boys to grow and make friends. Yet the last fifty dollars he'd needed to buy it had been more than he could scratch up. The day after tomorrow, they would move to the parsonage and try to make a home there.

Max scrubbed his hands over his face. Home. How could any place be home without Essie there? In the three days since she'd climbed into her father's carriage and gone home, there'd been little joy around here. He'd gone by the store to see her only to be told she was home sick with the flu. The pain of losing her had been almost palpable, not just for himself but for the boys too. Memories of their time together. Her open smile. The shy way she looked at him whenever she'd made her point. How her eyes went all soft the night he'd kissed her by the carriage.

Max sighed as he reached the front door. Dwelling on how he missed Essie wouldn't do him any good. Besides, it was Christmas, and there were six little boys ready to celebrate. He couldn't let them down.

He opened the front door, but there was no merriment or Christmas greeting to welcome him. "Merry Christmas, boys."

"We're in here!"

Max shrugged out of his coat and gloves, then headed to the parlor. Instead of counting presents or stealing candy canes off the tree, Billy and Neal stood guard at the scarred table at the door. "Where is everyone?"

"John, Jacob, and Noah are in the kitchen, trying to put together a pudding from the recipe Miss Essie sent, and Tommy is upstairs, finishing his Christmas presents," Billy explained, his eyes never leaving the table.

Max glanced over their heads. Lying on the table was a letter addressed to him. "What is that?"

Billy snatched the sealed envelope from the table and waved it in the air. "This came for you today."

"A messenger brought it." Neal jumped, swatting at the letter, but Billy held on tight. "He said it was important."

"He said it must be important to have him delivering it on Christmas Eve," Billy corrected, holding it above Neal's head.

"It's too small for a Christmas present, so what could it be?" Neal asked.

Max snatched it from Billy's hand. "Let's see." The return address was a lawyer's office he was unfamiliar with, and his stomach sank. It was the eviction notice; it had to be. Davidson had all but told him he would have them out of the house before the first of the year. He broke the seal, then took out the folded paper. Closing his eyes, he lifted a short prayer to the Lord. *You are our Comfort and our Strength through this life and forever.*

When he unfolded the stationery, another piece of paper fell to the floor. Neal picked it up and, after studying it, glanced up at Max. "What's this?"

Taking it from the boy, Max glanced over it, then studied it further. It was a check for a rather large sum of money. It must be some mistake. But when he looked at the envelope again, his name was printed on it. He looked at the check again, glancing at the signature. *Charles Banfield.*

Bile rose in his throat. Was Banfield trying to pay him to stop seeing Essie? He could understand if Banfield thought so little of him. He was just a pastor who would never be able to provide for Essie the way she was accustomed to living. Well, he may be poor, but he still had his pride.

He had to return the money. Today.

"That's a check," Noah said, grabbing it out of Max's hand. "And look at all those zeros!"

Tommy tugged on Max's sleeve. "Does that mean you're going to buy the house?"

Max glanced around. John, Jacob, and Noah stood in the kitchen doorway while the younger boys had gathered around him. He truly was blessed. He loved each one of these boys as if they'd come from his own body. They were his family. Just like Essie was. As long as they were together, anyplace would be home.

It just couldn't be here. Max took a deep breath. "As much as

I'd like to buy this house, I don't have the money for it. So, the day after tomorrow, we're going to move."

"Where are we going?" Tommy asked.

"You know the house beside the church? That's where we're going to live."

Jacob nudged Noah. "I bet we can tell some really scary ghost stories in that graveyard. Maybe even scare some girls."

Max made a mental note to sit down with the older boys and go over the rules regarding girls, the first one being no ghost stories in the graveyard. He felt a tug on his sleeve and looked down to find Billy. "What is it, son?"

Billy's blue eyes widened. "You've never called me that before."

He put his arm around the boy. "Well, I should because that's what you are. My sons, and if you like, you can call me Papa."

"I like that." Tommy smiled up at him. "Papa."

Never had a word sounded so sweet! "There's more than enough room for all of us, so we won't be stepping on each other anymore." They laughed at that, and for the first time in three days, Max felt a bubble of joy well up inside him.

"Is there room for Miss Essie?"

Max glanced at the check. It was past time Essie knew how he felt about her. No matter what her father thought, she was a grown woman, capable of making decisions for herself. And if she broke his heart? It couldn't be any worse than the last three days had been.

Tucking the check into his pocket, Max hurried over to the rack and grabbed his coat. As he shrugged into it, he turned to his sons. "If Miss Essie will have me, there's more than enough room for her too."

"Bring Mama home to us, Papa."

Neal's words were music to Max's ears.

Essie stood by the full-length window, watching the landscape turn a snowy white, and smiled to herself. The boys would be ecstatic about a Christmas snow, especially Tommy. That boy had been practicing for just this moment since before she'd met him.

A sharp pang lodged deep in her chest, and not for the first time today, tears clogged her throat. She missed her boys. Missed their silliness and how Billy had cuddled up in her lap and fell asleep when he was sick. She missed the grousing and the way Tommy would slip his hand in hers. But most of all, she missed loving them.

She missed Max too, more than she'd ever thought possible. Everywhere she went, something would remind her of something he'd said or done, and then the tears would start again. She hadn't been back to work since the morning Father had found her at Max's. The last two days had been spent in bed, nursing a slight fever. But the truth was, she was a coward. What she had to say to Max was between them, not for some public display.

The door opened, and her father strolled inside, looking hale and hardy and quite pleased with himself, though for what reason she didn't know. "How was your day, Papa?"

"Good, though I'm hoping this evening will be even better."

What a strange thing to say. But then her father had always loved Christmas. As much as she'd looked forward to sharing it with Max and the boys, she didn't care if she stayed in bed all day tomorrow. "I'm glad we're not entertaining any guests tonight. I don't think I'm up for it."

"Oh, Essie." Papa came to her and pulled her into his arms. "Is it as bad as all that?"

"I miss him, Papa, more and more each day," she croaked

against his chest. "I miss the boys and the life I was building for myself. I even miss Mr. Sum's crazy early morning sales. What am I going to do?"

Before Papa could answer, their butler, Matthew, came to the door. "A Pastor Max Warner to see you, sir."

Max? Why was he here? And why did he want to see Papa? Essie glanced up at her father, who handed her his handkerchief. "Dry your eyes now. You don't want your young man to know you've been crying."

"Why is he here?" She wiped her nose, then handed the square back to her father, who stuffed it in his pocket.

"Let's just say he's the man I thought he was." Papa turned and walked over to the door just as Max entered the room. "Pastor Warner, so good to see you. Merry Christmas."

But Papa could have been talking to the wall for all that Max noticed. Because he was too busy watching her, drinking her in as if he'd been without for an eternity. She looked her fill too. Did he look pale, or was she just imagining things? He was so handsome, even more so now that she knew the compassionate and caring man he was.

"How is everything, Pastor?" Papa asked.

His words broke the connection between them, and Max pulled something out of his waistcoat, then thrust it at Papa. "What is the meaning of this, sir?"

Essie had never seen Max so angry. Whatever Papa had done had insulted him deeply.

Papa casually loaded his pipe with tobacco. "Was it not enough? There's plenty more where that came from."

Oh heavens, what had Papa done? The sound of paper being torn into bits reached her ears. Max tossed the pieces on the table, then pointed at Papa. "I don't want your money."

Papa had sent Max a check? Why would he do such a thing? "Papa, please tell me you didn't do this."

But her father was preoccupied. "Then what do you want, Warner?"

"Your daughter, sir. I want to marry your daughter."

Essie's heart skipped more than a beat. She stepped toward him, uncertain if she'd heard him correctly. "What did you say?"

"Oh, Essie." He came and stood in front of her, staring at her as if she was the wonderful gift he wanted the most. "I've loved you from almost the second I first saw you, so prim and proper, waiting on your customers. You looked like an angel to me."

She shyly touched his cheek, loving the feel of it against her palm. "I love you, Max. So much."

"It's about time the two of you cleared the air," her father groused as he made his way to the door. "I can't handle a sick, moping woman, especially when there's a way to fix things."

The door clicked shut, and Max wasted no time. He lowered his head, his fingers caressing her cheeks, and he tilted her head back. His lips came down on hers in a slow, deep kiss that had her clutching at his shoulders, dragging him closer.

A few minutes later, he reluctantly pulled away, resting his forehead against hers. "That was. . ."

"Wonderful," she breathed, her body a mass of delicious tingles.

Max drew in a deep breath and sighed. "We'd better marry sooner rather than later."

"Is that a marriage proposal, Pastor Warner?" she murmured, leaning in as he brushed a kiss against her temple.

"No." He stepped back, and Essie mourned the loss of him. Watching her, Max lowered himself to one knee and took her hand in his. "Essie, will you marry—"

"Yes," she nodded, her heart threatening to beat out of her chest.

He rose, and they shared another bone-melting kiss before finally breaking apart. When they'd caught their breath, Max kissed her nose, then stepped back. "You know what I want to do?"

She smiled at him. "Probably the same thing I do."

They stared into each other's eyes. "Go tell the boys."

Dear Reader,

I hope you enjoyed Essie and Max's story as much as I loved writing it! One of the favorite memories of my childhood is eating lunch with my mother and grandmother at the Woolworth's lunch counter. While we waited for our food, Grandma would give me a little bit of money and send me off to the book aisle, where I discovered my love for historical romance. Woolworth's is closed now, but those memories live on in my heart even fifty years later.

One note about Woolworth's—we writers took some liberties in creating the store's departments. In 1881 Woolworth's wasn't divided into departments. Though they had people working the counters, the Five and Dime's claim to fame was the customer's ability to pick out their own merchandise. For fictional purposes, we changed that so each one of our heroines had her own department to run.

Blessings,
Patty

Multi-published author **Patty Smith Hall** lives near the North Georgia Mountains with her husband, Danny, her two daughters, her son-in-law, and her grandboys. When she's not writing on her back porch, she's spending time with her family or playing with her grandsons.

Website: www.pattysmithhall.com
Facebook: www.facebook.com/authorpattysmithhall
Pinterest: https://www.pinterest.com/authorpattysmithhall/boards/

The Light of Christmas

Christina Lorenzen

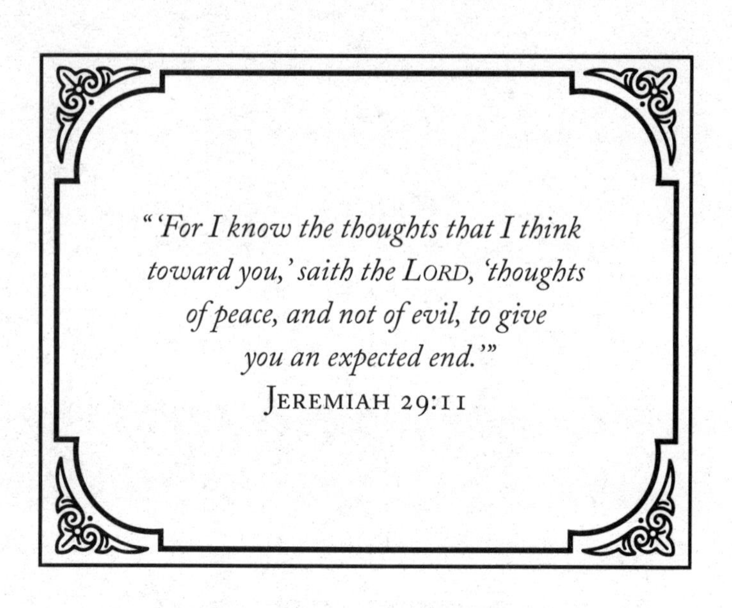

" 'For I know the thoughts that I think toward you,' saith the L*ORD*, *'thoughts of peace, and not of evil, to give you an expected end.' "*

JEREMIAH 29:11

Chapter One

Scranton, Pennsylvania, 1881
Woolworth's Five and Dime

Spotting a tall man at her counter, Lizzie Miller made her way through the aisles of assorted merchandise and slipped behind the housewares counter.

"Is there something I can help you with?" she asked.

A face with round wire glasses and a thin mustache looked up. Their eyes met. He looked surprised, as if he hadn't expected to see anyone behind the counter. He blinked and ran slim fingers through his hair, a very serious look on his face. *My goodness*, she thought, *not even the scents and colors of the season seem to bring a smile to this man's face.* She had always loved Christmas, and shortly after was her birthday on the thirty-first of December. For a brief moment, she remembered this birthday she would be alone again. She ignored the dismal thought and focused on the very serious man in front of her. Perhaps he was looking to buy something for his wife. The more sales she made, the more secure she would be in her job. Picturing the small envelope in the drawer of her bureau filling with the money she desperately needed, she got to work.

"We have several new items that would be wonderful for any woman to have in her kitchen."

He blinked again, this time looking taken aback. He cleared his throat. "I. . .I'm sorry. I was just getting an idea of the store inventory. I'm not shopping." He dropped his chin and stared at the clever layout she'd put together. Of course, when it came to housewares, she had a lot of experience, having run her family home since her father's passing and her mother's subsequent heart condition.

His words piqued her curiosity. Her mother had always said she was too curious for her own good. Her mother had also said if she ever wanted to find a good husband, she must stop questioning everything. A quick glance at the man's left hand told her he was not married.

"Why would you need to get an idea of the inventory in the store if you're not shopping?" she asked. If she didn't miss her mother so painfully, she might have laughed, imagining the aghast look on her face at hearing her daughter's boldness.

He looked right and left, adjusted his glasses, and cleared his throat again.

"Well, a good businessman should always be knowledgeable about what his store is selling."

Lizzie tilted her head as she took him in. What kind of businessman was he? She'd never seen him in Woolworth's Bros. Store before. Had Mr. Woolworth—or "Mr. Sum" as they called him, for his middle name, Sumner—hired on a partner she hadn't heard about? Lizzie talked to everyone at the Five and Dime, as the store was known. Everyone being the three clerks, Hattie, Estella, and Rose, and Maggie, the lunch counter gal.

"I hadn't heard word of a new partner coming to the store."

He took off his glasses and pulled back his shoulders.

"Partner? Oh no. I'm a new clerk. In the tool department." He tilted his chin in the direction of the counter across from housewares.

"Well, that is news to me. Welcome to Woolworth's, Mr. . . ?"

"Kimball. Henry Kimball."

Despite his attempt to appear businesslike, she thought he looked nervous. She also didn't miss the deep brown color of his eyes.

"Well, Mr. Henry Kimball, welcome to the floor. I'm sure you'll enjoy the tool department. It will be wonderful to have a gentleman in tools to help customers." She caught sight of a dark bowler in his hand and a slight tremor. He pulled a timepiece from his pocket, looked surprised, and dropped it back where it had been.

"It was very nice to have met you, Miss. . . ?" He gave her a distracted look.

"Oh, I'm sorry. How rude of me not to introduce myself. I'm Lizzie Miller. I've been here since the opening of the store." She was very proud of that fact. She wished her father could see her working and taking care of herself. He had been a laborer for the Slocum Iron and Coal Company. Making an honest living was very important to him. Now she was the one making a living, hopefully enough to take up where he'd left off on the house payments to Uncle Milton. She was sure her father would have bragged on her to the men at Slocum.

It was a different story with her mother. Even during her last days, she'd begged Lizzie to find a good husband. Her mother would have choked on the idea of a woman keeping a roof overhead. But that was exactly what Lizzie intended to do. Remembering how little she had saved made her stomach churn. But there was hope. The extra money would help fill out that envelope. Lizzie snapped out of her woes and stared at Henry Kimball. A brief smile crossed his face, making him much more attractive.

"Well, Miss Miller, it was charming to have met you." He turned to walk away.

"Mr. Kimball, you say that as though we won't be seeing one another every day."

She took him in from head to toe, dressed in a dark day suit. She would be lying to herself if she didn't admit he was dashing.

"Well, not for very long. You see, this is merely a step up the stairwell. . ." He gestured toward the stairs, the wood railing entwined with a thick pine garland for Christmas, leading to the office where Mr. Sum oversaw clerks. "My goal is to become a bookkeeper. I don't expect we will be working side by side for long." And with that he strode across the store to where tools and screws littered the tool counter. She would have offered a few tips about arranging his merchandise had she not been speechless.

It was a minute or two before she realized her mouth was gaping. She'd never met a man like Henry Kimball. Of course, she'd only spent time with her father, who'd been gone two years now. Then there was Dr. Evans. Between her father's and mother's health problems, she'd spent considerable time talking with the good doctor. Most of those times he'd have one of his six children in tow with him. She loved spending time with Dr. Evans's young ones, often reading them a favorite book from her childhood. No matter what the doctor said, she truly believed her mother had died of a broken heart. Only a month after her father's passing, her mother had been beset by the heart condition. She was gone a year later. Lizzie took comfort knowing her parents were in heaven. She was grateful they had given her a strong faith in the Lord. For without Him, where would she be now?

Lizzie gave herself a quick perusal. She smoothed her long

black skirt, checked the buttons on her white blouse, and straightened her apron. Within minutes, a group of women were standing at her counter, asking for the usual items needed in a home. The heels of her boots click-clacked across the polished wood floor as she darted to and fro, first helping one woman pick out the right color thread for a dress she was making for her little girl, next helping another choose a pie plate to bake a pie.

As she hurried about housewares, Lizzie glanced at the tool counter. The heavy hammer clutched in Mr. Kimball's slender hands looked as out of place as Henry Kimball himself. Well, he had said he wasn't planning to stay in tools very long. From his attire, she guessed he was better suited upstairs at a desk. She had to bite her lip to keep from giggling, thinking of the rough-and-tumble men from Slocum Iron and Coal who would be coming in for supplies. They'd have a field day with a fine gentleman like him.

With the last of her customers gone, her stomach reminded her of the lunch she'd brought from home. She was proud to carry her father's tin lunch pail to the store each day, containing an apple and bread. Another blessing her parents had bestowed on her was frugality. Right now every penny she earned had to go into that envelope.

She fished out her pail from under the counter. She'd sit on a stool at the lunch counter just long enough to eat. She enjoyed chatting with Maggie for a few minutes every day. Not wanting to take a stool away from a paying customer, she always ate quickly, then slowly made her way back through the aisles. This time of year, there were many things to see, but it was the light from the German Christmas ornaments in the window display that made her heart happy. She regretted not treating herself to one last year, when they first came to the store. While she might have spared the money then, this year it wasn't possible. But then, she didn't have a Christmas tree anyway. The thought of putting a small tree on the table in front of the parlor window without her family made her heart ache.

Lizzie took a small hand mirror from the cabinet behind the counter and quickly checked her hair. She'd worn the same simple hairstyle, bangs grown out and parted in the middle with her long blond locks swept up high, since she was a young girl. After replacing the mirror, she grabbed her pail and hurried to the lunch counter.

She placed her food on the white ceramic plate Maggie put in front of her. She felt a pang of sadness for the hardworking girl. Lizzie might not have any prospects for a husband, but she hadn't been left at the altar like Maggie. She felt they were kindred spirits. She finished her meal, nodded to Maggie, who was busy pouring coffee, and headed back to her counter.

She was disappointed Henry wasn't at the tool counter, but then she brought herself up short. She was being silly. What did it matter to her that Henry Kimball was working the tool counter? The man obviously thought he was too good for the sales floor. Spotting someone at her counter, her heart skipped a beat when she recognized the tall figure. What was he doing there now?

She tapped his shoulder, and he spun around. She found herself more interested in him than she cared to be.

"Mr. Kimball, can I help you with something?" Knowing he wasn't shopping made her more than a little curious about why he was there.

"Ah, yes, Miss Miller. I do have a bit of a predicament, and I was hoping I could ask for your assistance." He held out his hand. Seeing the sliver, she took his hand in hers. For a moment, they stood staring at their clasped hands before Lizzie felt her face flush, and he pulled his hand away.

"I seem to have gotten a sliver in my palm. Perhaps you have a pair of tweezers in your wares I may borrow?" He kept his hand a safe distance from hers.

Lizzie thought of the small table by the front of the store. Essie had insisted on displaying ladies' toiletries close to the entrance. Lizzie signaled for him to wait. She weaved through the aisles to the table, and within seconds she was back, holding the tweezers.

"Please give me your hand." Her voice sounded shaky. How silly she was being! She'd taken countless slivers out of her father's hands. Gooseflesh pricked her arms as she held his hand and took the tweezers to the embedded sliver. Catching it in the tweezers' tip, she gave it a good yank.

"Ouch!" Henry Kimball pulled his hand away and inspected it for damage.

"I'm sorry. I didn't think I pulled on it that hard. It's out at least." She held the tweezers up so he could see the sliver for himself.

"Yes, I see that it is out." He stood there looking uncomfortable.

"You're welcome." Her mother would have been quick to point out Henry Kimball's lack of good manners. Her father loved to tease her mother about "putting on airs," the two bantering back and forth. How she missed those days.

"Yes, thank you very much. I appreciate your help." He looked as if he wanted to say something more, but the sight of a man in front of his counter stopped him. "Thank you again, Miss Miller."

Lizzie watched him hurry to the tool counter. In his day suit, he looked out of his element behind the messy tool counter. He looked awkward holding the hammer as a skeptical customer listened to his sales pitch. Knowing it was rude to stare, she turned to her own counter. A little tidying up would do.

The day flew by. It seemed everyone in Scranton needed something or other on this afternoon. Lizzie glanced around the now quiet store. She moved to the back door and buttoned her long, heavy coat, wishing she had remembered her scarf. It was getting colder every day. Soon she'd have snow to contend with on her evening walk home.

She stepped out into the alley, closing the door firmly behind her.

It was growing dark, the time of day when the December sun had set and the moon gave off a faint light. The gas lanterns lit the way home for shoppers and working folks. Feeling a chill, she hugged her coat close. It felt like snow any day now. She enjoyed seeing people mill about Penn Avenue on her brief walk to her home on Walnut Street. Eager to get home, she set off when she heard a male voice call her name. She turned around. There was Henry Kimball.

Chapter Two

Lizzie was sure she'd been the last to leave the store. She stood clutching the small cloth bag with forget-me-not flowers her mother had embroidered specially for her.

"Mr. Kimball, you startled me. I hadn't realized anyone else was still in the store." She saw his serious expression soften. With a bowler hat on his head, he was buttoned tight against the cold December air.

"I apologize, Miss Miller. I should have announced myself instead of catching you unawares. Might I speak with you? I won't take much of your time."

By five o'clock when the store closed, it was already dark out. Lizzie wasn't completely comfortable walking alone and much preferred to be on her way home.

"Mr. Kimball, if you don't mind. . ." She stood under the streetlight at the corner, a warm glow reflecting on the Five and Dime's display window. It was a welcome contrast to the sound of the store banner flapping in the cold December wind. Maggie had done a magnificent job on the display. The streetlight sparkled on the glass ornaments Mr. Sum had brought from Germany. Lizzie pictured a small tree on the table in her parlor, a few of those ornaments shining against the dark green branches. But a tree would not ease her losses. Besides, there wasn't a penny to spare for a tree. If her heart were up to it, a string of cranberries was more affordable than imported German ornaments.

"Yes, I will get right to the point. As I said earlier, I am trying to get an idea of the inventory in the store. I can see you are a dedicated clerk. I thought you might be able to help me learn about housewares. I need to know what customers are buying and how much they are spending."

Lizzie flushed. Of all the clerks in the store, he was asking her for help. She admired his ambition.

"Mr. Kimball, I appreciate the compliment. But I take my position at Woolworth's seriously. I'm not sure that would be appropriate."

"Miss Miller, your loyalty is commendable. I apologize if I've made you uncomfortable. I can work with the other clerks I've spoken to. Of course, I would still like to have a look around housewares. There's no harm in that, you agree?"

She felt a twinge of disappointment. He hadn't singled her out. She wasn't the only one he'd asked. And he had asked them before he'd asked her. Despite the cold, the heat of embarrassment burned hot. She certainly didn't think she was the most important cog in the wheel, as her father used to say. Yet here she was, taking offense that Henry Kimball hadn't singled her out.

"Well, I suppose there's no harm in that. Now, Mr. Kimball, I must be on my way. Good night." She hurried past the store window, leaving him standing in the glow of the streetlight. Unable to resist, she peered over her shoulder. He was still there, but she couldn't see his face. It was just as well. He was a distraction. Remembering the small envelope in her bureau drawer, she picked up her pace. But the urgency had lost some of its appeal. What was the point of hurrying home to an empty house?

Henry spent his walk home deep in thought. He was a thinker, serious about his goals. He'd recently celebrated his twenty-fifth birthday. He had a deep desire to reach his goal of becoming a bookkeeper at Woolworth's. When doubt niggled at him as to whether he was pushing so hard for himself or to prove something to his father, he reasoned with himself. What young man didn't want to prove himself to his father? Wouldn't any man want to be a success in his father's eyes? William Kimball was a respected man in Scranton. Someday he would say the same about his only son.

The last several months had been strained after his refusal to join his father in the family business. Then there was his mother, Clara Kimball, née Brewster. He loved and respected his mother, but her attempts to find Henry a "suitable" wife were becoming more and more pronounced. In the last month alone, he'd come home five times to a Miss So-and-So having tea and an invitation to "unwind for a moment after a long day."

He heard the lilt of female voices as he stepped into the foyer. He would hang his coat, leave his shoes, and hurry up the stairs. He slipped off his bulky overcoat and padded to the stairwell as he heard his mother's voice. But before he could make his escape, the two women entered the foyer, their eyes staring at his stockinged feet.

"Oh my. Henry, your feet." One set of eyes he was quite familiar with, but the other belonged to a young, dark-haired woman. Unlike other past matchmaking attempts, he did not recognize this woman from church or any of his mother's other acquaintances. His mother took part in a ladies' aid group through the church, and charity was a vital part of upholding her status. He thought of Lizzie briefly. He'd felt her seriousness. He hadn't met a woman like her before.

"Good evening, Mother. I didn't realize you had company." Henry nodded to the young woman, who no doubt was not there to keep company with his mother.

"Henry, I would like you to meet Miss Emma Parker. Emma is Pastor Parker's niece. After the loss of her beloved parents, she's come to live with Pastor and his family." The wall sconces cast a glow on Miss Parker as his mother patted her shoulder with a look of pity on her face.

"So nice to meet you, Miss Parker."

Linking her arm with Miss Parker's, his mother entwined her other arm with Henry's. "Henry, do put your shoes on and join us in the parlor. The foyer is no place for conversation."

With Clara Kimball, there was no choice. Henry smiled congenially at both women. "Please give me a moment, and I will join you ladies." He gently broke free of his mother's arm and waited for the two women to leave so he could collect his thoughts and slip on his shoes. No matter how successful he became, nothing would derail his mother from her search for the perfect wife. If anything, she would strive harder, as a man of status required a certain type of wife. He slipped on the leather ankle boots and swiped the stray hair from his forehead.

The two women stopped speaking as he entered the parlor. His mother moved to the wing chair across from Miss Parker, who conveniently sat alone on the plush upholstered burgundy settee. Every cushion in the house was stuffed to the point of bursting, every piece of furniture the best money could buy. His father was a respected man, and their house reflected that. Henry's taste was much more basic. He wanted a simple home. And if he was to take a wife, he wanted one with similar tastes. A wife of his own choosing. His thoughts went to Lizzie Miller. No doubt she lived with her parents.

"Henry? Please join Emma on the settee." His mother gestured to Miss Parker, who looked uncomfortable, a faint blush on her cheeks. Feeling sympathetic for yet another of his mother's matchmaking victims, he sat down, leaving ample space between them.

"I was telling Emma about your new position at Woolworth's. Today a clerk, tomorrow a bookkeeper, and who knows from there? You could very well join Charles Sumner Woolworth as partner in a year's time." As she spoke, his mother's eyes were more on Miss Parker than Henry. While he had felt his father's chill after his decision to work at the Five and Dime, his mother seemed to understand his reasoning for taking the clerk's position. But even his own ambitions hadn't gone as far as his mother's. Partner in a year's time? He could only wonder if his mother had already set a date for his marriage as well. For that was Clara Kimball's goal. Seeing the way Emma Parker was staring at him, he wanted to say something before matters went any further.

"Mother, let's not get ahead of ourselves. These things take time. I have much to learn."

His mother's beaming face looked from him to Miss Parker. The young woman looked as impressed as his mother did. If only his father could see him this way. Once again Lizzie Miller came to his mind. He had shared his goal with her today. But instead of looking impressed, she'd looked amused. He hadn't seemed to make any impression on her. So why was he spending time thinking about the woman?

"Henry? Henry, I was just saying it might be nice for Emma to sit with us in church this Sunday. You could introduce her to the Walkers and Brainards." The Walkers and Brainards were two prestigious families his mother entertained occasionally. It was Mr. Brainard with whom his father was eager to establish a working relationship. Mr. Brainard managed the St. Charles Hotel, one of the finest lodgings in Scranton. Henry had done this before. Sat through Sunday service with a young woman his mother had hoped would be a match. Well, enough was enough.

"Mother, I am sorry, but I won't be able to. I am planning to attend services this Sunday with a young lady who works with me at Woolworth's." The words came out before he could think. He could only hope he didn't look as surprised as he felt when he said them. He was sure of one thing at least—he couldn't possibly look as surprised as his mother did.

Chapter Three

Fridays had always been Lizzie's favorite day when her mother was alive. Before her mother had taken ill, they had spent Friday afternoons walking along Penn Avenue, arm in arm, window shopping and chatting. Lizzie hadn't lost just her mother; she had lost her best friend. After her beloved father passed, it had been the two of them. They'd spent their days cooking together and tidying up the two-story home on Walnut Street that was too big for two women. Most evenings, Lizzie would read the Bible to her mother, and her mother would tell Lizzie every day her only comfort was her devoted daughter and knowing she would be reunited in heaven someday with her beloved Thomas. Now each morning, Lizzie took comfort in the Bible she had shared with her mother.

This morning she chided herself as she rushed to get to work. She'd been distracted from her morning prayers, her mind wandering to what she had to do today. She pushed away any thought of Henry Kimball's request. Today another shipment of the beautiful hand-blown glass Christmas ornaments would arrive all the way from Lauscha, Germany, from Frank Woolworth, Mr. Sum's brother. Woolworth's was the only store in Scranton, perhaps the country, that sold the shiny glass replicas of fruits and nuts.

Lizzie could watch the light shine on the ornaments all day long. Her mother had often talked about "the light of Christmas." She said that Christmas was a time for the light to shine on God's plan for a future and a hope. Lizzie thought of the verse in Jeremiah as she walked past the window to the entrance of the store. She would have to be content with seeing the light from the store display. Her small savings would not allow her to buy one. Saving every penny was more important now.

She passed her white clerk's apron over her head and tied a bow at the back. Gathering the sides of her skirt in her hands, she made her way through displays of a variety of wares to her counter. Everything was as tidy as she had left it the evening before. She gave a wave to Hattie Scott, the strawberry blond whose mother was an invalid. She prayed for Hattie and her mother every morning. Hattie and her brother, Zebedee, were working hard to get out from their parents' mountain of debt. The young woman juggled working at Woolworth's in the mornings and secretarial work in the afternoons. She spotted Essie tidying a display of hankies. She'd been crippled in a carriage accident but wore her leg brace as bravely as a soldier.

As Lizzie turned to pick up the feather duster, she spotted Henry slipping behind the tool counter. He was chatting with an older man, a hammer in his hands. She'd gotten a look at Henry's hands. There was no doubt he'd spent little time with a hammer. He was holding the tool carefully, as if it might injure him. She remembered him flustered over the tiny sliver in his palm. It wasn't until their eyes met that she realized she was grinning.

Maggie, the lunch counter gal, whizzed by, boxes in both hands. Lizzie guessed the shipment had arrived. She knew Mr. Sum was in the store hours before anyone else. She imagined him in the dark hours of the morning waiting for those glass ornaments. They had already sold every last one from the shipment that arrived before Thanksgiving.

"Oh, Maggie! Tell me those are the fruit and nut glass ornaments!" Lizzie waved as Maggie bustled past her.

Head bent, her chin pinning the boxes to her chest, Maggie nodded. "You'll have to pop outside to have a look!" she chirped.

Lizzie admired Maggie's positive spirit despite all she had been through. She couldn't imagine the pain she had endured being left at the altar. Just recently, she'd had to take several days off to care for her mother, who'd come down with influenza. And yet she had a smile for everyone who sat at her lunch counter. Lizzie had been pitying herself last night, dwelling on her losses, feeling lonely. She would not spend any more time feeling sorry for herself when Maggie was carrying on with such a merry heart.

"Good morning, Miss Miller." The greeting startled Lizzie from her thoughts. Still holding the feather duster, she turned to see Henry Kimball. He looked much the same as he had yesterday, in a dark suit and tie. She noticed the absence of his hat.

"Good morning, Mr. Kimball. Please call me Lizzie. We're not much for formality on the floor here at Woolworth's." His shoulders visibly relaxed. Perhaps she'd been a bit harsh in her judgment of him. Maybe like everyone else in the store, Henry Kimball had struggles of his own.

"Very well, Miss. . .Lizzie. And please call me Henry." A genuine smile crossed his face.

"Wonderful. Henry, please tell me your hand is fine today."

He stuck out his hand, palm up. She made a quick inspection of it, remembering its softness. She might have been harsh in her judgment, but it was not a hand that had spent much time with a hammer.

"Oh yes. I must thank you again. I didn't want to wait until

I got home to remove the sliver. They can be nasty, you know."

Lizzie had all she could do to keep from laughing. She'd removed countless slivers from her father's hands without him batting an eye. Yet the look of concern on Henry's face softened her. His mention of home also piqued her interest. She hadn't seen a band on his left hand. Not that she'd been thinking of such a thing, but with the sliver in his left palm, it had been hard not to notice.

"You're most welcome. It was nothing at all. I used to take them out of my father's hands all the time."

His smile faded. "And now? Is your father deceased?"

"Yes, he passed two years ago. Then a little over a year ago, I lost my mother. That's when I came to work here." She had a tendency to talk too much, but the sympathetic look on his face made her heart flip-flop and her mouth babble on. He looked at her with compassion. Not like the looks of pity she saw on the faces she passed in church.

"I am sorry for your loss."

"Thank you." Feeling flushed, she tugged at her apron. From the look on Henry's face, she wasn't the only one feeling flustered.

"Miss. . .Lizzie, I ought to thank you for your assistance yesterday. May I buy you a cup of coffee today? Perhaps you could join me at the lunch counter."

Lizzie felt like a silly schoolgirl as her thoughts skipped to what this might lead to. She imagined how pleased her mother would be. Her father would ask, "Who is this young man?" But her parents were gone, and there was no one to chaperone a gentleman caller. *Lizzie, he is not a gentleman caller. He's just kindly repaying a favor, silly girl.*

She surprised herself when she answered, "Yes, Mr. . .Henry. I would enjoy that."

Henry had felt like a schoolboy all morning. It was just coffee at the lunch counter with a fellow clerk. But this "fellow" was a she. Heart thumping, he sat and waited on the wood stool. A small child sitting a few stools down chattered to his mother, pointing to the shiny glass ornaments hanging from pine boughs above the lunch counter. Maggie was busy pouring coffee and slicing pie. A festive mood hung in the air like the scent of pine. But Henry was determined not to let the festivities of the season distract him. It was just a season, after all. When Christmas was over, Mr. Woolworth would need new plans for a new year. And Henry planned to offer Mr. Woolworth something that would take him from the tool counter up to a bookkeeping desk.

He hesitated when Maggie asked for his order, wanting to wait for Lizzie. A gentleman approached the stool he was saving for Lizzie. He patted it apologetically, and the man moved to another stool. It was early still, and the counter wasn't full. He checked his pocket watch to see it was a quarter to noon. He glanced toward the sales floor but couldn't see Lizzie in housewares. Perhaps she'd gotten too busy to eat. Or she had changed her mind. His heart sank at the thought of the latter.

"Sure I can't get you a cup of coffee, Henry? I'm guessing you don't have much time." Maggie leaned against the counter, staring at him curiously. He was sorry he'd mentioned he was waiting for someone. At least he hadn't said whom he was waiting for. The last thing he needed was his name being bantered about in gossip. He had to remember that being a clerk was temporary. It was just a stepping-stone to the stairs leading to the office of Charles Sumner Woolworth. If his plans went accordingly, he might very well be at a desk by spring.

"I guess that would be a good idea. Thank you, Maggie." He adjusted his tie. One never knew who one might meet even at the lunch counter of Woolworth's. Why, Mr. Woolworth himself could walk by at any moment. Everyone in Scranton knew the man occasionally liked to help customers here and there. Henry admired his approach to business. It was Mr. Woolworth's hands-on style that made Henry decide his best chance to get upstairs was to do the same and learn everything he could about the store. Deep in thought, he jumped when Lizzie sat down on the stool beside him.

"I apologize for being so tardy. I had a very indecisive customer. She needed help deciding on whether to buy a pie plate or a cake tin." Lizzie waved to Maggie, who promptly hurried over with a plate.

"Yes, decisiveness is very important—although I can't imagine choosing one over the other would matter so much." He lifted the cup to his lips and took a sip of the black coffee Maggie had set before him.

"Oh, but it is. One must plan according to what one is baking. I personally prefer a pie to a cake. My mother always said my apple pie was the best in all of Scranton." She waited as Maggie filled her cup with steaming hot coffee.

Henry thought of his own mother. She was a very efficient woman but spent little time in the kitchen. She had help for that. He wondered if his mother would consider Lizzie Miller marriage material. Well, he wasn't trying to court the woman. He felt a pang of guilt, remembering why he'd invited Lizzie for coffee. Not solely a thank-you. He summoned his courage. He wasn't one to shy away from business propositions, and this could be considered one. Even so, his stomach felt unsettled.

Lizzie had taken an apple and bread out of her pail and

placed it on the ceramic plate Maggie had set in front of her. He'd already told his mother he was going to church with Lizzie, and he wasn't one for being dishonest. He had no choice but to ask if he might join her.

"Miss. . .Lizzie, do you attend church on Sundays?" It sounded awkward to his own ears.

"Oh yes. I sit in the same pew my family sat in, but of course I'm alone now. I try never to miss Pastor Parker's service." Curious blue eyes stared at him. He couldn't blame her. First he invited her to coffee. Now he was sitting here asking her about church on Sunday.

"I imagine it must be difficult for you to be alone. I. . .I was wondering if I might join you this Sunday. I would be happy to escort you in the morning." He shifted on the wood stool, aware he should be behind the tool counter. He glanced toward his counter to check for customers, hoping she wouldn't think him rude.

"Well, Mr. . .Henry, that would be fine. But perhaps we can meet outside the doors a few minutes before eight. I don't want to be late." He saw her hand shake as she held her apple. His own hands a bit shaky, he stood and thrust them into his pants pockets.

"Well then, I should go. I shall see you on Sunday morning outside the church doors." He barely knew the woman. He did know she took her job as seriously as he did his aspirations. He could still see his father's disappointment when he declined to follow in his footsteps, the footsteps of all the men in his family before him. He would show his father he could succeed on his own. He stepped away but then heard her call his name.

"Henry?"

He stopped and turned to her.

"Yes, Lizzie?"

"It's only Friday. I will see you before Sunday morning." She turned on her stool and went back to her lunch. Henry hurried across the floor. He slipped behind the counter before anyone important could notice he'd been away from it far longer than he should have been.

Chapter Four

Lizzie was grateful for the whirlwind of customers buzzing about housewares on Saturday morning. After her very brief coffee with Henry yesterday, she'd returned to her mahogany counter with barely a customer. Too much free time left one with too much time to think. She had spent the rest of the day wondering whether she'd been too hasty accepting Henry's invitation to attend church together. She thought it odd he had invited himself to sit with her instead of the other way around. Didn't a gentleman invite a young lady to join him and his family when they were attending a service together? From the look of him, she imagined his family kept company with a certain circle of friends.

She'd been alone for some time now in her family's pew. Henry had most likely not been aware of that. Regretfully, she'd missed many services during her mother's illness. With no one else to look after Mother, it had been impossible to attend on those Sundays. Returning to the Adams Avenue church had given her some consolation after her mother's death, and her job at the Five and Dime made up for the loneliness at home.

Lizzie enjoyed helping the women of Scranton find what they needed. Nothing pleased her more than having a woman hand over her shopping list and ask Lizzie to advise her with her purchases. She had a natural instinct for what would make a woman's kitchen chores easier. Her father had always praised her for her efficiency. Her mother had delighted in the way Lizzie had taken the reins of their home, easing the bad days. Lizzie was sure her homemaking knowledge had helped her the day she had come to inquire about a clerk's position at the Five and Dime. The housewares counter was a perfect match, and she had been thrilled to take the position. She only wished her father were alive to see her working and earning her way.

Going from one customer to another left little time to think about Henry Kimball. Of course, that didn't mean she didn't glance his way every once in a while. It seemed he too was being kept on his toes. She recognized a few of the young men hovering around the counter. Some she remembered from her time spent helping in Sunday school long ago. The young teens were the newest hires at the Slocum Iron and Coal Company. She saw their eager faces as they rushed to buy what they wanted, only to see Henry's face take on a stern look. No doubt he was giving them a lecture about money, being he was a man of numbers. He wanted to be a bookkeeper. It seemed a better fit for him than selling hammers.

After spending a considerable amount of time helping Mrs. Martin, Lizzie returned the woman's list to her along with the bit of change due to her, and thanked her. She cast a quick glance in the small handheld mirror. She'd spent a good part of the day fighting a lock of loose hair that kept falling to her forehead. As she worked to make herself presentable, she looked up and caught Henry watching her from behind his counter. She felt a flush of heat as their eyes met. She was surprised to see the corners of his mouth curve into a smile. She smiled back. She should check in and see how he was holding up on such a busy day, being so very new to the store. Just then a familiar voice interrupted her thoughts.

"Looks like you found a moment to breathe." It was Maggie. Lizzie had grown very fond of the young woman who worked the lunch counter. While she got on with all of the clerks, Maggie was an instant friend. She was one of the kindest people Lizzie knew. Maggie made everyone feel at home at her counter, whether a small child enjoying an ice cream or a weary traveler in need of a cup of coffee. Lizzie's mother would have said a woman like Maggie would make a wonderful homemaker. Lizzie would have to agree.

"Yes, it's been quite the busy morning. I'll be grateful to get off my feet for a few moments to eat." Lizzie brushed at her white apron. In her busyness, it had become slightly crooked.

"I'll be sure to save you a stool. Or should I save two stools?" A teasing look in Maggie's eyes told Lizzie her friend had not missed the exchange between her and Henry.

Heat spread from her toes to the top of her head. She bit her lip to keep from saying something foolish. Maggie wasn't going anywhere, her elbow propped on the counter between the apple corer and gravy strainer displays.

"Oh no. Mr. . .Henry invited me to join him for a cup of coffee as a way of thanking me for getting a sliver out of his palm. It was merely a thank-you." The pesky lock of hair fell to her forehead again. There was no harm in her accepting his offer. The look on Maggie's face made her stomach flip-flop. She didn't want all the clerks in the store talking about her and Henry. There was no "Lizzie and Henry." They were coworkers. Her mother had taught her to avoid gossip as much as idle hands. No good came from either.

"Lizzie, it's fine. Henry Kimball seems like a good man."

"Maggie, it was nothing more than a cup of coffee between two. . .two coworkers." She wanted to say she had no thoughts of anything more than that. After years of caregiving, she was well aware that prospects for a husband had dwindled to less than nothing. But knowing about Maggie's heartbreak, she held her tongue. She looked over Maggie's shoulder and was never more grateful to see two women heading toward housewares. Maggie pulled herself up from the counter and stepped aside to let the women browse.

"Then I'm glad he appreciated what you did for him." Her friend scurried back to the lunch counter, leaving Lizzie feeling flustered. She did her best to put on her most professional look and attend to her customers.

Henry was in his glory. While he had enough basic knowledge of sales to make do at the tool counter, he considered his expertise finances. He was a numbers man. He was pleased when one of the new hires from Slocum Iron and Coal asked for his advice on how much he should be spending on tools for his job. Few things fired him up like talking about saving money. He easily had ten years on this young man—and enough wisdom to know at this point the boy need not buy all he was holding in his hands. Unfortunately, he had let his passion carry him away. When he glanced away from the young man, he saw several agitated-looking men staring at him.

"Yes, well then, you're making the right choice going with these pliers. Start small. Hold on to your money. Now that you're working, you might want to think about putting some of your earnings in the bank." He would have spent more time imparting advice, but the waiting customers told him he needed to move on. He clapped the young man's back, wished him luck, and turned to the cluster of men in flannel shirts and work pants. He hadn't even been on the job a week. Today he was more than getting his feet wet.

He wasn't quite sure how working the tool counter at Woolworth's would advance him in a bookkeeping career, but he had to start somewhere. He knew what people would think if he went to work for his father. That the only reason he got the position in the mill's office was because his father owned the mill. What else could they say? It would be true. It was a tradition. His great-grandfather had founded the mill. All the men in his family had skipped getting their hands dirty cutting logs and had started at the walnut desk in the office. His father had intended for Henry to be next sitting at the desk, in charge of finances and bookkeeping. Part of him worried what would happen to the mill if he didn't follow tradition. But another part of him longed to make his own way, and being handed a position didn't fill that longing. At least by working at the tool counter, he was earning his way. He planned to work hard, and one day Charles Sumner Woolworth himself would take notice of him. The Five and Dime mogul would ask who the sharp man behind the tool counter was. And once Mr. Woolworth saw the potential in Henry Kimball, it would only be natural he'd want to move him upstairs. Henry Kimball would become invaluable to Woolworth's.

He'd assisted the last of his customers. Having noticed a film of fingerprints on the glass countertop, he thought it might be a good idea to give it a cleaning. He searched under the counter for a rag, only to find boxes of hardware. No rag. He stood up and glanced over at housewares. From the looks of Lizzie's counter, he imagined she would have a rag he could borrow. Perhaps he should buy one from housewares to have on hand for his own department. This was the perfect time to do so.

Straightening his tie, he slipped out from behind the tool counter. The housewares counter was close enough that he could catch glimpses of Lizzie. It was also just as close to the stairs that led to the store office. He wanted to make sure he looked tip-top. What if Mr. Woolworth were to come down those steps just as he was standing there talking to Lizzie?

"Good day." He nodded to the woman leaving Lizzie's counter, a small brown paper bag in her hands. Lizzie was arranging the shelves behind her, unaware he was standing there. Her blond locks were held high on her head with a plain black comb. Not wanting to startle her, he cleared his throat, and she whirled around. The look of surprise in her eyes told him she'd been expecting a customer.

"Hello, Lizzie. I was wondering if you might have a rag I can purchase. My counter is quite a mess, what with all the men putting their hands on it." He fished in his pocket for loose change. Lizzie bent down behind her counter and then popped up, a small white rag in her hand.

"Here you go." Spotting the coin in his palm, she gently pushed his hand away, shaking her head. "Oh, that's not necessary. The store provides these rags for everyone. I'm sorry there wasn't one under your counter. I have several myself."

"You're sure?" He stood there clutching the rag and coin in one hand, his other hand holding the counter's edge. Lizzie smiled.

"Oh yes. Appearance is everything. If only my counters could shine like those ornaments on the tree in the window. Have you seen them? Mr. Sum's brother sent them from Germany. We just got another shipment of them." Lizzie gazed at the glass baubles strewn from the boughs on the ceiling above them.

Her distraction was a contrast to the woman who seemed so focused on her work.

Henry tugged at his tie. Despite the cold air spilling in from the door as customers entered the store, he felt a bit warm. "Yes, they are quite nice. An excellent business decision on Mr. Woolworth's part."

Essie, who worked in personal care, walked by them, her eyes darting from Henry to Lizzie. Realizing he was standing there idly, he took his hand from the counter. He'd been so busy today, he hadn't even eaten lunch. He wondered whether Lizzie had or if she'd been talking to Maggie. The two women seemed close. He hadn't missed the look on the counter girl's face yesterday when he and Lizzie had coffee together. He'd seen the arch of her brow when he'd said he would see Lizzie on Sunday, a day the store was closed. The last thing he wanted was to be fodder for the gossip mill.

"Yes, well, I must get that counter clean. Thank you for the rag. Have a good day." He hurried across the floor. Without another look in Lizzie's direction, he busied himself wiping away fingerprints from his counter. It was a good time to replenish the small display boxes as well. He wasn't even thinking about Lizzie. There was nothing to think about. He kept telling himself that as he busied himself at his counter for the rest of the day. But as the day drew to an end and the last customers walked out the door, he couldn't help but think about his mother's latest matchmaking attempt and why he'd asked Lizzie if he could join her at church. He only hoped Lizzie hadn't read too much into his invitation.

Later that evening, he excused himself to retire to his room with the newspaper, despite the disapproving look from his mother. Reading was to be done in the parlor. Beds were for sleeping unless one was reading their Bible before turning in. He checked the *Daily Times* for anything about Charles Woolworth importing those German glass ornaments. Unlike Lizzie, he was interested in the financial aspect of importing a product no store in Scranton carried. Seeing nothing about the store's success, he placed his glasses on his nightstand and saw the Bible passed down from his mother's mother. He slipped his glasses back on and reached for the "book of answers" as his grandmother had referred to the Bible. He opened it randomly, his eyes drawn to 1 Peter 5:5. "Submit yourselves unto the elder. . . . Be clothed with humility."

His mind went back to the day he had refused his father's offer to follow in the Kimball tradition. He closed the Bible, leaving it beside him in bed. He'd never doubted his decisions before. He closed his eyes and whispered a prayer for guidance.

Chapter Five

Nothing had changed, and yet as Lizzie walked the short distance to church, she felt as if something was different.

After reading her Bible last night while lying in bed, she had left it at her side as she had begun to do since her mother's passing. The weight against her was comforting as she drifted off to sleep each night. But last night she'd known no peaceful slumber. She'd alternated between fluffing the down pillow and tossing from side to side. She had been grateful to finally see daybreak. She'd spent more time than usual in front of her grandmother's mirror, taming the stray lock escaping from her hair comb. Seeing a peaked look on her face, she'd patted pink-tinted face powder on, something she rarely did. Natural beauty was a gift from God, and Lizzie was comfortable just as she was. She would rather read than spend her time fussing with hair and makeup.

Despite temperatures predicting a green Christmas, goose-flesh covered her arms as she approached the white clapboard church. A white picket fence ran around the perimeter of the building and its property. The heavy wood doors of the church were wide open, parishioners milling about the threshold, greeting one another. Lizzie scanned the growing group. While most of the men wore dark suits and bowlers, it was easy to spot Henry

Kimball. He stood with a woman dressed in finery her mother would have deemed rich. Instinctively, Lizzie knew the matronly woman was Henry's mother. Her heart thumped against her rib cage. She would never feel comfortable around a woman like that. Lizzie and Henry's eyes met as she began approaching him. As if he could tell how she felt, Henry hurried toward her. She saw the displeased look on his mother's face. She felt her face flush but smiled when he stood beside her. The lenses of his round-framed glasses were fogged, his cheeks a bright red.

"Good morning, Lizzie." He tipped his hat and extended his right arm. Hoping he didn't notice how nervous she was, she slipped her arm in his. They walked the short path to the doors of the church. Lizzie had passed through these doors with her parents her entire life. But today the familiar surroundings felt different as she held on to Henry's arm. As she pointed to the pew in which she'd sat with her parents her entire life, she saw the look on Mrs. Canterbury's face. Mrs. Canterbury was a seamstress and a dear family friend. Lizzie felt her face burn. The woman knew Lizzie's mother's dream had been for Lizzie to marry a good man.

Curious eyes took in Lizzie and Henry as they reached the pew. Lizzie was pleased when Henry waited for her to enter the pew before stepping in and sitting down. She slipped off her gloves and placed them on the bench, hoping to leave an appropriate space between them, but she needn't have worried. He was sitting at least two feet from her. She reached for a missal just as Henry did, and their hands brushed.

"Excuse me." Henry pulled his hand away and waited his turn.

Lizzie handed him the better of the two books, keeping the battered one for herself. The simple act of passing the hymnal to her parents on Sundays past had been a ritual that pleased both her parents. Handing Henry the prayer book felt oddly natural despite the flushed look on his face.

"Thank you. . . ." His voice trailed off as if he had forgotten what else he wanted to say. She felt at ease there in church beside Henry, but being in the Lord's house had always eased her soul. She'd turned to greet Mrs. Canterbury when Pastor Parker's booming voice stopped her. She straightened up and looked to the front of the church. Out of the corner of her eye, she could see Henry sitting "ramrod straight and no nonsense," as her father would say. Her mind wandered. Maybe her mother had been right. Maybe she had put off any potential suitors with her independence. Yet here she was seated beside Henry Kimball, a man her mother would have been pleased to have as a son-in-law. She tried to focus on the pastor's sermon, trying not to make the fact that Henry Kimball was sitting just inches away from her into anything more than his being kind.

Without taking his eyes from the front of the church, Henry fished in his pocket for his handkerchief. After quickly dabbing his forehead, he thrust it back into his pocket. It was rather warm for a December morning. From the looks of it, there would be no snow this Christmas. There had been a day or two when a quick flurry of white flakes fell from the sky only to melt just as quickly. The traditional white Christmases his favorite author Charles Dickens had written about would be a figment of the imagination this December.

It wasn't like him to be thinking of such foolishness like a white Christmas during the pastor's sermon. Grandmother Brewster would have taken a switch to him. Disrespecting the

Lord's house was a serious sin in his grandmother's eyes. Even still, he had loved going to church with her. She'd passed more than ten years ago, having lived with him and his parents after his mother had begged her to come.

Pastor Parker's passionate sermon boomed through the church as the gas lanterns flickered. Henry wasn't a daydreamer. On the occasion when he did drift during a sermon, it was about business. Now here he was thinking about Christmas and snow. From the corner of his eye, he could see Lizzie staring straight ahead.

If he had not gotten distracted by his mother's matchmaking attempts, he would not be here thinking about snow and Christmas. Or peering out of the corner of his eye at a young woman he had met only days before. His mother had cornered him, attempting to thrust him and Miss Parker together. But the silly thoughts of a white Christmas no doubt had come from seeing Lizzie admire the window of Woolworth's. He had to admit the window was an eye-catcher. A great way to get shoppers in a festive mood to buy Christmas presents. Charles Woolworth had made a brilliant move importing those German glass ornaments. He'd watched women from all over Scranton scrambling about, eager to have the shiny ornaments on their trees. Of course, word had it that Mr. Woolworth's brother, Frank, was the mastermind behind the plan, but Henry had nothing but great admiration for Mr. Woolworth.

A gentle tug on his right arm startled him, and he turned to see Lizzie and the rest of the congregation standing. She was looking down on him with raised brows. He gave her an apologetic look and jumped to his feet. He paid attention to Pastor Parker as he stood a bit closer to Lizzie. He had missed the entire sermon, but Lizzie looked intent on hearing the pastor's last words.

"But the greatest of these is love."

As Lizzie turned to acknowledge the service was over, she caught him staring at her. Now he was hot under the collar, flushing in embarrassment. She looked as flustered as he felt. He told himself it was just too warm in church this morning.

He exited the pew, stepped back, and held out his arm to her. Without a word, they walked to the doors where other congregants were stopping to speak to the pastor. Over a small sea of Sunday bonnets and bowlers, Henry caught his mother's eye. The displeased look she'd had before the service had not changed. She knew he'd made no promises to Emma Parker. And Lizzie Miller was a lovely woman. Surely his mother could see that. But he knew the kind of woman his mother wanted for him. He'd seen the way she'd looked when he'd said Lizzie worked at Woolworth's.

He offered his hand to Pastor Parker. He only hoped the man would think no less of him for not joining his niece for this morning's service. To his relief, the pastor seemed oblivious to any goings-on between Henry's mother and his niece.

"Wonderful sermon, Pastor." He felt a twinge of guilt. He'd barely heard a word. He'd make up for it next week. Perhaps his absence today would curb his mother's matchmaking efforts. *You could invite Lizzie to sit with us next Sunday.* He ignored the impulsive thought and watched Lizzie as she chatted amicably with Pastor Parker. Finally, they were outside in front of the church.

"Well then. . ." he fumbled.

"Yes then." Lizzie shifted her bonnet. She smiled, a playful twinkle in her eyes. "Did you enjoy the sermon today?"

He slipped his hat on and nodded. "Yes, indeed. Yes, indeed. I am always inspired by Pastor Parker's sermons."

Her laugh took him by surprise.

"Did I say something funny?"

"Oh, Henry. I don't think you were in church this Sunday."

He stared at her incredulously. "What do you mean? I was sitting there beside you."

He wasn't as interested in her reply as much as he was in her laughter. There was a lilt in her laugh. He wished he could think of something clever just to make her laugh again.

"Come now. I saw the faraway look on your face. You're lucky you aren't in Sunday school anymore. Miss Retch would have a sharp tongue for you."

She was having fun with him. And he was enjoying it. He was laughing. When was the last time he'd laughed like this? When was the last time he'd been in the company of a woman as fascinating and pleasant as Lizzie? Had he ever? The few young women his mother had attempted to match him with had had the wit of sawdust.

"I apologize, Lizzie. I'm afraid I have much on my mind these days with my new position at Woolworth's. I guess I wasn't listening to Pastor as I should have been."

She laughed again. He wasn't one for folly and fun, but there was something about Lizzie.

"Oh, come now, Henry. Woolworth's is closed on Sunday. It's the Lord's Day. Business can wait."

"Yes, yes it can. Well then. . ." He stood there, unsure what to do next. Normally, he would be on his way home for tea with his parents and oftentimes a guest or two. He looked over to see his parents standing beside Pastor and Emma Parker. His mother saw him. He looked away before she could summon him. He was not eager to have tea with the pastor and his niece, and he was sure that was his mother's intention.

"Lizzie, may I escort you home?" He braced himself. They were not courting. They were not betrothed. She might think it inappropriate for him to walk her home.

A lovely flush of pink colored her cheeks. She smiled and nodded.

"Henry, I would like that very much."

Pretending not to see his mother's hand in the air, he held out his arm. Lizzie seemed comfortable now as she linked her arm through his. *Too warm for snow*, he thought. He pulled himself up short. *These romantic, silly notions won't get you where you want to go.* But as he listened to Lizzie chatter about pie tins and cake plates, he wasn't thinking about the future. With her on his arm, thoughts of the upstairs office were as distant as a white Christmas.

Chapter Six

Lizzie stood outside her home with Henry. She saw him scan the house and small front yard.

At one time, the garden had been lush with petunias and verbena. Her mother had enjoyed gardening. Now nothing remained of her mother's beautiful blooms, only Lizzie's memories of them. At first Lizzie had attempted to keep up the garden for her mother to enjoy. For a few months, her mother would walk to the kitchen window and admire Lizzie's tender care of the blooms. But as she declined and took to her bed, she lost interest. Lizzie had all she could do to keep up with the household chores and her mother's needs. The garden was pushed to the back of her mind and eventually completely forgotten.

She'd been so consumed by her mother's needs she hadn't planned for a time beyond caring for her, and at her passing, she was at a loss as to where she would live. Uncle Milton had assured Lizzie she was welcome to stay on in the house a bit longer, but she knew that soon he would need money to keep the place going.

Lizzie had a good, sensible head on her shoulders. She understood her uncle's need. The house would not keep itself up. She knew she must find a way to earn her keep. If she could send her uncle the same amount her father had been paying him each month for so many years, it might convince him to let her stay on. Uncle Milton had written right after her mother died, inviting her to come live with him and Aunt Susanna. She'd only met her uncle once; she'd never met Aunt Susanna, his second wife.

Now, standing in front of the house with Henry, she was seeing it through a stranger's eyes. Seeing how neglected it appeared, with her father no longer there to repair and restore. She hadn't even noticed the missing shutters until this moment. The cedar-shingled roof had also seen its share of loss, likely during last winter's storms. The remaining shutters cried for a fresh coat of paint.

She glanced up at Henry. He was looking at her with a mixed expression. Was it pity? Or genuine interest? She wouldn't be pitied. She was fine on her own. But the thought of him being interested in her quickened her pulse. Were coworkers at the Five and Dime allowed to keep company? Meeting someone at the store had been the furthest thing from her mind when she'd started working there over a year ago. But the thought of possibly losing her job by breaking any rules made her heart pound harder than it already did because she was with Henry. She could not afford to lose her job. It meant the difference between staying in her home or living with family she barely knew. Or worse, ending up in a boardinghouse like poor Mrs. Canterbury. The very thought made her feel physically ill.

"Lizzie, are you all right? You look upset."

"I'm sorry. I guess you're not the only one with much on their mind today." She hoped he wouldn't ask what she was thinking about. He was probably eager to get home. She imagined his parents might be waiting for him. And perhaps the pastor and the pretty young woman who was standing beside them.

It was cold enough to snow, but it felt as if the earth was stuck in late fall's hold. The trees had lost their leaves, and all of God's creatures had taken to their winter hideaways. In her mind, she imagined it beginning to snow as they stood there. She pictured Henry offering her his coat. *You're wearing a perfectly good coat, Lizzie.* It was time to say goodbye and let Henry be on his way. He'd been a gentleman, seeing her home as he did, and it probably wasn't appropriate to ask him in. But she did need help. . .

"Henry, may I ask you for a small favor?" She didn't know if it actually was a small favor, but if she didn't ask someone for help, she would have to go to Uncle Milton. The last thing she wanted was to remind him that his destitute orphaned niece was still living in his house rent-free.

He answered cautiously. "Well, if it's advice you need, I am sure there would be no problem."

She tried to keep a serious look on her face. He thought she needed financial advice. On the contrary, she was proud of how well she was handling her money.

"Would you mind coming in and having a look at the flue?"

"The flue?" He looked puzzled.

Perhaps she should have asked Mr. Netherby, the church maintenance man, for his help. "Never mind. It's Sunday, and you're in your church clothes. . ."

He surprised her with a wave of his hand and started for the door of the house.

"Nonsense. If there is something amiss with. . ." He looked back to her for help.

"With the flue," she supplied.

"Yes, with the flue, I am sure there is something I can do. After all, I work at the tool counter at Woolworth's."

She hurried to open the door, a twinge of regret flip-flopping in her stomach. Knowing what she knew about Henry's tool experience, she was almost sorry she had said anything. Almost. Her heart thumped in her chest as she showed him the way to the kitchen, where her ailing woodstove was.

He'd been standing there wondering why a woman who lived in a fairly nice home like this was working at Woolworth's. Even a bit neglected, it seemed rather too much for her to afford on her own. He was sure she'd mentioned her father had worked at Slocum like so many of the men in Scranton. He hadn't missed the dented tin lunch pail Lizzie brought to work every day, common among laborers at the mill. He wondered how she afforded the two-story home. How could she manage it on her own, working in housewares? Had her parents left her an inheritance to remain in the home *until she married*? Until she married. The thought rattled him.

As he followed her into the kitchen, he wished he had more skill with odd jobs than numbers. Numbers would do him no good when she needed someone who could fix her cast-iron stove. They stood together, staring at the stove as if it might tell them what the problem was. He knew nothing about cooking stoves. He'd always been told a woman's place was in the kitchen; a man waited at the table. On weekends, his mother had a "kitchen girl" to help with cooking and baking should a guest drop by, which was almost always. He imagined Lizzie and her mother working together in the small kitchen as he watched Lizzie reach inside a bucket beside the stove.

"This will get you started." She dropped a weighty metal tool in his hand and scurried to the table, tidying what looked like something left from her breakfast.

Henry clutched the coiled end of the tool and tapped on the stove's top. He was bungling like a fool in front of her.

"Oh, you take the lids off with that." Her hand brushed his as she patted the tool in his hand.

"Yes, well, I guess that is where we should take a look." She'd soon see he was useless in these matters. He poked the square end of the tool into the small opening of the lid, surprising himself when it caught. He moved the lid to the side. Peering into the cavernous opening, all he saw was a partially burned piece of wood. He was so busy staring at it, he was startled when she came nearer to him. He almost dropped the lid lifter.

"Perhaps it's just a matter of emptying the ash box? Would you mind helping with that? It's been some time, so I'm afraid it might be a bit heavier than usual." She was gazing out the kitchen window as she spoke. "I'm a bit behind on these things. Before working at the Five and Dime, I never fell behind on chores. It must sound terribly lazy, but some evenings I'm too tired to keep house. Then last evening I noticed smoke. My father always took care of these matters and..." To his relief, she turned her back to him. He was grateful she couldn't see the emotion stirred in him.

Henry put down the clunky tool and swiped his grimy hand across his pants leg, smearing ashes on his trousers. His mother was a "chin-up" kind of woman. Of course, she also had led a very comfortable life. After seeing inside Lizzie's home, he knew that wasn't the case for her.

"I wouldn't call that lazy at all. It must have been quite a shock to go from being at home to working at Woolworth's. Many women would not be able to do so after all you've been through."

She was standing in front of the kitchen window now, the light from the morning sun casting a halo around her. In that moment, she looked fragile. He had to fight the urge to pull her into his arms.

"You're too kind." She walked over to a small sconce on the wall. Within seconds, the small kitchen was bathed in light. "Life doesn't always go the way we wish."

Swiping at the corners of her eyes, she straightened herself up. "Listen to me going on like this while I take up your time. I'm sure your family is waiting for you. I can manage that ash box just fine on my own." She walked to the entrance of the kitchen, signaling it was time for him to leave. Then he saw her eyes widen when she saw the ashes on his trousers.

"Oh, Henry! Let me at least see if I can get those ashes out of your trousers."

Henry waved a hand at her.

"Lizzie, it's no worry at all. It's not the first time I've gotten a bit of soot on my clothing." Here he was, telling a lie after coming from church. He'd have a lot to answer for next Sunday.

"No, please. If it weren't for me, you wouldn't be such a mess. I can't let you go home looking like that. . . ." Her words faded. He imagined she was worried what his family, particularly his mother, might say. He'd seen the look on Lizzie's face when she'd spotted him with his mother outside the church.

He'd been so taken by Lizzie that he'd almost forgotten Sunday tea with his parents. And no doubt they'd invited Pastor Parker and his niece.

"No, it's quite all right. It's no trouble. Let me help you with that ash box while I'm here."

After persuading her, they worked together to empty the ash box, carrying the heavy steel bucket to the heap in the yard behind her home. After an awkward pause, he gathered his coat from the coatrack in the hall. They exchanged a few words about seeing one another in Woolworth's in the morning and parted.

Henry picked up his pace, knowing he would be facing his mother's ire. He would simply explain the poor woman's emergency and apologize to Pastor and Emma Parker. But what weighed on his mind was the thought of Lizzie spending Christmas alone. Perhaps his mother would forgive him for missing tea if he were to bring home a lovely young woman for Christmas Eve dinner.

Chapter Seven

Monday mornings had become her favorite day since coming to work at Woolworth's. Lizzie crossed off the eighteenth of December on the small calendar on the kitchen table. She filled her lunch pail with an apple and cheese, then neatly covered the top of it with a handkerchief her mother had embroidered. The simple gesture felt like her mother was with her. She debated on her woolen hat and decided against it. A quick glance out the window said it didn't look like snow. The hat made such a mess of her hair, and she'd gotten the hair comb perfectly in place this morning. She remembered to grab her scarf and was wrapping it around her when she bustled out the door. As she hurried down the walkway, she bumped into Mrs. Canterbury.

The woman lived in a boardinghouse a few doors down. She had no family, and financially it was her only choice. She'd been a comfort to Lizzie's mother during her final days and to Lizzie. Lizzie had enjoyed their teatimes together. The thoughtful woman had tried to sway her mother's appetite, but even Mrs. Canterbury's sweet, buttery biscuits couldn't get her mother to eat.

"Lizzie, heavens, but you are in a hurry." Mrs. Canterbury had her customary carpetbag in one hand, a small paper bag in the other. The oversized cloth coat she'd gotten from the church box exaggerated her size. Gray locks of hair sprang from her bright blue hat. She looked frazzled, and Lizzie suspected she'd again taken on more work than she could handle. She hoped one of the bags held something good for her.

"Oh yes, Mrs. Canterbury. I'm on my way to work. What with Saturday being Christmas Eve, it's sure to be a busy day."

"Well, I'm glad I caught you. I thought with your evenings free, you might be able to help an old woman out." She reached into her bag and held up several blouses. "With Christmas coming, many of my ladies need their holiday clothes mended. Pure silk, these are. Hoping you could help me out, as they'll need them back the day before Christmas Eve. It's a tall order all by myself. 'Course, they don't realize these things." She rolled her eyes, but Lizzie knew how grateful the woman was to have the work. Such finery would take careful stitching, and it was short notice. Perhaps a pickle for Mrs. Canterbury but an answer to prayer for her.

"Oh yes, I would be happy to help you. This is just perfect timing for me." She needed to be on her way. There was no time to take the bag home. Mrs. Canterbury was shaking the small paper bag at her.

"And besides the money I can pay you, I have these to thank you for your help. If it wasn't for your handiwork, I wouldn't have been able to complete the last few orders, Lizzie." Tears pricked the woman's eyes. It made Lizzie's heart heavy to see her alone in what should be her golden years, sewing to pay for a room in a boardinghouse. Imagine not having any children in your elder years to take care of you. A knot of panic stuck in Lizzie's throat. *Lord, I took care of my mother. Will there be someone to take care of me someday?*

"Mrs. Canterbury, are those what I think they are?" The smell of butter permeated the air. Her stomach growled in response to the sweet aroma. "Would you mind bringing those blouses around this evening when I get home? And would you mind if I put those biscuits in my pail? They'd be such a treat for lunch."

"Mind? Of course not. I'm glad I was able to catch you before you left." She handed the small bag to Lizzie.

Quickly, Lizzie tucked the biscuits into the pail beneath the handkerchief. Something to look forward to on her break. And perhaps Henry might be at the lunch counter when she was. She shook her head as if she could erase the thought.

"I'll pop over in the evening once I see you're at home. Thank you, Lizzie."

Feeling hopeful at the thought of additional money for her envelope, Lizzie hurried to work. She prided herself on being one of the first clerks in the store each morning. She'd not been late one time. She heard Mrs. Canterbury call to her. She turned around.

"He looks like the perfect husband, Lizzie. Your mother would approve."

Lizzie was grateful the woman couldn't see her red cheeks. Husband. My goodness, all they had done was sit together at church. The woman had her married. *Don't pretend you haven't thought the same thing, Lizzie.*

Stepping in the back door of Woolworth's, Lizzie hoped for a busy day. There was nothing like a busy day to keep a person's mind from wandering. She tossed her apron over her head, smoothed her hair, and hurried to her counter. Everything was as she had left it. She smiled at the small display of biscuit cutters. Even from under the counter, the heavenly scent of Mrs. Canterbury's biscuits wafted in the air. They would be a wonderful treat with a cup of hot coffee. She'd be sure to share one with Maggie.

She couldn't help looking over at the tool counter. Henry was settling in. He caught sight of her, tipped his hat, and smiled. His smile was so much more appealing than his serious side. Still, having her own serious plan, she understood why Henry needed to give off an air of professionalism.

They were both still smiling at each other from across the floor. She hadn't seen him smile like that at anyone else. Not for Maggie as she poured him a cup of coffee nor for his customers at the tool counter. Mrs. Canterbury's words rang in her ears. Oh, she was acting like a silly schoolgirl. She was about to stroll over to offer Henry a buttery biscuit when she saw Mrs. Hill, one of her very first customers, waving to her. The stout woman was huffing and puffing as she approached Lizzie's counter.

"Oh, Lizzie. . ." The woman stopped to catch her breath, her small pudgy hand clutching the collar of her cumbersome winter coat. Her face was scarlet with excitement. Lizzie knew Mrs. Hill well enough to know there was always something going on in the woman's life. She was easily excited over what, most times, Lizzie considered frivolous. Last time she'd approached Lizzie in a huff like this, she'd been thinking her neighbor had the newest pie tin and might drop in on her unexpectedly to gloat. She wanted a new pie tin to be ready in case the woman did. Mrs. Hill's five daughters had all married. Lizzie suspected she was lonely, as Mr. Hill worked night and day at the St. Charles Hotel.

"Good morning, Mrs. Hill. How can I help you today?"

"Oh, Lizzie." She was calming down, the normal doughy color of her cheeks returning. "I just got a telegram from my sister. My youngest niece is getting married on Christmas Day. Goodness, in all my years, I have never been to a wedding on Christmas Day. But my sister says it's quite the thing to do in New York City. I must find a gift for my niece and her fiancé.

You're so wonderful at picking out just the right thing."

Lizzie became caught up in the whirlwind of Mrs. Hill's niece's wedding. As she looked around for something special for the impending city wedding, she knew she wouldn't have time to take a biscuit to Henry. She put her all into the task in front of her and tried not to look at what was happening at the tool counter. She would invite him to join her for a cup of coffee this time. Then she'd surprise him with a biscuit. The man had ruined his Sunday trousers for her. It was the least she could do.

Henry tried his hand at creating displays that would catch more than the customers he had coming in from Slocum. Those men would always need hammers and nails and what-not. It had occurred to him the tool counter wasn't reaching all the men of Scranton. Men like his father, who had never shopped for repair items. There was more to the tool counter than just serving the new hires and senior laborers from Slocum. If he could sell to the men who sat behind desks, the clean-hands type, he imagined sales for his department might double. Wouldn't Mr. Woolworth be impressed?

But even as his mind calculated the possibilities, he was thinking about Lizzie. He'd been distracted since their eyes had met from their counters. He needed to focus. It was a new week, and Saturday was Christmas Eve. Shoppers were sure to be filling the aisles of the Five and Dime. Mr. Woolworth might even come downstairs one of these days during what was considered the most important week for sales. The man was known for helping customers himself. Henry planned to have his notes ready to show to Mr. Woolworth when the opportunity arose. Who knew? Maybe his mother was right, and he'd be upstairs at a desk sooner than he'd planned himself. Perhaps he'd be ringing in 1882 with a whole new life. He pictured himself behind a desk on the second floor of Woolworth's.

He'd come up with a clever idea for a repair center for his counter. He'd grouped the glue and repair tape in a small box he'd found. Besides selling tools to the laborers, he planned to attract the man of the "make do and mend" mind. Already, he'd helped a half dozen or so men find what they were looking for. He surprised himself with his ability to convince customers of their need for this and that. Staying behind the counter wasn't his goal, but he was better at it than he'd expected.

He wiped away any stray smudges from the glass. Satisfied with what he had gotten done and at the behest of his rumbling stomach, he pulled out his pocket watch and checked the time. Almost noon. It wouldn't hurt to sit at the lunch counter for a few minutes. A quick cup of coffee from Maggie, and he'd get back to work.

He glanced at housewares and felt a pang of disappointment. Lizzie was nowhere in sight. He could take a stroll over there and ask her if she would be able to join him for coffee. Just two coworkers enjoying a break after a busy morning. He suddenly remembered her in her small kitchen. Even the mess of ashes on his good trousers couldn't stop him from smiling.

The counter was nearly empty. It was early yet, the best time to take a stool and eat a quick lunch. Maggie's back was to him as she juggled a pot of coffee and a cheese sandwich. He waited for her to notice him. She caught his eye and scurried over.

"Good afternoon, Henry. Can I get you a cheese sandwich and some coffee?"

"Yes, please, Maggie. I'm famished."

He was so busy eating his sandwich and coffee, he almost

missed her. Lizzie had sat down on a stool at the far end, out of the way of the now crowded counter. The stool beside her remained empty. His plate was empty, and he'd finished his coffee. *She might want a little company*, he told himself. He walked to the end of the counter. She looked up and smiled.

"Might I join you?" He waited before sitting down.

"Henry, why yes. As a matter of fact, I was hoping to see you. I was going to bring something over to you, but you were helping a customer, so I came here. I have to get back to work. Perhaps you noticed how busy housewares has been."

Henry flushed. Had she seen him looking over at her as she hurried about housewares? He didn't want her to think he'd been staring at her, but he'd glanced over more times than he should to see her busy with the women of Scranton.

"Oh yes indeed. It's sure to be a busy week." He sat down. "You were saying you were going to bring something to me?" His curiosity raced like his heart. Such foolishness. They were two coworkers sitting at the lunch counter of Woolworth's.

He watched as she reached into the dented tin pail she had with her every day. She held out a biscuit to him.

"I thought you might enjoy one. My mother's friend bakes them. They are the best butter biscuits you will ever have."

He took the biscuit from her, already enticed by the scrumptious aroma. He was touched she had wanted to share her lunch with him. Perhaps he wasn't a fool spending time thinking about Lizzie. She'd been thinking about him. He took a bite of the biscuit. He had never tasted anything like it before. He finished the rest of it in two bites.

"You say your mother's friend bakes them?"

"Yes, she brought them when she visited my mother. After my mother would fall asleep, we'd enjoy them with a cup of hot tea. It was a sad time, but I enjoyed her company so much."

Henry saw the sadness in her eyes. It pained him to see her so grieved. So much loss in such a short time. He thought about her alone in that home, the cast-iron stove not working quite right. It had weighed on him since the day he'd walked home from her house. He hadn't said anything yet to his mother. Now he spoke before he could think.

"Lizzie, I was wondering if you might like to join my family and me for the Christmas Eve service and then dinner on Saturday." He wanted to tell her how his family gathered after Christmas Eve service for the evening meal. It was a bit formal, but his mother always invited a friend or two who had nowhere to go that evening. He didn't want her to think he pitied her. He wanted her to join him. For more than a cup of coffee at a lunch counter. He wanted it more than he wanted anything else.

"After Christmas Eve service we go home and. . ."

"I'm afraid I have plans for the service. . ."

Henry felt heavy with disappointment.

"But I would be happy to join your family afterward for Christmas Eve dinner. May I bring something?"

He was grinning like a fool. Now Maggie was looking at them, no doubt catching bits of their conversation. He didn't care. He was extending a kindness to a coworker who had no one to spend the holiday with.

"Well, if you would like to bring something, I am sure Mother would be grateful." He hoped she could make something as wonderful as the butter biscuit she'd shared with him. He wanted his mother to be as taken with her as he was.

Chapter Eight

She blamed it on the scent of pine in the air. Or the way the light made the German glass ornaments sparkle from the small tree in the display window of the store. Whichever was to blame, before she could think, Lizzie had jumped at Henry's invitation to Christmas Eve dinner. Sitting there next to him at the lunch counter, it had just felt right.

She was almost giddy. She'd gone a ways from the store before she realized the top buttons of her coat were unbuttoned. The scarf she'd tossed about her neck blew wildly in the wind as she rounded the corner of her street. She'd just dropped her coat on the rack when she heard the door knocker. Mrs. Canterbury. Their morning conversation seemed like a hundred years ago. Smoothing the folds of her dress, she opened the door.

The seamstress's cheeks matched her reddened nose as she smiled at Lizzie. She held out the needlepoint bag she'd been clutching.

"Mrs. Canterbury, do come in. It seems like every day it's getting colder." Lizzie held the heavy door open and gestured for her to come inside. "I was just going to make a fire in the parlor. Please come sit down."

Lizzie cringed as they stepped into the parlor. Since her

mother's passing, she'd barely spent any time there. It was a simple room with a sofa and two hefty upholstered chairs. One of the chairs had been her father's favorite place to relax after a hard day of work. Her mother would sit in the other beside him so they could spend time together before retiring for the evening. Her father was an "early to bed" man, but his day began at five in the morning either way. Her mother would turn in with him, and Lizzie would spend her time alone reading by the fire. The room was too quiet with them both gone. She took her tea at the kitchen table now, before she turned in.

"I'm afraid I haven't given this room much attention lately." She hurriedly turned on the sconces, one on each side of the fireplace. A warm glow began to fill the room, chasing some of the chill away. She attempted to get the fire going, not wanting to spend too much time distracted from the woman's visit. Mrs. Canterbury was sitting on the sofa, waiting for her.

After assuring herself that a fire was building, Lizzie sat down beside her friend. She saw the look of sadness on Mrs. Canterbury's face. Lizzie had not shared with her why she needed to work at Woolworth's so desperately, but she suspected the woman knew how important the mending work was for her.

The mix of sadness on her face was exactly why Lizzie wouldn't share her financial worries with her. If Mrs. Canterbury found out about her money situation, she would take pity on her having no family and possibly no home. Lizzie could understand why. Mrs. Canterbury was in the exact same boat, only thirty-plus years older. She had no family, no husband, and no children. She'd resorted to living in a boardinghouse among other women who suffered such misfortune too. It made Lizzie even more determined to work harder to keep her family home.

"It's a lovely room. I remember your parents loved sitting by the fire in here." Mrs. Canterbury held the needlepoint bag in her lap. "So then, I shall leave these blouses for mending with you. I will need them back by Friday. Tomorrow is Tuesday, and I know you must be busy in the Five and Dime, but do you think you can get them done?" She tugged at the tangle of blouses in the bag and handed them to Lizzie.

Lizzie gently sorted through the half dozen blouses. What else did she have to do in the evenings? If she started tonight, she had four nights to get the mending done.

"It will be no problem. I spend my evenings reading, so I'll just put down my book and pick up my needle. I appreciate your faith in me." She clutched the blouses.

"Such a help. You know these mending jobs are all I have to pay my board." Mrs. Canterbury's eyes went to the pictures of Lizzie's parents on the table across the room. "Your parents were a lovely couple. Perfectly suited to each other. A love like that is a gift from the Lord. Sometimes He blesses you when you least expect it." She tilted her head at Lizzie.

Lizzie flushed. "My father adored my mother and she him. I miss them terribly." She bit her lip to stave off the trembling, but tears welled in her eyes.

"Oh, my dear, I am sure you do. So much heartache for a young woman to endure." She shook her head and continued. "But I see you had a fine gentleman keeping you company in church last Sunday."

Lizzie had wondered how long it would be before Mrs. Canterbury asked about Henry Kimball. She'd been behind them in church. Lizzie hadn't missed the look on Mrs. Canterbury's face as they had sat down.

Her cheeks were burning hotter than the fire, and she shifted on the worn sofa cushion.

"That was Henry Kimball, a coworker. He offered to accompany me to church as a thank-you for my help. He works at the tool counter and had a sliver in his hand. It was nothing to help him. It was a lovely gesture."

"Yes, and you did enjoy his company, did you not? I could see he is quite smitten with you." The woman's eyes twinkled. "He's very distinguished. You surprise me when you say he works at the tool counter."

Lizzie felt the need to defend Henry. He was a very distinguished man. She hadn't known him long, but she could see he was smart. Perhaps he was too sophisticated for the tool counter, but he had shared his ambitions with her.

"Well, he only started last week. He's at the tool counter now but aspires to work upstairs alongside Mr. Woolworth. He plans to become a bookkeeper." Seeing the amused look on Mrs. Canterbury's face, she worried she'd said too much. She felt as if she was gossiping, as some of the clerks did at Woolworth's. She was fond of all the ladies at Woolworth's but had to stay away from anything that might cause her to lose her job. *Like getting involved with a coworker.* She ignored the thought.

"One has to start somewhere. Mr. Henry Kimball sounds like a hardworking young man. I've heard of the Kimball family. His father owns the mill. Your mother would be pleased."

Lizzie fiddled with a lacy collar.

"It was just a thank-you." She stared at the fancy silk blouses. She would never have need for such finery as a working woman. "Besides, if he's from a family like that, he wouldn't be serious about the girl behind the housewares counter of the Five and Dime." She was thoughtful for a moment. "I saw his mother outside the church. I imagine I would not be her idea of a suitable wife."

Mrs. Canterbury shook her head. "My dear, I saw how you

cared for your mother. You were a blessing to your parents. She would be blessed to have you in her family." She turned to look at the sofa table in front of the parlor window. Lizzie used to open the heavy curtains each afternoon for her mother to look out at the garden and watch the birds. Now they remained closed.

"Are you not going to have a tree this year?"

Lizzie hadn't had a tree last Christmas either. She thought about those lovely glass ornaments in Woolworth's. No matter. Even if she had a tree, she couldn't afford them. And with working and mending, she had no time to fuss with decorating. As for next year, well, she didn't even know if she would be in this house next year. The lovely mahogany table and everything else in the house belonged to Uncle Milton.

Mrs. Canterbury stood to her feet. "I'm sorry. I shouldn't have said anything. I know how hard it is to be alone at Christmas. I should stop talking and get on my way."

They said good night and promised to see each other on Friday. The December wind grabbed a lock of Lizzie's hair as she closed the door. She felt the full weight of the sadness she'd been trying to avoid by keeping busy between the Five and Dime and her mending work. Not only for her losses, but the sadness of knowing she was alone in the house. Being able to stay in her family home was so important to her. She was proud to work hard and be independent, but perhaps her desire to take care of herself was costing her a chance to marry and have someone to share the house with.

The emptiness of the parlor and lack of Christmas cheer felt cold despite the roaring fire in the fireplace. She sat down on the sofa and stared at the blouses waiting for her. She glanced at the picture of her parents, the sconces illuminating young and happy faces. A pang of loneliness knotted her stomach.

It's just the grief. She'd find her sewing basket and get to work. Idle hands led to idle minds. She would have neither.

It was Henry's customary routine to retire to his room in the evening after spending time with his parents. Saturday was Christmas Eve, and he had to discuss his plans with his mother now before she planned otherwise for him. She'd spoken of Emma Parker several times since church. She'd not said one word about his sitting with Lizzie. He knew his mother. If she didn't acknowledge something, then it didn't exist. Lizzie had been on his mind all day, and he had an uneasy feeling. He was worried his mother was arranging the Christmas Eve table with a setting for the pastor's niece. He'd already invited Lizzie. Now he needed to make the invitation official.

His father was sitting beside the fire in the plush chair his mother had insisted upon from the upholsterer. Holding the *Daily Times* in front of his face, he was absorbed in the goings-on in the world. And keeping his distance from Henry, since Henry turned down his offer to work at the mill.

No matter. Henry's mother managed the guest lists. Clara Kimball came from the respected Brewster family of Boston. She'd grown up under the tutelage of Abigail Brewster, a woman who had taught her daughter the importance of high standards. His mother had carried those standards and married William Kimball, a family that owned the biggest mill in Scranton. Thus the drive behind her need to find her son—her one and only child—the right wife. He'd heard tales of matchmaking in the family and had heard whispers between his parents about one very unhappy cousin. He may not believe in fairy tales, but he wanted to be happy. He'd thought out his business goals. A wife could wait as far as he was concerned, but his mother's persistent attempts to find the perfect wife would continue. After meeting Lizzie, he'd found himself for the first time thinking not just about a wife but love.

"Mother, may I speak to you about Christmas Eve dinner?"

His mother put down the letter from her sister she had long been waiting for and looked up at him.

"Why, Henry, I don't think you've ever shown interest in our Christmas Eve dinner before. Goodness knows, your father shows no interest in all the hours I spend planning for a successful holiday. Of course, a man's place is not in the kitchen, but one would like to know if someone has invited a guest not on the list." His mother looked toward his father, who turned the pages of his newspaper, seemingly blissfully unaware of the conversation.

"Of course, Mother. That is exactly why I wanted to speak to you this evening. I know you have already sent invitations, but I should like to invite someone not on your list."

His mother folded her sister's letter and slipped it back into the envelope. She arched a brow and waited.

"And who might this person be, Henry?" Her tone implied she already knew.

His mother was not Mr. Woolworth. He wouldn't have butterflies speaking to Charles Woolworth. Business was so much easier than. . .than what? What was this he was doing?

"Miss Lizzie Miller. The young woman I escorted to church on Sunday."

"Ah, yes, and the one who delayed you from Sunday tea."

He hadn't thought she would be pleased. But he'd prepared himself should she refuse. He'd rehearsed the words that would make his mother understand why she must invite Lizzie. He wasn't ready to divulge anything more than Lizzie's being alone at Christmas.

"Yes, well, she had some troubles in the kitchen and asked for my help. . ."

"Troubles in her kitchen? Henry, you're no handyman. So that explains the soot on your Sunday trousers. It took the kitchen girl hours to clean them. I fear those trousers won't be the same again." She shot him a perturbed look despite them both knowing Henry could easily replace the trousers. They'd had the same family tailor for years.

"I apologize for the inconvenience, Mother. No, I am not a handyman, but her father passed just two years ago. There is no man of the house to help her."

His mother's expression softened a bit. "And her mother?"

"Her mother passed just over a year ago, I believe. She has no one to spend the holiday with. I believe you said some time ago we who have more than enough should open our table to those who have little." He'd written her sentiment down on an envelope before the evening meal, being sure to remember it word for word.

He watched his mother look around their elaborately furnished parlor. Their Christmas tree glistened in front of the window, covered in tinsel and the German glass ornaments she'd wanted. Of course, she hadn't bought them herself. The Five and Dime wasn't a store she frequented. The kitchen girl had done a good job picking them out and decorating the tree.

His mother prided herself on her charity work. She'd contributed dozens of baskets for the poor that Pastor Parker and his wife hand delivered. What would it look like if she didn't invite Lizzie to her table for dinner at Christmas?

"Very well, Henry. If she has no one else, I cannot say no. Tomorrow when you go to work, you may tell her we would be delighted to have her join us."

"Thank you, Mother. I am sure she will appreciate it." Feeling the weight off his shoulders, he excused himself. As he prepared to turn in, he looked at the Bible he'd been given as a young boy that sat on his night table. He felt led to pick it up. He ran his fingers over his gold-embossed name, something his mother had had done specially for his birthday all those years ago. He opened the book and glanced at the words halfway down the page. *Whoso findeth a wife findeth a good thing, and obtaineth favour of the Lord.* He placed the Bible back on the night table and pulled at the blankets to cover the gooseflesh on his arms, which had nothing to do with a cold December night.

Chapter Nine

Lizzie was absentminded Wednesday as she tied her apron at her waist and slipped behind her counter. Last night she'd read from her Bible longer than she usually did, but sleep still had evaded her. She'd tossed and turned until after midnight, her mind churning. She had more on her mind than just the envelope sitting in her drawer. There was the mending she needed to get done by Friday. There was the Christmas Eve dinner with the Kimball family.

Until Mrs. Canterbury had told her about the Kimball family, she hadn't thought much about who Henry was. Why would the son of a family that owned the largest mill in Scranton work at the tool counter of Woolworth's? Why would he spend his time working as a salesclerk when he could make a handsome sum working in the family business? She knew he wanted to work in the upstairs office of the store. She imagined a fancier desk in his father's office. All this thinking had gotten her little sleep. She was wiping her counters with the vigor of a woman with much on her mind when she saw two familiar boots.

She looked up to see Maggie staring at her, a silly grin on her face. Lizzie's stomach fluttered. Maggie had been within hearing distance when Henry invited her to Christmas Eve dinner.

"Good morning, Maggie. How are you today?"

"Good morning, dear Lizzie. I am fine. You look tired. I would expect you to look excited, with Christmas Eve only four days away."

Lizzie was very fond of Maggie. She prayed every day the Lord would bring someone wonderful into Maggie's life. She was such a kind woman. She deserved a good husband after what she'd been through. She saw the way Maggie looked at Seth Jamison when he delivered the milk. She was sure the widower was taken with Maggie too. Maggie was good with his little girl. Wouldn't that be a wonderful happily ever after? Her mother had wanted that for Lizzie.

Grief pricked her eyes again. The season of light was making her more emotional than she cared to be. Maggie's smile reminded her she would be spending Christmas this year with a family, just not one of her own. Remembering Henry's mother, she said a silent prayer, asking the Lord to help her not judge the woman. After all, she was opening her home to Lizzie.

"I'm afraid I didn't get much sleep last night. Tossed and turned for hours before finally drifting off." Once she said it, she knew what Maggie was thinking.

"Something or, rather, some*one* on your mind?" A devilish twinkle lit up her eyes.

Lizzie turned and poked at the shelves behind her, hiding reddened cheeks. Composing herself, she turned to Maggie. She wanted to make sure there was no gossip about her and Henry. The last thing she needed was trouble at work. Thinking of Henry's aspirations, she worried gossip might hurt his plans. He was so serious about moving to the office upstairs. She would hate to see him disappointed.

"Mrs. Canterbury gave me a bundle of fancy silk blouses for

mending. I need to have them all ready for her by Friday. I'm just worried I won't be able to get it done."

A disappointed look came over Maggie's face.

"Oh dear, that would keep one tossing at night. I wish I could help. While I've got little time left, what with the church play, perhaps my mother might like something to do during her evenings." Christmas bells jingled from the front door, and she glanced at her counter. "I've got a customer. We can talk later." And with that she was off, the folds of her skirt whipping between the displays as she made her way to the lunch counter.

Lizzie had never been so happy to be alone. She finished cleaning her counters. The festive atmosphere in the store was contagious. Last night, after Mrs. Canterbury's visit, the starkness of her home had hit her for the first time. Happy Christmases of the past had kept her mind from settling in to sleep. Her mother would be saddened by the bare parlor. She considered Christmas Day, the celebration of the birth of Jesus, to be the most special day of the year. They didn't have many decorations, but they always had a small tree on the mahogany table in front of the parlor window. More importantly, the nativity set passed down from her mother's family was displayed beside it. It was one of their few and most precious family heirlooms. Lizzie thought of her mother's nativity set wrapped in newspapers and tucked away in a closet.

The rest of the day was a good distraction as she helped customers buy what they needed for Christmas dinners with their families. The women of Scranton were eager to buy pie tins, cake pans, apple corers, and more. But despite all the busyness around her, her thoughts came back to her tree at home. And her mother's nativity set. And the Christmas Eve dinner with Henry's family. What could she bring to dinner that would impress Henry's mother? Mrs. Canterbury's biscuits came to mind. She might ask the woman to pay her in biscuits this time. But no, that was foolishness. She needed that mending money.

A wave of panic set in. She hadn't baked in a long time with the exception of bread that she brought to the store each day for lunch. From what Mrs. Canterbury had said, bread would hardly be looked upon as a Christmas dessert for the Kimballs. She was beginning to regret saying yes to Henry's invitation.

What she needed now was a distraction. And what better distraction than a Christmas tree? The thought of having a bit of Christmas in the house slightly eased the sick feeling in her stomach, knowing she'd be taking money from her envelope to buy it. *Oh Lord, please show me everything will be all right.* Just as she sent up the silent prayer, her eyes met Henry's. He gave her a sweet smile and continued speaking to his customer. *I'm leaving it all in your hands, Lord.*

The busy tool counter didn't surprise Henry. It was the Wednesday before Christmas, a busy day for any store. Not all of his customers were men from Slocum. He'd helped several women choose hammers or another tool for husbands and sons. What did surprise him was how much he enjoyed helping customers. He loved numbers but was enjoying helping people. While he was prepared to work as long as it took, he pictured Charles Sumner Woolworth "discovering" him as a man who had a mind for numbers and money. So much to think about, and he'd already been distracted by the upcoming Christmas Eve dinner with Lizzie.

He had expected his mother to refuse to invite Lizzie to dinner. He had been sure she'd been waiting for a chance to remind him of missing Sunday tea not only with her but with Pastor Parker and his niece. But he knew she would not turn away someone who was alone on Christmas Eve. He had seen her soften when she'd heard of Lizzie's losses. She herself had only her sister left and cherished getting letters from her. It had been years since Aunt Lavinia had visited, and he wondered if his mother filled their table to ease the ache of missing her family. Still, he knew as long as Emma Parker was living with the pastor, his mother would try to bring him and Miss Parker together.

A year ago he might have enjoyed Miss Parker's company, but marriage had been the furthest thing from his mind. There was time for that, he had told his mother. He'd never felt pressured to get married, even at the ripe old age of twenty-five. His mother understood his ambitions. But evidently her understanding didn't mean she would stop her attempts to find him a wife.

Now he'd met Lizzie. At the Five and Dime, of all places. And in just a week's time, his thinking had become less clear, his thoughts changing each time he saw her. He couldn't help but consider how foolish he was being. He barely knew the woman. He'd spent more time talking to the tailor who made his last suit than he had with Lizzie. Yet he couldn't deny the feelings she stirred in him. He'd never felt like this before. The way he couldn't get her off his mind. The way his heart beat faster when she spoke to him or laughed.

With the tool counter quiet, it was a good time to take a look at his inventory. He must learn what was and wasn't selling in tools. He'd asked a few clerks for their help in learning more about the store and had been disappointed at their lack of interest. He saw their dedication to helping customers, but to Henry it seemed they lacked any ambition beyond being clerks. But he'd heard several of the women had money woes. He imagined they were grateful just to have their jobs. He was aware no one knew his own circumstances, and he was grateful no one had connected his name to the Kimball mill. At least that he knew of.

He thought back to that day in Lizzie's kitchen. His ineptness might have given him away. He wasn't hiding anything, and Lizzie was a smart woman. He imagined she could tell he wasn't a handyman. He'd heard the admiration in her voice when she spoke about her father taking care of the repairs around the house. He wondered what Lizzie was looking for in a husband. That day in her kitchen, he'd felt he was lacking one thing she would want—the ability to fix whatever needed fixing.

Spreading the rag across the glass countertop, he dumped a box of screws out and began to count when he heard a woman cough. He looked up and saw Lizzie. His heart nearly skipped a beat. She'd looked so busy today, he hadn't thought he'd get to speak to her.

"Good afternoon, Lizzie. It's been a busy day, hasn't it?"

"Good afternoon, Henry. Indeed it has. I rather enjoyed it. I see you had your share of customers."

She had been watching him. At one point during her busy day, she had looked for him. The thought made his stomach flip-flop.

"Yes, it was quite a good day for sales. And housewares has done well today?" He wasn't asking for numbers or details. All he wanted was to keep the conversation going. Thoughtful blue eyes watched him. Her hand swiped at a stray lock escaping from a comb. She looked tired. Protective feelings stirred in him. He wanted to ask if she was all right, but that seemed too personal while they were working.

She nodded. "I must take a look to see what items need to be replenished before the next rush of customers."

There wasn't much else he could say about the tools. He wished he was better at small talk. He wanted something to talk about. About anything. He wanted to be around her. *Don't go just yet.*

"Good thinking. I was doing the same with these screws. It's sure to be busy before the doors close for the day."

She hesitated, glancing about as if she too wanted to prolong her visit. He had the feeling there was something she wanted to say.

"Always a good idea to be prepared. Four days until Christmas." He saw her expression change at his words. His heart sank. She'd looked so pleased when she'd accepted his invitation. Had she changed her mind in just three days?

"Yes, Christmas is coming." She paused, then said, "I'm actually going to pick up a Christmas tree today." Her face brightened, and a sense of relief washed over Henry.

"Ah, that's sure to be a cheerful task." Before he could think it through, he blurted, "If you need any assistance, I would be happy to accompany you." He held his breath as he waited for that pleasant look he'd seen twice now, once after inviting himself to church with her and just the other day after inviting her to Christmas Eve dinner. He was beginning to believe she might think of him as more than a coworker.

"Oh, thank you, but that won't be necessary." She waved to a woman waiting at her counter. "Time to get back to work. Have a good afternoon, Henry."

He stood there silent, feeling as if he'd been slapped, as she hurried away.

Chapter Ten

The days had flown by since bringing home the small tabletop tree. It hadn't taken long to decorate. She had found the wooden apple crate of ornaments her mother had stored in her closet. Holding the delicate embroidered fabric her mother had placed on top of the crate only made her yearn for her mother more than she already had been. Each of the dozen or so handmade ornaments stirred Christmas memories that seemed so long ago. She'd lovingly arranged her mother's nativity set beside the tree as her mother had done since Lizzie was a small child. Even though it was a small tree, there were a few bare spots.

Thoughts of Henry had come and gone that evening as she'd gone to the street corner to buy the tree. She'd felt terrible rejecting his offer to help, but she didn't want him to see her little tree. Or the few precious ornaments her family had. She had seen the way he'd looked around her kitchen. After hearing Mrs. Canterbury speak of the Kimballs, she pictured a large tree covered in fancy store-bought ornaments. She'd never seen Mrs. Kimball in the Five and Dime, but she imagined that like so many women in Scranton, she would have to have those ornaments. She felt guilty for wanting one when she had all she needed.

She was feeling tired, still not having gotten much sleep. She'd also lost some mending time trying to bring some Christmas cheer into the room. She'd stayed up far later than she should have decorating the tree, then mending two of the half dozen blouses Mrs. Canterbury was waiting for.

The Five and Dime had been a whirlwind of activity on Thursday. Every clerk had been on their toes, bustling about to find customers what they were requesting. Woolworth's was becoming known throughout Scranton for its array of notions, and it seemed everyone in Lackawanna County was shopping for gifts. Women had waited elbow to elbow at her counter on Thursday. She'd come home with aching feet, determined to finish up the remaining blouses.

Now it was Friday. Tomorrow was Christmas Eve, and she'd barely spoken to Henry since turning down his offer to help with the tree. He hadn't sought her out or come to her counter to ask for advice or assistance. Had he come to agree with his mother that he shouldn't be keeping company with a woman like her?

The sounds of shoppers, children's laughter, and the steady *click-clack* of boots on the wood floor this morning echoed throughout Woolworth's. The scent of pine boughs and linseed oil from floors polished overnight mingled in the air. Lizzie dropped items in a paper bag for a frazzled-looking young mother. Two small children stood at her sides, clutching the folds of her skirts as they peered up at Lizzie. Memories of her own childhood Christmases welled up in the corners of her eyes. She was feeling sentimental today. What had happened to the independent working woman she had been since the day she started at Woolworth's?

She glanced at the tool counter and saw Henry chatting amiably with two men passing a tool between them. She waited for him to look up and notice her, but he was engrossed in conversation. Her heart heavy, she turned to the children clutching their mother's skirt.

"Are you two ready for Santa? I'll bet you've been good boys for your mother, haven't you?" Shy smiles and giggles did her heart good. One little boy sported a gap where his front teeth should be. She couldn't help but smile back.

"Oh, they have their days, now don't you both?" Their mother shot them a flustered look. Her face softened when she turned to Lizzie. "But I wouldn't trade them for all the money in the world." Guessing from her purchases, Lizzie imagined the young mother didn't have much beyond these two sweet angels at her sides. Tears threatened again as she saw the loving look on the mother's face.

"How very blessed you are." Lizzie handed her the small bag. Clutching her skirt and the hands clinging to it, the mother made her way through the women waiting for Lizzie's help. One by one, she helped them all, proud she could find what they were looking for. Scattered words of praise from customers were just the tonic she needed to get through the rest of her morning.

At noon she barely nibbled the food in her lunch pail, causing Maggie to give her a questioning look. She wondered if Henry had had time to sit at the lunch counter, but she didn't want to ask Maggie. The woman's curiosity was already stirred up. It bothered her more than she cared to admit that he might have been sitting there without her. *You're acting like a schoolgirl again instead of a woman with responsibilities*, she chided herself.

The afternoon flew by. It was just minutes before closing time when she leaned against the shelves behind her and gave her aching ankle a rub. Her old boots needed replacing. Another item to add to her list of things needing replacing or repair. She nearly took a tumble when she looked up and saw Henry standing near her with an amused look on his face. She dropped her foot and stood up. Fiddling with her apron, she smiled, feeling the sudden warmth on her face.

"Henry, I didn't. . .didn't expect you. Just getting off my feet for a moment." A quick glance at the tool counter, and she guessed he was done for the day as well. She wasn't surprised to see his workstation left in immaculate shape, his display boxes neatly lined up.

"So sorry to startle you, Lizzie. It's been a busy few days. I apologize I haven't found the time to speak to you sooner, but tomorrow is Christmas Eve."

Lizzie felt a wave of panic. She had always been a calm woman, not a woman to get flustered easily. Until Henry had come to Woolworth's, and she found herself with a pounding heart or butterflies in her stomach. But she hadn't felt worried like this since she'd lost her beloved parents. Why did she feel as if she were about to lose something again?

Seeing the look on Lizzie's face, Henry was a bit nervous to speak to her. She'd agreed it best they speak outside the store. He wasn't sure if something between them had changed. He hadn't gotten to chat with her as he would have liked. The store had been too busy. He had also spotted Mr. Woolworth on the floor on two different occasions. After seeing him stop to speak to a clerk, he didn't want to be caught away from his counter.

But his opportunity to speak to Mr. Woolworth had probably come and gone. Tomorrow was Christmas Eve, and the man might not have the time to walk the aisles and mingle with customers. It inspired Henry that Charles Woolworth was exactly his age and so successful. It also reminded him of how much work he had to do to climb those stairs to Woolworth's office. He didn't have years to spend at the tool counter when his skills were better suited to a desk upstairs. Not that he wasn't doing an outstanding job in tools, but a bookkeeping job would provide a better living and a good future. Lizzie came to mind when he thought about his future. He had glanced over at her counter more than once.

Now they stood awkwardly facing the front window of Woolworth's. Lizzie was bundled up against the cold in her bulky winter coat. The ties of her navy blue bonnet blew gently in the wind, and he watched her gloved fingers toy with them. She seemed nervous. Perhaps she had changed her mind about Christmas Eve. The thought hit him in the gut. The heavy sky looked like it might snow, and he could see she was getting cold. He didn't want to keep her. He fiddled with his mustache then touched her elbow gently, and she turned to him. In the glow of the streetlights, he saw tears glistening in her eyes.

"Lizzie, is there something wrong? Have I done something to upset you?" He clutched her elbow, fighting the urge to pull her to him. They were in public. Customers were walking about Penn Avenue, finishing up their holiday shopping. She dabbed a gloved finger in the corners of her eyes and shook her head. A blond lock fell to her forehead. The familiar sight warmed his heart despite the cold air.

"You've done nothing wrong. You're such a gentleman. Perhaps that's the problem." Her eyes brimmed with tears.

"I don't understand. Tell me what's wrong. I may not be able to fix a stove, but there are a few problems I can fix." He'd hoped mentioning his fumbling in her kitchen might bring a smile to her face. He hadn't realized how tight he'd been holding her elbow. Seeing she was still looking grim, he reached for her gloved hand, no longer concerned who might see them. He wanted to comfort this distraught woman. A woman he was ready to admit he was falling in love with.

"I saw your mother at church last Sunday, Henry. I don't want to cause any trouble for you by coming to dinner on Christmas Eve." She raised her chin determinedly, and her strength impressed him once more.

"Lizzie, I asked to speak to you out here to tell you how much I'm looking forward to your dining with us on Christmas Eve. With me." He felt his face flush. "Mother wanted to make sure I let you know how delighted she is you will be joining us."

Henry felt as relieved as Lizzie looked. He had seen the look his mother had given her at church. He had hoped Lizzie hadn't noticed. He was sure she wasn't what his mother would call the perfect wife for him. But tomorrow his mother would meet the woman he was beginning to think was the perfect wife for him.

"Then you didn't ask me out here to cancel plans for Christmas Eve?"

Henry was stunned. He had never intended to cancel his invitation. If anything, he wanted assurance she was still coming. He wanted his mother to greet Lizzie with open arms. He'd prayed last night for his mother to take Lizzie under her wing and see her potential as a wife.

"I only wanted to confirm the time for dinner. As you know, the store will be closing early so everyone can enjoy the holiday with their family." He waited before he spoke again. "Will you be attending Christmas Eve service alone?" His heart pounded. Surely there was no one else she'd be attending with. His heart dropped when she shook her head.

"I promised Mrs. Canterbury we would sit together. She has no family, and she's been so kind to me."

Relief washed over him.

"I'm glad you won't be alone. Shall I come by afterward so I can walk you to my home?"

She was shivering. Whether it was the cold or nervous anticipation, he wasn't sure. The sky looked heavy but still not a snowflake in sight. *A little snow might make Christmas a bit cheerier for Lizzie*, he thought.

"Yes, I would appreciate that, Henry. I'll wait for you outside my door." Her face was a bright pink.

"Well then, we're all settled." That felt too much like a business arrangement. He wanted to say something else. He watched her gazing at the display in Woolworth's window.

"Isn't this the prettiest window in all of Scranton? There weren't any of the German ornaments left after today." Her eyes took in the shiny glass fruit and nut ornaments Maggie had strewn about the small tree in the window.

"Did you purchase one for your tree, Lizzie?" he asked softly.

A wistful look came over her. She shook her head. "I've got other things to take care of." She stuck out her chin. "Well, it's getting colder by the minute, Henry. I must get home, but I will see you tomorrow. . . ." She hesitated.

Henry waited for her to finish speaking.

"I look forward to Christmas Eve dinner."

He wanted to tell her more about how he could hardly wait to spend the evening with her, but he would wait. There was something else he would need before he could tell her how he felt.

"Yes then. Tomorrow it is."

Even with the wind growing colder, Henry was warm from head to toe. He could barely contain his excitement as he walked the short distance home. As he passed cheery shop windows on

Penn Avenue, thoughts of moving upstairs to a bookkeeping desk were the furthest thing from his mind. Tomorrow he would introduce his mother to the woman he intended to marry.

Chapter Eleven

After parting with Henry last night, Lizzie had gone home and waited for Mrs. Canterbury to come by to pick up the mending she'd done for her. She was proud she hadn't let the woman down. If only her father had been there to see her as Mrs. Canterbury placed the money in her hands, thanking her profusely for her hard work. Between working at Woolworth's and mending, Lizzie could see hard work was the only answer to her dilemma. If she did her best at the store and took on more work from Mrs. Canterbury, she could stay on in her family home. Uncle Milton would have to agree to let her stay once she gave him the envelope. She'd had to fight the battle in her mind as her self-confidence surged then faltered.

Then there was the matter of her dining with Henry and his family. It was just a Christmas Eve dinner. Surely that wouldn't jeopardize her job. Mr. Sum wouldn't even know about it. She remembered Maggie's expression as she overheard Henry inviting Lizzie. Surely a friendship with another clerk in the store wouldn't be going against the rules. *But is he just a friend?*

Her mind was busier than her hands. That was her problem. She must get her wits about her and help the women in front of her, some scrambling for a last-minute gift and others shopping for what they needed to prepare Christmas dinner.

While she knew Henry admired Mr. Sum's business smarts, she admired her employer's heart. The store would be closing early today. They were all eager to leave work behind to attend Christmas Eve services and spend time with their families. Lizzie found herself torn between being nervous and happy to be spending Christmas with family again. Only they weren't her family. Lizzie handed a woman an apple corer, her mind distant on the evening ahead. She and Mrs. Canterbury had arranged to meet outside Woolworth's so they would not be late for church. She'd been worried about wearing her Sunday dress to work. She could only hope her work apron would protect the finest dress she owned. It was also the dress she would be wearing to dinner at Henry's family home, and that worried her more.

Her mother had made the dress for her right before she'd taken ill. It was a lovely woolen muslin in a shade of rose that her mother had insisted complemented Lizzie's blond hair. She'd yet to wear the dress, and she had tucked it away as carefully as her mother had the nativity. Until today. She'd made an effort to twist her hair up into a smooth do, securing it with the mother-of-pearl comb that had belonged to her mother. The gift had marked the first five years of marriage for her parents. Since her mother's passing, it remained in the small wooden box on her parents' nightstand. As Lizzie checked to be sure it was still in place, her hand shook as she remembered how precious it had been to her mother. What if it fell out and she lost it? She'd been so torn as to whether she should wear it, she'd stopped to pray about it before fastening it in her hair this morning.

A sense of peace stayed with her as she stood in front of Woolworth's watching shoppers on Penn Avenue and hoping to spot Mrs. Canterbury by the hat she always wore to church. She hadn't been waiting long before she saw the woman and took her arm. Bundled against the brisk early evening air, they made their way to church.

After the service, Lizzie was ashamed of how little attention she had paid to Pastor Parker's Christmas Eve sermon. She hadn't missed the beautiful altar covered in holly and pine boughs, the smell filling the air. She'd been daydreaming, staring at the flickering altar candles, when Mrs. Canterbury tugged at her arm. She saw the woman's eyebrows arch as she caught Henry staring at Lizzie.

The two women had walked back to Lizzie's home in an awkward silence while Lizzie waited for her friend's questions. Neither she nor Henry had paid much attention during the service. He'd appeared as distracted during the sermon as she was.

Mrs. Canterbury clutched her hand-me-down coat against the cold. "Well, my dear, I can stay with you until Henry Kimball arrives." She exaggerated Kimball, as if to remind Lizzie who she was spending the evening with. The butterflies in Lizzie's stomach had already taken on the task.

"Oh no, I wouldn't want you to get sick, not with influenza going around. You can go home. He'll be here any minute. The cold isn't bothering me. Perhaps we shall see a white Christmas after all." Lizzie was certain the chill she felt had little to do with the cold air. Mrs. Canterbury smiled, a twinkle in her eyes.

"Good night then, dear, sweet Lizzie. Enjoy your dinner. Merry Christmas. And thank you for spending time with a lonely old woman."

"Merry Christmas, Mrs. Canterbury. And thank you again for having faith in me. You've helped me more than you know." Lizzie watched Mrs. Canterbury slowly make her way to the boardinghouse, back to the small room on the third floor. She wondered how she made her way up all those stairs, limping as she did. She was so busy watching out for Mrs. Canterbury that she didn't realize Henry was there until she turned and bumped straight into him.

"I hope I didn't frighten you." He gave her a slight bow. She grinned at his playful formality.

"Not at all. I was just making certain Mrs. Canterbury got home safely." Lizzie looked at Henry. She had grown accustomed to seeing him in his bowler hat. How could he possibly look even more dashing? The dark overcoat and Homburg hat told her she hadn't been the only one making an effort for their dinner together.

"Well, if all is well, perhaps we should be on our way." He extended his arm to her. She took it with an ease that surprised her. She was growing comfortable with Henry. *Just two good friends sharing a Christmas dinner*, she told herself.

She was surprised to learn Henry's family home was on Ash, only two streets from her home on Walnut Street. The thought of Henry being so close warmed her despite dropping temperatures. But as she took in the sight of the large and elegant house, panic overcame her. She felt the urge to run, and as if sensing her jitters, Henry patted her hand. She remembered Mrs. Canterbury's praise. *Lord, help me to make a good impression on Henry's mother.* She had never cared what anyone thought about her before.

But this dinner felt like more than two friends sharing a holiday meal. Suddenly it mattered that Mrs. Kimball approve of her. *You're being a silly goose, Lizzie. He's just being kind. He knew you were going to be alone at Christmas*. But as Henry opened the door and they crossed the threshold, the look on his face appeared to be more than kindness.

Henry watched Lizzie's eyes widen at the sight of his family's formal dining room. He heard the sharp intake of her breath and pulled her arm close as they entered the large room. Remembering the stark kitchen in her home, his heart ached for her. He wanted her to feel at home.

He watched her take in the room, eyes darting from the rich burgundy-papered walls to the fine linen cloth covering a table set for eight. His mother took great pride in her hostessing skills. Christmas Eve was one of several occasions where she went all out. At each end of the table, a silver wine bottle holder rested. An elaborate arrangement of silver and crystal culminating with a cut-glass bowl of fruit on top looked as if it would topple at any moment. Behind the chair where tradition dictated his father would sit was a crackling fire in a white marble fireplace. A dozen flickering candles surrounded by holly boughs reflected in the ornate brass mirror above the mantel.

Henry felt a bit uncomfortable himself but likely not for the same reasons as Lizzie. Seated at the table were Pastor Parker; his daughter, Anna; and his niece. They had not dined with them the previous Christmas Eve, and their presence caught him unawares. It hadn't crossed his mind that his mother might invite the pastor and his family, though he'd wondered if his niece might be at the table. The pastor's wife was absent. He recognized Charles Netherby from church. He'd been the church handyman since before Henry was born. Mr. Netherby had lost his wife and daughter to influenza more than twenty years ago.

If he and Lizzie had arrived only a few minutes earlier, perhaps she would have had a moment to socialize before sitting at the table. It might have given her a chance to get comfortable before heading into the elaborate setting.

His father pushed his chair back from the table and stood up. Henry saw his father take in Lizzie. She was wearing a lovely dress, and he imagined it was one of the finest she owned. He caught his breath. He was twenty-five years old, a grown man, and hoping for his father's approval. His father stepped toward them and reached his hand out to Lizzie.

"Welcome to our home. It's Lizzie, I believe?" His large hand held her small one as he waited for her to speak.

"Yes, sir. Lizzie, short for Elizabeth. Named for my father's mother." She flushed as he released her hand.

"Merry Christmas, Lizzie."

"Merry Christmas, sir. Thank you for your generous invitation."

As the exchange between Lizzie and his father went back and forth, Henry could barely breathe. Out of the corner of his eye, he saw Pastor Parker stand up, pulling his fifteen-year-old daughter from her seat as his niece stood beside her. Miss Parker looked as ruffled as Henry felt. A crimson flush spread across her face, and he felt sorry for her.

He began introducing Lizzie to the pastor and his family. Before he could ask after the man's wife, the pastor answered his question.

"Catherine had to travel out of town for the week. Her mother is ill with influenza, and she needed Catherine's help. The church will be praying for her until we hear news of her recovery."

Seeing Lizzie visibly relax a little when Mr. Netherby took her hand, Henry felt the tension in his body ease. Still, he felt a bit uncomfortable each time he looked over and saw Miss Parker watching him. While it was likely his mother invited the pastor and his daughter due to illness in the family, he imagined she still hoped to bring him and Miss Parker together. He hoped that after his mother spent some time with Lizzie, she would see what he saw in her.

Miss Parker was chatting with Mr. Netherby when Henry's mother made her entrance into the dining room. Everyone rose to their feet as she stood beside his father, her hand resting on his arm.

"We are blessed to have you all with us this Christmas Eve. I do hope you enjoy your meal. The kitchen girls will be serving now." Puffed with pride, she sat in the first seat on the right side of the table beside Henry, who had Lizzie to his right.

"Mother, you haven't made Lizzie's acquaintance yet." He turned to her. "Lizzie Miller, I would like to introduce you to my mother, Clara Kimball." He felt stiff and awkward, but etiquette was of utmost importance to his mother. He would not do one thing to prejudice her against Lizzie. Instead of coming to Lizzie, his mother stood up and leaned behind Henry to extend her hand.

"Very nice to meet you, Liz. . .is that the name you go by, or is it a nickname of sorts?"

His stomach felt like lead. He saw the discomfort in Lizzie's face.

"Yes, ma'am. It's short for Elizabeth, for my father's mother."

Henry was grateful to see the kitchen girls carrying trays of food into the room. The two young sisters worked quickly to fill plates around the table.

Pastor Parker held out a hand. "May I bless the food before we begin, Mrs. Kimball?"

Henry's mother nodded, and the pastor said a short blessing. The room grew silent while the guests began to eat the meal before them. Henry watched Lizzie cut up the goose on her plate. He saw the pleasure in her face as she chewed the potatoes and root vegetables. Feeling relieved, he began to eat.

"Elizabeth, Henry tells me you are a clerk at the Five and Dime. How do you find the time to work and manage your household?"

Henry nearly choked on his potatoes. He wanted to answer for her, to protect her from his mother's scrutiny.

"Yes, I have been with Woolworth's since the store's opening. It is difficult, but with it being only myself at home, I can manage what needs to be done." He heard the tremor in Lizzie's reply. Before he could add anything in her defense, his mother continued.

"Yes, what a shame for a young woman to have to work outside the home. I would imagine at your age the work gives you something to do. But there's nothing as fulfilling as having a family and home to tend to."

Henry clutched his fork and shot Lizzie a sympathetic look. Across the table, he saw Miss Parker staring at Lizzie as if she understood what Lizzie was feeling. He felt badly for both young women. Lizzie, who had been flat-out shown her station in life, and Miss Parker, who despite what his mother wanted, could see she would not be his wife.

"Oh, I'm fine. I enjoy my work at Woolworth's. I spent so much time as a caretaker for my parents. Someday I hope to have a family that can fulfill me as well."

Once again Henry heard the nervous tone in Lizzie's voice. Everyone at the table could see her reddened cheeks. A shaky hand put down her fork.

"It is good to hold on to hope no matter your age. A family is the highest blessing the Lord can bestow upon a woman. Don't you agree, Pastor?" She turned to Pastor Parker, who looked as if he'd much prefer to finish eating the food on his plate.

"Yes, yes, Mrs. Kimball. One of the highest blessings." The

pastor's eyes darted between Henry's mother and Lizzie. Henry liked the pastor. He was a good man. He knew Pastor Parker would not say anything to offend Lizzie. His mother, he had his doubts about. His heart ached for Lizzie, who was squirming in her seat. He looked at her shaky hands as she picked and smoothed the folds of her dress.

"Mother, how many families did the ladies' group aid this Christmas season?" Henry could see he wasn't the only one relieved for a change in conversation. As his mother regaled her guests with her efforts to "save the poor from a bleak and dreary Christmas," he reached for Lizzie's hand and squeezed it.

As the dinner guests proceeded to the parlor, Henry offered his arm to Lizzie to accompany him into what he hoped would be a more relaxed setting. She did not take his arm but instead walked down the long foyer to the door they'd come through only a short time before.

"Henry, I'm afraid I'm feeling a bit peaked. I think it best I go home. Would you please pass along my thanks to your mother and father for a lovely meal."

The disappointment he felt was nothing compared to how upset Lizzie looked. "Lizzie, I want to apologize for the way my mother spoke to you."

Lizzie was struggling to put on her winter coat, not bothering to button it as she pulled open the heavy door. A gust of cold air snapped at them both. Henry followed her outside into the cold night air. He needed to find the right words. To tell her he would not stand for his mother's treatment of her like that ever again. That she meant more to him than anything. Even a desk in the office of Woolworth's.

Instead, Lizzie turned to him, her coat flapping in the wind. With her lips trembling and tears in her eyes, she blurted out,

"Henry, I am sorry. I like you. Very much. Too much, I'm afraid. But we both can see we are from two different worlds. I'm not blind. I know what your mother was doing. You belong with someone like her."

He knew she was referring to Emma Parker. She might as well have slapped him. He could barely breathe.

"You don't understand, Lizzie. It's not Miss Parker. It doesn't matter what my mother's intentions are. I—" She stepped back from him and held up her hand.

"Henry, I understand. There is you and there is me. We could never be." She glanced at the large parlor window, where the curtains were open and candles flickered on the tree. His mother stood by the tree, Emma Parker beside her. Numb, he stared as Lizzie hurried away in her unbuttoned coat, nearly tripping on the hem of her dress. He would have blamed the moisture blurring his vision on the snow that was beginning to fall, but he couldn't. Lifting his glasses, he wiped at his eyes before going back inside.

Chapter Twelve

In her hurry to get inside her home, Lizzie nearly slipped on a patch of ice outside her front door. Steadying herself, she entered the small, darkened entryway. She closed the door behind her with relief. Even in the dark, she knew every inch of her house. The familiarity was comforting. She walked to the parlor and busied herself lighting the sconces. Within seconds the room came to life. Her minimally decorated Christmas tree greeted her as she crossed to the brick fireplace. She bent in front of it and took a match from the fire bucket beside the fireplace. After striking it against the charred bricks of the firebox, she tossed it onto the half-burned logs. Careful not to let embers catch hold of her dress, she straightened and watched as flames began to grow.

She sat on the sofa and looked about. She'd spent months avoiding the empty room. Now here she sat alone on Christmas Eve. She turned to her small Christmas tree in front of the parlor window. Unlike the window of the Kimballs' house, she still kept the curtains drawn tight. After seeing the Kimballs' tree, she imagined Henry might think it a pitiful sight with its handmade ornaments, even though she knew those fancy ornaments had nothing to do with what mattered at Christmas. Her family tree had always felt magical in years past. It wasn't the lack of decorations that bothered so much as the lack of family. She was missing the feeling of being loved and having someone to love back.

She walked to the gateleg table and picked up the photograph of her parents. The sconce above cast a warm glow on two happy faces. They had been so in love. They had adored one another until only one remained. Despite her heavy loss, it comforted her to know they were together again with the Lord they worshipped. Clasping the frame to her chest, she took it to the sofa table in front of the window and placed it beside the small tree. She walked back to the fireplace and held out her hands, feeling colder than she had outside.

She had let herself get carried away by the festive mood. She'd worked so hard at Woolworth's this past year. She had set out to make enough money to show Uncle Milton she could pay the rent her father had paid so she could stay on in her family home.

Thinking of the bulging envelope, she felt a swell of pride. She'd done it. After Christmas, she would send her uncle a letter letting him know that he could send for the rent money. She would make it clear she could do so every month. *But*, she wondered, *is this all my future holds*? Years of hard work alone in an empty house? Was it enough just to work at the Five and Dime and take mending jobs from Mrs. Canterbury? Mrs. Canterbury was getting on in years. What if that work ceased? Where would that leave her? She'd been so busy working, she hadn't given any thought to a future. A future alone that no longer felt like enough.

Henry. He would be at the tool counter at Woolworth's every day. She wouldn't be able to look at him anymore without her heart hurting. Her only hope was that Mr. Sum would soon see his value and promote him to a desk upstairs. At least that way there would be less chance of her running into him during the workday. She thought back to the times she and Henry had sat at the lunch counter. After seeing the elaborate dining table in the Kimball house, she couldn't believe he had been comfortable at the simple counter with its crude wood stools.

She sat back down on the sofa. She wasn't ready to go to bed. Even sheer exhaustion wasn't enough to stop her thoughts from straying back to Henry.

She'd left him standing out in the cold. She hadn't missed the grieved look on his face, the pain in his eyes. She believed he was genuinely sorry about the way his mother had treated her. She was sure his intentions had been pure when he invited her for Christmas dinner. He didn't want her to be alone.

She could still see the way he looked as they crossed the threshold of his home. She had almost believed there was something more. That maybe the invitation was more than two coworkers enjoying a meal together. She had almost convinced herself that Henry had feelings for her. She'd almost believed her mother was right and that it was never too late to find love. A husband.

"She would be blessed to have you in her family." Mrs. Canterbury's words rang in her ears. It had been obvious Lizzie was not the blessing Mrs. Kimball had in mind for her son.

Lizzie didn't realize she'd been crying until she tasted salt on her lip. Swiping at her cheeks, she walked to the fireplace. She moved the charred log to the back of the firebox and nearly dropped the poker when she heard a knock on the door. Who on earth could that be? Thinking Mrs. Canterbury might need her, she felt a rush of panic. The woman was all the family she had left.

It didn't take Henry long to go after Lizzie. But first he'd gone to his room. There was something he had been waiting to give her. He'd thought Christmas Eve dinner would be the perfect time to do so. But dinner did not go as he had hoped. Lizzie had left like a storm, fast and furious. It took only minutes to grab the gift-wrapped box he had tucked away three days ago. As he buttoned his overcoat and put on his hat, he heard his mother approach from behind. He wasn't a confrontational man, but he was ready to stand up for Lizzie. When it came to her, he would do or say anything.

"Henry! Where are you going? It's Christmas Eve, and you have guests in the parlor waiting for you." The indignant look on his mother's face didn't deter him.

"Mother, forgive me, but *you* have guests in the parlor waiting for *you*. My guest has gone home in quite the tizzy. And I have every plan of righting a wrong." He threw his scarf around his neck and reached for the door handle.

"Henry, you're upset. Why don't you come into the parlor? Spend some time with Emma. You will feel better. She's a lovely girl."

"Mother, that would make *you* feel better. I'm sure Emma Parker is lovely. But Lizzie is a lovely woman too, and you would have seen that if you'd only given her a chance." A gust of wind met them both as he opened the door.

Now he was standing outside Lizzie's door. Realizing she might not have heard him rapping on the door with gloved hands, he slipped a glove off and gave a firm knock. This time the door opened. The glow of the hall sconce behind her illuminated her blond hair. She stared at him, wide-eyed. He thought she looked as if she'd been crying. He wanted to take her into his arms and comfort her, but he needed to be sure of his welcome first.

"Lizzie, forgive me for coming at such a late hour, but I need to speak to you. May I come inside?" She surprised him by stepping aside to let him in.

They stood in the small entryway with little room between them. She gestured for him to follow her into the parlor. The room was a good deal warmer than her kitchen had been the day she'd asked for his help. It was on that day that he knew he wanted to be there for her for everything. A fire roared in the fireplace. He looked around and spotted the small tabletop Christmas tree in front of the parlor window with its curtains tightly drawn.

"Henry, I believe I have said all I had to say. If you've come to apologize, it's not necessary. I know you meant well. I appreciate your kindness."

"Lizzie, my inviting you for Christmas Eve was not a kindness." Seeing the arch of her eyebrows, he tried again.

"What I mean to say is that I was not just trying to be kind. I was not taking pity on you because you were alone. It was. . .it is more than that. Lizzie, this past week I have enjoyed the time we have spent together. The little time at the lunch counter. Our lively chats at the counters. Even my bungled attempt to fix your stove." He flushed, knowing how foolish he must have looked that day.

The urge to take care of her was more pressing now as he saw her red eyes and sad expression. He stood there in his coat, holding the small gift-wrapped box. He saw Lizzie take notice of the gift as she listened to him. She was standing by the window now, putting some distance between them.

"I have enjoyed our time together as well." Her voice was barely a whisper above the crackling of the fire.

He approached her slowly. "Lizzie, I have become very fond of you. More than fond. What I'm trying to say is that if you would have me, I would like to spend all my Christmases with you." He waited for her to tell him all the reasons why it could never be. Instead, she drew closer to him, letting him see the tears in her eyes.

"Henry Kimball, I would love nothing better than to spend the rest of my Christmases with you. But what about your mother? What will she say?"

"She would say she has the luckiest son in all of Scranton, Pennsylvania." He put the small box on the table, pulled her close to him, and gently kissed her. After a moment, she pulled away.

"Henry, what is in that box?"

He placed it in her hands. It took seconds to rip the paper away and open the small box. Staring in disbelief, she gingerly took out the shiny glass apple ornament, the one he knew she'd been watching in the Woolworth's store window.

"Oh, Henry!" She drew close to him for another kiss and then turned to the small tree. She looped the shiny ornament onto a branch and hurried to draw the heavy curtains from the window. As she did, they saw snow falling from the sky. It would be a white Christmas after all.

"What a perfect Christmas!" She rushed into Henry's waiting arms and looked up at him, tears sparkling like snowflakes in her eyes.

He kissed her forehead.

"Merry Christmas, my dear Lizzie."

"The first of many merry Christmases, Henry."

Epilogue

December 25, 1882

It had been a whirlwind of a year since last Christmas Eve, when Henry had come looking for Lizzie after she had fled from the Kimballs' dinner. Her knees shook with excitement. She was grateful to be seated at the table in her home. Uncle Milton had personally brought the papers for them to sign this morning.

God had blessed her so many times. He had given her the opportunity to earn the money she had needed through her job at Woolworth's. Then He had brought her and Henry together. The last thing she'd been looking for two years ago when she'd come to the store was a husband. Now here she was, a married woman. Their wedding had been held at his parents' home under the rose-covered trellises in their yard.

Lizzie had been a bundle of nerves, worried her future mother-in-law would kick up a fuss over the small guest list they had insisted on. Neither she nor Henry were much for big events. A small, cozy wedding suited them both. After spending a few weeks wedding planning with her soon-to-be mother-in-law, she'd come to relax. The woman had been as excited as the happy couple over the impending nuptials. Henry had teased that his mother was probably relieved her job was done. No longer would she have to look for a wife for him. Lizzie believed it was more likely the promise of her daughter-in-law supplying her with the best apple pies in all of Scranton for her future dinner parties.

She sat across from her uncle and her husband of just six months, her in-laws also there, watching as Henry signed the contract to buy what had been her family home. After their wedding, he had insisted they not only live in her uncle's house but buy it from him. The envelope she'd worked so hard to fill remained in her drawer, a nest egg for another blessing the Lord had bestowed upon them. Their first anniversary would be a celebration of both their union and the birth of their first child. They were abundantly blessed, and at times she had to pinch herself to be sure she wasn't dreaming.

"Thank you, sir." Henry shook the older man's hand. The two rose from the small kitchen table.

"Please, Henry, call me Uncle Milton." Uncle Milton, a big burly man, gave Henry a firm clap on the back.

Lizzie stood up to get the kettle. "Shall I make you some tea, Uncle?"

"No, thank you, my dear niece." He took her hand. "I must be on my way if I'm to be home in time for Christmas dinner."

Arm in arm, Lizzie and Henry walked Uncle Milton to the door. Overcome by emotion, Lizzie stood on the tips of her toes and kissed her uncle's cheek. "Thank you, Uncle Milton. For everything."

He smiled, and in that moment, she saw her father in her uncle's face. He was her father's only brother, the only remaining kin she had. It felt wonderful to be here with family.

"Your aunt Susanna and I could not be happier for you. And

the child we hope to meet next year, God willing." Lizzie was pleased Henry had wanted to share their joyous news of the coming blessed event with her uncle. Watching the big man walk out the door, she felt as if she would burst with happiness. They walked hand in hand back to the kitchen to Henry's waiting parents.

Henry gestured to them. "Father, Mother, would you join us in the parlor? We have some news to share. It's much more comfortable in there with the fire."

This would be their first Christmas as husband and wife. Henry had insisted his parents come over for dinner. He and Lizzie wanted to share their news from their own home. Lizzie knew they had only been expecting to witness the signing of the contract. She beamed as she saw the look of approval on her mother-in-law's face as she walked into the parlor. She and Henry had chosen the two settees for the room together. Her shoulders relaxed when she saw her mother-in-law smile.

"Father, I have some news to share I think will make you happy." Lizzie watched her handsome husband pull his shoulders back. Only days ago, he had given notice to Sum Woolworth. He'd been so proud of his promotion that spring. He'd made it to the bookkeeping desk of Woolworth's. But after witnessing the two Woolworth brothers' relationship, and now with the impending birth of his first child, he realized how important family ties were. More important than anything else, he had told her.

Henry's father leaned in, his glasses sliding down his nose. The resemblance between father and son fascinated Lizzie. Who would their child resemble? She touched her stomach and waited for Henry to speak.

"Father, I am leaving Woolworth's to join you in the mill."

It was the first time Lizzie had ever seen William Kimball taken aback. She thought she saw him tear up, but he quickly took off his glasses, rubbing at "a spot of dust," he said. He stood and came closer to the settee she and Henry were seated on. Henry stood, and the two men shook hands. When his father grabbed Henry for a hug, Lizzie thought she wasn't the only one with a "spot of dust" in her eyes. A quick glance at her mother-in-law confirmed her thoughts.

"Henry, that is wonderful." Clara Kimball stood up and embraced her son. Lizzie watched Henry take it all in, a mix of relief and gratitude flooding his face. Catching his eye, Lizzie nodded for him to go on.

"Well, perhaps we all should sit down now. I. . . We have more news to share." Henry sat down next to Lizzie and reached for her hand. Lizzie would never grow tired of seeing the light reflect off the ruby in her wedding ring, a ring that had belonged to Henry's grandmother. Each time she looked at the ring, she was touched by Henry's mother's generosity in giving it to them.

The four of them were seated. Henry cleared his throat, looking as nervous as Lizzie felt.

"We are expecting a blessed event in the spring." He and Lizzie sat pressed together, their hands entwined tightly. Lizzie had no doubt Henry's heart was beating as fast as her own.

Henry's mother and father stood again, and Lizzie rose from the settee to hug her mother-in-law. Henry stood beside his father, several claps of congratulations landing on his back.

"Oh, this is wonderful. I don't think I can wait that long to see if the baby will be a boy or a girl." Henry's mother fanned herself as she held Lizzie's forearm.

Lizzie glanced at the small tree on the table in front of the window. The flames from the fireplace cast a light on the new glass ornaments from Woolworth's that Henry had surprised her with last night. And as she turned to look for her husband, she saw that light in his eyes. The light of love. The light of Christmas.

Christina Lorenzen started writing as a teenager, filling composition notebooks with imaginary worlds. Her first typewriter fueled her love of writing as well as her writing speed.

While she tried her hand at a variety of jobs, even selling cosmetics door-to-door, writing was her true calling and a lot less walking.

An Amazon bestselling author, she is busy working on her next small-town romance. When she isn't writing or reading, she can be found walking her dog, talking to her herd of cats, and spending time with her husband, grown children, and grandsons, Charley and Hudson.

Cynthia Hickey

Prologue

Spring 1881
Scranton, Pennsylvania

Finally, the day had come. The day Marjorie Larson fulfilled her dream of becoming a wife. The second part, being a mother, would come later. Within the year, she prayed.

She ran her hands over the pointed waist of the satin wedding gown she wore. An extravagance few could afford, but her mother had sacrificed a long time for this day.

"Worth every penny, Maggie." Her mother stood in the doorway, hands clasped under her chin and tears in her eyes. "You're a vision for sure. Your brown cashmere traveling costume is hanging, ready for you to wear after the ceremony."

"Thank you, Mama."

"Daniel isn't here yet." Her mother sat on a velvet settee. "I've sent someone to see whether he's had an accident. You know as well as I do that he often drives his buggy too fast."

Always in a hurry, her Daniel. Maggie smiled and adjusted her veil. "He'll be here."

When an hour passed with no word, fear crawled into her throat. Maggie paced the room. Where was the man Mama had sent to check on her groom-to-be? Would she be widowed before she could be wed? Could that really happen to her? Would God allow such a thing?

She wanted to sit down, but doing so would wrinkle her gown. Her feet ached in the new boots. Her head started to itch under the veil. "Oh, Daniel." This was not how she'd pictured her wedding day. "I don't think he's coming, Mama."

"Don't give up yet. Let me see what I can find out." She bustled from the room.

The murmurs of impatient wedding guests drifted into the room when her mother opened the door, only to be cut off when the door closed. They shouldn't be made to wait any longer. If Daniel—when Daniel—showed, they'd marry with just their families in attendance.

Maggie reached for the door handle, then stepped back as it opened. One look at her mother's face, and she forgot about wrinkles. She plopped into a chair. "He's dead, isn't he?"

"Worse," her mother choked, holding out a sheet of paper.

Her hand trembled as she reached for the note.

Dear Maggie,

This will come as a shock. I do hope you're sitting down. I will not be attending the wedding. I've discovered that marriage is not for me. I thought it was, but no, not even to a sweet, lovely girl such as yourself. I wish you all the luck in the future, but I am moving to New York to pursue a career as a journalist.

Daniel

Not a single word of affection. No *Love, Daniel.* Not even the word *goodbye.*

Maggie wadded the paper in her fist and raised tear-filled eyes to her mother. "Why would God do this to me?"

Chapter One

Early fall

Maggie smoothed her black skirt, straightened her white blouse, slapped a hat on her head, and squared her shoulders. Excitement rippled through her. A new store had opened in town a year ago, Woolworth's Five and Dime, and she was the lunch counter girl and window decorator. Her, Maggie Larson, a career woman! After Daniel's cowardly flight to New York, Maggie didn't think she'd be anything more than her mother's receptionist.

She practically skipped down the stairs of the Larson Boarding house, where she'd helped her mother for as long as she could remember. "How do I look?" She paused outside the kitchen door.

"Very professional." Her mother smiled. "Thank you for setting the table this morning."

"You're welcome. I'll help out more when I return from work."

"No, that's fine. I'll hire a part-time girl. You focus on your job."

Mama really was the best. Maggie planted a quick kiss on her mother's cheek and headed out. A few blocks over, she turned onto Penn Avenue, past the dry goods store, the outfitters. . . There. One more store over was the Five and Dime.

A pretty girl with strawberry blond hair and a name tag stating her name was Hattie stood outside the door, a smile on her face. "You must be Maggie. I've just opened the store. Welcome."

"Thank you." She thought her face would split from grinning.

"Your apron is hanging in the back room, where you may store your purse and hat."

Maggie nodded and entered the store. She closed her eyes for a moment and breathed deep of polished wood. Then she let her gaze roam the display cases that stretched from the front of the store to the back. Clerks stood behind the cases that held a myriad of goods for sale. Every square inch of the place was filled with treasures.

And against the right wall ran the lunch counter.

"Miss Larson."

She turned to see her boss, Frank Johnson, headed her way. "Sir."

"I'll walk with you to the staff lounge. No sense in wasting time. Now is as good a time as any to go over your job list for the day."

She laughed. "Jump in with both feet, right?"

He joined in with her laughter. "I guess I'm excited to start the day."

So was she. After removing her hat and hanging it on a peg, she faced him for her instructions.

"I know that Christmas is almost two months away, but there's no time like the present to get folks in the holiday spirit. I'd like you to spend the morning working on the store window display before tending to the lunch crowd. Use anything in the store, but make sure to let the clerk in that department know so they can mark the expense. The other women will decorate the rest of the store."

"Yes, sir." She donned her white apron and left the lounge, eager to get started.

She nodded at two of the clerks, Lizzie and Essie. Maggie wanted to feature a bit of everything from each department, along with Christmas decorations. Before choosing what to display, she stood outside and stared in the window and tried to envision the end result.

Someone jostled her on the busy sidewalk. She planted both hands against the glass to keep from falling. Wonderful. She'd have to clean it now.

"Excuse me. Are you all right?"

She turned at the deep baritone and stared into eyes the color of a meadow in spring. Hazel with flecks of brown the same shade as the brown hair. "Oh. Uh. Yes, I'm fine, thank you."

He tipped his hat and sauntered away, leaving her with her mouth hanging open.

Mama would be aghast. Maggie snapped her mouth closed. She shouldn't act like such a ninny. She'd sworn off men since Daniel.

Okay, back to business. Time was flowing through her fingers like water. She strolled through each department of the store, choosing a set of scalloped plates, animal cake cutters, fire shovels, red jewelry, and a toy dustpan. Enough to start with.

She set the items near the window and went in search of decorations. Armed with garland and bows, she climbed onto the window platform and got to work.

She placed empty boxes under red satin to raise some items above others. She draped a necklace around the neck of a wig dummy, doing the same with a scarf. Toys she displayed the closest to the window in hopes excited children could persuade their parents to purchase what their little hearts desired.

"That is looking really wonderful," Lizzie said.

"Thank you. It's taking me much longer than I anticipated." Maggie glanced at her watch. She might have to finish after the lunch rush.

She turned around. The handsome man who had bumped into her earlier walked past the window.

Seth Jamison finished all but one of his deliveries and strolled the sidewalk with Annie to have lunch at Woolworth's. They entered through the back so he could drop off the weekly milk order, then went into the main part of the store. The pretty lady he'd stumbled into earlier that week served customers at the lunch counter.

He took a closer look and recognized her as the daughter of Mrs. Larson, the woman who ran the boardinghouse. He'd only caught a glimpse of her once, when he'd left the milk on the back doorstep and she'd been in the kitchen washing dishes.

"Let's look around first, sweetheart. Maybe you can point out what you want for Christmas to Daddy." His late wife had always done the Christmas shopping.

He smiled as Annie headed straight for the toys. Several dolls stared open-eyed from their boxes. Near them, someone had set up a porcelain tea set perfect for little hands. The first Christmas without Susan would be tough on both him and his daughter. He needed to do everything in his power to make it special for his little girl.

Annie pointed out far more things than she'd receive, but at least Seth had an idea of what to get her. "Let's go eat." A weekly tradition he'd started upon learning the new store had a lunch counter. His daughter enjoyed perching on the stool and ordering a cheese sandwich by herself.

"Good afternoon. I'm Maggie. What can I get you?"

Seth glanced up, his gaze locking with blue eyes that were almost gray. Like the sky right before a storm. Her dark hair was pulled up in the poufed style women seemed to favor.

"I want a cheese sandwich and milk, please." Annie folded her hands on the counter in an attempt to be proper.

"The special is fine with me." Seth preferred switching things up each week, unlike his little girl, who always ordered the same thing.

"Chili and corn bread." Maggie jotted down their order. "Coffee?"

"Yes, please."

She took their order to the cook and returned a few minutes later with coffee and a mug. She filled his cup and set a creamer in front of him before moving to the next customer.

"Will God send Mommy back for Christmas?" Annie asked softly.

"No, sweetheart. She lives in heaven now." A boulder lodged in his throat. He needed to change the subject and fast. "Are you excited about playing Mary in the Christmas play?"

She shrugged. "I'm more happy about holding the doll. It's made of glass."

The laughter that shot from him had him on the receiving end of another of Maggie's smiles. "The baby Jesus doll is porcelain, not glass. Maybe you'll get a new doll for Christmas."

"I don't want one. I still have the one Mommy gave me."

"It's missing an eye."

"I don't care."

Maybe he could find someone who knew how to repair dolls. That would put a smile on Annie's face Christmas morning. The trick would be getting the doll away from her long enough.

Their server brought their food, refilled his coffee, and moved down the counter, doing the same for the others. She definitely added some beauty and cheer to the place. The other woman, probably ten years older, had been overworked before Maggie arrived. She'd complained enough to everyone who would listen.

Seth paid for their lunch, left a tip for Maggie, and led Annie from the store. He had another stop to make at the feedstore. The cows ate mostly hay, but the rest of his animals needed something more.

He hefted Annie into the wagon, then drove to the feedstore a few blocks away. "Wait right here. Holler if you need me. I've already placed the order, just need to pay."

She nodded, the crowd on the street attracting her attention.

Less than five minutes later, Seth started loading feed into the back of the wagon. Despite the winter chill, he worked up a sweat he knew would quickly make him cold once he started the drive home.

"Annie, grab the blanket behind the seat, would ya?" He tossed the last bag of feed in the back and scampered into the wagon.

Snuggling close to him, Annie spread the faded quilt around the both of them. Seth smiled. There was nothing better in the world than his little girl sitting close at his side.

"Miss Maggie is pretty, isn't she, Daddy?"

He cut her a quick glance. "I reckon."

"She's nice too."

"She seems to be."

"Maybe you and her can be friends."

Maybe. The idea wasn't horrible to consider. Not at all.

Chapter Two

First week of work behind her, and things were grand. Maggie smiled at her reflection. She'd finished the Christmas display window yesterday. Her heart almost stopped when Mr. Woolworth himself commented on how good it looked. Today Maggie would be floating to work from the effervescence of the store owner's kind words.

"You sure are happy this morning." Mama handed her a biscuit with butter. "Thank you for setting the table."

"I'll do so every morning." And she had, but it was nice that Mama appreciated the gesture. Maggie breathed deeply of the warm biscuit. "I'll bring home some honey if there's any to be found."

"That would be nice. I plan on coming to the Five and Dime this afternoon to begin preparations for Christmas. Maybe I'll see you there."

"Of course." Maggie quickly made a sandwich for her lunch, then grabbed her shawl. "Watch for ice on the sidewalks. We had a freeze last night."

She ate the rest of her biscuit on the walk to work, carefully checking her face in the window before entering. Showing up with food on her face would be so embarrassing. Convinced her face was clean, she entered the store, greeting the other clerks on her way to hanging up her heavy wool shawl.

Now that the window decorations were done, she'd help with decorating the rest of the store before the lunch rush arrived. She donned her apron and went to the stockroom for the box of garlands that would grace the ceiling.

"Oh." She peered in a box to see delicate glass tree ornaments. Why were these back here? They'd be beautiful in the display window. After locating a small Christmas tree, she carried it and the ornaments to the front.

"Mr. Woolworth had those shipped from Germany," Hattie said as Maggie rushed past her. "I bet we sell a lot of them."

"I think we will too." Maggie stopped and handed her the box. "There are several more cases in the back room. I only need a few to decorate this little tree."

When she finished, she stepped outside to get the viewpoint of those passing by. The ornaments glistened under the lights.

"Good morning."

She turned to see the man who'd had lunch with his little girl last Friday. "Good morning."

He smiled, his gaze warm, as he hefted a crate of milk bottles from the back of his wagon and carried it across the street as if the full bottles weighed next to nothing.

Stop it, Maggie. Remember what happened the last time you set eyes on a handsome man you thought was kind. He'd turned out to be a viper. She tore her gaze away from the man's broad back and entered the store.

Her career was the important thing. Working allowed Maggie to be able to take care of herself. She didn't need a husband. She'd be fine living with Mama and going to work six days a week. Her life was plenty fulfilling.

"I could use some help in the kitchen if you've time." The head chef, Mr. Winters, waved at her. "I need the bread cut, and I'm running behind." He handed her a serrated knife. "Same thickness as the slices over there."

Maggie's eyes widened at the sight of five loaves waiting. She'd barely have time to get through them before diners started arriving. Nor had she written the day's special, pot roast, on the board. She'd spent far too long on the display window.

The three other lunch counter girls, part-timers only, arrived. Maggie delegated the bread cutting to one of them and went to the chalkboard above the counter. There. Pot roast, green beans with potatoes, and a roll.

The milkman came from the kitchen with his little girl and took their seats at the counter.

"Are you here every Friday?" Maggie set a coffee cup in front of him and filled it.

"Ever since the store opened. I deliver the milk here, so I pick up my daughter, Annie, from the lady who watches her for me, and we have lunch together." He smiled at his daughter.

Maggie's heart leaped at the tender way he gazed on the little girl.

"My mommy is in heaven," Annie said, pretending to read the menu.

"I'm sorry to hear that." She looked at the man. "You're brave raising her alone."

"Why?" He tilted his head. "Women do it all the time."

"Oh, I didn't mean. . ." She sighed.

"Don't fret. I know you meant no harm. I'll have the special. Annie?"

"Cheese sandwich."

He chuckled. "She has the same thing every time. I'm Seth

Jamison, by the way. Might as well get acquainted since you'll see me every week. Call me Seth."

Grateful he hadn't taken offense at her blurting her thoughts, silly ones at that, Maggie hurried to place their order.

"Why is your face so red?" the chef asked.

"Just flushed." Mercy. She ducked her head and began pouring coffee for the diners. Maybe next Friday she'd do better at thinking before speaking.

"My daddy thinks you're pretty," Annie said as Maggie set her sandwich in front of her.

Maggie's eyes widened.

Seth's face burned. The food in front of him suddenly became the only thing he could think about. Keeping his head down, he started eating.

It seemed like an hour before Maggie was far enough away that Seth could tell Annie there are certain things people kept to themselves. "That was between me and you."

"You said to always tell the truth." She took a big bite of her sandwich.

"Yes, I did, but you weren't asked a question by Miss Maggie. Just eat. I still have work to do." Not deliveries but work at the farm.

Mrs. Bookman, the widow who watched Annie for him during the day, would expect them back soon. The woman was indispensable. Having Annie with her for most of the week allowed Seth to work without worrying about what a five-year-old could get into.

"All right, but I think Miss Maggie is pretty too."

His head snapped up as Maggie paused in refilling his coffee.

"We. Uh. Weren't talking about you."

She arched a brow, a smile teasing at her lips. "The things little ones say."

Returning her smile with a grateful one of his own, Seth held a hand over his cup. "Thank you, but I've had enough." He paid for their meal and escorted Annie back to the wagon.

"I don't want to go to Mrs. Bookman's. There's nothing to do." Annie crossed her arms and pouted.

"You took your doll, didn't you?"

Tears welled in her eyes. "I can't find it."

"We'll look tonight." If he found it first, he'd hide it in order to get it repaired. "Isn't Mrs. Bookman teaching you needlework?"

"I guess."

Seth stopped the buggy in front of Mrs. Bookman's single-story cottage and helped Annie down. "It's only for a few more hours. I'll be back after I take care of the cows."

Mrs. Bookman opened the door, her round face split by a grin. "My daughter has arrived for the holidays. Please spare a moment to meet her."

Seth followed his daughter into the parlor.

A lovely woman with hair the color of corn silk stood when they entered the room. Statuesque, her eyes came to Seth's nose. "Who is this, Mother?"

"Deborah, this is Seth Jamison and his daughter, Annie. Seth owns the largest dairy farm in town."

"My pleasure." She held out her hand.

Seth gripped the soft hand in his, gave it a short shake, and stepped back. He recognized the predatory look that had come into the woman's eyes when her mother mentioned he owned a farm. "Nice to meet you. Enjoy your stay." He gave Annie a quick kiss on the top of her head and rushed to the buggy.

His mind went to work as he drove home. Mrs. Bookman's daughter wasn't the first to set her cap for Seth after the death of his wife. Unfortunately for all of them, he had no intention of getting married again. Maggie's face flickered through his mind only to be shoved aside. He wanted nothing more than maybe a friendship with the pretty brunette.

He'd seen her mother at church plenty of times but not Maggie. The past Sunday, he'd asked her mother whether Maggie would attend. The woman had evaded the question, which only made him more curious. Not that it was any of his business, but when a person was noticeably gone, he noticed.

Next time he saw Maggie, he'd invite her. With the holidays rapidly approaching, there were several opportunities at church to help Scranton's less fortunate. Seth was building the stage and backdrop for the Christmas play, but he wasn't much of a painter. Maybe Maggie would like to help him.

It didn't hurt to ask, and Annie would be happy. She'd taken a liking to Maggie, and Seth didn't want to discourage his daughter from having a good female role model. His daughter might want to have a career of her own someday. Not every woman aspired to marriage.

He thought of Susan as he went about the business of caring for his cows. Maybe it was too early to think about friendship with a woman. What if it turned into something more?

He forked hay into the paddock. What if Annie got too attached and Maggie married and moved away? Should he chance her having a role model if the woman could up and leave?

Doubt about his ability to be a single parent rose in his chest. Susan had made him promise to find another mother for Annie when she died, but Seth just couldn't do it. His heart still ached with memories of her slowly suffocating as influenza riddled her body.

He had a lot of praying to do about his future.

Finished with the day's chores, he went to claim his daughter so he could cook their dinner. Maggie had been right. Men rarely raised a child alone. He knew several that married right away after the deaths of their wives.

Seth wasn't like that. When he loved a woman, he loved her with all that was in him. He loved her as God loved His church. It would take a very special woman to claim his heart.

Chapter Three

At her mother's warning they were running late, Maggie snatched her straw hat from the top of her armoire and thundered down the stairs. "Sorry."

"A lady does not come down the stairs like a buffalo." Mama frowned. "I have a lot on my list today, most importantly, packing boxes at church for the poor. We must make haste."

Having a rare day off that wasn't a Sunday, Maggie had agreed to help. She no longer attended church with her mother but wouldn't stop helping the less fortunate. It wasn't their fault her faith had been shattered. She grabbed her coat from the foyer and followed her mother outside.

They strolled in companionable silence, nodding and smiling at folks they passed, until they reached the church. Once inside, Mama burst into action, telling those willing to help what to do and where to go.

Grinning, Maggie hung up her coat and turned to move to her assigned position, the food boxes. She found her way blocked by a solid chest of blue flannel. "Excuse me." She raised her gaze. "Mr. Jamison."

"Seth, remember?" He smiled. "I've been sent to help you pack the boxes."

She peered around him to see who else would be helping. "Just the two of us?"

"I reckon." He seemed unfazed by the daunting task.

Maggie knew better. Mama was playing matchmaker. Her thought was confirmed by the satisfied look on her mother's face. "We'd best get started then. There's a lot of food to be divvied out."

"How should we do this? In a line?" He set out the boxes. "Then go down the line putting in the supplies?"

"Sounds good to me." She grabbed an armful of bags of flour and started dropping one into each box. While Seth's idea had seemed sound at the time, they kept bumping into each other, which slowed their progress. "For heaven's sake." She couldn't take any more close contact with the man no matter how handsome he was.

Maybe that was the problem. His handsomeness. She moved to the other side of the table.

"I kind of liked bumping you." Seth chuckled.

Her face heated. "Slows down the work."

Shrugging, he returned to placing food in the boxes. As they filled, he closed them and stacked them on a nearby table. "I'll be delivering these. A couple of widows have offered to go with me, but I wondered if you'd like to, since you helped box them."

She widened her eyes, then burst into laughter. "You want me to protect you. Widows will look at you as prime food."

"What would you know about that?" He tilted his head.

"I've seen the way the women in Woolworth's look at you. You'd have to be blind not to see. You're obviously good husband material. You're raising your daughter alone and you own land." She arched a brow.

"What's good husband material?"

She could tell he enjoyed their conversation way too much

and bit her cheek to keep from laughing. "You have the means to support a family."

"I inherited the farm from my father. It's been in the family for generations."

"And you keep it going." She folded a box closed and scooted it toward him. "But yes, I'll go with you to make the deliveries. We'll also have boxes of clothes. Let me tell my mother I'll be gone."

She located Mama with a cluster of women, all whispering and casting curious glances to where Maggie and Seth packed boxes. Maggie heaved a sigh. Telling them she was going to help Seth make the deliveries would fuel the gossip for sure.

"Well, isn't that nice." Mama's eyes rounded, and she nodded at the ladies, who all bobbed their heads like chickens. "Why don't you invite Mr. Jamison and his little girl over for dinner? It's fried chicken."

"I'll see if he's free."

The murmurs started back up the instant she turned her back. Squaring her shoulders, she returned to her appointed station. "Mama has invited you to dinner. And Annie, of course."

"We can pick her up after the deliveries. I'd love to have dinner with your family."

"Not only us. Mama runs a boardinghouse."

"I know. I deliver the milk."

"You do? Why have I never seen you before?"

"I deliver there while it's still dark. I'm sure you're slumbering away."

"No, I'm not." She frowned. "I'm a working woman, and I help Mama before I leave for the store."

"Have I offended you?"

"No. Let's finish up here so we can leave." She knew exactly what made her words sharp. The nosy looks of Mama's friends. She didn't like being the main attraction at any time, especially if it involved a man.

She fetched her coat, and they started carrying boxes to Seth's wagon. When they'd finished, boxes with labels showing where they were to be dropped off filled the back. Her heart ached to see so many people in need so close to home. When Christmas neared, they'd do the same again, only with toys. Perhaps Mr. Woolworth would donate some things.

"I may make good husband material, Maggie, but you make the same for a wife. Hardworking, soft heart, and a clever mind."

"Are you flirting with me?" She narrowed her eyes.

"Is it working?" His smile widened, sending a twinkle to his eyes.

Maggie steeled her heart. "You're wasting your time. I have no desire to marry."

His heart dropped, but he forced his smile to remain in place. "Friends then."

"Friends." She nodded and held out her hand. "Shake on it."

He returned the handshake, her small hand warming as he held it. Her declaration of not wanting to marry shouldn't bother him. He wasn't actively searching for a wife. If he were, there were plenty of women who would jump at his proposal. But Maggie was different. Something about her drew him, and it was much more than her pretty face.

He helped her onto the seat, then climbed in on his side. With a flick of the reins, the two bay horses pulled away from the church. From the corner of Seth's eye, he caught sight of Mrs. Larson, hands folded under her chin, watching them drive away with a smile on her face.

Uh-oh. Having seen the same look on many a mother's face, he recognized the matchmaking gleam. Perhaps Maggie had neglected to tell her mother she had no plans to wed.

Maggie glanced back and groaned. Shaking her head, she pulled her coat tighter around herself.

"There's a quilt behind the seat if you're cold." Seth reached back and pulled out the blanket.

"Thank you." She spread it over her legs. "I've helped Mama with these boxes for the last five years and don't recall ever seeing you there."

"I've only recently started attending church again." He cleared his throat. "After my. . .Susan died, I didn't go for quite a while. Then Annie started asking why we'd stopped. I felt it was time to go back and chose this church. My heart couldn't allow me to return to the one I'd attended with Susan. Perhaps you'd like to go with us this Sunday?"

"No, thank you. I don't attend." She lifted her chin and kept her stare forward.

Seth could take a hint and didn't ask questions. Maybe eventually she'd let him know why church was so distasteful to her. He'd heard rumors about her being jilted at the altar but found it hard to believe that someone wouldn't want Maggie.

"Here's the first place." He hopped from the wagon.

Before he could get around to assist her, Maggie jumped down and reached for a box of clothes. He took one of food, led the way up a couple of steps in bad need of repair, and knocked on the door.

A woman so thin a stiff wind would blow her away answered the door. Three very small children peeked around her skirt. "May I help you?"

"It's we who can help you, Mrs. Wells. We've brought food

and clothes for you and the little ones."

Maggie stepped to his side. "From the church."

Tears welled in the woman's eyes. "God bless you. It was going to be a sparse Thanksgiving."

Seth wished he had some bottles of milk in the wagon. He vowed right then and there to leave a bottle free of charge each morning as he headed into town. "Is there anything else we can do for you? I can come by one day and do some minor repairs."

"I've no money to pay you."

"I'm not asking for payment, but perhaps if I brought some mending by. . ."

A weary smile graced her face. "A barter, then. Yes."

Back in the wagon, Maggie faced him, her eyes shimmering. "You are a good man, Seth Jamison."

House after house was the same. A widow with children more thankful for the boxes than they could say, and house after house, Seth vowed to leave milk. At that rate, he might very well go broke.

"You're going to need more cows," Maggie said with a laugh.

"I might at that." He stopped in front of Mrs. Bookman's house, hoping her daughter wasn't home.

Unfortunately, Deborah Bookman stepped onto the porch with Annie before Seth reached the house. Her sharp gaze landed on Maggie. Her forehead creased. "You aren't alone."

"Church work. Hello, darlin'." He held out his arms for Annie, who wrapped her small ones around his neck. "Thank you for watching her."

"It was only for a few minutes while Mother ran some errands." With a wrinkle of her nose, she went back into the house.

"You remember Miss Maggie, don't you?" He sat his daughter

on the seat between him and Maggie. "We're going to her house for dinner."

Annie shot him a glance too old for a five-year-old, then grinned and snuggled under the quilt with Maggie. "That sounds just fine."

Seems Mrs. Larson wasn't the only matchmaker around. Seth had second thoughts about accepting the dinner invitation. But at least there would be more people than just the four of them to make the meal less intimate.

Seth parked the wagon near the house and looped the reins over a fence post before helping Annie and Maggie down. Annie slipped her hand in Maggie's and skipped toward the house.

Sighing, Seth followed. What could he do to keep his little girl from becoming too attached to Maggie?

"Welcome, Mr. Jamison. Who is this pretty thing?" Mrs. Larson bustled from the kitchen. "Why, it can't be Annie? She's much too big. This isn't the same young lady I saw at church last Sunday."

"It is Annie." His daughter pointed at herself. "I am big now."

Maggie shot Seth an amused look. "I'll help you in the kitchen. Seth, why don't you and Annie head into the parlor with our other guests? We'll call everyone in when we're ready."

He led Annie into a room full of comfortable furniture and men smoking cigars and reading newspapers. Mrs. Larson's business must be good, since he counted five men lounging. Her home couldn't have more than seven or eight bedrooms, even with it being as large as it was. Since the boardinghouse seemed prosperous, why was Maggie so intent on being a career woman rather than helping her mother, as most young ladies did?

After introductions were made, Seth found an empty space on the sofa and sat, pulling Annie into his lap. Several minutes later, a bell rang calling everyone to the dinner table.

Before Seth could claim a seat next to Maggie, two others took the seats on either side and another straight across from her. Despite her reluctance to wed, if men kept flocking around her, she might give in and get married.

The thought left a bad taste in Seth's mouth.

Chapter Four

Mama rushed into the dining room, clearly flustered, her hands twisting in her apron. "Maggie, I've run out of milk. That simply will not do. I know it's early, and I know you have to be at work, but I really need you to run out to the Jamison farm and pick up a couple of bottles to get us through. Tell Mr. Jamison to up our order by two."

Maggie glanced at her watch. If she hurried, she could make it to work on time. "I'll need the buggy." She grabbed her coat and purse and darted out the door. She'd make better time on horseback, but that would muss her hair, and she had no time to redo the style.

After tying a scarf around her head, she entered the barn, grateful to see the horse already hitched. One of the boarders had come to their aid. Too bad they couldn't have also fetched the milk.

"Yah!" She flicked the reins and galloped out of town.

She raced for the milking shed, hoping to find Seth. There was no time to hunt him down. What if he'd already left for his deliveries?

"Seth?" She ducked into the dim recesses of the shed. "We're in need of more—"

A lovely blond woman stood improperly close to Seth, one finger trailing down the buttons of his shirt. Maggie backed out of sight and cleared her throat. "Seth, are you in here?"

"Yes, Maggie." He greeted her with a smile. "What can I do for you?"

"Mama is in need of two bottles of milk and would like you to up her order." She squared her shoulders.

"I'm on my way to make the deliveries. Couldn't she have waited?"

"Obviously not. You're late, thankfully for me, and she needs the milk." Her gaze flicked to the blond, who watched them with amusement. "I really must get back so I can get to work."

"I'll apologize to your mother when I stop." His face darkened. "I got detained."

"So I see." *Bite your tongue, Maggie. You have no claim to Seth.*

"Follow me." He led her to a crate of bottles filled with milk and handed her two. "Hurry on or you'll be late. I'll make sure the order is increased."

"Thanks to a full house." She forced a smile and rushed to the buggy, racing from the dairy farm.

What was wrong with her? Why the spark of jealousy? She'd told him she wanted to be nothing more than friends. Maybe the fact he'd shown interest and moved to another so quickly had her irritated.

She hitched the buggy in front of the house, set the bottles near the front door, knocked, and practically ran down the sidewalk toward the Five and Dime. Mama would have to get one of the boarders to care for the horse.

"You're late, Miss Larson." Her boss glanced at his watch.

"I'm so sorry. I had to run an errand for my mother." She hung up her coat and donned her apron.

"Perhaps your mother should hire an errand boy. Do not let this happen again or I will have to write you up. The chef is in need of your assistance today." He spun on his heel and marched away.

Maggie's throat clogged. Reprimanded! Heart heavy, she headed for the kitchen. She'd have to put her foot down if Mama asked something of her that could cause her to be late. This job meant too much to her.

Chef Winters frowned and set her to kneading the dough on the counter. "We're down a girl. She sent a message that she's sick. I think she's lazy. That means your job today just doubled. And the milk delivery is late. What is going on with these people?"

A tall blond woman delayed Seth. As for her coworker, Maggie simply shrugged.

The back door opened, letting in a blast of cold air. Maggie turned, her gaze clashing with Seth's. "Milk is here," she called to the chef.

"I also got the rest to your mother." He set the diner's supply on the counter.

"Thank you." Maggie set the kneaded dough aside to rise.

"Sorry for the delay. I found myself detained by my daughter's babysitter."

"Babysitter?" Maggie arched a brow. She didn't look like the type to watch a child, but looks could be deceiving.

"Well, her mother actually watches Annie."

Maggie pasted on a smile. It really was none of her business, but Seth continued, babbling with what seemed nervous energy.

"Have a good day," she said, wiping the flour from the counter, turning away from the pained look that crossed his face.

He sighed and nodded. "See you tomorrow."

"See you tomorrow." In the meantime, Maggie needed

to control her emotions and stick with her resolve not to get involved with a man. Ever.

The rest of the morning sped by. By lunchtime, every stool held a hungry customer.

Maggie soon found herself run ragged, having to apologize when they ran out of the day's special of chicken and dumplings. By the time lunch was over, she wanted nothing more than to go home and fall onto her bed no matter the early hour.

Alas, Mama needed her help with supper.

"I think it might be time for you to hire that help you keep saying you're going to." Maggie stirred the pot of stew on the stove.

"I suppose, although I had hoped you'd quit the job at Woolworth's and help me here. That's what most proper young ladies would do."

She shook her head. "I want more than this, Mama."

"What do you want? You've rattled around like a bean in a jar since Daniel left."

Maggie raised her chin. "I don't want to be dependent on anyone but myself."

Seth continued his late deliveries, having to appease upset customers, then dropped off the promised bottles to those he'd vowed to help. By the time he passed by the Five and Dime on his way home, one glance through the window showed a full counter.

Why had Maggie given him the cold shoulder? Oh, he hadn't missed the shocked look on her face when she walked into the barn. That had to be it. What must she think of him?

It made no sense for Deborah to come and offer to pick up Annie. Not when Mrs. Bookman was his first delivery each day.

Not to mention the woman had been entirely improper. Seth didn't want to be rude to anyone, but Miss Deborah would have to be put in her place if her advances continued. If Seth did remarry, it would be to someone like Maggie, not a vixen like Deborah.

If his daughter needed a mother, and that was a big if, it wouldn't be someone who would hire a nanny. He shook his head. No, he was all his daughter needed. They were doing just fine.

At the Bookman home, he sat in his delivery wagon, reluctant to enter the house where he knew Deborah would be. When the curtains at the window parted for the third time, he exhaled heavily and climbed from the wagon.

"Annie has been telling us all about a Miss Maggie." A hard glint shone in Deborah's eyes.

"We're just friends. Annie and I eat lunch at Woolworth's every Friday. Maggie works the lunch counter."

"They sure do," Mrs. Bookman said. "That allows me to get some errands run after Seth picks her up. It works well for both of us."

"That it does." Seth smiled and helped Annie into her coat. "See you tomorrow."

Once he had Annie in the wagon, the quilt tucked firmly around her against the afternoon chill, she tapped his shoulder. "I don't like Miss Deborah."

"Oh?" He tilted his head. "Why not?"

"She's mean. She won't talk to me and tells me to go away." She pouted.

"What do you do then?"

"I go find Mrs. Bookman, and she gives me a cookie."

"Then all is good." He tapped her nose and climbed into the driver's side. "Try to leave her alone, all right?" Hopefully, Deborah would return to Philadelphia soon.

A brisk wind picked up when they were halfway home. Seth pulled the collar of his coat up and shivered.

Black smoke billowed in the distance. An iron fist squeezed Seth's heart. The farm!

He flicked the reins to spur the horses faster, stopping a safe distance from the burning house. "Stay in the wagon." He leaped down, grabbing the quilt from Annie, and sprinted for the well.

The fire seemed to be contained to the kitchen so far. With God's grace, he'd get it out before it spread. After soaking the quilt, he slapped at the flames over and over until his lungs burned from inhaling smoke and from exhaustion.

"Daddy!"

He whirled to see sparks land in the dry grass near the milking shed. "I've got it." He quickly stomped out the glowing embers.

He had the fire well under control by the time help arrived in the form of his closest neighbor, who lived three miles away.

"Saw the smoke." Herb glanced down from his wagon. "What will you do? The house ain't fit for a child right now."

"Tonight we'll sleep in the milking shed. I'll figure something out tomorrow. All we lost was the kitchen and this old quilt." Seth leaned against the rock wall of the well and beckoned for Annie to join him.

"Quite a bit of wind we had." Herb shook his head. "Most likely stirred up the embers in your kitchen stove."

"Most likely." Thank God that his father had the foresight to build most of the house out of rocks he'd carted in.

"I'll gather up a crew, and we'll get you fixed up this weekend."

"I appreciate it, Herb." He and Annie would only be misplaced for a few days.

"That's what neighbors do." Herb turned his wagon back to the road and drove off.

"Looks like we'll be camping out tonight." Seth put his arm around Annie's shoulders. "I'll go into the house and get some blankets. They might be a bit smelly, but they'll keep us warm." So would the heat from the cows' bodies. Things could have been a lot worse.

It had been quite the day. With orders for Annie to head to the milking shed, Seth entered the house and fetched enough blankets to make them comfortable. After making a bed, he would take care of the horse and wagon.

Tonight's meal would be. . . "Looks like we're headed to the diner in town." Anything they had to eat in the kitchen lay in ashes.

Seth cleaned himself up the best he could in the trough, gasping as he splashed cold water over his face and arms. First, the day had started with Deborah, then he'd gotten a cold shoulder from Maggie, now it ended with a fire. *Please, God, let the rest of the year go smoothly.*

Shivering, he put his coat back on and helped Annie into the wagon. The diner in town was a rare treat. Seth usually stayed too busy to make the trip. He would still have cows to care for when he got home. The rough day would also be a long one.

"Good evening, Mr. Jamison, Annie." The hostess, a middle-aged widow named April, greeted them as they entered the diner. "It's been a long time since you graced this place."

"Had a kitchen fire."

"Oh, I'm sorry." She led them to a table in the corner. "Anything we can do? I'm sure the chef wouldn't mind sending you some extra food for your breakfast."

"That would be kind, thank you." Seth glanced at the menu. "Two bowls of beef stew and corn bread, please." It would fill their bellies and warm them up.

Mrs. Larson rushed into the diner. "I need the pie I forgot to pick up earlier. My boarders are clamoring for their dessert." She smiled, spotting Seth and Annie. "A night on the town?"

"We had a fire," Annie said. "Our kitchen is gone."

"Oh dear. Where will you sleep? I know," she said without waiting for an answer. "We have an attic room that hardly anyone wants to rent. It's clean and warm with two cots. You may use it as long as you need to."

Seth's heart warmed. "We will accept with gratitude. I'll have to care for my cows before we arrive."

"The back door will be open. Collect a few things. I'll wait up for you." Pie in hand, she bustled from the diner, leaving Seth feeling very much cared for.

Chapter Five

Maggie lay in bed and stared at the ceiling. Something had awakened her earlier than usual. There. A rustling in the attic. She tossed off the thick quilt she'd slept under and grabbed her robe.

"Mama, I think there are rats in the attic again," she called as she rushed down the stairs.

"I've been called many things," a voice said behind her, "but never a rat."

She whirled, her gaze clashing with Seth's as he and Annie came down the stairs. "What are you doing here?" She clutched the neckline of her robe closed.

"Don't be rude, dear. Come on in, you two. Maggie, get dressed, please. Mr. Jamison had a kitchen fire, and he and his daughter will be occupying the attic for a few days." Mama led them into the dining room.

Gracious. Maggie stood there for several seconds, mouth hanging open, hair tousled, until she caught the amused glance of one of the other guests. She thundered upstairs and quickly donned her work clothes.

Once she'd composed herself and gotten over the shock that Seth was living under the same roof, she returned to the dining room at a more ladylike pace. Since she'd gotten up early, she had time for a quick breakfast of biscuits and gravy.

"I can give you a ride to work," Seth said. "We can drop Annie off and get you there in plenty of time. It's drizzling rain this morning."

"Thank you. I accept." A chilly walk in the rain did not sound appealing.

"Today is Friday, Daddy." Annie took a bite of a biscuit without gravy.

"So it is." He gave her an indulgent smile. "What's the day's special, Maggie?"

"I won't know until I get there, but I'm sure it'll be something delicious." She finished her breakfast and went to gather her things.

"Maggie, please bring me a new biscuit cutter and gravy strainer. Mine have seen better days, and with Thanksgiving next week. . ." Mama called when Maggie came back downstairs. "I'll pay you when you return home."

"No need." Maggie tied a scarf around her hair and snatched an umbrella from the stand near the door. "Ready?"

"Yes, ma'am." Seth held the door open, allowing Maggie and Annie to step out first.

Maggie shared her umbrella with Annie, and Seth set his hat on his head. It didn't take long for water to drip from the wide brim. "Thank you again for the ride."

"You're welcome. You'd be soaked by the time you got to work. It's more than drizzling now, and the wind is blowing."

"What about you on your deliveries?" He'd be soaked through.

"I've got my slicker." He grinned and helped her onto the wagon seat, where Annie sat as close to her as possible. "It isn't the first time I've delivered in the rain." His warm gaze showed he appreciated her concern.

Maggie's face heated, and she turned away. How was she going to survive a few days of him under the same roof without looking like a ninny? Sure, the other guests were all men but much older and not nearly as attractive. Well, she'd just have to hold on to her resolve and live each day as she had been.

The woman who watched Annie met them at the wagon with a large umbrella. "See you at lunchtime, Seth."

"Yes, ma'am." He touched the brim of his hat and flicked the reins.

Less than five minutes later, he pulled in at the rear of the Five and Dime and helped Maggie down before retrieving the store's milk delivery from the back of the wagon. She glanced at the chalkboard as she entered the kitchen. The special was chili. Not something Annie would enjoy, but then, she always ordered a cheese sandwich.

"See you at lunch." Seth set the wet bottles on the counter.

"See you then." Maggie strolled through the kitchen and into the back room to don her apron. She smiled at Hattie as she passed her coming out of the room. When Maggie entered the main area of the store, she waved at Lizzie and Essie, who were already at their posts.

"New glass ornaments," Lizzie called out. "I kept one separate in case you want it for the window display." She handed a bronze-colored bell to Maggie.

"Thank you." The ornament sparkled under the store lights. "These are so beautiful. I'd like to purchase six of them for my mother as a gift."

"I'll wrap them and set them aside. All bells or an assortment?"

"An assortment. Could you add a biscuit cutter and gravy strainer to my order? Those don't need to be wrapped."

With long strides and smiles at arriving customers, Maggie hung the bell on the tree in the window and went to help Chef Winters prepare for lunch. He immediately set her to work on bread again, the other girl having quit. So, another day of being shorthanded. She sighed and got to work.

By the time Seth and Annie arrived, she'd made her third pot of coffee and felt as if she'd worked a full day already. She tossed them a smile, waved them to the last two stools at the counter, and quick-stepped to the end to take an order.

Poor Maggie looked as frazzled as a worn-out tassel on his mother's old curtains. She stood, wide-eyed with a forced smile, as an irate customer complained about the wait.

"I'm sorry, sir. We're shorthanded today."

"As you were yesterday." He slapped the counter. "Why haven't you hired another girl yet?"

"Not all women want to work outside the home." Her smile started to falter.

Seth told Annie to remain seated and stood behind the angry man's stool. "She's doing her best, sir. If it isn't to your liking, perhaps the diner would suit you better?"

"Trying to run off my customers, Mr. Jamison?"

He turned to the store manager, Frank Johnson. "No, just trying to soothe some ruffled feathers."

"I'll take things from here. Sir, follow me to my office, please." Frank gave a nod to Maggie and led the customer away.

"Thank you, Seth." High spots of color appeared on her pale face. "He's right though. Especially with the approaching holiday rush, we need more help. I'll be down to take your order in just a moment."

"No hurry." He returned to his stool.

"If I was bigger, I'd help her," Annie said.

"I know you would." He gave her a quick one-armed hug. "You'd be a great help."

"What can I get you?" Maggie took a deep breath, her smile fading.

Knowing she felt comfortable enough around him to let her guard down filled him with warmth. "I'll have the chili. Annie wants a ham and cheese sandwich with milk."

"Ham and cheese?"

"I'm big now," Annie said, as if that explained the change.

"Coming right up." Maggie took another deep breath and pasted the smile back on her face.

When Seth had first spotted her behind the counter, she'd been full of pep and bright spirits. Now her steps dogged, and she looked as if she forced herself to be cheerful. Had the job become too much for her? Did he know anyone who might be willing to fill the vacant spot behind the counter? Surely someone at church needed a job. There were several single women, some widows, that could use the extra income. He'd check with the pastor.

He said a quick prayer for Maggie's health and strength, wrapping his hands around the cup of hot coffee in front of him. If Susan were alive, she'd have stepped behind the counter and helped, asked to or not. She'd had the biggest heart of anyone he'd ever known. Annie showed signs of having the same compassion for people. Maggie, now, she had the mental and emotional strength of three men. He admired her very much. His gaze followed her as she served customers. Perhaps he admired her too much.

"Hot chili and one sandwich with milk." Maggie set their order in front of them.

"Would you like a ride home after work?" Seth crumbled his corn bread into his chili. "It's no trouble to stop by here on my way to the farm."

"Only if it's raining." Her smile seemed genuine this time. "The walk helps me wind down after a hard day. That way I don't take my work home with me, and I'm in a better frame of mind to help Mama."

"She won't accept rent. Says the fire will cost enough. What repairs need doing around the house? I can do them without asking." He grinned.

She tilted her head. "You're a special man, Seth Jamison. Free milk to the needy, repairs when my mother is trying to help. Do you ever tire of doing good?"

"No. My body grows weary sometimes, yes. But there is Someone whose shoulders are broad enough. He keeps me going when it seems like I can't take another step, do another good deed."

"He's talking about God," Annie said, a milk moustache on her face.

"She knows, sweetie." He wiped her face with a napkin.

"I can no longer rely on someone who will allow the rug to be yanked out from under me, sending my world and my future spinning." She overfilled his cup, stopping when he yelped as the hot coffee hit his skin. "I'm so sorry."

"It's all right." He used the same napkin he'd used on Annie.

"You need church." His daughter gave a definite nod.

"Not me, honey, but thank you." Maggie helped sop up the spilled coffee, casting an anxious glance to where Frank watched them. "The coffee is on me. Are you burned?"

"Not a bit." He put his hand over hers, stilling her movements. "I'm fine. No harm done. Frank won't reprimand you. I'll tell him I distracted you. It's the truth after all."

Her eyes shimmered. "You really are special," she whispered before moving down the counter.

He wasn't special enough to convince her that God had yanked out that proverbial rug for a reason she couldn't yet see. Her being ditched at the altar hadn't been a surprise to Him. He had something better for sweet Maggie. It was up to Seth to help her find out what that was.

After paying for their lunch, he set a nice tip on the counter for Maggie and helped Annie into her coat. His daughter called out a goodbye and waved.

Maggie smiled and waved back. "I'll have a list of what Mama needs doing by the time I get home."

Seth dropped Annie off at Mrs. Bookman's, then rode to the farm to begin the afternoon's work. His Friday lunches with Annie took a large chunk out of his workday, but he wouldn't trade that hour with his little girl for anything. Having Maggie there only sweetened the time.

As he milked the cows, his mind drifted to Susan's last words before God took her home. "Marry again. You're too good a man to live life alone."

He felt as if he might be ready to fulfill her dying wish. The obstacle in his path was the fact that the only woman who interested him since his wife didn't have a relationship with God. Nor did she ever want to marry.

He leaned his forehead against the cow and prayed for Maggie to reunite with her Creator. For her sake and Seth's.

Chapter Six

Thanksgiving morning, and Maggie was up before the sun to help her mother with the meal. The week of Seth living under the same roof had gone smoothly, without any embarrassing moments. The house ate breakfast together, and then he dropped her off at the store before his deliveries and returned after dark.

His kitchen had been repaired, and he and Annie would return to the farm in the morning. If not for Mama asking them to stay through the holiday, they would have left yesterday.

Regardless of her feelings about a relationship, Maggie had enjoyed having Seth there. He had made many minor repairs around the place despite Mama's protests. Having a man around did have some benefits.

She smiled at her reflection in the mirror and smoothed the sides of her best dress, a gown the color of the sky after a rainstorm. Taking such care with her appearance when she wasn't out to impress anyone seemed silly, but she was a woman and enjoyed the glimmer of admiration that appeared in Seth's eyes when she looked good. What a conflicting mixture of emotions she was.

After tying up her hair, she skipped down the steps and into the kitchen, where Mama was working over a hot stove. "I'll make the stuffing. Chef Winters sent me home with some dried bread."

"Thank you, dear. I've just about got the turkey ready."

"Is there anything I can do to help?" Seth stood in the doorway with hair still wet from a bath and wearing a green cotton shirt that matched the specks in his hazel eyes.

"You know your way around a kitchen?" Mama widened her eyes.

"I used to help my wife all the time, and now that I'm raising Annie. . .yes, I spend quite a bit of time in the kitchen."

With a grin, Maggie tossed him a ruffled apron. "How about you get the potatoes going?"

"With pleasure." He gave her a bow and donned the apron that barely tied around him.

Mama looked every bit like a cat who finished off the last of the cream. "Once the turkey is in, I'll leave the two of you to finish up the side dishes. I've some last-minute chores to do."

Since when did Mama relinquish a chore she loved? She lived for holiday cooking. Maggie cut a quick glance at Seth, who looked adorable in her old apron. Since he arrived, that's when.

Maggie slid the bowl of stuffing to her mother and started cutting potatoes as Seth peeled them. The more she got to know him, the more she knew how correct she was about him being husband material. Why hadn't he remarried? She cut him another sideways glance.

"Do I have something on my face? You keep sneaking peeks at me." He arched a brow.

"No." She ducked her head, pretending to concentrate on the task at hand.

"Are you inwardly laughing at me in this apron? Don't I look good in a floral print?"

A laugh escaped her. "You look a bit silly." And more alluring than a man had a right to be.

The knife slipped, cutting her finger. She hissed and grabbed for a nearby towel.

"Let me see." Seth stopped what he was doing and took her hand. He pressed the towel against the cut, then removed it, bending over her injury. "It's not too deep, but it does need to be bandaged. Where is the first aid kit?"

"Closet under the stairs."

"Sit right here." He helped her into a chair and moved swiftly from the kitchen, returning a few minutes later with Mama's first aid kit.

"We'll have to toss a couple of the potatoes." Maggie winced as he poured disinfectant over her cut.

"Don't worry about that. I can handle the potatoes." He blew on her finger to take away some of the sting.

What he did was take away her breath. She forgot all about the pain in her finger.

He raised his head, his face so close she felt his exhale. His gaze landed on her lips.

Gracious. Was he going to kiss her? Did she want him to? Her eyelids drifted closed.

"Is she all right?" Mama's question jerked them apart.

Thank goodness. A kiss would change the friendship she had with Seth. A friendship she cherished. "I'm fine, Mama. Really."

"You can set the table with our good china, and I'll take over in the kitchen. Obviously, working with Seth caused too much of a distraction." Mama moved to the counter, tossed the potato Maggie had been cutting into the garbage, and started chopping like a pro.

Seth put a hand on Maggie's shoulder. "There you go."

"Thank you." Without meeting his gaze, she moved to the dining room.

Once free from Mama's watchful eyes, she leaned against the wall to catch her breath. Seth would have kissed her if Mama hadn't entered the room. The disappointment flooding through Maggie confused her. She didn't want Seth to change her resolve of being a career woman. Life was good as it was, wasn't it?

"Miss Maggie?"

Maggie opened her eyes. "Good morning, Annie." The little girl stared with wide eyes and mussed hair. "Do you need help getting dressed?"

"Where's my daddy?"

"In the kitchen."

The girl darted past Maggie. "Why are you wearing an apron?" Maggie heard her say.

Seth answered in a deep rumble that Maggie couldn't make out. Seconds later, Annie reappeared. "Yes, I need help getting dressed."

Relieved to have something to occupy her mind before she set the table, Maggie followed Annie up the three flights of stairs to the attic. She sat on the edge of one of the cots, then leaped up when she realized she'd sat where Seth slept. She really needed to get ahold of herself.

Because one by one, the bricks erected around her heart were starting to tumble.

"Thank you for making the first Thanksgiving without my wife easier." Seth set a stack of dishes in the sink.

Mrs. Larson glanced up at him. "I'm glad to have helped.

How will you do at Christmas?"

"I'll buy Annie some gifts, attend the Christmas play at church, and read from the book of Luke. The same thing I did every year with my wife. I'd like to keep it as traditional as possible." He plunged his hands into the hot soapy water as Maggie brought in more dishes.

He smiled in her direction, marveling at the blush that rose to her cheeks. How would she have responded if he'd succeeded in kissing her?

Her lashes lowered, and she turned to head back to the dining room.

"Give her time," her mother said after Maggie was out of earshot. "Being left at the altar and hearing the news through a letter takes time to heal. My Marjorie will come around."

"How could anyone walk away from a woman like Maggie?"

"I never liked Daniel. He always seemed like a stuffed shirt to me." She dried the plate he'd washed. "But some things a person needs to find out for themselves no matter how much it hurts. You must have loved your wife very much."

"I did." Thinking of her sent a pang through his heart.

"You should remarry."

"So say a lot of people." He scrubbed at a pan.

"I remember when I lost my husband. I thought I'd never find joy again. This house, the guests, friends at church, and my charity work helped immensely. Maggie told me of your kindness toward the widows in town. You'll find your joy again. Now take off that silly apron and spend time with your daughter. I can finish up here."

"Thank you." Seth dried his hands and hung up the apron.

He found Annie curled up on the sofa while Maggie read a book to her. His daughter's head rested on Maggie's shoulder, her eyes on the page. Seth wished he could draw. He'd love an illustration of that moment.

Yes, Annie needed a mother. It was time. The problem was the only woman he could see himself marrying didn't want to wed. He settled himself into a chair opposite them and laid his head back to listen and rest.

Maggie smiled up at him, then returned to the book in her hand. Something about a hare and a tortoise, it sounded like to him. Whatever the story, Annie seemed enthralled.

"Where did you get the book?" he asked when Maggie finished.

"The library. I figured there would come a time when Annie would be still long enough for me to read to her. Do you?" She gently slid from under his sleeping daughter and placed Annie's head on a pillow before pulling a crocheted blanket over her.

"Read to her?" He shook his head. "There's never been any time. As it is now, I've got to head to the farm and take care of the cows. I made my deliveries before you or your mother woke."

"Early bird."

He shrugged. "I wanted to help with the holiday meal. Feel like taking a ride with me? I'm sure your mother won't mind watching Annie when she wakes." Which wouldn't be for at least an hour.

Conflicting emotions flickered across her face before she said yes. "I'll speak to Mama and change my clothes. I don't want to traipse through a barn in my best dress."

"Wonderful. I can show you my new kitchen. It's got all the modern amenities." Susan would have been pleased.

She nodded and left the room, returning a few minutes later with her mother.

"I've some mending and reading I want to do," Mrs. Larson

said. "I'll be happy to watch Annie. She can help me bake some cookies when she wakes. Take your time."

"We'll be home in time to eat some leftovers," Seth said. "Thank you." He placed his hand on the small of Maggie's back. Heat rose from the contact. He half expected her to step aside and enjoyed the fact that she didn't.

They rode through a bright clear day. The air held a winter chill despite a cloudless sky.

"Are you warm enough? I have an old blanket in the back. I haven't been able to replace the one that burned yet."

"I'm fine." Maggie had her hands tucked into the fur-lined sleeves of her coat. "Thank you for stepping in and helping Mama with the meal."

"It's a lot for one person."

"It is, but it's something she enjoys. Taking care of others. That's what makes the boardinghouse work so well."

"But it isn't something you want?"

She shook her head. "I don't think so."

"You don't want a home of your own someday?"

"Maybe, but there really is no point. I'd rattle around like a pebble in a tin can." She tilted her head. "Why all the questions?"

"Just passing the time." Plus, he wanted to know her better. "What are you most thankful for?"

"My job at Woolworth's." She laughed, the sound like the trickling of a creek. "That sounds strange after the craziness of being shorthanded, but I do enjoy my job. Oh, and thank you for finding help."

"How did you know I had anything to do with finding help?"

"The woman is from your church. Knowing how much you enjoy helping others. . .it wasn't hard to figure out."

"I can find just about anything I need at church or within the pages of the Bible."

"Don't start, Seth, please. It's a wonderful day."

It pained him that she thought talk of God and church could ruin a day. Maybe someday, if he was subtle, he'd succeed at breaking down the wall around her heart. *With a little help from above, that is.*

Chapter Seven

Maggie spent the next Sunday afternoon reading in the parlor. At least until Seth entered the house.

"You busy?" The corner of his mouth quirked. "I've got an adventure, if you're interested."

Closing her book, she arched a brow. "What kind of an adventure?" She had to admit, her curiosity was piqued. She hadn't seen hide nor hair of Seth since Thursday. Now, here he was, hat in hand, wanting to go on an adventure.

"The helping people kind." He tilted his head. "You coming?"

Since Mama was at church, Maggie was free. "Let me get my coat." She snagged it from the coat tree near the front door. "Which family are we helping, and what will I need to do?"

"Mrs. Mason is ill. I thought maybe you could take care of her five children while I do some repairs around the place. I'm surprised the house hasn't fallen down on their heads."

Maggie paused in donning her coat. "Give me five minutes to pack a box of food and see what medications we might have." With the mother ill, food might be scarce. She rushed to the pantry, glancing at the menu Mama had tacked to the door so she wouldn't take anything planned for the week's meals.

Seth followed her to the kitchen and a few moments later

lifted the heavy box from the counter. "You've a good heart, Maggie."

Maybe not as good as his, but a flush of warmth flooded her face as she jotted a quick note explaining to Mama where the food went. "Thank you. Where's Annie?"

"Spending a few hours with a friend from church." He led the way to the wagon. After setting the box in the bed, he helped Maggie to her seat. "I appreciate you coming. If I had to take care of the children, I wouldn't be able to get any work done. Not sure how much I'll get done before dinner as it is."

"I wasn't doing anything more than reading." Which she rarely found time for anymore. Still, it would do her good to help someone less fortunate.

The Mason home, quite a ways out of town and backed up to a thick woods, was one of the ones where they'd dropped off food and clothes a few weeks back. Had they received any help since then? Surely the children weren't left starving. What if they'd had little more other than the milk Seth dropped off each day?

Her heart ached as five little faces peered from a grimy window. "Why can't more be done for the widows and children of this town?"

"There's a group of us who do what we can." Seth hopped down, holding out his hand. "Careful. It's muddy from last night's rain."

That put it mildly. Her boot sank up to her ankle, making a squishing sound when she pulled her foot free. "We'll track it inside."

"I have a feeling it won't matter much."

It didn't matter. They entered a house with dirt floors. A thin blanket hung over a broken window doing little to keep out the cold. Five small children huddled on the single bed with their mother.

"I'll start a fire first thing," Seth said, setting the food box on the rustic table before heading for the woodstove in the corner. "Then chop as much wood as I can in an hour."

Maggie approached the bed. "Mrs. Mason? I'm here to get the children fed and cleaned. What can I do for you?"

"Water," she said in a raspy voice. "Well out back."

No water in the house? Maggie widened her eyes, searching for a bucket. The only one she found had been used as a chamber pot. That wouldn't do at all. She took the bucket outside and dumped it at the edge of the woods before rinsing it out with well water. Surely they had another bucket. One clean enough for drinking water.

She followed the sound of wood being chopped. "There's no clean bucket, Seth."

He frowned. "I've a couple in the bed of the wagon. They've had nothing but milk in them and are made of tin. Rinsed out, one of them should work perfectly. I also saw a tub hanging on the side of the house if you've time to bathe the children."

She'd make time. How could people live like this? She lugged the tub to the front porch, then went to fetch a pail from the wagon. She'd need to heat water for a bath, so she took all three buckets. She'd return the other two once she'd finished with them.

First, a drink for Mrs. Mason. The woman gave a weak smile. "Bless you."

Next Maggie handed each of the children a day-old biscuit and set a pot of stew Mama had set aside for their dinner that night on the stove. It would be nice and hot by the time the children were bathed.

By the time she'd carted and heated enough water to fill the tub, perspiration ran down her back and the hem of her dress was soaked and muddy. She'd never worked so hard in her life.

While Seth worked on the sagging front porch, the children were bathed and Mrs. Mason given a bowl of broth. Maggie set the children at the table, gave them each another biscuit, and ladled stew into bowls.

She fixed one for Seth, who declined to eat. She didn't blame him. There was enough stew left for another meal for the Masons. Mama would understand if their guests had to eat sandwiches that evening.

Now that the children were eating, Maggie turned her full attention on their mother. "What ails you?"

Mrs. Mason struggled to a sitting position. "Fever, aches, chills, and until the broth, I couldn't keep anything down. The little 'uns wiped my brow best they could, but this bed reeks something awful from my sweats."

"Do you have clean linens?" Maggie glanced around the one-room house.

"In the trunk under the bed."

Maggie helped the woman to a chair. "You sit right here while I get this taken care of." She'd need to wash the dirty bedding and hang it up before they left.

"I've got to pick up Annie. You ready?" Seth entered the house, wiping his brow with a handkerchief.

Maggie took his arm and led him outside. "I can't. You'll have to come for me in the morning. There's far too much undone. Neither Mrs. Mason nor the children can do the laundry."

"It's growing late."

She nodded. "I've work in the morning. Come as early as you can."

"I'll bring someone this evening to take over for you." His expression left no room for argument.

When Maggie entered the house again, her shoulders sagging

from weariness, Mrs. Mason said, "Bless you. You're a true gift from God."

Maggie didn't know about that. She'd simply come to help a family in need.

"I'll be more than happy to go," Mrs. Larson said. "The guests have been fed. You can pick me up in the morning when you deliver the milk. I'll leave a note so the guests will know they must fend for themselves at breakfast." She put more food in a box.

"The house is little more than a shack," Seth warned her as they headed for the wagon. "I doubt you'll be comfortable."

"Pshaw. I've slept sitting up before. I'll be fine."

After picking up Annie, Seth started the long drive out of town again. When they reached the Mason home, drying bedding flapped in the chilly breeze.

The glow of a candle flickered in the window. The aroma of baking bread beckoned them to enter. Maggie had been busy indeed.

"Stay in the wagon, Annie. I'll only be a minute." He hopped down and helped Mrs. Larson to the ground.

"Oh." Mrs. Larson paused in the doorway.

Seth glanced over her head. Maggie slept at the table, her head resting on folded arms. The five children, now clean, lay in the bed with their mother. The dirt floor had been swept, everything in sight wiped clean, the dishes done, and a pail of clean water sat on the counter. Two of his milk pails were stacked near the door.

"That girl of mine is something else." Mrs. Larson grinned up at him. "Why, there's hardly anything left for me to do except get the bread out of the oven before it burns." She bustled forward, tapping Maggie on the shoulder as she went by.

"What?" Maggie sat up, blinking. "Oh, you're back." Her gaze fell on Seth. "With Mama? What about the guests?"

"It's only until morning, dear. Seth will bring another woman from church when he comes to get me. We've got it all planned out. Go home. You've done enough."

Maggie groaned, arching her back as she stood. "Tomorrow will be a rough day for sure."

"Maybe a hot bath will help." Seth helped her into her coat. "I could draw one for you before heading home."

"I'll be fine, but thank you. Annie needs to get home. She's asleep in the wagon."

Seth glanced back to see his daughter curled up on the seat. "Guess you'll have to climb in back."

"Which sounds perfect. I can sleep on the way home." She smiled, then hugged her mother. "See you in the morning. I'll make oatmeal for the guests."

"No need. I've told them to fend for themselves. You sleep as long as you can." Mrs. Larson flitted around the small house like a hummingbird.

Maggie wasted no time falling asleep. Before they'd reached the road leading into Scranton, soft snores came from the wagon bed.

Seth smiled, remembering what he'd heard Mrs. Mason say about Maggie being a gift. Bringing her along with him might be the best way to guide her back to God. Actions spoke louder than words. Maggie's heart wasn't as hardened as she pretended. She'd gone above and beyond what anyone could have expected her to do that day.

The streets of the city were empty of pedestrians at that late hour. Seth stopped the wagon in front of the boardinghouse, jumped to the ground, and looped the reins over a hitching post.

He stared into Maggie's sleeping face. Beautiful, like a porcelain doll under the gas lamps. But not as lovely as when she was awake. Then her face was alight, her expressions, her smile, brightening any room she entered.

Softly, he shook her. What he wanted to do was carry her inside. He would have if not for his sleeping daughter. He couldn't leave her alone at night on a city street. "Maggie."

"Hmm."

"Wake up, sweetheart. You're home." The endearment slipped from his lips.

Her eyes opened, and she sat up, holding out her hand. "Seems as if I just lay down."

When she moved to the edge of the wagon bed, he lifted her down, his hands almost meeting around her slim waist. Why hadn't he noticed before how small she was?

Her eyes glittered in the light as she gazed up at him, her head barely reaching his chin. He so very much wanted to kiss her, he actually lowered his head.

"Daddy?"

Saved from making a public spectacle of himself by his daughter. Not that there were many people out and about at that time of the night, but who knew who might be watching from behind their curtains? And what kind of man would he be, kissing her in public?

"Let me walk Miss Maggie to her door, and I'll be right back to take you home." His day wasn't near over. He still had cows to milk.

He escorted Maggie to the door and pushed it open for her. "I'll bring your mother safely home."

Her teeth flashed. "I know you will. You're the most trustworthy man I've ever met. Good night." She stepped inside and closed the door.

"Good night," he whispered.

Chapter Eight

Although the night had been short and the day before the longest and most physical she'd ever lived, Maggie found her steps light as she headed for work. She'd declined Seth's offer to give her a ride when he'd brought Mama home. He'd almost kissed her yesterday! And he'd called her sweetheart.

What frightened her was that she knew he'd wanted to kiss her, and she hadn't been the one to step back. Despite her good feelings that morning, she could not risk being in close proximity with him for a while. She might lose all the good sense she had left.

"Good morning." She smiled and waved at her coworkers as she headed for the staff lounge.

"You're in a good mood," Lizzie said, returning Maggie's smile.

"It's a glorious morning." She hung up her coat and donned her apron, ready to start the workday. Nothing could dispel her good mood. Absolutely nothing.

She came to a sudden halt in the middle of the store. Mr. Woolworth widened his eyes as he passed but said nothing. What was Maggie thinking? She was acting very much like a young girl in love. That could not be. She wouldn't allow herself to feel that way again. Not ever!

"Working today, Miss Larson?" Her boss marched past. "The window display needs updating, and the chef is asking for you."

They must have gotten some new items in. Maggie forced her worries aside. She could dwell on them later. She strolled the store, gathering a few toys and household items that might generate interest should a window shopper spot them, and placed them strategically in the front window.

A tap on the glass caught her attention. She turned to see a smiling Seth watching from the other side.

She smiled and returned to work, her face heating despite her resolve not to get involved with any man. Convincing her heart might be a challenge though. Why couldn't she and Seth simply be friends without hearts and emotions getting involved?

She climbed from the window to the sound of someone clearing their throat. This time she found herself face-to-face with the blond beauty she'd seen at the farm with Seth. "Hello. Miss Bookman, correct?"

"You are correct." She did not return Maggie's smile.

"How may I help you?" Maggie folded her hands in front of her.

"I've heard from many witnesses that you've been spending a lot of time with Seth Jamison."

"Yes, we helped the Mason family yesterday." Maggie frowned.

"I'm here to tell you to stay away from him. I've set my sights on him." She leaned closer. "And I always get what I want."

"I have no claim on Mr. Jamison." Maggie squared her shoulders, ready to do battle if the woman became more unreasonable. "We simply help the less fortunate together. Perhaps, if you showed an interest in charity, Seth would invite you along." She had no idea where the woman stood in regard to the needy, but from the flashing of her eyes, Maggie could safely deduce she'd struck a nerve.

"Do not toy with me, little mouse."

"Would that make you the cat?" Seeing Mr. Johnson staring in their direction, Maggie made sure to keep a pleasant smile on her face. "Again, I must stress that you are mistaken. Seth and I are simply friends. Now, please excuse me. I do have a job to do." Her skirts flared as she whirled and marched to the kitchen.

The nerve of the woman. Maggie banged a pan into the sink and filled it with water. Today's special was potato soup. Peeling, cutting, and boiling so the chef could work his magic would take time.

Potato peelings flew as she worked. How dare that woman ruin Maggie's day. Of course, some of the shine had come off when Maggie realized how very much she had wanted Seth to kiss her, but the woman's high-handedness simply made her angry.

"You'll cut off a finger if you aren't careful," Chef Winters said. "What's got your apron twisted?"

"Foolish people."

"That'll do it every time." He placed a calming hand over hers. "Take a deep breath, shake it off, and resume without bloodshed, please."

"Thank you." She resumed peeling and chopping at a more reasonable pace.

She glanced at the clock to see how much time she had before the lunch crowd would arrive. Today wasn't Friday, so she wouldn't have to pretend everything was fine while Seth sat across the counter from her.

The rest of the day passed without incident. Maggie stopped at the dry goods store down the street to pick up some woven fabric for Mama, then the general store for basics like flour and sugar. Laden down with packages, she headed home with heavier steps than when she'd left. Drat that woman.

She entered through the kitchen door and set the purchased items on the counter with a thud. "I've had the most exasperating day."

"Oh?" Mama glanced up from removing biscuits from the oven. "Want to talk about it?"

"If you promise what I tell you doesn't leave this room."

"I would never betray your trust by repeating things." Mama's brow furrowed. "Sit. I made cookies today. Tell me what has you so upset."

"You know Mrs. Bookman's daughter?"

"Deborah? I've seen her but never had the pleasure of meeting her."

"It's no pleasure, I assure you." Maggie sat at the small kitchen table. "She came into the Five and Dime this morning."

"To shop?"

"To warn me away from Seth. Said she'd set her sights on him and always got what she wanted."

"What makes her think you and Seth are a couple?" Mama set a plate of cookies on the table.

"The amount of time we spend together, I suppose. All we're doing is helping the community, Mama. Not forging a relationship." She wisely kept silent about the near kiss.

"If it isn't true, why does it bother you so much?" She handed Maggie a cup of hot coffee.

"I don't know," Maggie said softly.

"Perhaps you have feelings for Seth and don't want to admit to them." Mama sat across from her.

"No. I've told you I do not plan on marrying. Ever."

"Then one woman's comments shouldn't upset you so."

True. Maggie's shoulders slumped. She'd failed to keep her

heart safe. All it took was a handsome man with a heart of gold to break down her defenses.

She pushed to her feet and turned.

Seth, a shocked look on his face, stood on the other side of the kitchen door. Without a word, he stomped away.

He hadn't meant to eavesdrop. Hearing voices, he'd merely paused to make sure he wasn't interrupting something important. Hearing Deborah's name, then the conversation that followed made his blood boil.

"Seth? Wait, please."

His steps faltered. He glanced over his shoulder.

"Did you need something?" A crease appeared between Maggie's eyes.

So, she wanted to act as if the conversation hadn't occurred. Very well. He would follow her lead and not wonder, as her mother did, why Deborah's words bothered her so much. Dare he hope Maggie had feelings for him?

"You left your shawl in the wagon last night." He held it out to her.

"Thank you. Seth. . ."

He shook his head to stop her. "Miss Bookman will not bother you again."

"It's not my place to come between you and a potential courtship."

"Courtship?" He gritted his teeth hard enough to make his jaw ache. "You think I would choose a woman like her? Someone shallow and self-absorbed? What kind of man do you take me for?"

"I. . ." Her mouth opened and closed. "I'm sorry. I meant no harm."

"You did nothing wrong." He exhaled heavily. "I shouldn't have stood there without making my presence known. See you on Friday, Maggie."

He'd gone to her home not only to return her scarf but to ask her to help him with the backdrop for the upcoming Christmas play. He needed help and couldn't think of anyone he'd enjoy working with more. Instead, he didn't ask and returned to his wagon.

Next stop, the Bookmans'. Deborah had no right saying anything to Maggie. Seth had never spent time alone with the woman except that one time in the milking barn, and Annie hadn't been very far away.

He knocked on the door and stepped back as Mrs. Bookman answered. "Annie is ready. Get your coat, sweetie."

"I'd like a moment in private with Deborah, please."

Her eyes widened. Curiosity shone in her eyes. Was that a spark of hope he saw? Surely not. "You may step into the parlor. I'll let her know you're here."

He gave Annie a quick hug on his way to the overly decorated parlor and stood in front of the roaring fireplace.

"You wanted to speak with me?"

He turned to see Deborah, lovely in a gold-colored gown, standing with a demur expression. "Yes. You might want to sit. This is not a pleasure call."

"Oh." Her features hardened. "I'll stand, thank you."

"I have recently discovered that you have made claims on my person and warned Maggie Larson to stay away. You have no such claims, Miss Bookman. None at all."

She narrowed her eyes. "So, the little ninny ran tattling to you."

"No, she did not." He crossed his arms. "My business is my business. You had no right accosting my friend in that way. Stay away from her and from me."

"I'll tell people you made untoward advances, then cast me aside like an unwanted toy."

"Go ahead. No one will believe you. I have a good reputation in this town." He marched from the room. "My apologies, Mrs. Bookman, but circumstances have risen that cause me to seek out someone else to watch Annie." He took his daughter's hand and headed for the door.

"But. . .Deborah?"

"Let him go, Mother. I'm not cut out to be a milkman's wife anyway."

Some of the tension left his shoulders. The woman had seen reason and wouldn't cause him or Maggie any more trouble.

"Who will watch me now?" Annie asked.

"Perhaps Mrs. Larson until we find someone else." It wouldn't hurt to ask, although he wasn't thrilled to return to the boarding house so soon after hearing Maggie and her mother's conversation.

Thankfully, Maggie was nowhere in sight when he knocked on the kitchen door of the boardinghouse. "Mrs. Larson?"

She turned from the sink. "Come in."

"Thank you. I've a favor to ask." He took a deep breath. "I need someone to watch Annie until a more permanent person can be found."

"Is this because of what you overheard?" She tilted her head.

He nodded.

"Of course I'll watch her for as long as you need. She likes to help me cook. I've got a young woman coming in to help me clean the boarders' rooms. Annie and I will get along fine. I'm pleased that Deborah Bookman doesn't catch your eye." She lowered her voice. "Don't give up on Maggie."

He blinked, surprise flooding through him. "She has no desire to marry."

"So she says." Her mother winked. "See you in the morning. Now go before Maggie comes downstairs."

Feeling very much as if Mrs. Larson and he shared a secret, he rushed Annie back to the wagon and set off for home. Maggie's mother seemed to think her daughter could be saved from life as a single woman at least. Could she also find her way back to God? If not, Seth couldn't dream of asking for her hand in marriage.

In fact, he should probably stop spending as much time with her as he had been. He sighed. His brain made sense, but his heart said otherwise. During Friday's lunch, he'd ask for her help with the play. Let his brain try to convince him otherwise. Seth would follow his heart and God's leading.

And his heart chose to believe Maggie's mother.

Chapter Nine

As the days passed, the Christmas spirit in Scranton increased. The Five and Dime had been fully decked out for the holidays. Even the street boasted colorful decorations. Maggie had decided not to dwell on Deborah's nastiness from a few days ago and entered the store to start work.

Life had returned to normal after helping the Mason family, although Maggie felt certain Seth still dropped by there regularly. It would be one of the town's widows that eventually got him to the altar, she knew. His heart was too kind not to marry one of them.

The thought pricked her heart. She shoved the emotion aside. Why should she be upset? She planned on sticking to her vow not to marry.

She spent the morning chopping vegetables for the day's lunch special. A thick beef stew that ought to warm the cold shoppers and those enjoying their lunch break. The monotony of cutting eased any worries, and she thanked God. . . Hold on. Thank God for her job? He hadn't helped her get hired. She'd done so on her own.

"You're taking out your frustration on the vegetables again." The chef patted her on the shoulder. "I need you and all your appendages."

Laughing, Maggie slowed her actions. "I do need to keep my mind free of the things that bother me when I'm holding a knife."

"I'd hate to see you with that knife and the person who has you riled." He laughed with her.

It wasn't a certain person that had her irritated. Other than herself, that was. When would she be able to control her emotions?

Maggie poured the first cup of coffee a few hours later to a man from the bank. While she explained the day's special, she spotted Seth holding the store door open. A smiling, clean Mrs. Mason and her five children, along with Annie, trooped inside. Seconds later, they occupied half the lunch counter.

Maggie's hand shook. So, she was right. A widow had stolen Seth's heart. "Excuse me." She set the pot down and raced for the staff restroom.

Leaning heavily on the sink, she fought to control the tears blurring her vision, the boulder stuck in her throat. Why had she let him weaken her resolve with kindness and near kisses?

She splashed her face with cold water and hurried past her frowning boss back to the lunch counter, where she pasted on a smile and carried the coffeepot to where Seth sat. "Hello. I didn't expect such a crowd."

"This is a special treat for sure," Mrs. Mason said. "A celebration after my recovery from influenza. Thankfully, none of the children caught it, and you seem right as rain."

"I feel fine, thank you." She cut a quick glance at Seth. "Today's special is beef stew."

"Sounds wonderful. We'll have seven bowls of it." He motioned when she could stop pouring and reached for the cream.

The Mason children turned on their stools, wide-eyed at all the things in the store they most likely had never laid eyes on. Perhaps she could convince Mr. Woolworth to donate some penny whistles when the church made up the Christmas boxes.

"Mrs. Mason has kindly agreed to watch Annie a couple of days a week in order to give your mother a break." Seth lifted his cup. "I know your mother enjoys having my daughter, but she is also a very busy woman."

"This also puts funds in my pocket." Mrs. Mason motioned for her children to turn back around. "Mr. Jamison laid a fine wood plank floor for me last Sunday afternoon. The house is shaping up just fine."

Of course Seth would find a way to help the woman and her children without making it seem too much like charity. "He is a good man." She cast him a soft look and left to place their order. Perhaps the lunch was as innocent as it seemed, after all.

"Maggie? Would you like to take a walk with me when you're off work?" Seth held out his cup to be topped off. "I've something I need, and you're the perfect person to help."

"Oh?" She tilted her head, refilling his cup. "Of course. I'll be waiting right inside the door at five." What could it be? Another family needing help? Advice about Annie?

She wondered what it could be for the rest of the day. Precisely at five p.m., coat buttoned against the winter chill, she stood right inside the door and waited. At five past, Seth's wagon pulled up out front, and he jumped from the driver's seat.

She stepped outside. "Where would you like to walk?"

"How about here?" He smiled. "I could do a little window shopping, maybe stop if I see something for Annie's Christmas."

Thankfully, she'd purchased Mama's gift already, the glass ornaments, but window shopping sounded like fun. She nodded, wondering exactly why he hadn't outright asked her for what he needed help with. He'd tell her in good time.

He crooked his arm in invitation. She hesitated for a moment before joining her arm with his. It was only a gentlemanly gesture, nothing more.

"The stores are pretty, aren't they?" Seth led her toward the Scranton Dry Goods.

"Yes. I love Christmas. The anticipation of gifts, the excitement in a child's eyes. . ."

"Celebrating the birth of Jesus."

She sighed. "Yes, that too." She might not be happy with God, but she did know the reason for Christmas. Besides, God's shoulders were large enough to carry her anger.

Seth paused in front of a clothing store, where a red wool coat that looked to be Annie's size hung in the front window. "Annie would love that."

"Then you must get it for her. A new Christmas coat. How fun." Maggie grinned, seeing something she'd like for herself, a blouse in a lovely shade of red. But she didn't need more clothes. She wore a black skirt and a white blouse sometimes six days a week. She sighed and followed Seth into the store.

She did purchase a new pair of stockings though while Seth had the store clerk take the coat out of the window. Thankfully, since it was the last one, it happened to be just a little big for Annie, but it was wearable and would serve her next winter too.

As they stepped back outside, Maggie turned to face him. "What do you need help with?" Her stomach rumbled, reminding her of the time.

"Let's discuss it over dinner. Annie is fine at the Masons'." He motioned his head toward the diner.

She seemed hesitant, something he'd noticed since he'd

arrived for their walk. Had he done something wrong?

"All right. Dinner sounds lovely. You sure are feeding the women of Scranton today."

He laughed. "Can't pass up an opportunity to brighten someone's day."

"Are you developing feelings for Mrs. Mason?"

Was she jealous? His heart leaped. "No more than as friends and the woman who watches Annie while I work. Mrs. Mason's oldest and Annie will both start school next year and are developing a friendship."

He opened the door to the diner for her and held up two fingers for the hostess, who then led them to a small table. Seth helped Maggie out of her coat, then pulled the chair out for her.

Once they'd looked over the menu, Maggie ordered a meat loaf plate and he ordered pork. He folded his hands on the table and gazed into her face. "Annie is playing the part of Mary in the Christmas play at church. I've volunteered to do the backdrop. After seeing how well you decorated the window at Woolworth's, I'm hoping you could lend me a hand for a couple of hours each evening."

"There's only a couple of weeks until Christmas." She straightened in her chair.

"That's why it would be something we'd work on every evening after you get off work. But not Sundays. I do need some time to rest."

"But. . .your farm."

"I'll manage." He smiled, touched at her concern. "Will you help?"

"I do believe you'll resort to almost anything to get me to grace the doors of church." She laughed.

"Perhaps." He returned her smile. "Please?"

"As long as the hours don't interfere with my ability to work the next day, I'll help you. Beginning when?"

"Tomorrow?"

"Tomorrow."

Seth had accomplished two things in that moment. The opportunity to spend a lot of time with the woman he grew to like more every day, and she'd be in church. Maybe not sitting in the pew listening to a sermon, but she'd still be within its four walls. God could work with that.

"The play will take you away from helping the widows of Scranton."

"I'll manage that too."

"You aren't invincible, Seth. Even you have your limits. You can't work yourself into the ground. You have a daughter to raise. Perhaps it's time you married again."

He arched a brow. "Are you offering?"

"Heavens, no." She paled. "You know my stand on marriage."

Unfortunately. "I'll marry again when the time is right. I promised Susan that."

The waitress brought their food, and they ate for a few moments in silence before Maggie spoke again. "That was kind of your wife. Even dying, she thought of you and her daughter."

"Susan was a good woman. A bit like you, in fact. Hardworking, kind, ready to lend a helping hand."

"But a faithful church attendee, I'd wager."

"Absolutely."

"Hmm." She took a sip from her water glass. "That's why she was perfect for you. I hope you find another woman like your Susan."

He already had. What he needed to do was convince her of that. When they'd finished eating, he dropped Maggie off with the promise of meeting her tomorrow at five, then drove to pick up Annie.

She sat at the Masons' table, a bowl of milk and bread in front of her. Not the meal he'd have chosen, but he'd brought his leftovers from the diner. Annie would be all right. "Ready, sweetheart?"

She jumped up. "Yes, Daddy. Can I milk a cow today?"

"When you're six. What brought that up?"

"Mrs. Mason showed us a book with a little girl named Heidi."

He shrugged. Knowing his daughter, there could or could not be a girl milking a cow in the story. She had a tendency to insert plotlines not in the original stories. "Thank you." He gave Mrs. Mason a nod. "She'll be with Mrs. Larson tomorrow, then back with you."

Since the Masons lived so far out of town, his days would be a little shorter having Annie with Maggie's mother. He lifted his daughter and carried her to the wagon. "You're almost too big to be carried."

"No I'm not, Daddy."

He laughed. She was right. She would never be too big for him to carry if she needed it. "I've some food for you if you're hungry." He handed her the bag from the diner. "Still a little warm."

"You ate in town?" She narrowed her eyes.

"I took Miss Maggie to dinner to ask her to help me with the backdrop to your play."

She nodded, obviously having decided his reason met with her approval. "I like her."

"I do too." He flicked the reins and headed for home.

Soon, Susan. Soon, I'll have fulfilled the last words you said to me. God was working on Maggie's heart. Seth saw how she felt about him in her eyes. Once they got past the big obstacle of her running away from God, all would be good. She'd see that her fiancé leaving her at the altar had all been part of God's grand plan for her life.

A plan that, unless Seth was wrong, included him.

Chapter Ten

As had become the routine, Maggie waited for Seth to arrive at precisely five minutes past five. Christmas was next week, and they still had a lot of painting to do on the background. No hanging sheets for Seth. He wanted painted wood.

It didn't come as a surprise to know Seth wanted everything as good as it could be. It was one of the traits she most admired in him.

The wagon pulled up exactly on time, and Maggie rushed out to meet him. "Good afternoon."

He smiled and helped her into the wagon. "Feel like painting about a hundred stars on the backdrop? If there's still time, I'd like some paper cutouts too."

"And what will you be doing, sir, while I'm cutting away?"

"Sawing animals."

"Out of wood, I hope." She laughed, with Seth joining in as they drove to the church.

She'd been there so often over the last few days, the building no longer bothered her. So far she hadn't had to step foot in the sanctuary. The last time she had, she'd felt judgment laid across her shoulders. She'd turned to see the pastor's wife scowling at her. That had been the last time.

She stiffened. She'd promised to attend the play. It would be in the sanctuary. Everyone would stare at the jilted woman who had turned her back on God. But she couldn't not go. Annie would be devastated.

"You've grown quiet." Seth cut her a quick glance.

"Busy day."

"Then we'll make it a short night."

Doing so would cause more work another night. "We'll do what needs done tonight. I'll be fine. I brought sandwiches from the kitchen. I hope that's fine with you."

"Most definitely. How much do I owe you?"

"Absolutely nothing, Seth Jamison. Let me pay for once, please. Don't take away my joy. I do so little as it is."

His brow furrowed. "Little? Have you forgotten all these late nights? The day spent with the Masons? The many boxes you fill for the needy? Give yourself some credit, darlin'." He patted her arm, sending her senses tingling.

Controlling her growing feelings for him was a lot easier when he didn't touch her, even when the contact was done so innocently. When he called her by an endearment, well, her heart leaped. Not good at all. "But I wait to be asked. You go looking for ways to help."

His laugh startled a bird from a roof. "Someday, you'll see your worth."

She waited for him to spout a Bible verse or tell her how she was a child of God. When neither of those came, she wondered if he'd given up on saving her soul. Sadness washed over her. Even though the times he tried to convince her that God waited with open arms rankled, she'd at least known he cared. She sighed as they pulled up to the back of the church.

"Let's get in where it's warm to eat our sandwiches." Seth

leaped down and came to her side, holding out his hand.

She put her gloved one in his, feeling his warmth through the wool. "There's no one else here." She motioned to the empty lawn.

"Afraid of being alone with me?" His eyes twinkled.

Yes. "People will talk."

"The pastor and his wife are in the parsonage. I'm positive one of them will come right over when they see the wagon."

Maggie wasn't worried at all about seeming improper. Anyone who knew Seth wouldn't bat an eye. It was herself she didn't trust. But under the shrewd gaze of Pastor Samson's wife, Maggie couldn't dwell on the fact she was falling hard for Seth. Mama would never let her hear the end of it if she were to find out that Maggie's resolve never to marry was wavering.

"There she is." Seth's voice pulled her from her thoughts.

They hadn't gotten inside before Mrs. Samson bustled their way, her bag of knitting slung over her shoulder. "Good evening. More work on the play?"

"Yes, ma'am." Seth smiled. "I guess the children have already gone home?"

"Except for Annie. She's with my husband, having milk and cookies. I'll send her over when she's finished. Her friend didn't show for practice tonight, although we did receive a note the child wasn't feeling well."

"How did Annie get here?"

"Mrs. Larson dropped her off."

"I do hope it isn't the influenza going around." Maggie stepped gratefully into the warm fellowship hall.

"I fear it very well may be. We'll have to pray it doesn't ruin the holiday festivities." She sat in a chair in the corner and started knitting.

Unwrapping her ham and cheese sandwich, Maggie headed for the backdrop. She'd drawn and painted the city of Bethlehem. The dark navy sky called for a myriad of stars. Off to the side sat the simple stable, complete with a manger, that Seth had built during his free time. She didn't think he ever had a spare moment just to sit. Maggie took every opportunity, no matter how few, simply to be still and read. She glanced his way.

"What?" Seth asked, his voice low. "Do I have something on my face?"

"Do you ever relax?"

"I'm relaxing right now. It's also relaxing to milk the cows, drive the wagon, and see smiles on people's faces when I deliver their milk."

She stared at him in disbelief. "You're too perfect, Seth Jamison. There must be something wrong with you. Tell me what it is."

His laugh attracted the attention of Mrs. Samson. "Here, start painting." He thrust a paintbrush into her hand.

"That's it. You're bossy."

"You really want to know?"

She nodded, opening a can of white paint. Why did she feel as if whatever he told her shouldn't be said?

"I'm sometimes so angry that God took my Susan that it takes everything in me to get out of bed in the morning."

She jerked to face him, tears welling in her eyes. "I'm sorry."

"It's the truth." He shrugged. "Helping others, staying busy, keeps me from dwelling on what can't be changed." Getting through the day had gotten a lot easier when he'd met Maggie. Now he had more to live for than just Annie, although his little girl had kept him going through the darkest days of his life. Her and his faith. "Please don't cry on my account. I'm doing well. I'm enjoying life again."

"Mourning the loss of your wife isn't a bad thing, Seth. It proves my point that you are perfect." Tears shone from the tips of her lashes.

He laughed again, turning as Annie barged into the room. "Give your daddy a hug. I've missed you."

She wrapped her arms around his neck and squeezed. "Hello, Miss Maggie." She narrowed her eyes. "Why are you sad?"

"Your father said something sad." She ducked her head and dipped her paintbrush into the paint.

"That's not nice, Daddy." Annie pursed her lips.

He chuckled. "I bet Mrs. Samson has some paper you can draw on until we're finished here."

When she darted away, he turned his attention back to Maggie. "See? From my daughter's mouth, I'm not nice."

Maggie's shoulders shook and a laugh escaped. "Oh yes, you're a bad one."

"I'm far from perfect," he said softly. "I overcommit myself on a regular basis." He exhaled long and slow, wondering why he felt compelled to dispel her notion that he was what she thought he was.

Her paintbrush paused over the painted night sky.

"I'm resentful of that sometimes," he said.

"Yet you press forward."

"Yes. Because I said I would."

"Let your yes be yes?"

He arched a brow.

"I never said I didn't read the Bible." She painted a five-pointed star. "Mrs. Samson watches me as if I'll sprout horns and corrupt you though."

"Shhh." He grinned. "Like you, she thinks I'm wonderful, raising my daughter alone. I don't really though. I get plenty of help."

"Now who's not giving himself credit?" She returned his smile and painted another star.

Christmas was approaching with the speed of a freight train. Once the play was over, how could Seth spend time with Maggie? Should he? She didn't seem any closer to reconciling with God than the first day they'd met. Maybe, after the holidays, he should stop seeing her other than the lunch on Fridays.

The thought was like a cold fist squeezing his heart. He liked her being a part of his world. Annie looked up to her. Why couldn't the first woman he cared for since Susan share his faith?

He carried large pieces of wood from the warmth of the fellowship hall to the chill of a winter's eve. Several feet from the building, he'd set up his saw. For the next hour, he cut out a few sheep, a donkey, and a camel. A few more nights of painting, and the backdrop would be ready for the Christmas play.

The play would be over, Christmas would come and go, and Seth had a hard decision to make. None of his efforts with Maggie had worked. While she seemed content to be his friend, for which he was grateful, she hadn't given him any reason to think she wanted more from their relationship. And over it all hung the fact he couldn't be unevenly yoked. That would bring more heartache in the end. Not just for him but for his daughter too.

He carried the wooden animals inside. "Ready, ladies?" Annie looked ready to fall asleep at the table. Not much longer before she'd be home at a normal hour.

"Yes." Maggie wiped her hands on a towel. "I've done the last star but didn't get to the paper ones."

"Those aren't important. If there's time, there's time. If not..."

She tilted her head. "You all right? That doesn't sound like you."

"Trying to get my priorities straight."

"Why do I think you aren't talking about the play preparations?" she asked as he helped her into her coat.

He glanced over to see Mrs. Samson watching them with interest. The woman didn't try to hide the fact that she eavesdropped. Let her. He'd be saying nothing improper or anything to fuel gossip around the quilting bee.

"Let's just say I'll be relieved when all this busyness is behind us." He helped Annie put on her coat, then lifted his sleepy child into his arms. "My daughter needs more stability in her life than I'm giving her right now." He opened the door to let Maggie exit first.

"The holidays are busy for everyone." She glanced back. "Want to tell me what's really bothering you?"

"No." How could he tell her his heart, a heart he didn't ever think would heal after Susan's death, was breaking all over again? "I'm tired. That's all." He laid a sleeping Annie in the bed of the wagon.

"Liar. I hope you know I'm always here if you need to talk." She put her hand in his and climbed onto the wagon seat.

"Look at her. I'm keeping her out too long. She should have eaten a hot meal and already been in bed."

"She ate a hot meal with the Samsons, and she's right where she wants to be. With you." She reached back and covered Annie with the old blanket he kept behind the seat. "Things will be different when she starts school."

"You're right. I'm sorry." He forced a smile. "See? Not perfect."

"Worrying about your daughter is pretty good to me." Her teeth flashed in the moonlight. "That isn't all that's on your mind, but I'll not press the matter."

"Thank you." He climbed into his seat and flicked the reins.

Her house was dark but for a small light in the parlor. He hated her going in alone but couldn't leave Annie. "I'll sit right here until I know you're safely inside."

"Mama left the light on. I'll be fine." She jumped down before he could help her. "See you tomorrow. If you're concerned about Annie, then leave her here with Mama tomorrow and spend tomorrow night in the attic room. Annie can get to bed on time, and you won't have to worry."

Another night under the same roof as Maggie? He'd have to think long and hard on whether he could handle that. He didn't think so. He waited until the door shut behind her. "Good night, Maggie," he whispered.

Chapter Eleven

Maggie moved slowly down the stairs. No delectable aromas came from the kitchen. No lamps burned in the dining room or parlor.

She entered the dark kitchen. No fire burned in the stove. "Mama?"

Fear coursing through her, Maggie thundered up the stairs and barged into her mother's room without knocking. Her mother lay under a pile of quilts, groaning.

"What's wrong?" Maggie moved to the side of the bed. "Are you ill?" She placed the back of her hand against her mother's forehead. Her skin burned to the touch. "What can I do?"

"Water. Fever."

Maggie had made it halfway down the stairs when the front door banged open and Seth rushed inside, Annie in his arms. "Help me."

"Is she ill?" Maggie raced down the rest of the stairs.

"She's burning up with fever. I'm not a nurse. All I know how to doctor is cows."

"Mama is ill too. Bring Annie upstairs. When you deliver the milk, please let the Five and Dime know I won't be in today. Also, send the doctor as fast as you can." She barked orders as she climbed the stairs again. She might sound in control, but her heart beat in her throat like a runaway team of horses. "There's a foldable cot in the closet. Lay Annie at the foot of Mama's bed and fetch the cot, please. Oh, and bring blankets and a pillow." It would be best if the two were in the same room. Running back and forth would be as tiring as the day she'd cared for Mrs. Mason.

Seth gently laid Annie at the foot of Mama's bed and hurried to do Maggie's bidding. Annie was dressed in a flannel nightgown a size too small.

"Come on, sweetie. Let me change you out of that sweat-soaked gown and into one of Mama's old blouses." At least until she could wash the girl's nightclothes.

Seth set down the cot with a clatter. "What now?"

"Change your daughter while I make the bed, then fetch the doctor. Your milk deliveries can wait."

He took the faded blouse Maggie held out to him. When he'd changed Annie and moved her to the cot, he said, "I'll be back as soon as my deliveries are done. We'll take shifts watching them."

"That would be a big help, Seth, thank you."

His gaze settled on her face as if he wanted to say something more. Instead, he gave a nod and darted from the room.

What Maggie needed now was a plan. She glanced at her work clothes. A change into something more serviceable. She first went to the kitchen, lit the fire, and put a kettle of water on to boil. Tea with a healing dose of honey would help. At least that's what Mama used to do when Maggie was ill as a child.

While the water boiled, she quickly donned her oldest dress, then returned to the kitchen to fix three cups of tea. She'd need the nourishment herself. Grabbing a day-old biscuit from the pantry, she added it to the tray and headed back upstairs.

"Miss?" One of the guests exited his room. "Something amiss?"

"Mama is ill. I'm sorry, but there's no breakfast this morning."

"That's all right. I'll get something from the diner. Can I get you anything?"

"I. . .don't think so." In fact, she had no idea what Mama might need from town.

She'd barely made it to the top of the stairs when a knock sounded on the front door. "Would you please answer that for me on your way out?"

"Most definitely." The man opened the door and let in the doctor.

"That was fast, Dr. Ward. Please, up here." Leaving him to follow, she set the tray on Mama's bedside table.

The doctor glanced at Annie, then at Mama. "Which should I check on first?"

"Mama seems the hottest." Maggie thrust her hands into the pockets of her skirt. Could it be influenza? God, don't take my mother. "She can barely talk."

He set his bag on the bed and pulled out a stethoscope. "Mrs. Larson, I'm going to listen to your chest and take your temperature, all right?"

After a tense half hour of asking questions and checking vitals, the doctor announced both of them had influenza. "Bad cases too. How long have they been ill?"

"The house was dark when I came home last night, but Mama never mentioned anything about not feeling well earlier. Annie seemed fine, maybe a little tired." *God, please. Why?*

"They'll need their fevers brought down. This medicine should help. Keep them warm and give them plenty of fluids. As much as they can manage. Lots of folks are ill right now, but these two seem strong. Call me if they get worse." He put a hand on Maggie's shoulder. "Chin up. You've a rough few days ahead of you."

"Thank you." Her voice barely rose above a whisper. Fear closed her throat. Papa had died of influenza. God couldn't do this to her again, could He?

Once the doctor left, Maggie fell into the chair opposite Mama's bed. She could do this. She'd helped Mrs. Mason, taken care of her children. This was only one woman and one child.

She covered her face with her hands. What if she couldn't? Most likely Mama had helped Mrs. Mason get better. Fluids! She pushed to her feet and propped pillows behind her mother's back.

"Try to drink this, Mama. Please." Maggie poured in some of the medicine the doctor had left. "All of it if you can. Doctor's orders." She did her best to keep her voice calm when what she wanted to do was scream.

Mama coughed and reached for the cup. "I have it. Go to Annie. I promise to drink it all."

Maggie did the same with Annie, moving back and forth between the two of them until they both slept again. Exhausted already, she headed to the kitchen to make soup.

After his deliveries, Seth entered a quiet house. His heart stopped when he spotted Maggie, head bowed, leaning against the kitchen sink. "What happened?"

She turned, face pale, eyes rimmed with red. "Influenza."

He took a deep breath and nodded. "They'll be okay. It isn't a death sentence."

"It was for my father."

"We'll pray." He reached for her, only to have her shrink back.

"The church prayed for my father. The church prayed for my wedding. It didn't work in either case." She lifted a lid from the pot on the stove. "I'm making soup. Why don't you go check on them? There's medicine on Mama's nightstand. She gets a teaspoon, Annie only half."

"Maggie..."

"I don't want to hear it." She turned away from him.

With a sigh, he headed upstairs and cared for their patients. When they'd had their medicine and their feverish foreheads dabbed with a cool rag, he sat in the armchair and bowed his head. Prayer and willing hands were the only things he had to fight the illness. Well, the stuff in the brown bottle might help, but God was the Great Physician, after all. He prayed for a quick recovery for his daughter and Maggie's mother, for others in Scranton suffering from the same illness, and for Maggie to turn to God to help carry her burden.

By the time Maggie entered with bowls of soup, his spirit had calmed. He got up and took the tray from her. "This smells delicious."

She gave a thin smile and took one of the bowls. Sitting on the edge of the bed, she helped her mother eat.

"What's wrong?" Mrs. Larson asked.

"I'm afraid." Maggie's voice broke. "You have what Papa had."

"Doesn't mean it will claim my life."

Seth's hand stilled, hoping, praying Maggie's mother could get through to her. He'd failed miserably.

A knock from downstairs lured him from the room. He opened the door to see the pastor and his wife standing there.

"We heard Mrs. Larson and your little girl have taken ill. I've brought a casserole." Mrs. Samson held out a dish. "What else can we do?"

"This is very much appreciated. Come in." He stepped aside.

"No, we'll keep our distance, thank you." The pastor smiled. "We'd like you to know the church will be praying."

"That means a lot to me. Thank you." Seth closed the door.

Maggie, expressionless, stood at the top of the stairs. She glanced at the dish in his hand, then turned and went back into her mother's room.

Shaking his head, shoulders slumped, Seth put the dish on the counter to be reheated later for supper. There should be enough to feed the guests. Another knock had him returning to the door, where a neighbor woman also brought food.

"We know the guests rely on being fed and brought a meal large enough. It's a breakfast dish."

"I've got something for tomorrow evening." Another woman bustled down the sidewalk toward the house.

Grinning, Seth stepped back and ushered them inside and into the kitchen. Catching sight of Maggie once again watching from the top of the stairs, his grin widened. Let the good deeds of caring neighbors do what he couldn't. Let them show her God's love.

By the time the ladies left, with promises to keep them fed for the week, Seth's heart overflowed. These women from his church, Mrs. Larson's friends, had made the next few days so much easier.

He climbed the stairs. "I've got to milk the cows. Will you be all right?"

"They're sleeping. I'll close my eyes for a bit too." She waved him away.

"Aren't the women of this town wonderful?"

"Very kind." She laid her head against the back of the chair and closed her eyes.

Dismissed, Seth checked on Annie, kissed her hot forehead, and rushed to do his chores so he could take over watching her and Mrs. Larson. One day in, and poor Maggie looked exhausted.

At the farm, he fed and milked the cows, storing the milk in the back of his wagon, where it would stay cold throughout the winter night. As he drove back to the boardinghouse, he thanked God for the kindness of neighbors and prayed again for a quick recovery for Annie and Mrs. Larson.

Once back at the house, he relieved Maggie, who went to the kitchen to warm up a casserole. The houseguests trickled past the bedroom, sending their well-wishes as they headed to their own rooms.

When dinner was ready, Maggie rang a bell. Seth remained where he was. If he stayed, then she would take the opportunity to eat, something he doubted she'd done all day.

An hour later, she returned and handed him a plate. "How are they?"

"Resting. No change otherwise." He dug into the meal, which tasted a lot like venison. "I think they'll feel better by morning. We caught the illness early."

She narrowed her eyes, fear etched on her lovely face. "How can you be so calm?"

"Someone much stronger than me has our loved ones in His hands."

"That didn't save your wife." Her eyes widened, and she clamped a hand over her mouth. "I'm so sorry. What a horrible thing for me to say."

Seth stared at the plate in his hand for a moment. "I don't know why Susan was called home. That wasn't my decision, but I've come to terms that it was her time."

"She suffered."

"Yes, she did." He set his fork on his plate, appetite gone. "That's something I will ask God about when He calls me home. Until then, I have to trust that He knew what He was doing."

"What if he takes Annie?" Tears sprang to her eyes. "Or my mother?"

Seth set the plate on the bedside table and gathered Maggie into his arms. "Then I'll cry, I'll be angry, and I'll push on. That's what we do, darlin'. Push on with faith that what happened was for the best."

She raised her eyes to his. "How do I do that?"

"By talking to Him." He cupped her cheek. "I don't know what was in Susan's future, but God did. Maybe he took her home to spare her." At least that's what he told himself.

"I think I'll go to church with you on Sunday."

"Really?" He arched a brow.

"If Mama is feeling better." She returned to her mother's side. "I hope you're right, Seth."

He did too.

Chapter Twelve

Throughout the course of the week, Mama and Annie made steady improvement. Maggie's mind took her places she hadn't gone in a very long time. When Sunday rolled around, she donned her best dress and joined her mother downstairs, where she sat wrapped in a quilt in the parlor. Annie sat next to her listening as Mama read a book aloud.

"Where are you going?" Mama glanced up.

"Church." Maggie smiled, smoothing her hands nervously down her skirt. "Hopefully, I won't be struck by lightning when I enter the sanctuary."

Tears glimmered in her mother's eyes. "What prompted this, dear?"

"I made a deal with Seth. If you and Annie pulled through, I'd go talk to God." She glanced to where a couple of boxes sat under the window. "You're going to put up the Christmas tree?"

"It's way past time. We've only a week until Christmas. Seth says he'll bring us one before church. Annie and I will take our time decorating, I promise."

"I've something for you." Maggie rushed to her room, where her mother's present sat wrapped on top of her armoire. Returning to the parlor, she handed it to her. "You'll need this then."

"Oh?" She tore into the wrapping and removed the lid from the box. "They're beautiful."

"I bought them at the Five and Dime. I knew you'd love them."

"Daddy!" Annie tossed off her blanket and raced for the front door.

Seconds later, Seth dragged in a five-foot tree. "In the corner?"

"Yes, please." Mama motioned to the tree stand. "Now, you'd best hurry before Maggie changes her mind." She laughed.

"Mama." Maggie shook her head and reached for her coat. She knew her mother teased, but her nerves already rang like the church bells across town. She didn't need to be made more nervous.

Seth crooked his arm. "I'm going with the prettiest girl in Scranton."

Her face warmed. "Oh hush." But the way he looked at her made her feel as if his words were true.

Her steps faltered as she neared the church building.

Seth put a hand over her trembling one linked with his arm. "Relax. God doesn't bite."

"With me He might make an exception." She chuckled. "I haven't been very nice to Him lately."

"He's waiting for you." Seth opened the church doors.

Maggie squared her shoulders and entered, immediately surrounded by Mama's friends asking after her welfare and stressing how pleased they were to see Maggie. Her nerves settled, her spirit calmed, and her gaze rested on the simple wooden cross behind the pulpit.

A woman she didn't know sat at the organ. A man she hadn't met requested a hymn.

Maggie settled into a pew with Seth and opened her hymnal.

The normality of the service, something she remembered from before, soothed her. What was it about a group of believers congregating together?

"You all right?" Seth shared the hymnal with her.

"Yes." In fact, she'd never been better.

The irony of the pastor's sermon on the prodigal son wasn't lost on Maggie. In fact, it brought a smile to her face as she realized how right Seth had been all this time. She fixed her gaze on the cross again. She was home in the arms of her heavenly Father.

She wanted to let Seth know, shout it over the rooftops of Scranton, but she held back. It wouldn't hurt to savor the renewal of her faith for a while.

"Welcome back, Marjorie," Mrs. Samson said after church. "Will you and Seth be finishing the backdrop this week?"

"Yes, ma'am." She glanced up at Seth. "Care to join us for lunch?"

"Annie would shoot me if we didn't."

"See you at rehearsal." Seth smiled and led Maggie outside. "No lightning, no sour looks, only pleasure in seeing you again."

"You were right, I was wrong." She lifted her chin, trying not to smile at his teasing.

"Thank you for being honest." He laughed and helped her into the wagon. "Any idea what's for lunch?"

"Nope." She smiled, spreading the blanket over her legs. "I'm sure Mama thought of something. She really is doing quite well and hated missing church."

"I think both she and Annie will be fully recovered by next Sunday, Christmas." He moved to the driver's side. "I want Annie to rest as much as possible except for rehearsals."

Mama turned from the stove when they entered. A knowing gleam shone in her eyes after one look at Maggie's face.

"Is it that obvious?" she asked, giving her mother a hug.

"It is to me. I've made a stew of leftovers. Would you set the table for four, please?"

Maggie did as she was told, getting a glimpse of the decorated tree in the parlor. Candles were perched on branches, waiting for nightfall to be lit. The new ornaments glistened from the sunlight streaming through the windows. It all looked very festive, but Maggie had already received her gift. The gift of renewal.

The Friday before Christmas. The last day of rehearsal. Seth sat in the church pew and watched his baby girl cradle the doll portraying the baby Jesus.

Behind her, Maggie put the finishing touches on the wooden animals Seth had carved, something that had gotten pushed back when Annie and Mrs. Larson fell ill. Now, fully recovered, his daughter beamed as Mary.

Seth's gaze again landed on Maggie. He'd noticed the change in her after church the previous Sunday. Why hadn't she told him she'd reconciled with God? His heart had leaped when he'd seen the transformation on her face. All he needed now was to hear her say the words.

She smiled his way and moved from a sheep to the donkey. He still had some minor things to do, but Annie had asked him to watch her despite the fact he'd see the play the next night.

When they went into their second and final run-through, he got up. A pile of quilts sat on the front pew, waiting for him to hang them on the wire he'd strung the week before. They'd have a colorful curtain for one of the church's youth to open and close on cue.

"We can't thank you enough, Seth." Mrs. Samson handed

him a quilt. "If not for your and Marjorie's untiring help, this play would not be near as wonderful. Oh, the story can't be beat, that's for sure, but thanks to you two, it will look beautiful as well."

"Glad to help." He really was, but he also looked forward to things settling down. He felt as if he'd been galloping for months.

By the time he'd hung the quilts, Maggie had finished painting eyes on the donkey, Annie had milk and cookies supplied by Mrs. Samson, and he was ready to go. Maggie's mother had invited them over to exchange gifts since he planned on spending a quiet Christmas at home with Annie.

They parked in front of the boardinghouse to the sight of the tree lit with candles.

"So pretty." Annie pushed against him. "Hurry, Daddy. Presents."

He laughed, meeting Maggie's amused gaze. "Go on in. I'll take care of the horses. Give me five minutes."

His daughter scowled but raced into the house, squealing in delight. Most likely at the sight of wrapped gifts under the tree.

He glanced heavenward. "Thank You, God, for making this Christmas nice for Annie." He'd worried so much about how the first Christmas without Susan would affect his little girl. Worrying had done no good. God had handled things, as usual.

After securing the reins to the hitching post, he entered the warm house and shrugged out of his coat. Annie sat in front of the tree, two gifts on the floor next to her.

"Sit there, Seth." Mrs. Larson pointed to the sofa where Maggie sat. "Why don't we let Annie go first?"

"I think that's best, before she goes rabid." He sat and crossed his ankle over his knee.

"Daddy!"

"Just joking, sweetheart." His arm brushed Maggie's shoulder as he stretched it out along the sofa back. He smiled at the sudden intake of her breath.

"I got a doll." She held up a curly-haired doll with a green velvet dress. She narrowed her eyes. "This is my old doll, and somebody fixed her."

"That's from me," Mrs. Larson said. "Someone told me your doll needed some care. Now, open the one from Maggie."

She unwrapped a white flannel gown adorned with a pink ribbon. "Thank you, Miss Maggie!"

"Her other one is too small," Maggie said. "And I couldn't get out all the stains from when she was ill."

"It's appreciated. Open yours from me." Seth handed her a slim box.

His grin widened as she opened the box. A necklace of red beads winked up at her. "I thought you could wear it to the play tomorrow evening."

"It's beautiful." She ran her fingers lightly along the beads.

Seth received a red and black flannel shirt from Mrs. Larson. "Store-bought?"

She shrugged. "I didn't have time to sew one. Not only us gals should have something new to wear at Christmas."

"It's very nice." He opened the gift from Maggie and burst into laughter. "A blanket?"

"For the wagon." She smiled, leaning over to whisper in his ear. "I'm hoping for many more rides this winter, despite the end to the holidays."

His heart threatened to beat free. "I think I can manage that."

"Oh, Seth." Mrs. Larson held up a glass cake plate. "It's beautiful. Are you hinting for me to bake something?"

"Perhaps." He chuckled.

"Here, Maggie. You'll need this for tomorrow night." Mrs.

Larson pulled a gift from behind her chair.

Maggie opened it. "It's the blouse I admired. How did you know?"

"A little birdie told me." She smiled in Seth's direction. "Let me get us some coffee. It's too early for the night to end."

Maggie scooted closer to Seth. Her hair carried the faint aroma of roses. Closing his eyes, he breathed deep, relishing in the feel of her next to him.

"It's been a nice Christmas," she murmured. "And Mama's ornaments look so pretty on the tree."

"Yes. Annie will be pleased with the coat you had me get her. I'll give it to her in the morning so she has it for the play."

"Hmm. What else did you get her?"

"A tea set."

She gave a sleepy laugh. "Be prepared for a multitude of tea parties."

A few moments later, Mrs. Larson paused in the doorway. "Looks like you and I are the only ones not sleeping."

He glanced down to see Maggie's eyes closed. "Annie fell asleep under the tree seconds after you left."

"Would you like coffee?"

"Sure. I still have to care for the cows." He accepted the cup she offered. "Why hasn't Maggie told me she's turned back to God?"

"I don't know." She settled back into her chair. "She has her reasons, I suspect."

"I've been waiting for what seems like a very long time."

"You love my girl."

It wasn't a question. He nodded. "I never thought I'd feel this way again," he said softly, checking to make sure Maggie truly was asleep. "I couldn't express my feelings until she turned back to her faith."

She nodded. "It was only a matter of time before her heart melted. I had faith all along, although it did disappoint me that she wouldn't accompany me to church. After a while, folks stopped asking about her."

He took a sip of his coffee and stared at the tree. "You and Annie did a good job."

"So did you." She smiled over the rim of her cup. "If not for you, Maggie might still be wandering. For that, I thank you."

Whether she told him about turning back to her faith or not, he had something to ask Maggie after the play.

Chapter Thirteen

Maggie felt very festive indeed in her new red blouse and beads. She tied her hair up with a red satin ribbon and twirled in front of the mirror. She had one more Christmas gift to give Seth that evening. She wanted to look her very best. Not that the way she looked mattered. Only how he would feel when she told him.

As ready as she'd ever be, she joined Mama in the kitchen, where she was putting cookies in a lined hatbox. "I'm sure there will be more refreshments than needed, but folks love my gingerbread."

"Yes, they do." Maggie gave her a quick kiss on the cheek. "Merry Christmas Eve."

"Merry Christmas Eve, dear."

Tiny thundering footsteps on the porch, then the excited voice of Annie, signaled their ride had arrived. "It's snowing." She grabbed Maggie's hand. "Come look."

"I'm coming." Laughing, Maggie grabbed her coat as Annie tugged her out the door.

A light snow, magical in the waning light at the day's end, drifted lazily from an almost white sky. Seth sat in the wagon seat, his dark coat sprinkled with tiny flakes. Garland and red ribbons adorned the horses.

Maggie stood still, taking in the postcard scene. If only she could take a photograph. She'd frame it and treasure the moment forever. "Merry Christmas Eve, Seth."

"Same to you. You look beautiful tonight."

"Must be the beads." She donned her coat. "I really like your coat, Annie."

The child preened. "Daddy gave it to me." Under her coat, she wore her Mary costume. A simple, biblical times robe of blue. "Let's go. I can't be late." She scrambled into the back of the wagon.

Maggie followed, leaving the seat for Mama.

Seth hurried to take the box of cookies from her mother, then helped her into the wagon. "We won't be late, sweetie. See? We're leaving now."

Maggie's smile stayed in place as a very excited Annie practically bounced around until they pulled in front of the church. Already, buggics and wagons filled the lawn. Snowflakes continued to fall. Some of the child's excitement rubbed off, and Maggie quickly climbed from the wagon.

Inside the church, folks stood in small groups or had already chosen their seats. Maggie scanned for the best available pew and hurried to spread her coat over a space large enough for three adults. She managed to save them a spot in the third row near the aisle. Unless someone very tall sat in front of them, they'd have a good line of sight.

"I do believe you're as giddy as my daughter." Seth sat beside her. "The play doesn't start for another twenty minutes."

"I don't want to have to sit too far back."

"No longer afraid of lightning?" His smile widened.

"No, I'm not." She bit back a smile and kept her gaze forward.

Now was not the time to tell him her news. This was Annie's moment. She cut him a sideways glance. He acted as if he already knew. She narrowed her eyes. Had Mama told him? No, she wouldn't have. Mama always respected Maggie's privacy.

Excited chatter started behind the quilt curtain. Someone shushed them. The organist began playing Christmas carols. Soon, everyone in the pews began to sing.

Seth took Maggie's hand in his calloused one, his deep voice rumbling over her. He had a wonderful singing voice. She lifted her eyes heavenward and added her voice to those around her as the lyrics to "Silent Night" filled the church.

After several carols, the pastor stepped to his podium and opened his Bible. As he read the Christmas story, the curtain opened, and the children acted out the story.

Annie, a pillow under her gown, smiled and waved before putting on a serious face and following Joseph as he pulled the wooden donkey along. Maggie was sure she'd never seen anything more precious.

From the tears in Seth's eyes, neither had he. Maggie squeezed his hand. "Susan would have been very proud."

He glanced over at her. "Yes. I think she's seeing this. I like to believe that God allows glimpses once in a while, when it's important."

Maggie liked that idea. Maybe Papa knew how well she and Mama were doing.

When the play ended, Pastor Samson invited folks to stick around and fellowship with one another. Only those with infants left, the rest happy to visit with friends and neighbors.

"You know, don't you?" Maggie smiled and tilted her head.

"Know what?" The corner of Seth's mouth twitched.

"That I've returned to my faith. Who told you?"

"No one did, my dear Maggie. It's been written all over your face since last Sunday." He took both her hands in his. "That's the best Christmas present you could give me."

"Why is it so important to you?"

Before he could answer, Annie ran over, cookie crumbs dusting her gown. "Did you see me?"

"You were the best Mary I've ever seen." Seth gathered his daughter in a hug, glancing over her head at Maggie. "I'll answer your question later."

His gaze held a promise that took her breath away. Was Maggie ready for his answer?

By the time they left the church, Maggie's mind whirled with possibilities. She kept her hands clenched to control their trembling, telling herself Seth wasn't Daniel. The two didn't resemble each other in the slightest. Would she be risking heartbreak again?

Seth stopped the wagon in front of the house. "Mrs. Larson, could I trouble you for a hot drink for Annie? I'd like to speak with Maggie."

"Of course." She flashed Maggie a grin and ushered Annie quickly into the house.

Maggie moved to the end of the wagon bed.

Seth's hands circled her waist as he helped her to the ground. He brushed a snowflake from her cheek. "Is it too cold to stand out here for a moment?"

She didn't feel cold at all. The opposite in fact. She shook her head, her heart racing.

"I'm ready to answer your question."

"Which one?" she asked breathlessly.

"About why your return to your faith means so much to me."

"Oh." Her gaze lifted and locked with his.

"I love you, Maggie. From the first time I saw you at

Woolworth's, my heart was ready to move into a future I didn't think I wanted." The vulnerable look on his face tore at her. "I know you said you never wanted to marry, but please, will you reconsider and be my wife?"

His face blurred from her tears. "You're the only man I would reconsider for." She caught a glimpse of Mama and Annie watching from the parlor window. She smiled and cupped Seth's cheeks. "I love you. I will marry you."

"Let's give the audience something to watch." He lowered his head and claimed her lips in a kiss that was everything she'd dreamed of.

Epilogue

Maggie stood in the same church in the same wedding gown as the year before, with some minor adjustments, of course. While she didn't have the funds for an entirely new gown, she didn't want it to look exactly like the one she'd planned on marrying Daniel in. The gown had been modified with fewer frills; it was simpler, more elegant. Maggie had grown a lot since that day.

"What a strange sense of déjà vu," Mama said from the doorway.

"There's nothing at all similar as to how I feel on the inside." Maggie smiled. "Seth is the complete opposite of Daniel in every way."

"I've never seen such a glow on your face. Are you ready?" Mama crooked her arm. Since Maggie's father had passed years ago, she'd asked her mother to give her hand in marriage.

"More ready than I've ever been for anything." God, in all His amazing glory, had sent Daniel away, breaking Maggie's heart, only to renew her better than ever and make her free to love the man He intended her to wed.

Tears sprang to her eyes as she waited for the sanctuary doors to open. The soft melody of the wedding march sounded from the church piano. The doors opened and those in attendance stood.

Annie stepped in front of Maggie, a big grin on her little face, and strolled down the aisle, strewing pink rose petals. When she reached the end, she dropped her basket and ran into her daddy's arms before taking her spot beside him.

A nervous giggle escaped Maggie. She choked it off, her breath short, as she walked toward Seth, who wore a new dark suit. *Thank you, God. He's perfect.*

Maggie stepped away from her mother and beside her soon-to-be groom. She took a deep breath and blinked away tears in order to see him better.

His eyes weren't dry either.

This man was hers. A true gift from God, and in a few minutes, the pastor would declare them husband and wife.

"You may now kiss your bride," the pastor said just moments later.

Seth lifted her veil and lowered his head, kissing her with a sweetness that took her breath away. When he stepped back, she sighed, wanting more. Her gaze locked with his. A warm gaze full of promises.

He took her hand and led her down the aisle and out of the church, where their friends waited to rain rice on their heads. Seth's buggy, decorated with white streamers, waited to take them to the farm after the wedding potluck. Long tables stretched across the lawn, the fried chicken and biscuits they held filling the air with delectable aromas.

She smiled at her friends from the Five and Dime. Having quit her job a few days ago, she'd miss them and the customers, but Seth had promised they'd continue the Friday lunches he'd started with Annie.

"Come with me." Seth drew her behind the church. "I have

something for you and want to give it to you away from prying eyes."

Curiosity piqued, she gazed up at him. "Oh?"

"I want you to have something that never belonged to Susan. Something more than beads from Woolworth's." He pulled a jeweler's box from inside his jacket.

"Oh, Seth. That doesn't matter to me."

"It does to me." He handed her the box.

She opened it, revealing a strand of pearls with a teardrop diamond dangling from the center. "It's beautiful."

"May I put it on you?"

"Yes, please." She turned.

His hands trembled as he hooked the clasp then put his hands on her shoulders and turned her to face him again. "I love you, Marjorie."

She laughed. "You've never called me that before."

"I like Maggie better." His eyes twinkled. "We should get back before someone comes looking."

She agreed, though she'd prefer to be alone with him. Mama would watch Annie that evening, but tomorrow, Maggie would take the role of the little girl's mother in addition to being Seth's wife. Her future shone before her as bright as the sun.

Glancing heavenward, she said, "Thank You."

Dear Reader,

Woolworth's Five and Dime is a store everyone recognizes. For years it served the communities well. There was not a lunch counter until 1823 though. Forgive the four of us authors for stretching the timeline a bit. That's one of the beauties of fiction. An author can manipulate time. I couldn't think of a better way for jilted Maggie to meet Seth and, with regular conversations, realize she could love again.

I hope you're enjoying these sweet Christmas romances.

God bless,
Cynthia Hickey

Multi-published and bestselling author **Cynthia Hickey** has taught writing at many conferences and small writing retreats. She and her husband run the publishing press Winged Publications, which includes some of the CBA's best well-known authors. They live in Arizona and Arkansas, becoming snowbirds with two dogs and one cat. They have ten grandchildren who keep them busy and tell everyone they know that "Nana is a writer."